The Goblin's Daughter

Publisher's Note: This is a work of fiction. Names, characters, places, and incidents are a product of the author's imagination. Locales and public names are sometimes used for atmospheric purposes. Any resemblance to actual people, living or dead, or to businesses, companies, events, institutions, or locales is completely coincidental.

Book Layout © 2017 BookDesignTemplates.com

www.mksawyerbooks.com

The Goblin's Daughter/M. K. Sawyer. -- 1st ed.
ISBN: 978-1-64316-434-2

For anyone who has ever felt like an outsider.

The Goblin's Daughter

M. K. Sawyer

"I'm no more your mother
Than the cloud that distills a mirror to reflect its own slow
Effacement at the wind's hand."

-From "Morning Song" by Sylvia Plath

Prologue

STOP CRYING. STOP crying. Please, just STOP CRYING!

Nolin wailed from her playpen in the next room in high, desperate cries. Sometimes she screamed so hard that she fell silent as she struggled to inhale, squashy face red, toothless mouth gaping open. Melissa knew the difference between hungry or dirty cries and the ear-splitting, colicky ones that went on for hours no matter how much she tried to comfort her baby. Feeding, changing, swaddling, massaging, rocking, she'd tried everything. Four months of nonstop crying and she still couldn't soothe her own baby.

Melissa could have sworn Nolin sensed her ineptitude. Those piercing eyes bore into her like termites. Nolin was unexpected, but throughout the rocky pregnancy, nausea, vomiting, the constant unease as the baby grew inside her, Melissa always told herself everything would get better. It had to. Once the baby came, everything would be all right. The mothering instinct would take over. Melissa would somehow know how to stop a baby from crying all day and night. She'd chanted it over and over—*this will get better, it will all be better...*as much a prayer for help as a mantra.

The messy living room darkened as the heavy autumn sun sank below the horizon. The sky glowed red through the trees outside the window.

Melissa wished Paul would hurry. The darkness made her nervous. When the sun went down, her wild imagination became downright unruly while the shadows of the trees curled up the walls and fireflies twinkled like eyes in the woods behind the house.

Melissa sprawled across the living room sofa and watched the ceiling with blank eyes, her head tilted back, the arch of her neck gripping the arm of the couch. She liked the way the room looked upside-down. It was easier to pretend she was somewhere else. The room was crowded with piles of laundry, stacks of diapers, forgotten books, and empty bottles clouded with dried formula. Paul often hinted that she should clean, but what was the point? The mess would come right back, like hurricane season.

Melissa tipped her head back farther, half-hoping her neck would snap. Glowing insects darted around the porch light out the window, bouncing against the glass again and again. The digital clock on the end table switched to 9:17 p.m. Melissa lifted her head from the arm of the couch. Paul would be home any moment. He'd make it all better. Melissa pictured how he'd sweep into the door and take her into his arms while the baby magically stopped crying. He'd tell Melissa she was wonderful, that he understood why she was so exhausted and that he'd handle it from there.

Go take a bath, babe. I'll put Nolin to bed, then I'll be back to give you a foot massage and you can tell me anything you want. I love you, and everything is okay.

Of course, it never happened that way. It was a nice fantasy, though.

The shrill wails faded as Melissa fought to tune them out, but then Nolin screamed so hard that she gagged. Melissa groaned and pushed herself off the couch to scoop Nolin up and hold her against her chest, patting her back, whispering half-forgotten fragments of lullabies, songs echoing from a childhood she barely remembered.

Nolin's soft, dark hair brushed Melissa's cheek. The shrieks softened to fussy whimpers, punctuated by sharp cries that rang in Melissa's ears. Nolin's hands twined in Melissa's hair. Her little feet poked into her stomach, soft as a punctured balloon.

Melissa could feel the delicate bones in Nolin's limbs. *So fragile,* she thought. *So tiny.*

Finally, the glow of headlights passed over the back wall. Melissa heard the groan of the station wagon lurching into the driveway. She stopped pacing, jiggling enough to keep Nolin's cries at bay, waiting to hear his key in the latch and the creak of the door.

The rattle of the latch. The moan of the door opening, followed by a slam. Melissa felt the rush of fresh air scented with wood and dying leaves. Her heart leapt at the sound of his footsteps down the hall. Nolin let out a deafening wail.

"Melissa, Nolin should have been in bed two hours ago," Paul said before Melissa could even see him. "She needs to be on a schedule." His voice sounded far away, underwater.

He emerged, his hair sticking up in the back from scratching the back of his head all day. He only did that on bad days. Something inside Melissa deflated.

The black briefcase bumped against his thin legs as he staggered into the kitchen. He slipped off his jacket, draped it over the back of a kitchen chair, and immediately opened the fridge.

Melissa wanted to run to him and throw her arms around him, but she knew Nolin would scream if she put her down. An embrace would be heaven.

Part of her couldn't face another limp, one-armed hug, which was worse than no greeting or embrace at all. She stood her ground, rocking on the spot, watching him rifle around the fridge.

"She won't sleep," Melissa said quietly. "And I thought you might want to see her when you got home."

"I'll see her tonight when she wakes up." Paul said tonelessly. He pulled a jar of raspberry jam from the fridge, then rifled through the cupboards. He hadn't looked at Melissa yet. The creases in his forehead and under his eyes carved his face into that of a man much older than twenty-five. His dark hair, shot with gray, was already thinning on top. "Hopefully, she'll grow out of this."

Melissa nodded. Paul still hadn't looked at her. He sat down at the table to eat.

"I love you," she offered.

"Love you too."

"How was your day?"

"Long."

"You say that every day." Melissa smiled, trying to prod some lightness from her husband.

"I deal with assholes every day," he said flatly. He tore his sandwich in half and took a bite. "Why did I become a lawyer? Brightest idea of my life."

4

"It'll get better. Things will get easier as you get more established."

He grunted in response.

Nolin tilted her head up and clamped her toothless mouth on the side of Melissa's face, her slippery tongue testing her mother's cheekbone. Melissa leaned away, offering her finger instead.

"I got an idea for an illustration today," Melissa said, suddenly remembering. She hadn't spent much time in her studio lately, but at least she was still getting ideas. The thought stirred a ripple of excitement in her chest.

"Yeah?" said Paul through a mouthful of bread.

"Yeah," Melissa went on. "Nolin was crying, and I closed my eyes and I saw this...this creature. Kind of like a little elf or goblin. Like the sound was coming from it instead of her. I could illustrate a whole story of these little elfish creatures that live in the woods..."

"Sounds neat. She really should be in bed, though."

Melissa chewed the inside of her lip. Her fist tightened around a fold of Nolin's jumper. "Okay."

She shuffled across the room and up the stairs to the nursery. Nolin's fussing slowed to soft whimpers. Melissa gently laid her on the changing table, stripped off the jumper, then changed her diaper. Nolin watched silently with piercing, dark eyes. Melissa felt a pang of guilt deep in her stomach. Her body felt hollow, transparent, her substance disappearing into this new little creature she was suddenly expected to care for, this tiny thing that stirred a deep, primal affection within her and terrified her at the same time. All she felt anymore was fear and exhaustion.

It's not like HE helps much, Melissa thought bitterly, thinking of Paul. She yanked the tape of Nolin's diaper across her slim tummy. Nolin cried out again.

"I'm sorry, I'm sorry..." Melissa murmured as she undid the diaper and re-taped it, looser this time.

She slipped Nolin into a fresh pair of pajamas, a white sleeper with pink giraffes. Nolin sucked on her fist and flailed as Melissa wrestled her tiny feet into the pink booties.

The shoes were still a bit big, but the soft pink yarn kept Nolin's little feet warm, and they were the only booties she didn't pull off and throw out of her crib during the night. Melissa ran her thumb over the even knots and tiny flowers on the toes before lifting Nolin into her crib. Nolin kicked and started to cry again. Her tiny face scrunched up like a raisin.

"Shh, shh," Melissa said. "It's time to go sleep now. Can you sleep for me? Sleep for Mommy?"

The cries faded to soft grunts like a puppy's whine. A faint smile tugged at Melissa's mouth. She leaned down to gently kiss Nolin's forehead.

She flipped on the baby monitor and left the room, closing the door behind her. The muffled screams started as soon as the door clicked shut.

***

Melissa stared at the back of Paul's white tee shirt. She'd pulled the edge of the down comforter up to her eyes, wrapped around herself like a cocoon. Static crackled on the baby monitor. She listened for the sound of Nolin gurgling or even breathing, but she heard nothing except soft cracks and pops of the speaker.

Then, whispering.

Melissa bolted upright, her heart in her throat.

Strange, hissing sounds and hushed fricatives emanated from the monitor. Words she didn't understand. Soft taps and the hush of wind. The scrape of the window opening or closing.

Melissa's insides froze. Throwing the covers off, she leapt from the bed, nearly tripping over the pajama pants twisted around her legs. Paul groaned as she ripped the bedroom door open and sprinted down the hall to the nursery.

The window over Nolin's bed stood wide open. The sheer, white curtains billowed into the room like ghost hands. Melissa's breath caught in her throat as she slowly stepped toward the crib, terrified of what she would find. She closed her eyes, gripped the edge of the crib, then looked down.

The baby gazed up at her with curiosity, dark eyes wide and toothless mouth open in what might have been a smile. The giraffe sleeper was streaked with dirt.

Melissa picked up the baby, raised her to her face, and stared. The baby stared back just as intensely, silent and still.

Something was different.

Melissa held Nolin to her chest and pressed her face into its curly hair. It smelled of wood and earth and was gritty with dirt. Melissa shivered. Ice filled her veins. Her arms went slack, and the baby dropped back down into the crib with a thud, but it didn't cry.

The baby flailed, squealing joyfully. Melissa noticed Nolin wore only one of the pink booties; the other foot was bare, with the toes curled like little pink mushrooms.

Melissa cried out, drawing sharp breaths as her heart raced and her mind whirled in a tornado of half-formed thoughts. She dropped to her knees and peered under the bed, around the floor, looking for the missing baby shoe, anything to prove her fears were irrational. She reached under the crib and into the corners, pawed under the mattress and through the blankets. Nothing.

Paul's footsteps pounded in the hall, and he burst into the room.

"Melissa, what the hell is going on?"

She didn't answer. The trees outside howled and swayed in the wind, the top of the forest dancing. The baby looked at Melissa as it played with its own bare foot, poking its toes into its mouth. Melissa stood, her shoulders slack and her hair plastered over her pale face. She stared out the window into the woods and blinked, sure she saw something moving in the trees.

Part One

Ten Years Later

Chapter 1

NOLIN CROUCHED AND clawed at the dirt, unearthing pebbles and rendering a few insects homeless. Minuscule, shining beetles scurried out of their dark hiding places and over her fingers. She didn't bother to brush them off. The damp soil felt good in her hands, moist and cool like pudding. The dark smell enticed her, reminded her of some distant place she'd never been but wanted to go. Nothing in the world smelled better than good soil.

A wild brown curl fell on her face, and she brushed it away. Her white tee shirt was streaked with dirt, and the knees of her purple leggings were soaked through and filthy. She didn't mind. She dug deeper, squeezing the clay and watching it squish through her fingers in clumps.

Nolin glanced over her shoulder to make sure the teacher was still on the other side of the playground. Far away behind the monkey bars, Mrs. Carson paced slowly, watching a group of children playing kickball, edges of her brown coat flapping in the breeze. Nolin turned back to her digging, drinking in more of the soil's aroma.

The other children sometimes glanced at Nolin, but quickly looked away as if she were something indecent that shouldn't be observed. Nolin noticed, but tried not to.

A fat earthworm wrapped around her finger. She paused, studying the slick, writhing creature, its body cool and pleasant on her skin. What would it be like to be blind and limbless? Does a worm think? Does it have any sort of mind, or does it just slither through the soil because that is what it was meant to do? She thought of an earthworm in the first chapter book she learned to read by herself in preschool, about a boy and a giant peach. The worm in that story wasn't a happy character at all. Were all earthworms so sad?

She closed her eyes and plunged her hands into the soil again. She wished she could bury herself.

A shriek of laughter shattered her trance. Nolin looked up at a clump of sixth-grade girls. They peeked over their shoulders at her, giggling with their hands over their mouths, speaking in hushed voices. Nolin heard her name but couldn't make out the rest. Surely nothing new or important. She loathed their stupid magpie chatter and would dearly have loved to grab their blond ponytails and rub their faces in the dirt.

Most of the time, she pretended she didn't care what they said, but their words stung. They sank into her bones, echoed through her head when she was sad. *Freak. Sicko. Disgusting. Goblin girl.*

The giggles grew louder. Then one of the girls shouted, "Teacher! Nolin's digging holes again!"

The girl met Nolin's eyes and sneered. Her friends snickered. Nolin clenched her jaw and shoved the dirt back into the hole. She heard a thudding sound approaching and looked up to see a pair of brown suede boots marching toward her.

"Nolin, we've been through this before," said Mrs. Carson. Fatigue hung in her voice like wet laundry on the line. "We don't dig up the lawn. If you want to dig, go in the sand."

Nolin stared at the torn patch in the grass and nodded. She hated sand—dry, scratchy stuff. No insects in the sand. No winding plant roots or tiny rocks to examine. Sand felt dead in her hands while soil teemed with life, every handful ripe with new things to discover. Soil and sand were like silk sheets and a gunnysack; different as two things could be.

"And please, put your shoes back on! You're ten years old, Nolin. Why can't you follow directions?" The boots turned and stomped away. Nolin sat in the damp grass and stretched her bare, calloused feet in front of her. Gritty black dirt lined her toenails. The seat of her leggings would be wet when she got up. The girls would make fun of her again, that was certain. Maybe she had time to swipe a few more worms to hide in the Ponytail Girls' desks if they gave her any trouble.

She'd only have a few minutes until Mrs. Carson blew the whistle to return to the windowless classroom for their math lesson. The thought made her stomach hurt. Nothing tortured her like sitting at a hard desk in a stuffy room listening to a teacher's babbling. She gazed longingly at the edge of the woods on the other side of the chain link fence and wished she could climb the fence when no one was looking.

"Hey shrimp, why were you digging in the dirt?" A stocky sixth-grade boy with a ketchup-stained shirt tossed a football between his hands as he approached her. The two boys he was playing with stopped to watch. The larger boy, his twin, snickered and hopped up from where he sat to join his brother while the other, a skinny boy with a mess of dark hair, hung back.

"Max, we only have a couple minutes..." the thin boy called. Max ignored him.

"Why are you so dirty?" he sneered. "You look like you've been rolling in the dirt!" He checked over his shoulder at Mrs. Carson, who patrolled the perimeter of the sandbox at the opposite end of the playground.

"You know, my cat digs like you do. But you know what? She only digs when she's burying her poop. Did you leave a little surprise in that hole, String Bean?" His brother shrieked with laughter. Max grinned, his mouth stretching to reveal a row of crooked teeth.

Nolin scrambled to her feet. Her shoulders and jaw tightened. Anger sizzled in her veins, built up over weeks of relentless teasing and disapproving teachers staring at her down their long noses.

"You probably wouldn't bother to bury it, though, would you?" Max jeered. "You were probably looking for a snack. Do you eat bugs, Shrimpy? Do you eat worms?" He grinned at her. *Come on, Shrimpy, say something,* that smile dared. He turned and tossed the football to the dark-haired boy, who caught it and sat cross-legged in the grass, staring at the ball in his hands.

"Max, come on, you're being a jerk," the boy said.

"Shut up, Drew," said Max's brother.

Max squatted and pawed at the ground, his tongue hanging out of his mouth like a dog's, then lowered his face to the earth like a dog eating. He pushed himself back to his feet, laughing until he gasped for air.

Nolin lunged and planted her fist into his jaw. Shocked, Max stumbled backward. His brother stopped laughing and the dark-haired boy, Drew, shot to his feet. Max's eyes narrowed on Nolin.

"Oh, you're going down, Peewee!" He charged her like a bull and swung his fist, grazing the side of her head before she ducked and pummeled his side. He coughed and seized a handful of her tangled hair to yank her head back. Nolin shrieked and shoved her shoulder into his stomach, knocking them both to the ground with strength that surprised even herself. She kicked and thrashed until long fingernails dug into her shoulders and yanked her off.

"Nolin Styre!" Mrs. Carson bellowed. Her hair had fallen out of its clip, and her lined lips pulled back over large, glassy teeth. Nolin thought she looked like a mountain lion. "I have had enough of this! You come with me right now!" She wrapped her clawed hand around Nolin's arm and dragged her toward the school. Before Nolin was pulled through the double doors, she looked back into the forest on the other side of the chain link fence, wishing she could disappear into those trees.

***

She'd forgotten her shoes. Nolin curled her toes to hide her dirty nails. Sitting alone in the hallway outside the principal's office, she gazed at art projects hanging on the opposite wall—flat, generic blossoms cut and collaged with scraps of cheap construction paper. She wasn't tall enough to flatten her feet on the floor. How many times had she sat in this chair this year? Twice? Three times? And how many last year? And the year before? It all ran together.

She noticed her knuckles were crusted with blood from Max's nose. Her jaw tightened again, and she tried to wipe the blood onto her pants.

The buffer groaned across the cafeteria floor, mingling with the gossiping of the secretaries in the office next to her. The artificial light made her head ache. The buzzing of the electricity raked her nerves.

If only she could just go back outside and listen to singing birds and rustling leaves. If only she had a book to take her out of this hallway for a little while, take her anywhere else. Her legs jiggled and her stomach gnawed when she contemplated the trouble she was about to be in.

The doorknob of the principal's office turned. Max stepped out into the hall, a smug grin plastered on his face. A plump woman exited the office after him. "Thank you Mr. Clark," she said before taking Max by the shoulder and leading him in the direction of the sixth grade classrooms. She threw a dirty look in Nolin's direction as they turned away. Max flashed her a toothy grin. Nolin took a deep breath and went back to studying her dirty toes.

Mr. Clark popped his head out. His eyes fell on Nolin. He sighed. She stood, and he held the door open while she passed under his arm into his office.

"Nolin, where are your shoes?"

Nolin didn't answer. She climbed onto the wooden chair before his desk with her hands in her lap. Mr. Clark eased himself into his own chair, which creaked when he leaned back. His white dress shirt stretched over his large stomach. His face was leathery from years of sun damage, but his deep-set eyes were bright and gentle. Nolin liked him; he was always kind to her, even when she was in trouble. But that was the problem: she only ever spoke to him when she was in trouble.

"Listen, I know kids can get nasty," he said. Nolin stayed silent, staring straight ahead. She felt like a prisoner of war, withholding information under torture.

Mr. Clark sighed again. "Have you been working on those exercises the counselor told you about? Taking deep breaths? Counting to ten? Walking away and telling a teacher if someone is bullying you?"

Nolin's eyes flicked downward. No matter how much she told herself that next time she'd be better, none of those things ever entered her mind before she snapped.

"You're such a smart girl, Nolin. Your teachers always tell me how bright and imaginative you are, but then you go and get into fights. I don't understand it."

The ticking of the clock on the wall synchronized with her pulse. She fidgeted and pulled her legs to her chest. Mr. Clark sighed and leaned forward.

"Is there anything you want to talk about, Nolin? Is everything okay?" Nolin knew he really wanted to help. She shook her head. "I'm sure things are hard for you at home right now, with your mother sick, but there are better ways to express yourself."

"I'm sorry," said Nolin tonelessly.

"I know, Nolin, but this is your third fight this year. You have got to learn to control yourself." He tapped the desk on the word *got*. "You're so smart. I know you can do better than this."

"No, I mean I'm sorry you're disappointed in me," Nolin said. "And that my parents are. I'm not sorry I hit him."

"You're not?"

16

Nolin shook her head. "He deserved it. He shouldn't treat people like that. He's mean to everyone, not just me. I've seen him." She spoke calmly, even though her fists were clenched in her lap. She forced herself to relax her jaw, keep her voice even. Grown-ups listened better when she stayed calm.

"Fighting doesn't solve anything, Nolin," Mr. Clark said. "You should tell a teacher if someone is picking on you."

Nolin stared at her dirty knees and dug her toes into the edge of the chair. She'd tried that, but the teachers always told her to stop tattling. She knew she couldn't tell him so. No one ever took her side over a grown-up's.

Mr. Clark leaned back and sighed again. "I called your father to pick you up. I'm afraid I'll have to suspend you for the rest of the week. You can come back on Monday."

Her face fell. Her father would be disappointed. Her mother would be distraught. Nolin wished she could run out of the office and hide somewhere until things blew over, but there was nowhere to go.

One side of Mr. Clark's mouth curled up into an expression of pity. "Is there anything I can do to make school more pleasant for you?" he asked. "Is the classwork too easy? We've already moved you up to the sixth grade. Maybe we could look into getting you more challenging coursework if you'd like."

Nolin shook her head. Then the door opened behind her and she smelled her father's cologne. She didn't turn around.

"Have a seat, Mr. Styre," said Mr. Clark.

Her father pulled a chair next to Nolin and sat. His eyes were flat behind his rimless glasses.

"I'm sorry I have to see you again, sir," he said to Mr. Clark. Nolin curled herself into an even tighter ball, pressing her chin into her knees. She could almost smell his disappointment, like smoke in the air. The atmosphere in the room thickened. Nolin thought she felt the temperature rise a few degrees.

"I'm sorry too, Mr. Styre. It seems Nolin is still having trouble controlling herself, and from the sound of it, she's not really concerned with improving."

"I won't do it again," Nolin piped up.

"That's good, Nolin, but you're still not sorry you did it."

"No, and I don't see why I should be. I'm sorry I've hurt you and my parents, but not him."

She looked over at her father. He stared down at his hands, the tips of his ears growing red. He was embarrassed by her. Nolin's face suddenly burned with shame. *Why can't I just shut up and do what they say?* She knew the answer: it was unfair. The other kids picked on her every single day. If the teachers wouldn't do anything, the only other option was to take care of it herself.

Mr. Clark cleared his throat. "Nolin, I'd like to talk to your father alone, please."

Of course. The grown-ups had to talk, because they knew best. Nolin clenched her teeth and pushed herself off the chair. Her father didn't look at her.

The door closed behind her, and she took her seat in the hall. Her insides twisted around themselves like the worm she'd dug up only a half hour ago. Her mother would be so upset. The last time Nolin got in a fight, Melissa didn't speak to her for days. Nolin tapped her head on the brick wall behind her chair, pinching her eyes shut.

Muffled conversation rumbled behind the door. Her bitter curiosity prickled. She glanced down the hall both ways before sliding out of her seat to press her ear to the polished wood.

"...so much pent-up energy, and I think a lot of it has to do with her mother being ill," came Mr. Clark's voice. "Has Nolin seen a therapist? Any kind of psychological help at all?"

Her father spoke next. "Child psychologists, doctors, you name it. Nothing they've done or prescribed has helped. She doesn't misbehave at home, though. It's just at school that she gets into trouble."

Why would I be bad at home? Nolin thought.

"Have you considered enrolling her in a special school? Gifted children often act out at school because they're bored. They may feel isolated or different. They're vulnerable to teasing. A different environment could be beneficial."

Nolin almost snorted. The teachers in those schools looked at her the way her classmates did, like she was a freak.

"We've tried. Nolin wasn't interested in any of them and the teachers found her behavior a little...odd. They turned us down. All of them. Some counselors suggested homeschooling, but it's just not possible with my work, and my wife...well, she just isn't up to it."

"Well, Nolin is a little different. Bright, though," said Mr. Clark. "She reads at a high school level. When she actually completes her classwork, when she can focus long enough to take a test, her scores are incredible."

"I know."

"I mean, we could advance her another grade or even further perhaps, but I just don't think she could cope with junior high with her limited social skills..."

Nolin didn't want to hear any more. She stood and paced the hall, forcing herself to block out the muffled exchange behind the door.

A few minutes later, the door opened and Mr. Clark leaned out.

"Nolin, can you come back in here, please?"

Nolin crept back into the room but did not sit down. Her father placed his elbows on his knees and rested his chin in his hands. His thin, graying hair was mussed. His eyes were ringed with shadows. Nolin wanted to rest her hand on his shoulder. She decided it was better not to.

"Okay, Nolin," Mr. Clark began. "We've looked over your records, and we're going to give you one more chance. I'm sure adjusting to the sixth grade has been difficult, but this can't continue. One more fight and we may have to expel you. Do you understand?"

Images of flying bats, swaying trees, and rushing rivers flashed through her mind. No school? Was that possible? She could play outside all day, read whatever books she wanted, be free from her classmates and teachers. Her insides fluttered. Then she pictured her weary, haunted mother rocking back and forth in the corner of her room, open bottle of Prozac on the nightstand. How this would burden her. Nolin aggravated her mother's condition as it was. Getting expelled from school could send her over the edge.

Nolin couldn't let that happen.

"Are we on the same page, Nolin?"

She nodded.

"All right, I think we're done here, Mr. Styre." Her father stood and shook Mr. Clark's hand. Nolin followed her father into the hall.

"I'm sorry." Nolin said. They pushed through the double doors and out into the parking lot. Spring rain sprinkled the pavement. The smell was extraordinary. Nolin filled her lungs. Her father shielded his glasses from the rain and sighed.

"Nolin, this has to stop."

"I know."

They climbed into the old station wagon. The inside was worn, spotless except for a tattered planner in the passenger seat. Her father tossed it into the backseat.

"Your mother is falling apart as it is," he said, gripping the wheel tightly and staring straight ahead. "The last thing she needs is an out-of-control daughter. This will not happen again, do you hear me?"

"Does she know?" Nolin asked. The car pulled out of the lot and onto the road. He drove slowly; Nolin knew he was in no hurry to get home.

"No. I want it to stay that way. I don't know what we're going to do about this suspension. We'll figure something out. If you get expelled, though, it'd be pretty hard for her not to notice."

Nolin laid her head on the window and watched the spray of rain on the sidewalk from the tires. Leaves uncurled on the branches of the trees lining the road. Bright flowers exploded in their beds in front of the small brick houses. Two toddlers in yellow raincoats danced with their umbrellas and jumped into puddles while their mother photographed them from the porch.

They passed by the road to their home. Nolin didn't have to ask where they were going.

Chapter 2

THE CAR STOPPED in front of the library, a small brick building with a large willow tree out front.

"Don't walk home until at least three," Nolin's father said. "Wait until you're sure the school bus has passed. Don't bother your mother."

Nolin popped the door open and stepped into the rain. The car started moving the moment her bare feet touched the pavement and soon disappeared down the street. She stood still for a moment to watch the willow vines flow like tentacles. The last time she'd been suspended, she had climbed up the willow with a book and stayed there all afternoon. She wished she could do it today, but she didn't want to ruin a book in the rain. After wiping her bare, muddy feet on the damp grass, she strode up the sidewalk, wrung out her hair, and stepped into the library.

A blast of cold air greeted her. The dark-haired young woman behind the front desk looked up from her computer. Her shoulders dropped slightly, though her heavily made-up eyes sparkled behind her thick tortoiseshell glasses. Nolin loved those glasses with their little rhinestones on the corners. The librarian had very dark-blue eyes, midnight-blue like the bottom of an ocean trench. Her dark hair was pulled back tightly from her oval-shaped face.

Nolin thought she looked like a chocolate truffle from a Valentine's box in her caramel-colored turtleneck and brown slacks.

"Hi, Ms. Savage," Nolin said sheepishly.

"Well, at least your nose isn't bleeding this time," Ms. Savage responded. She smiled with her red lips pressed together, not revealing the slightly crooked teeth Nolin knew she didn't like. "What happened this time?" Her eyes drifted to Nolin's feet, then back to her screen.

"I need something really challenging today," Nolin said. "But beautiful. Do you have any recommendations?"

Ms. Savage smiled and gave an understanding nod. "A good cure for a bad day." She rose from the desk, towering over Nolin in her high heels. Nolin followed her past the rows of books, watching the loose brown sweater fold and pull across Ms. Savage's slim shoulders.

Ms. Savage turned down an aisle and pulled a book halfway out, then thought better of it and pushed it back in. She placed a hand on the front of the shelf and tapped her fingers, eyes narrowing as she studied the row of books.

"Have you read any Shakespeare?" she asked.

"Just a few sonnets," Nolin said. Her mother owned a slim volume of romantic sonnets. Nolin read it one night when she was eight. She still returned to it sometimes when she was in trouble and wasn't allowed to go outside.

Ms. Savage tugged a small red paperback from the shelf and handed it to Nolin. "You might like this one. Very entertaining."

On the cover was a beautiful woman embracing a man with a donkey's head, surrounded by gold embossed flowers.

"*A Midsummer Night's Dream*," Nolin read.

"It's my favorite."

Nolin flipped through the pages. The text was tiny. She'd asked for a challenge, and she had a feeling she'd gotten it.

"Make sure you use a dictionary," Ms. Savage said, "and go slowly. It's okay if you have to reread things. Stop after every few lines to make sure you understand what you just read. You'll get used to the language. There should be a guide to Shakespeare's sentence structure and such in the front of that script."

Nolin tucked the book under her arm. "Thank you."

"Anytime, hon." Ms. Savage studied Nolin for a moment as if she were a particularly difficult line of text. Then she shook her head. "How does a ten-year-old who reads Shakespeare get into so much trouble?"

Nolin shrugged.

Nolin settled into her usual spot on the old couch in front of the large back window, *A Midsummer Night's Dream* open in her lap. Rain pattered on the glass, blurring the image of the woods on the other side of the garden. Her mind wandered. Though the play was beautiful, she couldn't stop watching how the water on the window distorted the trees. Nolin let her vision blur as she stared through the wet glass.

"Nolin, it's three o'clock." Ms. Savage pushed a book cart past the couch. Nolin jerked out of her daze. "What do you think of the Bard?"

"It's lovely," said Nolin, blinking her eyes back into focus. "I haven't gotten very far, though."

Ms. Savage nodded. "You'll get faster." She followed Nolin's gaze out the window. "Do you want me to walk you home?"

"No, thanks. It's not too far."

Ms. Savage shrugged and disappeared between the shelves with the cart. Nolin left the book on the table. She'd come by later tomorrow if it wasn't raining and check it out, but for now she didn't want it getting wet on her walk home.

The rain was warm for spring, just heavy enough to form decent puddles for her to jump in. She ran part of the way, relishing the feel of the water splashing her face. Lightning clawed the sky. Thunder growled. Her clothes were sopping, and her wild hair tangled like a mass of wet moss.

She slowed down and walked, taking care not to step on the cracks of the sidewalk, but walking through every puddle she could, savoring the cool rainwater on her feet.

Dread roiled in her stomach when she turned onto her street. Her father might scold her if he had the energy, but that was nothing compared to her mother if she found out. Nolin hated disappointing her. The look on her face when Nolin got in trouble at school...she couldn't even stomach the thought of it. Nothing made her feel worse.

It was her fault her mother was sick, after all.

Nolin took her time walking down her street.

The woods appeared in the gaps between the houses as Nolin passed by. They seemed to be watching her, those deep, dark spaces between the trees like sunken eyes that saw every move she made, read every thought. The woods almost felt like a kind of imaginary friend. She'd never had a real imaginary friend—she was far too old for one now—but she never felt alone with the woods watching her. They scared her. The forest was a companion that might shift its mood at any moment, like a wild animal, and devour her.

26

Chapter 3

HER FATHER'S FACE reminded Nolin of a zombie movie she once watched. He shuffled around the kitchen while he cooked dinner, sometimes pausing to stare at nothing, eyes glazing over and mouth hanging open slightly until he shook his head and returned to cooking.

"Dad, are you okay?" Nolin asked. He put a brick of cheese in the cupboard and a loaf of bread in the refrigerator, then shook his head and switched them, putting them both where they belonged. The circles under his eyes were more pronounced than ever.

"I just had a really long day," he said. "I didn't sleep much. Your mother was twitching around all night. Kept jabbing me."

"Was she talking?" Nolin often heard muffled words when her mother had nightmares, like she was talking to someone who wasn't there. Sometimes, Nolin got out of bed to creep into the hall and listen. Melissa mumbled nonsense in her sleep—whimpering, groaning, often crying. The next morning, Nolin would find her father sleeping in the armchair, pale with bruise-like shadows under his eyes.

"Not really. She nearly kicked me off the bed, though. I swear, that woman takes karate lessons in her..." He yawned before he could finish. His face stretched so far Nolin wondered if it would flip inside out.

His gaze didn't seem to focus on the cheese sandwich in the pan. He stared straight ahead, his gray eyes glazed over like those of the dead fish in the seafood case at the supermarket. Dark smoke started to rise from the pan.

"Dad, you're burning that."

He jolted back to life and cursed at the charred, black sandwich. Muttering, he slid it onto a plate and turned on the overhead fan. He ran his fingers through what was left of his hair, which made it stand on end. He looked like a mad scientist.

Nolin slid off her barstool and took the spatula from his hand.

"Go sit down; I'll finish," she said. He didn't protest, but silently staggered into the living room and collapsed into his favorite armchair.

Nolin scooted her little kitchen stool to the stove, then peeled the burned slice of bread off the sandwich and replaced it with another buttered slice and piece of cheese. She hadn't found any tomato soup in the pantry, but she did recover some carrots from the bottom of the crisper that weren't too wiggly. The milk should have been thrown out days earlier. She poured three glasses of water instead.

"Is she coming down for dinner?" Nolin asked, though she already knew the answer. She sliced carrots for her mother's plate and added the sandwich, neatly cutting it into triangles. When her father didn't answer, she glanced over her shoulder. His head had already tipped back, and he was snoring.

Within a few minutes, her father's snores practically rattled the windows. Nolin pulled off his shoes and laid a checkered fleece blanket over him. He wouldn't move until morning. Before placing his shoes by the chair, where he was sure to find them in the morning, Nolin slipped the right shoe onto her own small foot. It was still warm inside and slightly damp from workday sweat. When she was little, she used to waddle around the house in her father's shoes, quacking like a duck.

"Daddy, I'm a duck!" She'd exclaim.

"Yes, you are. I need those to go to work, Nolin. Give them back."

Her cheeks burned. She removed the shoe and laid it next to its mate.

When she returned to the kitchen, she flipped the sandwich onto the center of the plate inside the carrot design. She ran her fingers through her knotted hair and scrubbed her wet hands on her face before cautiously carrying her mother's dinner up the stairs.

She hoped with all her heart that her mother didn't know about her suspension. Nolin planned on going to the library during school hours to cover her tracks. She sometimes saw her mother at the window, watching her get on the school bus in the mornings; she'd know if Nolin didn't go. Maybe Nolin would tell her she was going to ride to school with a friend who lived around the corner.

No, that would never work. Melissa knew she had no friends.

Maybe she'd pretend to miss the bus and look like she was running to catch it at the next stop. Or she'd just fake sick.

That wouldn't work either. She'd never been sick.

A slice of dim light peeked through the crack under Melissa's bedroom door, casting a yellow square on the floor of the dark hallway. Nolin tiptoed to the door and knocked. Nothing. Carefully, she let herself in.

The room smelled of stale sweat and dirty laundry. Something ominous hung in the air, an odd tension like dust settling after an explosion. The hot, stagnant air made her head swim. She wanted to open a window, but Melissa never opened windows. She said she wanted to keep the outside out and the inside in, whatever that meant.

A little lamp on the nightstand cast sticky yellow light over the master bedroom, showcasing the unmade bed with sheets falling all over the mattress and floor. Thick curtains were drawn over the windows, the floor dotted with stacks of books and empty water glasses. Beside the door sat a bowl of untouched, dried-up oatmeal from that morning.

The flickering lamp threw dancing shadows over the walls. Nolin tried not to look at her own twitching shadow, distorted and hunched like a monster.

Breath hissed. She turned to see her mother lying on her back with her legs propped up on a wall, her arms stretched out to the sides with her curled palms facing upward, glasses folded and resting in her right hand. Her eyes were closed, her limp, pale hair spread around her head like a fan. The bony ribcage rose and fell as she drew in deep breaths and exhaled through her nose.

Without her glasses, Melissa looked much younger. Though her eyes were shadowed and sunken, her delicate features echoed a time when she smiled more, when her mind was clear and vivacious instead of haunted.

"Melissa?" Nolin stepped forward, closing the door softly behind her. "I brought your dinner." Melissa rolled her head to the

30

side, away from Nolin. Her jawbone standing out like gills on a fish.

"This is soothing," Melissa said softly. "Inverted poses prompt the circulation of stagnant blood in the legs and increase blood flow to the brain, calming the mind." She breathed in deeply and exhaled through her nostrils, her breath rattling in the back of her throat. The legs of her pajama pants had slipped down her calves, revealing her skinny legs and bony ankles. Under the old tee shirt, Nolin could see protruding collarbones, the sharp points of her mother's shoulders, and the peaks of her ribcage poking out below her flat chest. Melissa inhaled again.

"Did you have a panic attack?" Nolin asked. She didn't dare speak above a whisper in this strange room, where everything seemed surreal and even the colors were muted.

Melissa exhaled again. "That would have been a relief."

"Oh." Nolin cast her eyes around for clues about what Melissa had done that day. Crumpled papers. Books facedown to hold their places. After a moment she set the plate and glass on the floor, then sat cross-legged, slowly working her way into the invisible bubble that surrounded her mother and kept everything, everyone out.

Nolin noticed a plate of hard toast on the end of the bed from two days earlier. She leaned down and saw two other plates under the bed, one bearing what looked like an uneaten sandwich, the other with what Nolin assumed to be the enchilada she'd brought up the night before. She wrinkled her nose; the food was starting to smell in the warm room. How did her father sleep in here at night? No wonder he often slept in the armchair.

"When was the last time you ate?" she asked. Melissa didn't respond. Nolin eyed her mother's sharp elbows. "You really need to eat something."

Melissa let her legs slide to the floor. Slow as a sloth, she rolled onto her hands and knees and pushed herself up to her feet, swaying where she stood. She put on her glasses and parted her long, lank bangs.

"I saw the school bus come." She didn't look at Nolin. Nolin was glad. "You and Paul try to hide it from me. I'm not an idiot. You got suspended again, didn't you? You got in another fight." Her voice climbed higher. She looked over at Nolin. The glare on her glasses shielded her eyes, but Nolin knew they were wide with anxiety. She'd received that look many times. It stung like a whip.

"I...I'm sorry, Mom."

"Do not call me 'Mom.'"

"Sorry...Melissa."

Melissa sighed and clutched her face with her trembling hands. Her pale, papery skin pulled over her fine bones. She wasn't wearing her wedding ring. Behind her hands she drew in rattled breaths, shoulders quivering.

"I'm sorry," Nolin said again. She wished she'd just let stupid Max carry on until the whistle blew. Why did she have to hit him? Why couldn't she control herself? It was so hard in the moment, when that boiling rage swam in her veins. Her eyes filled with tears. She watched her mother shake.

"You can't do this anymore," Melissa squeaked from behind her hands. "You don't know what you can do. You can really hurt someone, Nolin! You *cannot* do this!"

Nolin fiddled with the frayed hem of her tee shirt. "I won't do it again," she whispered.

"You will *not* do this again," Melissa repeated, her hands dropping from her face. For a moment, she swayed, staring over Nolin's shoulder. She looked ill. Nolin worried she might be sick, though she probably couldn't vomit because she hadn't eaten in days. Melissa swallowed hard and straightened, still unsteady on her feet.

"Mom, I mean...Melissa?"

Melissa's eyes snapped back into focus and bored into Nolin's, then floated upward to rest on Nolin's hair. She took a few wavering steps forward, then reached out and touched a matted lock.

"Your hair. Go get the brush."

Nolin dreaded that phrase. Obediently, she stood and crossed the room to the adjoining bathroom. The floor was littered with towels and dirty clothes. The mirror was so covered in water stains that Nolin could barely see her reflection. She opened the top drawer to fish out the dreaded hairbrush, an awful object she regarded as an instrument of torture. For a few moments, she desperately pulled at her hair to untangle some of the knots before the brush ripped through. They remained hopelessly snarled.

Melissa was punishing her. Nolin knelt before her mother, facing away from her. Nolin saw Melissa's shadow raise the brush behind her. She gritted her teeth.

The brush dragged through Nolin's wild mass of knots, making a sound like Velcro unsticking. Nolin wondered how much hair she'd have left when they were finished. Her watering eyes squeezed shut. Tears dripped down her cheeks. Melissa held the top of Nolin's head still and raked the brush through, her grip strong for an emaciated woman. Nolin whimpered and pretended to be somewhere, *anywhere*, else.

"If you'd look after your hair yourself, we wouldn't have to do this."

Nolin bit her lips until she tasted blood.

"You listen to me: if you hurt *anyone* again, any child, any person, I don't care what they've done...you will not leave this house for a very long time. And I don't mean grounding. You will not set foot outside until I'm sure you will never harm anyone ever again. Do you hear me?"

Nolin nodded. She twisted the bottom of her shirt in her hands until the fabric tore.

When they finished, Nolin carried the plates of leftover food downstairs. Her face was stained with dried tears. Her hair puffed out from her raw scalp like a dandelion. Nolin tiptoed as she put the plates in the sink and retrieved her book from the counter before going upstairs to her room. She didn't want to wake her father, who still snored in his chair.

Her mother's words etched inside her skull, screeching like nails on a chalkboard. *You could have really hurt that child. You could hurt someone!*

She settled into bed with her knees propped up to support her book, *Where the Wild Things Are*. She couldn't remember where they'd gotten that book, just that the book had always been around. The idea of a child stumbling into a world of strange creatures felt so familiar. Her parents must have read it to her when she was a baby, because that idea had fascinated her when she was very young, determined to learn to read so she could pore through the pages herself, perhaps find the answer to a question she couldn't quite articulate.

Too often, she felt like the boy in his wolf suit, an animal among humans. If only she could crawl inside those pages and find her place with monsters. Turning the pages, she daydreamed of running away to a land of creatures who loved her so much they'd roar their terrible roars and gnash their terrible teeth at the thought of her leaving.

Chapter 4

SOFT SPRING LIGHT trickled through her bedroom window, the morning sky gloomy and bruised. Nolin cracked the window open for rain-scented air to waft in. Her head felt heavy. For hours she'd drifted in and out of sleep, her bedroom window swimming through confused visions of trees, mist, and wild-haired women with empty eyes.

She slid off the bed and changed into a fresh tee shirt and shorts. Her hair had matted again during the night. She tried to untangle it with her fingers as she descended the stairs, but her curls wound even tighter.

The green numbers on the microwave clock glowed seven thirty. Why wasn't her father getting ready for work? She looked to the chair where he'd fallen asleep the night before; he had slumped down so far in the armchair that his legs splayed out before him, his big toe peeking through a hole in his left sock.

"Dad?" Nolin touched his arm. He jolted forward so hard that his glasses fell off his face into his lap. He checked his watch.

"Damn!" He leapt from the chair and bolted upstairs without acknowledging Nolin at all.

Nolin listened to the bedroom door opening and slamming closed, his heavy footsteps pounding overhead as he stomped around. Melissa was probably already awake. At least Nolin hoped so. This would have made for a very rude awakening.

Water swished in the pipes. She listened for voices upstairs while she assembled a stack of peanut butter sandwiches and slid them into plastic baggies. Once or twice she thought she heard murmuring, but no shouts or sharpness. No clear ring of her mother's panicked voice. No low rumble of her father's toneless reassurances.

When the clock glowed 7:37, she heard her father's frantic footsteps like bowling balls bouncing down the stairs. She scooped up the sandwiches and rushed them to him as he pulled on his jacket and picked up his briefcase. With a tiny nod of appreciation, he took them and disappeared out the front door, one arm still out of his jacket. Nolin's heart deflated. She'd hoped for a good-bye hug or even a smile, but he was late.

The sudden quiet filled her ears. Blocks of gray light streamed through the windows. Everything stood eerily still. For a moment she stood between the kitchen and living room, listening to the roaring silence, hypnotized by the gently falling dust, sparkling as it hung in the air, some of it swirling in her own breath.

The whoosh of a passing car outside broke the spell. Nolin blinked. Breakfast. Her mother. Lots to do. Humming tunelessly, she cracked eggs into a pan, slipped bread into the toaster, poured water into glasses because the milk smelled like corn. She climbed on the counter to reach the serving tray.

Very slowly, she carried the heavy tray up the stairs, eyes trained on the water glasses, careful not to let them tilt too far. When she reached the bedroom door, she tapped a few times with her toe. No answer, of course. Nolin carefully laid the tray on the floor to let herself in.

Her mother lay on her back on the disheveled bed, studying something in her raised hand. Nolin stepped over the untouched remains of yesterday's dinner to approach the bed.

"Melissa?" she whispered. She felt like an invader, stepping in on something she shouldn't be seeing, like she always did when she visited her mother's room. "Breakfast."

Her mother didn't acknowledge her. She continued rolling the glinting object through her fingers. A wedding ring, Nolin realized. She hadn't seen her wear it in years. Melissa slipped the ring onto her finger and let her hand droop, allowing the ring to slide off. It landed on her belly with a soft thud.

"It doesn't fit," she whispered.

"Well, you've lost a lot of weight," Nolin said nervously. "Here, eat breakfast..."

"It was always too big, but it never fell off. Now..." Melissa put it back on and let it drop again.

Nolin wanted to suggest that the ring could be resized, but she knew better. This was about much more than a ring.

She settled on the bed and placed the tray next to her mother. "You need to eat breakfast," she said, her voice quavering.

"Is that so?"

"Yes. You haven't eaten in days." She eyed the harsh line of her mother's jawbone. Melissa pushed herself up and plunked the ring onto the nightstand. Nolin scooted the tray closer. The water glasses sloshed. She stabbed a clump of scrambled eggs with her fork, as if demonstrating for her mother, who might have forgotten how to use a fork. Melissa gingerly picked up her toast and nibbled a corner.

"It's a little burnt."

"Sorry," Nolin said. She made a mental note to turn the knob on the toaster down. Nolin devoured her breakfast while Melissa nibbled her toast. Nolin never took her eyes off her mother, making sure she chewed and swallowed what she ate. Melissa took a tiny sip of water. The sinews in her neck poked out when she strained to swallow.

"How did you sleep?" Nolin asked through a mouthful of toast. Melissa shot her a glare. Nolin held her hand over her mouth. Her mother hated when she talked with her mouth full.

"Badly," Melissa croaked before sipping more water. "Dreams...Paul never came up." The skin between her eyebrows folded into its familiar creases. Nolin reached out to touch her leg. Melissa flinched.

"Maybe you should draw today," Nolin offered, changing the subject. "You haven't drawn in a long time. I think that mermaid picture is still in there. You should finish it." Nolin sometimes slipped into the studio to see the drawings. She loved her mother's illustrations and paintings, the bright colors, swirling shapes, elongated figures, and perfect pen lines. She never dared touch anything or look through the sketchbooks that lined the shelves.

Nolin thought she saw a sparkle in her mother's eye at the mention of drawing. Then they darkened.

"I don't think I remember how." Melissa dropped the half-eaten toast onto her plate next to the cold eggs.

"If you don't want toast and eggs, I can make you something else. We don't have much right now, but I can make peanut butter and jelly, or oatmeal..."

"No, I'm done." Melissa nudged the plate forward.

Nolin stacked her mother's plate on her own empty one and set them on the tray.

"Okay, I'll make you an early lunch then. If we have some money, I can go to the grocery store. You could even come with me..."

"I'm not leaving this house, and you shouldn't either."

"Oh." Nolin fiddled with the fork on her plate. Melissa flinched at the clinking noise and snatched it out of Nolin's hand, placing it deliberately next to the plate.

"Okay, well, why don't you draw while I clean up today?" Nolin suggested again, her voice cracking slightly on "today." Melissa sighed.

"Maybe."

Nolin knew that meant no. She took her mother's hand. Melissa allowed Nolin's hand to close around her cold, bony one.

"Come on."

Nolin gently pulled Melissa to her feet, which wasn't hard even though Melissa made no efforts to aid her. Nolin felt her mother's pulse flutter in her hand as they walked to the room at the end of the hall. Melissa's studio. When had Melissa last left the bedroom? Nolin wasn't sure. She knew she wouldn't leave unless led.

The door yawned on its stiff hinges. Pens, pencils, and brushes poked out of cans and jars like strange flowers waiting to bloom. A dusty lamp arced over the work desk on which a half-finished sketch on watercolor paper was taped. Bookshelves lined the walls, filled with old sketchbooks, novels, boxes of art supplies, and other mysteries Nolin had never dared investigate.

Nolin pulled up the shades to flood the room with morning light. Melissa squinted and shielded her eyes, pale as a ghost in the blast of light. Her skin had the translucent, faded quality of someone who never saw the sun, like creatures in dark ocean caves.

Nolin pulled the faded office chair from the desk, inviting her mother to sit. Melissa took a few tentative steps forward and carefully sank into the chair, gripping the edge of the desk so hard Nolin worried her pointed knuckles would burst from her skin.

"I can get some water for your brushes." Nolin plucked a paint-stained marmalade jar from the desk and shifted on her feet. Melissa brushed the film of dust off the drawing without answering. Mermaids with hair swirling around their faces; eyes huge and sparkling looked up at her from the page, half-colored, expectant. Fish of all shapes and sizes flocked around them, emitting tiny ink bubbles from their open mouths. Seaweed and coral snaked around the borders. Nolin hovered expectantly.

Melissa traced the mermaid tails with her fingers. She opened the top drawer of the desk, filled with crumbled tubes of watercolor paints.

"A palette, Nolin?"

Nolin scrambled to retrieve a paper plate from a stack on a shelf. Melissa's hands trembled as she plucked colors from the drawer, twisted off the caps, and squeezed a tiny blob of each onto the plate.

Nolin loved watching her mother paint. The expert movements of her brush and pen captivated her as the magical creatures came to life under her mother's hand. Strange how a woman so haunted could produce such magic. Some misshapen chunk of hope in Nolin's chest told her that if she could just get her mother to make that magic again, everything would be all right.

Melissa slid a sleek sable brush from the can, thought better of it, and slipped it back in before picking another. This brush hovered over the palette for a moment, twitching between the red and blue paints. Again, she stuck the brush back in the jar.

Nolin's eyes wandered along the bookshelves as her mother agonized over paintbrushes. A sliver of pale pink peeked over the top of the bookcase next to the desk, standing out against the line of black sketchbooks. Nolin stood on her tiptoes and caught something soft in her fingers.

It was a baby shoe, candy pink, faded by time, with dust settled deep into the fibers. One of the tiny flowers on the toe held on by a single ragged strand of yarn.

"Melissa," she said. "What's this?"

Melissa's thin body shuddered under her tee shirt. She twisted her neck around to see. Suddenly, Nolin wished she hadn't said anything. She clutched the shoe to her chest. Melissa's eyes bulged behind her glasses. She stood up, still holding the brush, and threw out her hand.

"Give that to me." Her hand shook, her voice soft and deadly. Nolin stared and placed the shoe in her mother's palm. Melissa stuffed it into the pocket of her pajama pants without looking at it. "Do not touch that. Ever." Jagged terror flashed across her eyes before they turned to cold, steely gray.

Nolin nodded. Shame prickled in her stomach. She hadn't meant to upset her. Why was her mother so afraid of a shoe? Where was its mate?

Melissa looked down at the illustration she hadn't yet touched. "These damn brushes are full of dust," she said. She dropped the brush. It clinked and rolled until it caught on the lip of the desk. "Don't touch anything else," she said before stomping out of the room. Nolin heard the bedroom door slam.

Chapter 5

THE SHADOW WATCHED from the edge of the woods in the shelter of the undergrowth, her pale hand resting on a tree. Fireflies sparked in the trees and in the yard of the house she'd watched all afternoon. Nolin had fought at school again. Today, she had passed by the windows with dust rags and mops until the father came home from work with a pizza. Nolin and Paul ate in silence, then Nolin retired to bed.

The Shadow drew shallow breaths. Fireflies danced in her dark eyes.

Why did she torture herself like this? Watching this family, wanting what should have been hers but never would be, sneaking into the house to steal things, leaving tiny hints of her existence. A door cracked open, an object slightly moved. What good could it possibly do?

They'd all be asleep soon. At night, she often whispered to the child on the wind to help her remember. Nolin had no idea what she really was.

Melissa, on the other hand, understood.

The Shadow smiled grimly. She wasn't surprised the mother was unstable, knowing what she knew. It pleased the Shadow in a perverse way. She'd let Melissa see her many times. She knew it frightened her.

For years, the Shadow didn't think Melissa fully understood what she saw, but she understood now. Melissa spoke to the Shadow at night. Desperate as she was not to believe, Melissa couldn't deny what she'd always known.

The Shadow wanted Melissa to know she was still there.

The biting chill of the night raised the hairs on her pale arms. She broke out in goose bumps. Cold, a weakness she'd never overcome. Humans weren't meant for this life, but she wasn't human. Not anymore.

She wasn't quite sure what she was.

Part of the forest. At the same time, not.

She had been ripped from her life and replaced with a demon— a little beast that grew to bear her name, her identity.

Her.

She couldn't turn back time, travel back to the night when she was stolen from her bedroom window and carried off into the woods and changed into...whatever she was now. She could set things right, more or less. Revenge was petty, but goblin babies tore families apart. She'd seen it, watched her own human parents squabble, drive themselves mad knowing deep down the beast in their life wasn't the child they wanted. What's done was done. All she could do was pick up the pieces from the wreckage of her life, salvage what she could, and make things right.

She'd already begun.

***

Nolin woke slick with sweat. The full moon spied on her from its station in the ebony sky, its light oozing through the open window like a silvery liquid dripping off the windowsill and furniture. The potted plants on her dresser twitched in the breeze from the window.

Had she heard something? She couldn't remember.

Silently, she slid off the bed, tiptoed to the bedroom door, and crept into the hall. She listened. Nothing. Alert and suspicious, she inched back into her room.

She'd dreamt of the forest again, running barefoot, leaping over rocks and fallen logs, darting between trees like a deer. The dreams were getting more frequent, more vivid.

They were the same each time. Always running, but from what? Or toward what? She never felt afraid in the dreams. She only felt longing, like she was searching for something. The forest was misty in her dreams, hazy, only partially formed. She always stopped before a massive tree, a half-fallen timber whose five thick roots still gripped the ground like a gnarled hand refusing to surrender completely. The Claw Tree, she called it. She stood before it, marveling at its size, the strength of the roots that clung to the ground. She felt on the verge of solving some mystery she'd unraveled like a knot all her life, the answer a breath away.

She sat cross-legged on the mattress, looking out the window at the woods beyond the yard. Black trees stood like soldiers at attention, forming a striking silhouette against the sky. How would it be to slip out of the house and disappear into those trees forever? The thoughts scared her. She wouldn't be the same person among those trees. She could swear the forest whispered to her: an invitation into its depths.

She spread her hands wide on the cool glass. A mosquito bounced on the outside of the screen before darting away into the night. Lightning bugs twinkled, mirroring the stars above them. The tips of the trees swayed in the wind like hands.

Movement.

A small, pale figure slid into the trees.

Her stomach lurched. Goose bumps raised on her arms, either from fear or excitement. Had she really seen it? She trained her eyes on the spot where the figure had vanished. There was nothing there except the spark of a firefly.

She settled back into the bed, heart thudding in her chest.

It was nothing, she told herself. *Just a trick of the moonlight.*

Chapter 6

HER HANDS WERE red from scrubbing the kitchen floor. The hot water and soap made her hands wrinkled, dry, and raw. At least the downstairs sparkled: vacuumed, dusted, furniture polished, windows washed, everything in its place. Maybe her father would notice how nice it looked. Nolin imagined him praising her, telling her what a good job she'd done. Even more fantastic, she imagined her mother smiling, looking around the spotless house and nodding her approval.

That scene only ever happened in Nolin's imagination. Cleaning the house when she was suspended was a punishment. It was silly to expect praise.

Melissa was still in her room. Aside from that bedroom, Nolin couldn't think of anything else to clean. She dropped the rag into the gray water with a splash.

Wait. She hadn't finished the studio. That room held so much of Melissa, maybe more than Melissa herself did anymore. Maybe a clean, inviting studio would tempt her mother back to her drawing desk. Maybe it would make her happy.

She grabbed the feather duster, a few rags, and furniture polish and trekked upstairs. The house creaked around her. She felt a funny feeling of being watched that visited her so often.

Nolin crept down the hall to the studio and opened the door. The dirty carpet turned abruptly grayer at a line along the door, contrasting with the cleaner carpet in the hallway. Dust coated every surface. She'd need to wash the brushes out, rinse the water jars, and work a cloth into the cracks between drawers and books to get all the grime out. Cobwebs flourished in the corners of the ceiling and on the domed light fixture.

She stood on the chair to clean the bookshelves. She sneezed and blinked the flying particles from her eyelashes. She read the titles of the books on their worn spines while she worked. Which were her mother's favorites? What was she like when she had read them? Someone very different from the Melissa she was now, Nolin was sure of that, though she had no idea who that person might have been.

She imagined a different version of her mother, someone with the same pale eyes and thin face, with blonde hair thick and flowing instead of stringy and unwashed, who wore long dresses that curved along healthy, round hips, not jutting bones, who smiled instead of staring into space. That woman read fantasy novels, created worlds in her sketchbooks, ate entire meals, and savored ice cream cones on hot summer days. Her mother was alive and fiery once, she was sure of it. No one who could create such art could have been anything else.

Nolin ran the feather duster over the spines of the hardbound sketchbooks. Something whispered that she'd find answers there.

Heart thudding like a thief's, she slid a black sketchbook from the tightly packed shelf and opened the stiff cover.

Dark, angry scribbles covered the first page. If Nolin looked closely, she could see the faint outline of a half-finished human form, frantically scribbled out. The same thing on the next page. Nearly half the book was just scratched-out drawings, outlines of arms and legs hidden in the pencil marks.

Toward the middle, abstract forms started to appear: aimless swirls and zigzags, twisting tree branches, disembodied faces, and skinny, headless bodies. Faceless, deformed figures. Androgynous figures with long necks and pointed chins, all bending strangely.

She turned the pages. The figures gave way to trees, some of them sprouting limbs from their torsos or leaves from their heads. Soon they were dancing trees, bending and swirling in the invisible breeze. Puzzled, Nolin flipped through the rest of the pages, replaced the book on the shelf, and pulled out the next one.

She flipped through that one to find more of the same. Pencil marks smudged on the yellowed paper. The books smelled faintly chemical, like spray paint.

Three books later, Melissa was drawing large, elaborate trees in scratchy pen, sometimes with tiny, faceless figures with spindly limbs and wild hair. Nolin leafed through slowly, studying the pictures. The figures started to gain faces; tiny eyes and wide grins.

She turned another page. A stone dropped into her stomach.

A thick black tree tilted on the page, five massive roots curling up out of the ground like fingers and a forearm.

The Claw Tree.

The tree from her dreams. The same giant, half-fallen tree she saw almost every night, on the page in her mother's scratchy ink lines.

Nolin ran a trembling finger up the trunk, her heart beating like a kettle drum. How did Melissa know that tree?

The leaves seemed to twitch on the page. Nolin could almost smell dark soil and bark. Her hand jerked back as if she were afraid the page would suck her in. She slapped the book shut and shoved it back into the bookshelf.

Nolin's mind spun. She could only think of two possibilities: either her mother dreamed about that tree as well, or the tree was real.

Nolin wasn't sure which troubled her more.

Chapter 7

THIS HAS SURE been a rainy spring, Nolin thought. Thick droplets tumbled off leaves and tulips from a downpour that had ended moments before. Earthworms and snails stretched across the dark sidewalks. Clouds pulled themselves apart like cotton balls, allowing sun rays to shine through in golden pillars.

Nolin set off for the library with a gallon-size zip bag in her pocket to protect her book if it rained again. She needed to clear her head, and she'd run out of things to clean anyway, so she'd decided to return to the library while the sun was shining. Melissa hadn't made a sound all morning, so Nolin doubted she'd notice her being gone for a little while.

Her flip-flops scratched on the pavement as she carefully trod around worms and snails, occasionally stopping to bend down and examine them. Years ago, she'd collected dozens of snails in a box. Melissa made her throw them all out in the road so they'd get run over instead of eating the plants in the flowerbed in front of the house. Nolin hadn't told her there were no flowers in the yard. There hadn't been for years. The flowerbed was full of weeds.

An earthworm squished under her shoe. She resumed her watch on the sidewalk to avoid the creatures and cracks.

"Hey, Nolin!"

The call snapped her out of her thoughts. She turned and saw a skinny boy from class waving from his front walkway, which was littered with clumps of wet lawn clippings, clutching a broom taller than he was. Drew, Max's friend. Nolin didn't stop.

Drew stood still for a moment, grasping his broom. Nolin turned the corner so that she walked along the other side of the yard of his corner house.

"Max tried to come over today. I told him to get lost," Drew said. "He shouldn't have teased you."

"You didn't have to. I don't care who you're friends with." Nolin kicked a pebble, sending it skittering across the street. "Why are you sweeping that while it's wet?"

Drew scowled at the messy sidewalk. "I told Mom I'd sweep this up after my brother mowed yesterday, and I forgot. So I'm doing it now. It's not working very well. Anyway, where are you going?"

"Library."

"Oh," Drew said. "Can I come with you? I might have to wait until this dries anyway, and I have some books to take back."

Nolin shrugged. The tips of her ears grew hot, and her stomach backflipped. Drew ran inside, carrying the broom like a lance as he charged the house. The screen door banged, and he disappeared inside, leaving Nolin alone, unsure what to do.

A minute later, Drew scampered down the front steps with a few books under his arm. He jogged toward her, his sneakers squeaking in the grass. His brown hair stuck out in all directions.

"Mom said I can go," he said breathlessly. "She's cool."

Nolin nodded, not sure what to say. They walked. Drew made heroic attempts to keep the conversation moving.

"Have you read these?" he asked, showing her his books: *Maniac McGee* and *Tuck Everlasting*.

"My teacher read both of those to us last year when I was in the fourth grade," Nolin said. "I enjoyed them."

"Oh yeah, you skipped a grade, didn't you? You must be really smart."

Nolin shrugged again. "I think they just didn't know what to do with me."

If Drew found this strange, he didn't show it. He bobbed along with his bouncy walk. "Did you get in fights in the fourth grade too?"

"Sometimes."

Drew kicked a crab apple. It bounced down the sidewalk ahead of them. "Well, you fight really good. I've never seen a girl punch like that. Not even my sisters."

Nolin cracked a small smile. "Do you have a lot of sisters?"

"Four of them," he said. "And two brothers. I'm the youngest."

Nolin couldn't imagine so many people living in one house. "I don't have sisters or brothers," she said.

"Well you can have some of mine. It can be really fun, but most of the time my house is noisy and smells like perfume and there's not enough space. I share a room with my brother Mark. He's fourteen and he's nice. He's really messy, though. I mean, I'm pretty messy too, but at least my mess stays on my side of the room. Mark gets so mad when I shove all his stuff back to his side."

How can someone talk so much? Nolin wasn't annoyed; she was just used to silence, parents who didn't talk enough.

"Isn't it nice, though, to have other people to talk to and play with?" she asked. "You probably never get lonely."

Drew shook his head. "Nope, I definitely don't get lonely. I love them all, but girls are just...crazy sometimes."

Nolin laughed. "Crazy?"

"Yeah. They take forever in the bathroom, they like to watch movies that make them cry, and they eat all the ice cream when their boyfriends do stupid stuff. They don't all live at home, though. My oldest sister doesn't live with us. But she comes over a lot and then they all get out their nail polish and talk all night long and keep me awake."

They turned the corner. Nolin could see the giant willow in front of the library.

"If you need peace and quiet, you should come here," Nolin said. "It's always quiet. This is where my dad takes me when I get suspended. I don't walk home until I'd normally get home from school. It never fools my mom, though. I think she watches for me to get off the bus."

"Your dad wants you to lie?"

Nolin smiled grimly. "My mom gets upset easily. He doesn't want her to get any more worked up than she already is. She always knows, though, and she gets upset anyway."

"Oh yeah, I've heard about your mom..." He immediately turned red. "Oh, I'm sorry. I didn't mean that...I mean, I haven't heard much. Just that she has...you know...problems."

Nolin crossed her arms over her chest. "I know better than anyone else about her *problems*, thank you."

"I'm really sorry." Drew's cheeks flushed pink. "I didn't mean to hurt your feelings. I don't know what I'm talking about; I've never met her. I shouldn't talk about things I don't know."

The brewing anger in Nolin's stomach cooled a little. "It's okay," she said. "I know people talk about her."

It was true. She often felt the neighbors' eyes when she left for the bus stop every morning, heard the whispers of teachers about her "troubled" mother and her "unfortunate" situation. Words like "crazy" and "loony" had floated around her classes and the playground since kindergarten. Once or twice, she'd heard hushed whispers of "the incident" among some of the older teachers. She wasn't sure what they meant.

"They don't know what they're talking about either," Drew said. "People just get bored and like to gossip. Don't listen to any of it. I shouldn't. I won't listen to them again."

They walked in silence, Nolin kicking rocks with each step. She could almost hear Drew's mind working, searching for a grip on the conversation. He cleared his throat, like a car shifting gears.

"If I got suspended, Mom would whup my butt. I'd be scrubbing toilets and pulling weeds till my hands fell off. That's not even counting what Dad would do."

"My parents don't do much," Nolin said. "My mom stays in her room and Dad goes to work. I clean, though. I guess it's a good thing I get suspended or the house would never get clean."

Drew chuckled uneasily. "Do you get lonely?"

The question caught her off guard. She thought for a moment, still treading around the cracks and worms on the sidewalk. The willow tree grew closer. Its vines reached for them fluidly, like they were underwater.

"Yes, I do."

"No brothers or sisters, your dad goes to work, and your mom stays in her room. You don't have any friends at school."

"Most people don't want to be my friend. I don't really want to be their friend either."

"Why not?"

"Because they don't care about anyone except themselves. They don't like anyone who's not like them. They're boring and mean and I don't want to be friends with people like that. I'd rather be alone."

"Not all people are like that. You could play with me at recess. We can make you some friends."

Nolin shrugged again.

"You shrug a lot."

"I don't have anything to say."

They crossed the street to the library. Nolin paused under the willow to reach up and touch the vines.

"What are you doing?" Drew asked.

"I like to feel things."

"Why?"

Nolin thought, running the smooth leaves through her fingers. "It just makes me feel alive, because those things are living. I don't feel so alone."

Drew reached up and took a vine in his hand, running his thumb over one of the soft leaves. He smiled, crinkling the corners of his eyes and revealing large front teeth. "This feels cool."

"I like to climb this tree," Nolin said. "Sometimes I'll take a book up here."

Drew smiled. "I've never read a book in a tree before."

Nolin laughed softly. "Most people haven't. Let's go get a book, and I'll show you."

As they came up the walk, Ms. Savage's face appeared in one of the windows. Her red lips parted; maybe she was just surprised to see Nolin with someone who wasn't her father, but a child her age. A friend maybe. She smiled. Nolin smiled back.

Chapter 8

SPRAWLED OUT ON her bed, Nolin finished Act One of *A Midsummer Night's Dream*. Her mind stretched, struggling to translate the musical phrases into everyday language, pausing after nearly every couplet until she began to understand. The wordless part of her comprehended those artful phrases, though she couldn't have fully explained them. It was like learning a new language.

Helena's unrequited love fascinated her. Why did she pursue such a love when Demetrius obviously despised her? She saw it over and over again in books; characters torturing themselves, pining for the love of someone who would never love them.

Does love just makes people miserable?

I love Mom, she thought. *They never write about that kind of unrequited love.*

She shook her head and began Act Two.

Finally, the fairies! She was done reading about humans for now. As a fairy named Puck conversed with a fellow fairy in Shakespeare's musical words, the language filled her like cool water. Then her eyes snagged on a term she didn't recognize.

Changeling.

Puzzled, she scanned the footnotes. "*A child exchanged for another by fairies or goblins.*"

Nolin's eyes fell on a castoff drawing of her mother's, that was taped to the wall, one that Melissa had let her keep. It was a tree surrounded by skinny, elfish children with long fingers, their faces devious and frightening.

Changeling.

The word stuck in her mind like the name of an old friend she'd almost forgotten but might not have liked much. She whispered the word to herself. A strange mixture of emotions brewed inside her. Nervousness prickled her stomach. Excitement fluttered like wings in her chest; dark, hot dread bubbled in the pit of her gut. Her eyes locked on one of the children in the drawing, peeking around the trunk of the tree with a devilish grin. Before, she'd thought the elfish children in the drawing were funny, interesting, harmless. Now they scared her.

Melissa had never talked about that illustration, whether it was for a specific story or if she'd just drawn it for fun. Nolin decided to ask her sometime, if she ever had a good day.

The bed creaked as she stood up on the mattress. The light of the full, bright moon blazed through the window and lit the room pale blue. Long shadows of the trees mingled with Nolin's shadow on the floor and walls. Her shadow, the slight figure with the mass of wild hair, reminded her of the children in the drawing.

She ripped the drawing off the wall, jumped off the bed with a thud, and stuffed the drawing in her dresser drawer.

***

Night. The Shadow's favorite time.

She waited by the edge of the woods as she did every night, watching for the lights in the house to go out. Nolin's light went out first. The light in the living room where Paul stayed up to read burned late into the night. Eventually, it went out too.

When the house was finally dark, the Shadow inhaled the scent of the night, the aroma of their slumber on the air. She turned from the home and trekked deep into the woods. Her mind wandered, but her body knew the way through the subtle paths, around each exposed root and rock, every tuft of grass on the forest floor. She weaved around trees and slithered below fallen logs.

The massive black tree hid itself behind a cover of tight trees and mossy boulders, half-fallen, holding itself to the ground with five thick roots, leaving a spacious hollow underneath.

Home.

One of the few places in the world that felt anything like home. A place to hide, wait, and dream.

She crept between the roots into the soft bed of leaves and grass beneath the trunk to the bed of leaves below.

The Shadow inhaled and twined her fingers around a thin branch growing from a root of the ancient tree. She laid back into the leaves and inhaled the fresh, earthy air. Her hand tingled all the way up her arm and into her head, tickling her temples as if insects were crawling around her hairline.

Voices whispered. Thoughts that were not hers floated through her mind. There weren't many left. She knew some of them. Others were unfamiliar, other goblins unknowingly living as humans. There seemed to be fewer and fewer each time. She hushed them out, sorting through the babble with her eyes closed.

On the edge of the babble were the familiar, jagged thoughts of Melissa, jolting like wounded animals. The Shadow pushed them out. They hurt. If she let them, those thoughts would poison her, stain her mind until she'd be nothing more than a heap of torment, just like Melissa.

No, she needed her mind sharp, clear. She forced Melissa's ragged pain out and focused on the gentle trill of Nolin's mind drifting off to sleep.

Nolin's mind was imagination, hope edged sharply with worry, fear, and guilt that threatened to seep into the Shadow's own heart. She hardened herself like ice. These were not her thoughts, not her feelings. She was an observer. She could feel what she chose. The Shadow forced her breathing to stay soft as she settled into Nolin's mind. She had a message to send; one she'd sent many times before.

The Shadow thought of the woods, picturing the Claw Tree in her mind clearly. Nolin's thoughts flared like a cat bristling in fear. Ripples of anxiety shot through the Shadow's body. She breathed deeply. This wasn't hers.

The Shadow's thoughts raced, though she tried to slow them. Images flashed through her mind, propelled by the fear and anger of years past. Her brain burned behind her forehead.

She pressed images out of her mind until there was nothing but the Claw Tree. The message. Nolin knew the way. She has to, the Shadow thought. She wasn't sure if the desperation she felt was hers or the feelings of another whose thoughts flowed through the tree.

Nolin's mind would filter the images like tinted glass. The Shadow felt it along the edges of Nolin's thoughts, her draw to the forest.

Soon, she would come.

***

She was a tree.

Nolin reached to the sky with branches instead of arms. The swishing material on her head was not hair, but leaves. The canopy of the woods twisted, swirling like the dark clouds above them. Grasses tickled her trunk. She forgot everything about herself: her name, her family, her past. She danced happily in the wind, her strong roots twining deep into the earth. She couldn't remember feeling such peace. Being a tree felt natural, like she'd been born a seed and spent her whole life growing out of the ground.

When she remembered she was a person and not a tree, she suddenly stood on two legs. She reached with two arms instead of branches. Her spray of leaves had become her wild, curly hair. She closed her eyes with her arms out, willing herself to stretch taller and become one of the trees again.

Nearby, something rustled in a bush.

Twigs and tiny green leaves twitched violently. Whatever was hiding sounded terrified. Perhaps it was trapped. Nolin moved closer, instinctively crouching, making no sound. The bush shook. The creature inside it shrieked—an oddly human sound. Tension rippled through her muscles. The thing screeched again. Nolin reached out to the thrashing bush, her heart leaping with anticipation.

An icy hand fell on her shoulder.

With a gasp, she spun around to meet two liquid black eyes framed by a mane of wild dark hair, a red mouth set in a hard line.

Nolin's eyes shot open. Roaring wind rushed over her, filling the bedroom with the scent of the woods. She scrambled to her knees to close the window above her bed.

The rustling sound again—a frightened squeak.

The sound was inside the house.

Her toes gripped the carpet as she padded toward the door. A sense of déjà vu overtook her as she reached to push it open, like reaching for the thrashing bush in her dream. Her shoulders tightened, waiting for the hand on her shoulder.

Her fingers brushed the cold wood. The door swung open.

Shadows danced in the hallway, flickering in the yellow glow of the night-light. The sound was louder now, coming from her mother's room. Melissa was thrashing in her bed, Nolin realized.

"Melissa?" Nolin whispered. She crept to her mother's door with the caution of a thief. "Melissa?"

Another sound inside the room. Whispering.

Was Melissa talking to herself? Nolin strained to hear what was going on behind the door. A low, menacing whisper, words Nolin didn't understand.

"Melissa?" she called again, louder. She took a breath before turning the knob and pushing the door open.

The whispering stopped. Though the room was dark, Nolin could see her mother's narrow form under the comforter, rolling back and forth. Melissa whimpered, a pitiful sound that turned Nolin's blood to ice.

Her father wasn't there. He'd warned Nolin to never wake Melissa from her dreams, to let them play out on their own. Nolin desperately wanted to run inside, shake her mother awake, and end whatever terrors gripped her sleep.

A soft whistle blew downstairs; her body coiled back like a compressed spring. She backed out of the room and realized someone had turned on a downstairs light. The whistle stopped. Someone coughed downstairs.

It was just her father and the teakettle. Nolin let out the breath she didn't realize she held. Her raw nerves jangled as she forced her heartbeat to slow.

Nolin decided to leave her mother to her fitful sleep. She'd have to come out of it on her own, like her father said. Nolin felt both wide-awake and exhausted. Tea sounded nice. She went downstairs.

Her father poured hot water into a mug, steam rising in ghostly curls. He looked like he hadn't slept in days.

Nolin stopped at the bottom of the stairs, not wanting to startle him. He hadn't noticed her yet. "Dad?" she whispered. Humming to himself, he added a teabag to his mug.

"Dad!" she called in what she thought was her inside voice. It came out at a volume her teacher would have scolded her for if she'd used it in the classroom. Her father jerked, eyes wide and mouth gaping open. Then his face scrunched in pain as hot water sloshed out of the mug.

"Ow! Son of a...Nolin! Don't *do* that!" he ran his hand under cold water in the sink. Nolin's stomach twinged, the familiar feeling that she'd done something wrong.

"I'm sorry! I'm sorry! Did it burn you badly?" she scampered to his side and peeked over the counter to see his hand in the sink.

"No, it's fine," he grunted. Nolin shrank back to dab the spilled water with a dishtowel. Paul sighed and turned off the faucet, shaking his hand dry. "You couldn't sleep either, huh?"

Nolin nodded. She wiped his mug and paused to look at the picture of the Grand Canyon printed on it. "Did you really get this at the Grand Canyon?" she asked.

Paul nodded. "The only vacation your mother and I ever took. That was our honeymoon. Not long after we got back, you came along."

The tips of Nolin's ears burned. She hadn't missed the shadow of accusation, though she was sure her father hadn't meant it. "Maybe Mom would like a vacation," she suggested. "I've never been on one. Maybe something new would be good for her."

Paul snorted. "She barely leaves the house, Nolin. What makes you think she'd be up to a vacation?"

Nolin shrugged. She found her own mug in the cupboard, a pink polka-dotted one. She added a chamomile tea bag. "I don't know. Maybe she's bored being inside all the time. Wouldn't you be?"

Paul bobbed his head from side to side, adding honey to his tea. "Where would you want to go, Nolin?"

Nolin's mind cast around. She'd only left the town on school field trips. She'd never left the state. She thought of the places she'd read about or learned about in school, vacations she'd heard her classmates bragging about. "Alaska?" she proposed.

"Really, why there?"

"I think Mom would like it. And I'd like it. It's totally different from here."

Paul sat at the bar and sipped his tea. His brow wrinkled.

"Maybe. If she starts to get better."

Tiny butterflies danced in Nolin's chest. She joined her father at the bar. A hopeful smile tickled the corners of her mouth.

They sipped in silence. The overhead light cast eerie shadows over Paul's face, darkening the wells of his eye sockets and cheekbones. He reminded her of skeletons from old Halloween books she'd read.

"Dad?" she ventured.

"Hmm?"

"Was Mom ever happy?"

Paul tipped his head down. The shadows in his eyes grew darker and longer.

"Happier than she is now."

"When did she start getting sick?"

"Hard to say. When I met her, she'd barely graduated high school and her best friend had just died. She was in a pretty rough spot, but I don't think she was sick."

"Her friend died?"

He nodded. "She and your mom were hiking or something up in the mountains. I guess Alexa fell down the side of the mountain and into a river. Your mom tried to find her. She stayed there for most of the night, searching. Eventually, she had to go all the way back to town alone for help. She was all kinds of torn up. She still had a job and went to school, though. She wasn't like she is now."

Nolin bit the inside of her cheek. She watched the curling steam from her mug as if expecting to decipher some meaningful shape in the vapor.

Her father chuckled. *What could possibly be funny?* Nolin thought. He looked out the window, the corners of his eyes crinkling into long-forgotten laugh lines.

"She worked at a burger place when I met her. I was in town for school. I spent a fortune on burgers that semester. I'd always get the cheapest meal and leave her a big fat tip and my phone number on the receipt." He chuckled. Then the smile faded.

"We dated a year before I proposed. She was doing better. She started art school. She even got some freelance drawing work. Your mom used to be a fun lady. You've never known her like she was." His voice cracked on was. "I thought she'd be happy if we got married."

Nolin noticed his simple gold wedding band, scratched and bent. She knew he never took it off, even when he showered or mowed the lawn. His lips bunched together. Nolin had the feeling he was talking to himself more than her.

"Then you came along." It sounded like an accusation, as if she were a pothole in their road to wedded bliss. Nolin felt her cheeks flush.

"Mom said I was an accident," she said quietly.

Her father cocked his head to the side, his eyes crinkled in a soft smile. "Well, you weren't planned, but I wouldn't call you an accident. The usual...well, birth control didn't agree with her. All the hormones drove her crazy. Then one day that little pink line appeared, and we knew you were on the way. She had a rough pregnancy. Sick every day, lots of complications, bed rest. She had to quit school and work, and she stopped drawing.

"You came almost two months early. You cried and cried and cried; you never stopped crying. You stayed in the hospital for a couple weeks. The doctors didn't think you were going to make it at first; you were so tiny and frail. Your mom hardly left the hospital. Once we got you home, the crying started. Day and night. Taking care of a new baby is tough for anybody, but she really struggled. Then that one night, she just went over the edge."

He paused, looking out at the swaying trees, the wind blowing through the branches. The rustling leaves whispered, like the trees had spirits.

"Something happened that night," he continued. "It was the weirdest thing. You never cried after that. It's like you were a completely different child. You slept through the night, you weren't sick anymore, and you never cried."

"What happened?"

"I don't know. I just found your mom in your room in the middle of the night, and she was just...not right. She hasn't been right since."

Her suspicions prodded her. She knew that acting on them would only unleash a monster. Still, she couldn't resist.

"Dad?"

"Hmm?"

"Is it my fault Mom's sick?"

He paused and then gulped down the rest of his tea. Nolin waited, her insides twisting around themselves like a pit of snakes. Her father mopped his chin with the bottom of his tee shirt. A gush of wind rattled the windows. The tree in the front yard reached across the window with a branch like a witch's hand. Nolin thought of her mother's body, thin and gnarled.

Her father cleared his throat. "I don't know."

He didn't look at her when he answered.

Chapter 9

NOLIN WOKE TO pounding on the ceiling over her head. Faint sunshine filtered through the sheer curtains, bathing the living room in gray light. She sat up from where she'd fallen asleep on the carpet in front of the window. Her father snored in his arm-chair.

"Uh-oh." Nolin scrambled to her feet, dashed up the stairs to her mother's room, and threw open the door. Melissa faced the open window, sprinting in place. The back of her tee shirt was blotched with sweat, and her dirty hair clung to her neck. The stagnant air reeked of sweat. The bedsheets lay in a knotted pile on the floor. The naked mattress was littered with jewelry: a string of pearls, dozens of earrings, a jeweled bracelet. Tangled around a gold chain was a clay bead necklace Nolin had made in school for Mother's Day in the third grade; a string of blue and purple pea-sized spheres she'd spent hours shaping and smoothing, ensuring each was the exact-same size and shape.

Melissa coughed, a deep hack in her chest. Her face was pale and shiny.

"Is Paul mad at me?" she puffed. Her wild eyes were bloodshot. She stared out the window, dirty hair swinging around her face.

"He fell asleep downstairs." Nolin grabbed Melissa's clammy wrist and pulled her onto the bed. Melissa almost tripped, but caught herself on the mattress. She breathed.

"I was afraid he was upset when he wasn't here when I woke up. He hardly ever sleeps in the bed anymore. I couldn't sit still. I just had to do something. Work the energy out." Nolin didn't ask how long she'd been running. She'd never looked so old. Nolin knew her mother was only thirty-one, but her pale lips drooped at the corners, shadows rimmed her eyes, and a deep crease separated her eyebrows. Even now, with her skin red and blotchy and her white tee shirt stained with sour sweat, Nolin thought she was beautiful.

Melissa collapsed onto the mattress. "Paul bought me most of these." She picked up the gold chain by her index finger. The clay bead necklace dropped and slid off the end of the bed. "He loves me. Look at all these." She seemed to speak to herself, not Nolin.

"Why don't you wear some of them today?" Nolin said. "We could go for a walk, and maybe Dad will get home early enough to take you to dinner tonight." A twinge of guilt twisted her stomach. It was a lie. He'd probably stay late to make up for the time he'd missed earlier in the week when he picked her up from school. Melissa would never go anyway. Still, she had to try to get her out somehow.

"A walk?" Melissa echoed.

"Yeah, we could go to the park, or we could get sandwiches or something and have a picnic..."

"No, no picnics."

"Right, well, it's supposed to be sunny today. You'll like it."

Melissa dropped the pearls across her forehead.

Nolin pressed on. "I'll go make breakfast, then you can take a shower. We'll go for a walk." Melissa didn't respond. "I'll be right back."

Nolin went down to the kitchen, listening for any movement in the bedroom. Downstairs, her father hadn't moved. She put on a pot of water to boil and picked two mugs out of the cupboard. Seven-thirty, the clock read.

"Dad?" Nolin patted her father's shoulder. He stirred, opened his eyes and jerked, startled to see someone so close.

"Come on, Nolin. You're going to give me a heart attack. What time is it?" He looked at his watch and leapt from the chair, tripping over his shoes as he lunged toward the stairs.

"I started breakfast." Nolin called after him. "It'll be ready when you're done showering."

"No time!" he called from upstairs. Water gushed in the pipes. Nolin stirred oatmeal and raisins into the boiling water. While the oatmeal cooked, she made a sandwich, slipped it in a plastic bag, and set it on the table with an apple and her father's car keys. This was getting to be a routine.

***

Melissa scooped the scattered jewelry into a mound on the mattress, mentally cataloging each piece. The anniversary bracelet, the wedding pearls, the engagement ring.

Her eyes caught the simple necklace on the floor, a string of purple and blue beads. She leaned down to picked it up with her finger, then slid it over her head. The cool beads felt soothing on her sweaty neck. She examined her reflection in the vanity table mirror. The necklace draped across her collarbones, which were still graceful and feminine despite their alarming sharpness. The cool colors coaxed the last tinge of blush from her cheeks. She remembered her eyes were faintly blue. Unlike overpowering pearls and diamonds, this simple gift suited her, even made her feel pretty.

Any mother would be ecstatic to have a child like Nolin. She helped around the house without being asked. She was a pretty little thing, or would be if she would comb her hair and wear something decent. She was brilliant, probably a child genius if given the proper attention.

What kind of a mother feels ill at the sight of her own daughter? To feel disgust rather than love was despicable, inhuman. True, Nolin was different, but special. Why should her differences matter?

Melissa's stomach lurched. Her esophagus clenched. She doubled over, dry heaving. She hadn't eaten in days. There was nothing left to purge. The rough spasms clawed her lungs. She wished she could eat. And sleep. Couldn't she have one night free from nightmares? Just one day without having to look over her shoulder for shadows?

Maybe it was all in her head. She'd told herself that so many times. She knew it wasn't true.

At least, it wasn't *all* in her head.

A shower might help her feel better, like Nolin said. She hobbled into the bathroom, slipped her hand inside the shower curtain, and twisted the knob for hot water.

She slid off her filthy tee shirt and pajama pants. Blue veins pulsed under the thin, pale skin of her limbs and torso, crisscrossing like cracks in white marble. Her hip bones and ribs reached from under her skin, perhaps trying to escape. She looked down at her deflated breasts. Her body disgusted her.

The body: a sack of bones, veins, frail organs, a bloody mess held together by a weak sheath of skin that could be broken so easily by a kitchen knife, a cat's claw, a piece of paper. What good was such a fragile barrier? Just to hide the true appearance of the body underneath? Skin was a lie.

She slipped into the shower beneath the burning spray, gritting her teeth as the scalding water pelted her back. Smothering white steam wrapped around her as she scrubbed her arms, legs, torso, and back with a rough sponge until she felt raw, like she had no skin left. She wanted to see the body underneath the lie, see what she really was.

She dropped the sponge to scratch at her shoulders, digging with her nails to peel the skin from her back. The water ran red around her feet. She twisted her arms around to claw into her lower back, the front of her thighs, her hollow stomach. The steam and pain nearly blinded her. The hissing water drowned out all other sound.

Then she saw it.

A dark eye, staring at her through the crack in the shower curtain. She knew that eye, and it knew her.

Melissa screamed and ripped at the shower curtain. Then, she slipped.

***

Nolin balanced two bowls of oatmeal on her forearms and held a glass of milk in her hands, walking slowly so the milk didn't slosh. It was shiny and white as Elmer's glue.

A scream sliced through her concentration.

Ice shot through her veins. That scream, raspy and shrill at the same time, raised bumps on her arms and tingled like spiders under her skin.

Then, a thud.

The bowls and glass dropped, splashing on the carpet of the dining room. Nolin sprinted up the stairs two at a time. When she got to the top, she threw open the bedroom door.

Thick, white steam poured into the room from the bathroom. Something smelled wrong, coppery like pennies.

The wet steam settled on Nolin's skin. She ran into the bathroom. Through the shrill hiss of the shower, she heard whimpering behind the shower curtain.

"Mom..."

Nolin reached in and winced as the blistering water burned her arm. Gritting her teeth, she twisted the squeaky knob to shut off the shower. The water trickled to a stop. The only sounds left were the dripping shower head, Melissa's shallow whimpering, and Nolin's sharp breaths. Her heart pounded a bass line in her ears. Melissa cried softly, mumbling something Nolin couldn't hear.

Nolin pushed the curtain aside.

Melissa huddled at the end of the tub with her back to Nolin, naked and red as a stewed tomato, one hand over her forehead. The other arm wrapped around her knees. Angry red scratches crisscrossed her shoulders, white blisters bloomed on her back and arms, and blood ran down the side of her face and seeped between her fingers.

"Mom?" Nolin's voice quavered. Melissa's shoulders shook as she cried. Blood trickled from the gouges on her back.

Nolin squashed her racing thoughts and forced herself to focus. She ripped open the bottom drawer of the vanity and pulled out a clean, folded hand towel. Gently, she reached for Melissa's hand that covered her head.

Melissa shuddered. She pressed her face into the tiled wall, shrinking away from her daughter. Was she was afraid of Nolin? The idea that her mother feared her made Nolin sick. She would never, ever hurt her mother.

Nolin gently pulled Melissa's hand from her bleeding head and pressed the towel to the wound. Her skin was burning hot. "Hold... hold this," Nolin choked. Melissa pressed her hand over the towel.

"I...I'm going to get help. It'll be okay." Nolin yanked a bigger towel off the rack and carefully draped it over Melissa's torn back. Melissa flinched like Nolin had cracked a whip at her, then she reached a bony claw to pull the towel tighter around herself.

Chapter 10

THIS IS WORSE than waiting outside the principal's office.

The paramedics hadn't let Nolin ride in the back with her mother; instead, she was allowed in the cab with the driver. He assured her that her mother would be fine, they'd take good care of her, that the hospital had a playroom. His high, scratchy voice buzzed like a mosquito in her ears. She wanted to swat it away.

Now she heard the grown-ups talking inside the hospital room while she waited outside. She tried not to listen, instead focusing on the endless tapping of feet echoing around the hall. Words like "hallucination" and "self-harm" still fell on her like lashes from a whip. She might have only been ten, but she'd been Melissa's daughter long enough to know what those words meant.

The door opened. Her father stepped out. He looked exhausted.

"Is Mom okay?"

Her father put his hand on his mouth and sat next to her. His suit looked strange in a hospital full of doctors and nurses in their colored scrubs.

He leaned forward with his elbows on his knees, shaking his head.

"Seventy percent of her body is covered in first- and second-degree burns," he said. "Lots of minor lacerations. She has a concussion from when she slipped and hit her head, but the doctors say she'll be fine." His jaw stiffened and he avoided her gaze. "We don't think she meant to hurt herself," he finally said. "They think she had a psychotic episode." He glanced up at Nolin, looking horrified that he'd just uttered those words to a ten-year-old. Nolin stared straight ahead, her brow furrowed in concentration.

"Like a hallucination?"

"Yes, like a hallucination. We think she thought she saw something on her skin, and she tried to scratch it off. Do you understand?"

"I know what a hallucination is."

"Of course you do." He nodded, his eyes unfocused and glassy. "She should heal physically. We're more worried about what this means for her mental condition." He cupped his hands over his mouth and nose, like he was praying with his face in his hands. "They're going to keep her in this part of the hospital until her head injury gets better. Then they're going to move her to the psychiatric ward."

His eyes darted sideways at Nolin. Maybe he hoped she didn't know what that meant. She knew. She'd read "The Yellow Wallpaper," *One Flew Over the Cuckoo's Nest, The Bell Jar.* She was terrified for Melissa.

"Are they going to shock her?" Nolin asked.

"No, Nolin, they don't do that anymore." His words were reassuring, but he looked even more worried.

"Are you sure?"

"They won't shock her."

78

"Could you make sure?"

Nolin thought of *The Bell Jar*. Her stomach churned. She imagined her mother on a cold metal table with wires in her mouth, her body convulsing with electricity like Frankenstein's monster.

"I'll ask the doctor when I talk to him again."

"How long will she be here?"

"I don't know."

He turned to Nolin, biting his bottom lip. "Nolin..." he started. He looked at his hands clasped in his lap. "I need you to promise me something. Promise you'll be good. We can't have any more fights. No more trips to the principal's office or phone calls from teachers. It puts a lot of stress on your mom and me. It can't happen again. Not now. Promise me."

"I promise."

Two young nurses, one in dark-blue scrubs and the other in hot-pink, walked past them, laughing. Laughter sounded strange. All Nolin could think about was the woman in "The Yellow Wallpaper" crawling on her hands and knees, around and around the walls of her room until the wallpaper wore through.

"Can I see her?" Nolin asked.

"She's asleep. She won't know you're there. You probably don't want to see her right now anyway. She's doesn't look good."

"I want to see her."

He nodded, lips set in a tight line.

Nolin pushed herself off the chair and opened the door.

The shared room was bigger than she'd expected, full of hanging white curtains to shield the beds from one another. A medicinal odor stung her nose. The cacophony of clicks and beeps grew louder like a swarm of hornets.

Her mother was in the bed closest to the door, asleep. A half-moon of black stitches curved from the end of her eyebrow to her hairline and white bandages peeked out the neckline of her gown. Nolin had never seen anyone lie so still. Carefully, she placed her hand on her mother's chest to feel for her faint heartbeat. She wanted to hold her hand, but she was afraid to hurt her blistered fingers. There was still blood caked under Melissa's fingernails. Nolin's stomach turned.

Nolin wondered if Melissa had any idea where she was, in that odd room full of white curtains and injured women, if she knew her skin was a hot, bubbling mess, or that she might forever have fingernail scars running down her limbs and torso. Nolin knew her mother was sick. Her mind had a disease the way hearts or livers or kidneys get diseases. Something dark grew in her mind like an invisible tumor.

Her mother truly believed something was wrong outside of that dark place in her head. Melissa's eyes always widened with fear when she caught a glimpse out a window. Nightmares racked her sleep. Her mind never knew a moment's peace.

Nolin gingerly touched the back of Melissa's hand. It felt like a bad sunburn.

Could something in her head hurt her like this? Could her mother have seen something and believed in it so much that she hurt herself?

Outside the door, she heard her father grumbling. Something about supervision and "turn down that damn water heater." Nolin knew he thought it was all in her head. His crazy burden of a wife that dragged him out of work when things went wrong, just like her daughter. Things were always going wrong with the two of them.

Another woman somewhere in the room cried softly. Nolin's father called her from the hallway, sharply. Time to go. She gently touched her mother's hand again.

"I promise I'll be good."

Chapter 11

NOLIN'S HEAD ACHED from concentrating all morning, not on schoolwork, but on keeping her fists to herself. Max sat behind her in class, poking a pencil between her shoulder blades.

She wanted to turn around and punch his teeth down his neck. No, she was being good.

"Hey, Shrimpy," Max hissed. "Do you ever eat? Look at this bony chicken wing." Jab jab in the shoulder. Nolin reached into her desk and fumbled for the purple stress ball Mr. Clark had given her the previous year. She squeezed until her hands ached.

What a great day for Mrs. Carson to change the seating arrangements. Nolin swore she was being tested, punished, or both. Maybe she'd ask Mrs. Carson for a change after their grammar lesson. She'd ignore the rolling eyes and exasperated lecture that would probably follow.

"Huuuuggghh!" Max said, pretending to vomit. "Pukey pukey." Jab jab.

A tiny ball of wadded paper hit her ear. She breathed deeply through her nose and out through her mouth, the way her mother did when she tried to calm herself.

One, two, three...

Another wad of paper hit her neck.

Six, seven, eight...

Lunch was a welcome relief. When she reached the cafeteria she collapsed on the bench at the lunch table. Two blond girls at the other end glanced at her, whispered to each other, then moved to a table farther away. She might as well have had the plague for how she repelled people. The girls watched her from the other table, giggling to each other and mimicking Nolin's way of hunching over her food like an animal protecting its cache. It might have bothered Nolin if she hadn't been so used to it.

She chewed her peanut butter and jelly sandwich. The door to the playground opened and closed as students left, letting in pockets of natural blue light that made Nolin's heart flutter. She hadn't seen the sky since she arrived five hours ago. The school had no windows.

"Can I sit here?"

She hadn't heard him approach. Drew set his loaded lunch tray on the plastic table with a click and ambled onto the bench next to her.

"Why are you eating alone?"

She swallowed her bite of sandwich. "I always eat alone. I have the plague."

Drew chuckled. "You do not." He popped open his chocolate milk and sipped straight from the carton. "Are you not coming out to recess anymore?"

"Nope. I gave up recess for Lent."

"Really? I didn't know you were Catholic."

"I'm not," Nolin rolled her eyes, but her mouth curled into a smile. "I just decided to skip recess for a while, that's all."

"So you don't get in a fight?"

Nolin took a big bite of her sandwich.

"I saw Max poking you all morning," Drew said. "You should ask Mrs. Carson if you can change seats."

Nolin shrugged. "I don't want to make any more trouble than I already have."

Drew stabbed his lasagna with his plastic fork, looking down at his tray through a web of thick, dark eyelashes. His hair was a little long and curled slightly at the ends. He looked extra skinny in his too-big Spider-Man tee shirt and worn jeans. "I had fun with you the other day."

Nolin smiled. The sensation in her cheeks felt unfamiliar. "I did too. We should do that again sometime." Drew nodded, then shoveled a massive bite into his mouth.

"You know," he said once he'd swallowed, "you could play football with us at recess."

"I don't think your friends would like that."

"It won't be Max, just some kids from Mrs. Andrew's class."

Nolin looked up to see Max dumping his tray and laughing with his friends as they slipped out the door. Her hands tickled. *He deserved to get punched.* Her stomach jumped in horror at her own terrible thoughts.

"I think I'd better stay in," she said. "Just to be safe."

Chapter 12

MELISSA'S ROOM IN the psychiatric ward had a window. Small, double-paned, but at least she had a view of the courtyard garden behind the hospital. The rain had just stopped. Scarlet and lemon-yellow tulips in the flower beds reached to the empty clouds.

She couldn't remember the last time she had looked out a window without panicking. Aside from the ride in the ambulance, she hadn't been outside in months, maybe even years. For once, she wished she could open the window to let air into the stuffy room. She wanted to smell the rain, soak it in like the tulips. Her hands pressed on the glass to feel the coolness of the outside air. She thought of pushing the glass out, wondered if she was strong enough. She'd stand before the window-hole, nothing between her and the sky. Maybe she could fly if she really wanted to. What a strange feeling. So different from wanting to shrink until she disappeared.

"Mrs. Styre?" A young male nurse with a long neck and huge Adam's apple poked his head into the room. "You have visitors."

The tapping of two sets of feet—the light slap of flip-flops, the heavier fall of a man's shoes on the tile floor. Every sound in this place echoed.

"Leave the door open," the nurse told the visitors in a low voice. Melissa heard the soft shuffle of the nurse's sneakers as he left. He'd be back. He would casually pace the hallway until the visit was over.

"Melissa," Paul said. She could almost hear his heart beating. It was drowned out by gravity of the presence beside him.

"I brought you some things," said Nolin.

Melissa looked away from the window. Nolin's mass of hair was restrained into a ponytail. Tendrils shot out from the crown of her head like wire springs. Her slight body was that of a child, but her lovely face was oddly mature, with well-formed features devoid of childhood roundness. Her molded cheekbones swelled under her large green eyes, her chin pointed under a bow of full, pink lips, and her olive skin was smooth and glowing despite a green tinge that she'd never grown out of. Melissa sometimes had the sense her daughter was an adult trapped in a child's body. Sometimes, Nolin surprised her with her innocence. How she could she be such a gentle creature at home, yet a violent one at school?

"What did you bring?"

Nolin opened a canvas bag she'd slung over her shoulder. "I drew this at school and thought you might like it." Nolin handed Melissa a rolled-up piece of paper tied with a strand of blue yarn. Melissa took it and laid it on the bed without opening it.

Nolin's lips twitched. "Um, I also have some of your books in case you get bored. I didn't know what you'd feel like reading, so I brought a few options." Nolin pulled out Melissa's box set of the Chronicles of Narnia, her old copy of *The Hobbit*, and a volume of Emily Dickinson poems.

"Thank you," Melissa said, her voice hollow.

Nolin's shoulders dropped a fraction of an inch. Something about her darkened like tinted glass, but Nolin immediately straightened herself. Whatever had changed about her disappeared instantly.

Melissa noticed shadows under Nolin's eyes, faint purple streaks like strokes of watercolor. Maybe she wasn't sleeping well. Melissa could empathize.

She turned back to the window.

Paul cleared his throat. "Nolin, why don't you go check out the playroom for a few minutes?" A pause. Melissa felt that darkness again. Nolin's disappointment, anger at being dismissed. She could almost smell it. The door opened, and the flip-flops slapped out of the room and down the hall, taking that little dark cloud with them. Melissa knew Nolin wasn't stupid. She knew when she was being dismissed. Melissa felt a twinge of irritation at her husband.

"Melissa, what the hell?" Paul stomped to her side; Melissa turned around to face him. His gray eyes were bloodshot as if he hadn't slept in days. He looked so different from when she'd met him. His hair was graying and thin; premature creases lined his forehead. The purple shadows under his eyes gave him a hollow look, like something had been removed from him. His eyes pleaded with her. He didn't look angry, but desperate.

"Can't you at least try? She's your daughter!" he hissed. "You act like she's some stranger or something."

Melissa said nothing. What could she say? She couldn't defend herself.

For ten years, Melissa felt like two people inside. The mother, the part that understood just how special Nolin was, how brilliant and caring and selfless she'd always been, and the darker side that couldn't stand the sight of Nolin, that hated the pain she stirred up. Melissa hated this part of herself, the layer that lived on the surface. She didn't know how to pull it back down.

"I know we didn't plan on having a child," Paul went on. "I know she's different, but she's trying to make you happy."

"I know."

"At least humor her, for hell's sake! She works so hard to make you happy, and you just keep sinking and sinking and there's not a damn thing anyone can do! What do you want from us?" He threw his hands off her shoulders and turned away, pacing with his palms clamped to the side of his head.

Melissa wrapped her arms around herself. "This isn't about Nolin, is it, Paul?"

He pressed his forehead into the wall, his back heaving with his breath. He rubbed his temples and turned around.

"Paul, I know you work hard. I'm sorry. I just... can't change."

"Why not? You used to be fine. Accidents happen, but people adjust. So what's wrong with you?"

Accident. People adjust. What's wrong with you?

"Well? Hey, I'm talking to you." He gripped her shoulders then released her when she flinched. Her skin was still burned and bandaged beneath her hospital gown. "I can't hold this together anymore. Not by myself. I need your help."

She should have been furious. She was a sick, frail woman. Her husband accused her of tearing the family apart, as if she were in control. Like she could help what she was doing.

But she knew he was right. It didn't matter. She couldn't change what she was. Her condition was carved into her bones. The hallucinations, the depression, the voices...it would never go away. She'd never escape the face that haunted her dreams, the tiniest corners of her waking hours.

She was prepared to die this way. She only wished her family didn't have to suffer as well. Though she'd considered the way out, even daydreamed about it, she knew the act of saving her family would tear them apart.

Paul leaned forward and touched his forehead to hers. His face was damp with cold sweat. The sharp smell invigorated her, inspired something she'd thought was completely buried. She pressed her lips together. Her arms itched to throw themselves around his neck. Maybe for a moment, they could be a normal couple, comfort each other, figure things out together like a husband and a wife should. They'd always pulled their yoke in opposite directions. Maybe once, just for a minute, they could act together.

"I love you," she whispered.

Paul squeezed his eyes shut. "Please," he said. "I need a wife. Nolin needs a mother. We both need you."

What did they really need? A wife and mother, or a release from the burden of her?

"Bring Nolin by tomorrow," she said. "I need to sleep now, though. My meds...they make me tired."

Paul sighed and kissed her forehead, probably knowing she just wanted the conversation to end. He pulled her into his chest for a brief embrace, then turned and left the room.

The bag of Nolin's gifts rested on the flimsy pillow. The beige canvas was decorated with a swirling circle design in green and brown fabric paint, like the ring of a tree. Nolin must have decorated it at school.

Melissa unrolled a colored-pencil drawing of a willow tree. Scratchy green strokes formed leafy vines that swayed in the invisible breeze, and subtle stokes of crimson breathed dimension into the dark green leaves. Deep blue in the bark of the trunk brought out the texture. Nolin's drawing skills impressed her. How had she learned? Melissa sure hadn't taught her. She placed the drawing on the bedside table where it slid back into a loose roll.

She'd never known Nolin was so creative. She didn't know her at all.

Melissa looked through the novels, eager for a distraction. She selected *The Hobbit* and opened the stiff cover.

Her veins froze like tiny icicles up and down her body. Her fingers twitched, confused by the fumbled signals from her panicked brain. She wanted to slap the book closed and fling it across the room, and to press her hand to the page, close to the hand that had been there.

On the first page was a torn slip of paper. It was streaked with dirt and bore scrawled, lilting handwriting. Melissa's stomach dropped out. She clamped a hand to her open mouth to stifle a cry.

you never tried to find me

Chapter 13

A SPIDER SCUTTLED across the bedroom ceiling. Nolin could almost hear each tiny footfall as it moved in a zigzag pattern like a skier on a slope. Though the spring breeze from the window was cool, the roots of her hair were damp with sweat. Her clothes stuck to her back and the bottoms of her legs, and she'd kicked her covers into a wad at the foot of the mattress. Her breath felt hot and sour in her throat. She didn't move, but watched the spider progress across the white ceiling.

She floated in the limbo between dreaming and waking, where she didn't realize she was hot and sticky, or that the tiny dot she watched was a spider and not a comet or a fleck on the inside of her eyelids.

Groaning, she sat up. Her head felt like an overfilled water balloon. She rubbed her eyes and her tongue unstuck from the roof of her mouth like Velcro.

Water.

She stumbled to the door. Why was she so groggy? Was she sick? She didn't remember ever being sick. She blinked sleep from her eyes and raised a palm to her forehead. Hot.

The door creaked as it opened. The yellow night-light flickered in the hallway. Brighter light from downstairs illuminated the stairway; her father was already up. Maybe he couldn't sleep again, like her, and had gone downstairs to make tea. She tiptoed to the top of the stairs.

Then she heard her father's voice, just above a whisper. She could hear him if she held her breath.

"I can't leave."

Nolin froze. Was there someone else downstairs?

No, no voice answered him. He must be on the phone. Why would he be on the phone in the middle of the night? She crouched at the top of the stairs, sheltered in the shadows, and peered downstairs.

Her father sat at the bar in his rumpled work shirt with his back to her. His head rested in his hand with his elbow propped on the counter, cell phone held to his ear.

"I want to, but I can't. You know that. I've got a wife and daughter here that need me. I can't just abandon them... I know... I know. I love you too, but I have responsibilities."

Nolin's eyes narrowed. She felt sick.

"Someday maybe. My wife is sick, and Nolin is having a hard time in school... I know, she does... I can't take her away, either. I don't think she'd adjust very well. Can you blame her? No, I didn't mean it like that... can we just talk tomorrow? I'll meet you for lunch, okay? Same place?" A pause. "I love you. I want to be with you. You know it's not that simple. I've explained this to you before. I just can't. We'll figure something out, but not now." He ended the call, then put his head on his arms like a naughty child in school told to put his head down for five minutes. His shoulders rose and fell with his breath.

Nolin's rage boiled. She backed away from the stairs on her hands and knees, careful not to make a sound. Her torso contracted and expanded with sharp, furious breaths in and out her nose.

He wanted to abandon them.

Melissa in the hospital. Nolin was going crazy in school, trying so hard to do the right thing, to take care of her parents and hold them together while they fell apart inside, and he wanted to leave. The only thing that kept him around was duty, obligation. Not love.

Nolin slinked back into her bedroom and closed the door. She lay on her bed with the breeze blowing over her, burning with feverish anger.

The trees clicked like a chorus of snickers. She pinched her eyes shut and opened them several times, willing herself to wake from this odd dream. She heard and felt nothing until the tiny tickle of the spider worked up her arm. She didn't shake it away.

***

Nolin didn't move from her bed until her father called her, ten minutes before the bus would arrive. The sound of his voice infuriated her. That voice had crooned to some other woman on the phone only hours earlier, telling her he wanted to be with her instead of them, that he loved her.

He said he'd drive her to school. Nolin said nothing. She was afraid to open her mouth. She might scream at him, call him every bad word she knew and others she'd read in books that she knew meant something terrible. She didn't eat breakfast. She didn't make him lunch when she'd made hers.

Gravel spattered the sides of the station wagon as her father backed out of the driveway. Nolin's heart raced. He wouldn't believe she had a fever if she would have told him, or that her stomach hurt. She was a lousy liar. Red ears betrayed her every time.

He glanced at her, puzzled. "Are you okay?"

"I don't feel well." She pulled her legs into her chest and stuck her head between her knees. In health class, they'd learned to do that if they ever felt faint. Maybe she should have collapsed on the front porch like women in old movies, complained of a headache. Maybe he would have let her go back to bed, and she could wake up to find that it was all a dream. Her father and mother were in love. Everything was fine. Her mother wouldn't be in the hospital. She wouldn't be sick. Everything would be okay.

"You haven't been sick since you were a baby. You're going to school. Do you have an oral report or something today? Are you just nervous?"

"I don't know. I don't want to go." She needed to go for a long run in the cool air to clear her thoughts and calm her fever. Nolin hugged her legs. Nothing sounded more miserable than school. She couldn't do it, not today.

Five minutes later, they stopped in front of her school. Children poured out of school buses. Nolin always thought the buses looked like giant yellow caterpillars. Today, they were monsters, giant metal dragons spewing exhaust and squealing children. Nolin let herself out without saying good-bye.

Swarms of children bumped her shoulders. Their chatter echoed in her skull. She clamped her hands over her ears as she staggered through the classroom door. Max Fraser ran up behind her and jabbed her shoulder.

"How was your weekend, Pukey? Did you do a lot of digging?"

One, two, three...

She mimicked her mother's deep-breathing exercises, in through her nose and out through her mouth. It came out louder than she intended, a roaring hiss.

"Whoa, did Pukey hiss at me? Are you a snake now, Pukey? No, you're a kitty, remember? Because you dig like my cat after she poops in the yard."

She gritted her teeth, hung her pack on the hook, and stuffed her fists in her pockets. She plopped into her chair and thrust her hand into the desk for her stress ball. She squeezed it all morning until she held only a handful of white foam.

Chapter 14

THE MORNING CRAWLED by. When the lunch bell rang, Nolin bolted from her seat and practically ran to the cafeteria. She found an empty table and ripped open her lunch bag to retrieve her sandwich. It felt good to tear something. She chewed the ham sandwich slowly, focusing on the nutty grains of the bread, the saltiness of the ham, the sharp, smoky flavor of the cheddar.

Drew scrambled onto the bench across from her. He'd eaten with her every day for the past week since she'd returned. She was starting to look forward to seeing him. Drew was never grumpy or unhappy.

His hair stuck up in the back like a rooster's tail. He opened his chocolate milk and chugged half the little carton before dunking his corn dog in a glob of mustard.

"So, Nolin," he said through his mouth full of corn dog, "I know you haven't been going outside lately, but we really need someone else to make the football teams even. We keep getting our butts handed to us."

"I don't play football."

"You could if you wanted to. You just grab the ball and run to the other team's side. I know you can run real fast. Come play with us."

Nolin chewed the last bite of her sandwich. Maybe she could go out today; the fresh air would calm her. She wanted to run so badly. She pictured herself scoring a touchdown, her teammates smiling and congratulating her. Not that she cared. She didn't need any of them.

"C'mon, Nolin. The fifth graders creamed us yesterday. *Fifth graders.*"

Recess only lasted fifteen minutes. She looked to the table where Max sat across from his brother with his back to her. He wore a bright-yellow shirt, which gave him an unusually friendly appearance.

Only fifteen minutes. I can stay away from him.

"Okay. I'll play."

After they finished their lunch, she followed Drew out the door to the playground, where a group of sixth-grade boys sprawled on the grass.

"Hey, guys. I found another player," Drew called to them. "This is Nolin."

One of the boys, a freckled redhead with a buzz cut, wrinkled his nose, but said nothing. Nolin's stomach gurgled with nerves.

The group divided into two teams of four. Drew chose Nolin first for his team, and a soft heat filled her cheeks.

She kicked off her flip-flops to the side of the field so she could run. The redheaded boy on the other team hiked the ball to their quarterback. Nolin watched the ball spiral through the air. She didn't know the rules or even the point of the game, just that she needed to get that ball and run as fast as she could. She locked her eyes on the ball and ran, holding her arms out. Miraculously, the ball dropped into her arms.

"Run, Nolin!" Drew yelled. She hesitated from the shock of actually catching the ball, then she moved. Through her teammates' yells as she sprinted toward the end zone, she only heard Drew's voice.

"The other way!"

She locked her legs and skidded forward, then turned to shoot in the other direction. The other team charged her. Her blood churned. She dodged the four boys, zigzagging like a pinball until she heard cheering.

"Touchdown!" someone hollered. Nolin dug her foot into the ground and stopped. A touchdown? She got a touchdown?

"Good job!" Drew huffed as he jogged to her. He held out his hands for the ball. Nolin froze. She didn't want to let go. The ball was her trophy, but it was her team's turn. She reluctantly surrendered the ball.

"That was awesome, Nolin. You're really fast. Just remember to run this way, okay?"

She nodded. Bubbles of excitement tingled in her arms and legs.

She'd never had so much fun playing a sport. She ran hard, intercepted passes, got a bit of a reprimand for being a ball hog, but scored two more touchdowns and even earned a few smiles from her teammates. At the beginning of the final down, a jeering voice interrupted.

"Hey, Pukey! Are you a boy now? Only boys play football."

She laughed. Was that the best he could do? The ball flew, and she ran to catch it. Even from forty feet away, she sensed Max's surprise and frustration that his words had no effect.

"Why aren't you digging, Pukey?" he called louder. "Did you have enough worms, and now you're full? Did you puke up the worm sandwich you had for lunch?"

She ran past him without a glance. She caught the ball, pivoted, and sprinted toward the end zone. This touchdown would win them the game. The redheaded boy lunged at her, sweeping his arm low to tag her foot. She leapt. Max's frantic insults faded behind the cheers of her teammates.

"Go, Nolin!" Drew shouted. "Go, go, go! Run!" Two boys from the opposing team charged her. She darted sideways. Out the corner of her eye, she saw Drew running and jumping, pumping his fist, yelling for her. Time slowed. She felt blood moving through her veins, air rushing in and out of her lungs, each hair whipping in the wind. She met Drew's gaze. He smiled, his adult teeth still a little too large for his mouth. She felt a deep warmth for him. Without him, she'd be sitting in a stuffy classroom instead of running like a wild animal and breathing the sweet air.

Finally, she crossed into the end zone. Her team whooped. Nolin chucked the ball at the ground like she'd seen NFL players do back when her father watched football. She'd never won anything in her life, never been part of a team except for when she was forced to in P.E. The two boys on her team whom she'd never spoken to congratulated her. They even introduced themselves, though she knew their names from class.

"You can play with us anytime," Brock, the taller boy said, then lightly slugged her shoulder.

"Yeah, you did real good," said the other boy, PJ.

The whistle screeched. Drew picked up the ball and waited for Nolin to catch up before walking in. Max still stood nearby, scowling. Then, a nasty grin spread across his ruddy face.

"Hey, Pukey," he said. "I heard your mom's in the hospital."

Nolin's stomach sank. The balloon of joy punctured. *Don't listen.*

"My sister works there, and she said your mom is crazy. Psycho."

Nolin tucked her head down to avoid eye contact. *Ignore it. He doesn't know what he's talking about.*

Drew froze, looking between Max and Nolin.

"Shut up," he muttered. His face flushed.

"Oh, standing up for your girlfriend, Carrington? That's sweet. You'd better watch out who you get smoochy with, though. Nolin Styre's mom is crazy. They threw her in the loony bin, you know." He looked back at Nolin. "No wonder you're such a freak, Pukey. Your mom's a psycho!"

One, two, three...

"You can't fix crazy. I'll bet it's all your fault, too, that your mom's a loon. Maybe she'll die in there, Pukey. *Your psycho mom's going to die, and it's all your fault!*"

Nolin might have imagined that last part, but she was on him before she realized what was happening. He smacked the ground hard and screamed. Nolin's fists flew. With a shriek, she sank her fist into his face and felt the crunch of his nose snapping. She yanked his hair, clawed his face, beat the sides of his head. He cried as warm blood flowed from his nose, soaking his shirt and Nolin's hands. She bared her gritted teeth. She wanted to yell at him, something awful, but she'd forgotten how to speak.

"Nolin! Stop!" Drew yelled. She felt him yank on her shoulders, but she shook him off.

"*Nolin Styre!*" a voice shrieked. Mrs. Carson dashed across the blacktop, stumbling in her high-heeled boots, blowing the whistle and waving her arms like a drowning person. Nolin paused. She looked down at Max; his face was streaked with blood, tears, and dirt. Her hands were stained red. Air snagged in her chest as her mind crashed-landed back into her body.

She leapt up and stumbled backward. Mrs. Carson charged her, now only fifty feet away. Drew looked at her helplessly.

She was finished. They'd throw her out of school for sure. This time she wouldn't be coming back. What would happen to her mother when Nolin was expelled?

Your psycho mom's going to die, and it's all your fault!

She had no choice.

Nolin sprinted to the fence on the other side of the field. There were shouts behind her, gasps. Every eye on the playground, the field, the entire school was on her. Inside, she was alone.

Her consciousness shrank until it only focused on one point: Escape. From everything. Expectations she'd never fulfill, the family she'd betrayed. She'd never harm them again. Her mother would recover; her parents would get things under control and have the happy life they'd always wanted without the burden of a ruined child.

The sound of her breathing took over. Nolin reached the fence and leapt onto the chain link, crawled to the top like a spider, and swung her legs over. She hit the ground running and bounded through the dense foliage and into the forest.

The tree branches reached out in welcome after years of calling though her bedroom window.

She didn't stop until she couldn't remember the way back.

Chapter 15

THE TREES HELD their breath, waiting to see what Nolin would do next.

Nolin had never known trees could watch. They watched every move, listened to every thought.

The drumbeat of her pulse pounded in her ears. Nolin didn't know how long she'd been running. It didn't matter. Time meant nothing to her anymore.

She slowed to a jog, then walked and finally stopped. The air smelled like rain. The forest, usually a symphony of birds, insects, and the sound of rustling leaves, stood silent.

Something touched her head. She startled, grabbing at whatever it was, ready for another fight. It was just a leaf. Small, round, bright apple-green. She held the tiny leaf in her hand, studied it, examining each tiny vein, holding it to the light to see the sun shine through. The leaf felt smooth and waxy. She didn't know how she knew, because she didn't know much of anything at the moment, but she knew that little leaf pulsed with life, that the woods around her were alive and breathing.

Another leaf fell, taking its time before settling on her toes. It landed so lightly she didn't feel it.

Nolin looked up at the sky through the branches. The leaves were still. The air hovered, motionless. It was spring; the trees shouldn't be shedding their leaves now.

She picked up the second leaf from her toes and held the two in her cupped hands. Tiny, round, perfect leaves. Carefully, she tucked them into her pocket. A part of her felt that the forest had given her a gift, a good luck charm.

The lack of breeze made her uneasy. She walked. Her footfalls on the forest floor made no sound. Insects scuttled over her bare feet, tickling her toes. Her sweaty shirt clung to her back. Her hair was wet at the roots, speckled with bits of leaves and dirt.

Her stomach growled. She put her hands to her stomach, fascinated by the vibrations of her clenched insides. Automatically, her eyes scanned the trees and ground around her, searching for anything she could eat to stop this gnawing, hollow sensation. She strode to the nearest tree, dropped to her knees, and pawed at the dirt.

Tiny winged insects crawled over the bark of the tree. She didn't want those. She dug deeper until a glistening earthworm coiled around her index finger. She lifted the finger in front of her face. It writhed, groping for the soil. Gently, she squished it between her thumb and forefinger, testing the elasticity of the pink coil. Her stomach roared again, and she popped the worm into her mouth. The creature squished between her teeth, cold and rubbery, chewy, but surprisingly tasteless. Chewing and swallowing felt good. Her stomach grumbled for more. She dug deeper, slipping worms out of the soil and into her mouth as she found them. She swallowed one whole and felt it wriggle down her throat. Amused, she swallowed another.

After ten or twelve bites, the aching hollow in her stomach eased. She crawled to a patch of white wildflowers a few feet away. The flowers smiled at her with pure, round petals and delicate white spines in the center. She clutched a wiry stem, then yanked the flower out of the ground. Clumps of soil dropped off the web of tangled white roots. With her other hand, she snapped off a wiry root and chewed on it like a child gnawing a lollipop stick. The crunchy root tasted slightly bitter with an underlying sweetness, like turnips. She uprooted a few more flowers and nibbled on the roots until the rumbling sensation subsided completely.

She had nowhere to go. She didn't know where she was, so she sat in the dirt, surrounded by the litter of her meal, and stared into the depths of the woods. Nothing moved; not even a blade of grass. No insects or birds flew through her line of sight. She might have been staring at a photograph.

Eventually, the light dimmed. A deep-purple hue settled into the forest. How long had she sat here? Minutes or hours, it was all the same to her now. Her eyelids drooped. The trees blurred. A bubble bloomed inside her, and she yawned, stretching her mouth wide.

She pushed herself up and wandered farther. The brilliant cerulean of the sky had faded to midnight blue. Pinpricks of stars gazed down on her, surprised to see her in the woods instead of in her home with her family, playing her part. Light vanished, but she could still see.

The silhouette of the Claw Tree appeared in the shadows, its roots clinging to the ground. Nolin stopped, cocked her head to the side. There was something familiar about the tree. Had she seen it before?

Nolin's thoughts reached through the fog in her brain, searching for anything to grab onto. It was no use. The trees knew it. They knew a crack had been forming in Nolin's mind for months, years even, deepening each day until finally, her poor child mind had splintered open. She had no idea who she was, where she'd come from, or what she was doing in the woods under the watchful eyes of the forest. The trees whispered amongst themselves, their leaves rubbing together like fingers in the canopy.

What they whispered, no one could ever know.

Giving up on remembering and deciding there was no danger, Nolin approached the Claw Tree. At the base of the huge trunk, she dropped to her hands and knees and crawled into a soft bed of dead leaves underneath.

Nolin heard a sound like a sigh, and the roots around her seemed to move; the ground beneath her flexed ever so slightly. Then silence. Curious, Nolin waited to see if it would happen again. Seconds later, there was a soft whooshing sound like wind, and the ground inflated, raising her up an inch or two under the base of the tree.

Nolin filled her belly with air and felt it expand. A few seconds later, she heard a sound like an inhale. She let her air out.

Nolin's fingers played in the leaves, burrowing as she dozed off. They closed around something small and soft that crumpled when she gripped it. She opened her eyes to examine the object in her hand. It was a tiny pink shoe made of yarn with three little roses on the toe. Something twitched in the back of her mind, a memory struggling to rise to the surface. Sleep overtook her before she could unearth it from the depths of a mental archive she no longer wanted.

The tree leaned, cradling her as she fell into a dreamless sleep.

***

If the trees could talk to her, they would have. "Do you know what this means?" They wished they could say. "Do you know what you are?"

Even if the trees could speak the language of humans, or even the language of goblins, Nolin wouldn't have understood. Her broken mind had forgotten language, even the language of trees. She was, for all intents and purposes, an animal.

The trees nearly wept.

***

The Shadow slid through the darkness like liquid. Something was wrong. Nolin hadn't gotten off the school bus, Paul hadn't come home, and the air shimmered with excitement. Crickets chirped in the bushes. Fireflies twinkled. The woods sparkled with dew and insects creeping through the dirt and the wood.

Finally, the Claw Tree rose before her.

Her dark eyes scanned the edges of the clearing for movement or the glow of eyes in the darkness. Something was different. She slipped closer, closer, until finally, she crawled under the tree.

A pair of spindly legs tangled with her own. She tripped and caught herself on one of the thick roots. The intruder stirred and rolled toward her.

It was Nolin.

The Shadow crawled back between the roots, too excited to speak.

Nolin was here. She'd come on her own after all.

Had all these years of whispering through the tree, calling her into the forest, finally worked? The Shadow's thoughts chased each other. She'd dreamed of this for years. Now she wasn't sure how to proceed.

Nolin looked more peaceful in sleep than she ever had in her waking hours. Her face was relaxed, smooth as the inside of a seashell. Soft brown eyelashes curled from her closed eyes like tiny feathers. Her pale lips parted. Her chest rose and fell with gentle breath and her fingers curled softly against her cheek.

Leaves whispered in the canopy. A gentle breath of air moved through the woods and tousled Nolin's mess of dark hair.

Nolin's forehead wrinkled. With a gasp, her eyes snapped open, glowing like two fiery emeralds.

***

Wake up, the trees screamed.

A sharp, sour smell penetrated Nolin's sleep. Her eyes burst open.

A pair of wide black eyes stared back at her, reflecting her own alarmed face.

Nolin screeched and swung her arm, catching a handful of tangled hair. The intruder darted out from under the tree before Nolin could get a good look. Nolin only saw a flash of pale legs as the figure silently leapt onto the giant tree and disappeared.

Nolin scrambled between the roots and looked up the trunk of the Claw Tree. The intruder was gone. She scanned the clearing around her. The woods remained silent and empty. She lifted her hand to her face and examined the coarse strands of long, dark hair between her fingers, then let them slide off her hand and drift to the ground. They were almost the same color as her own.

She didn't notice the dark figure watching her from the canopy.

Senses narrowed, ears listening for the softest footstep, the tiniest rustle in the bushes. Her fingers curled like claws ready to tear through anything that dared to move.

She waited for any sound or scent, any sign of movement, ears pricked for the slightest rustle, the tiniest snap of a twig or click of stones shifting.

Eventually, the adrenaline drained from her veins and exhaustion overtook her again. Nolin stumbled off into the darkness in search of a safer place to sleep.

***

What's wrong with her?

The Shadow waited in the upper branches of the Claw Tree, watching Nolin disappear into the night. She'd give her a safe distance before she followed.

Nolin was different—not the intelligent girl the Shadow had watched for years, but a mindless animal operating on instinct alone. Nolin's eyes were fierce and wild, almost lacking human consciousness.

Had the woods changed her?

She'd spent most of a night under the Claw Tree, the tree of dreams and connection. Who knows what that could have done to her already-addled brain. This wasn't the way it was supposed to be. Yes, Nolin had come of her own choice, but how much control did she have? She had no idea what she was doing. The woods controlled her now; not just the nature around her, but the nature inside her.

When she could barely see Nolin through the tight gaps in the trees, the Shadow crept down to the ground, tiptoed across the clearing, and slipped through the trees, crouching low to avoid being seen. She'd follow Nolin and watch.

Nolin had to be aware. She had to choose.

Otherwise, the Shadow thought darkly, Nolin would be *stolen*.

The Shadow could never steal a child, even if that child never belonged to the humans in the first place. She'd be no better than the creatures who'd stolen her own life in the first place. She'd be as inhuman as they were.

***

Nolin sat cross-legged in the dirt, tugging squishy blackberries off a bush. The trees cut sunlight into slices, illuminating the forest with glowing shafts of light. A leaf spiraled down from the canopy and landed softly in the nest of Nolin's hair.

The Shadow watched from a few dozen yards away, crouched behind a boulder.

This wasn't right. It wasn't working. Two days since Nolin had run away, and she showed no signs that she had any idea who she was or that it was unusual and dangerous for a ten-year-old girl to live in the woods alone. She'd had no trouble finding food or shelter. It was both fascinating and frustrating to watch.

So close. Nolin was here, in the woods, just as the Shadow had wanted for years, but she was an empty shell. She needed Nolin to be *Nolin*, not this animal. Even if the Shadow stepped out in full view, Nolin wouldn't recognize her. She'd just be an ordinary threat in the woods like a bear or a hunter, and Nolin would react instinctively as an animal would: fight or flight. The Shadow had worked and hoped for this for years. She hadn't counted on a psychotic breakdown or whatever had happened in Nolin's mind.

She'd wanted Nolin to come into the woods willingly, with full knowledge of what she was.

The Shadow wanted to scream with frustration, but she composed herself, regaining her grip on endless patience cultivated over years of waiting.

Then, she heard a man's voice.

***

Nolin slipped another plump berry in her mouth, humming a tune her mind couldn't recall but her voice still remembered. Her humming flowed into words.

"Rock-a-bye Nolin, in the tree tops,

When the wind blows, the cradle will rock,

When the bow breaks, the cradle will fall..."

In her mind, a soft voice sang that song. It made her sleepy again. She closed her eyes and saw a woman's face.

Where had she seen that face?

She remembered someone holding her and singing in a soft, heavy voice.

"...and down will come Nolin, cradle and all."

She felt relaxed for a moment. Then her shoulders tensed. Something was different.

A soft snap in the trees. A sapling shook.

Something was there.

Nolin sprang up and darted through the blackberry patch. Thorns tore at her shirt, scratched her feet and legs. Behind her, she heard voices.

Her heart tried to outrun the rest of her. She hadn't been afraid when she'd woken to the dark eyes two nights ago. She wasn't afraid at night when the woods were silent.

111

Now she was afraid.

A shout, this time to her left. She veered to the right to leap onto a mossy boulder, climbing over and dropping to the ground.

As she scurried to her feet, two strong hands clamped her arms to her side.

A voice spoke to her. The words were gibberish in her ears. She kicked and thrashed.

The trees watched in horror.

"I've got her!" The man called, struggling to restrain her. Nolin screamed and kicked at her attackers, hair falling over her face.

More men emerged from the bushes, speaking into beeping black boxes. Nolin filled her lungs and screamed, every nerve in her body vibrating. She twisted in the first man's arms. The man in the red hat talked to her, frantically.

"It's all right, it's all right, calm down."

It's not, said the trees. *It's not all right.*

No one but Nolin could hear them. There was only a gentle breeze.

The man touched Nolin's face, brushing her hair away from her cheek. Nolin dug her teeth into his hand and held on.

The man shouted and swore. Nolin bit down harder, clenching her jaws until she tasted blood. He jerked his hand. She let go. He clutched his bleeding hand in his shirt and gaped at her in horror. "The little bitch bit me!"

Nolin tried to run. A man in a dark blue jacket rushed forward, diving to grab her around the legs. She shrieked and landed, hard. The man pinned her as she struggled, flailing her limbs, scratching, kicking. The man pressed her head into the dirt with his elbow shoved painfully into her back. She couldn't move.

Chapter 16

MELISSA CRUMPLED INTO a heap in Paul's lap, trembling. He wrapped his arms around her. Her breath escaped in husky whimpers. She cradled her head in her skeletal hands and rocked from side to side. Paul rubbed her back, whispering assurances.

"At least she's safe," Paul said, stroking her limp hair. "She wasn't hurt. Just confused. They'll take care of her, and she'll be out of here in no time."

Melissa opened her mouth to speak, but a choked sob burst out instead. She crossed her arms in front of her. Thoughts rocketed around inside her, colliding and spinning out of control.

She tried so hard. It was too much for her. I pushed her too much. She really hurt that boy; she could have hurt him worse. Now she's locked up in here like me. What have I done?

"What if she doesn't get better?" Melissa wheezed. She sat up. The shadows under Paul's eyes and the red blotches on his cheeks told her he was thinking the same thing. He shook his head without looking at her. His shoulders twitched as if attempting an optimistic shrug. He opened and closed his mouth wordlessly.

"Nolin's different," Melissa mumbled.

Paul slumped forward and dropped his head in his hands. "Not this again."

Hot anger shot through Melissa's veins. Suddenly, she wanted to slap him. "No, Paul, *listen to me*. She's not like other children." Her voice rose, quivering with rage. "It might be dangerous for her here."

"So what do you suggest we do?" Paul glared at her. "The last time I checked, you weren't a doctor. Let them do their job."

"They don't know how to help her!"

"She's sick!" he shouted. "So are you. Doctors help sick people. Let them figure it out. Do you think you know better than them?"

A male nurse walked in, pretending to read a form in the binder he carried. Paul didn't notice.

"I don't want to hear any more of this," Paul said. "Can't you hear how insane you sound? She's not an animal, for hell's sake. We can't just release her into the wild like some bear cub. She's a child, and she belongs with us, whether she wants to or not. She's not leaving here until she understands that."

"What if she never does understand?"

Paul shot to his feet like a firecracker and threw up his hands. He turned back to Melissa, his face red.

"You know, maybe you really are crazy. I don't know what I've done wrong, but two-thirds of this family is in a damn crazy house and I can't do a thing about it!"

"Sir..." stammered the nurse, looking up from his binder.

"Stay out of this!" Paul said, thrusting a warning finger toward him. The nurse's eyes grew wide. He rushed out the door and down the hall, calling for security.

Paul crossed to his wife and placed his hands on the bed on either side of her, leaning forward so their faces nearly touched.

"I've have done *everything* I can possibly do to hold this family together, and everything has gone to shit anyway. I can't do this anymore. I'm done."

Melissa's jaw stiffened. "You're done," she repeated tonelessly, glaring. Paul's shoulders dropped, almost shrinking under her gaze, but he didn't blink.

Two large men in white stepped into the room. "Sir, I'm going to have to ask you to leave immediately," the taller one said.

Paul stepped backward toward the door, swaying on his feet and locking his eyes on his wife's.

"I'll leave. No problem; I'll go right now." He walked out the door. The two men followed. The timid male nurse slid back into the room.

Melissa propped her elbows on her knees and laid her head in her hands. She'd always known he would leave someday. No one could live with this burden. Her hands twitched. She couldn't decide whether to sob in despair or scream in fury. She and her sick child, abandoned. She thought of her piles of jewelry she'd clung to for years. Tactile proof of his love. Evidence that he'd never leave her. In her mind, those jewels crumbled to dust and blew away like ashes. The only piece that remained was the clay bead necklace.

"I want to see my daughter," Melissa said to the nurse. He smiled nervously and shifted his weight to his other foot.

"Um, I don't think she's allowed to have visitors right now."

"I don't care; I have to see her."

"Ma'am, I'm sorry, I could lose my job."

"Then I'll go myself." Melissa stood up taller than she had in years and pushed past the nurse into the hall. He called after her as she marched toward the children's ward. She ignored him and followed the directions posted on the walls. She listened to the rhythm of her feet on the floor, imagining each footstep crushing the fear that gnawed her from the inside out.

Mozart played softly from a room down the hall. Somewhere, a child sobbed. The walls in the children's hall were sky blue instead of white. Bright crepe paper flowers decorated the doors. Melissa stopped in front of a door that only bore torn pieces of crepe paper stuck to loops of Scotch tape. The flowers had been ripped away.

She turned the handle and let herself in.

Two doctors crouched over the tiny figure in the bed. They looked over their shoulders at Melissa like two kids caught with their hands in the cookie jar. One of the doctors clutched a clipboard in a thickly gloved hand. The other gripped the sides of Nolin's head, holding her down. Her eyelids drooped and her mouth hung open; a shiny stream of saliva glistened on her chin. Melissa's heart stopped. She could never have imagined her daughter looking so weak, so... *defeated*. The flat, pale-green eyes looked like two dull stones—no glint of intelligence. That spark of knowing had fled.

"Ma'am, you need to leave," demanded the doctor with the clipboard. Melissa didn't look away from Nolin, all she had left. She stood still in the doorway.

"Ma'am, visitors aren't allowed in here."

"I'm her mother."

"Yes, but you're also in a hospital, and you have rules you must follow. Return to your room, or I'll have to call security."

The nurse poked his head into the room, breathless. "I'm sorry, Doctor," he wheezed. "I tried to stop her."

"Go get security," the first doctor ordered. The nurse nodded and skittered off in the direction from which he'd come.

Melissa lumbered into the room. Nolin's eyes rolled in their sockets like a frightened animal's. A soft moan escaped her open mouth.

"What the hell have you done to her?" Melissa's voice shook with rage.

The doctor stepped closer and reached out his hand, maybe trying to calm her. The other doctor released Nolin and twisted on his stool, his eyes larger than life behind his thick spectacles.

"You shouldn't be here," the first doctor said calmly. "You don't want to see your daughter like this. She's very sick."

"You people don't know how to help her," Melissa spat. "You and your needles. You can't do anything except pump her full of sedatives till she's a damn vegetable!"

"Ma'am, I've warned you. You need to leave." The doctor slowly placed the clipboard on the counter. The other stood up. Melissa took a step backward.

"You can't help her!" she shrieked, pointing to Nolin, who moaned again. "She's different!"

Melissa had no idea what those chemicals could do to Nolin, and she didn't want to find out.

The doctor's eyes traveled from Melissa to a point over her shoulder. The same two men in white appeared behind her. She jerked away from them.

The other doctor caught her and clamped her arms to her sides. The men in white stepped into the room, their mouths opening and closing. Melissa heard no words, only the soft moans from the girl in the bed. Melissa twisted and jerked as the men in white took her from the doctor's hold. She shoved her shoulder into the wide chest, stomped on a large foot. The man only grunted and nodded to the doctor. Melissa screamed at the pinch in her neck. The scream trickled away like a dried-up river. Her legs slackened. She moaned as she tried to call to Nolin. A strong arm around her waist dragged her from the room. She watched the crepe paper flowers on the passing doors. The colors blurred together until she forgot that those flowers weren't real.

Her mind swam. She felt she was finally in the flower garden in the hospital courtyard instead of watching it from the window.

***

The forest never looked so foreboding.

The Shadow huddled under the shelter of the Claw Tree. Rain poured from the night sky in torrents. The trees kept most of the water off, but she wouldn't have cared if she drowned. She choked and whimpered as tears ran down her face in streams, dripping onto her knees that she pulled into her chest.

So close.

Nolin and Melissa were gone now. Who knew for how long. Maybe they'd never recover at all. Nolin would forever be out of the Shadow's reach.

She'd have patience. No matter how long it took, she would wait until she could take action again.

The Shadow reached through the cover of leaves to touch the bloody scab on her scalp where Nolin had ripped out a handful of hair. Thunder boomed around her.

She didn't want to be here. She crawled out of the shelter and sprinted in the direction of the house, flying over the familiar rocks and fallen trees in the freezing rain. She could run this route in her sleep.

The dark windows stared blankly, with no signs of life inside. Paul wasn't home yet.

She slid out of the trees and across the yard, relying on the rain and darkness to conceal her. The back door was locked. She tried the knob, then put her lips to the keyhole and blew. The latch clicked inside the knob; she turned it and pushed the door open.

The silent house stood still as a photograph. She climbed the stairs, squishing the soft carpet between her bare toes. The stairs creaked like whispering ghosts.

Nolin's door stood open a few inches. The Shadow pushed it open wider. Her stomach clenched. This room, the memories, would always haunt her. She doubted that Nolin remembered, but the Shadow would never forget.

She stepped into the room and clicked the door shut behind her. The plants on the dresser drooped like sad children. The Shadow flopped on the stark bed, suddenly sleepy. She stretched out on her back and stared at the smooth white ceiling until her eyelids grew heavy.

***

She didn't hear Paul come home. She didn't hear his footsteps on the stairs, the creak of his bedroom door, or the muffled sobs from his room.

He didn't notice the damp footsteps on the carpet. He couldn't hear the soft breathing in the other bedroom, and he never opened

Nolin's door. The rain stopped, clouds sailed into the distance, and the sky opened to the winking stars.

The trees didn't speak to each other. They didn't know what to say.

So they stood silently, waiting, and watched.

Part Two

Ten Years Later

Chapter 17

THE BABBLE OF voices and clattering keys grated on her nerves. Melissa adjusted the microphone of her headset and clicked yet another phone number on the computer screen. Three rings in the ear of her headset, each one a fly she longed to swat away.

"Hello?" chirped a female voice on the line.

"Hello, my name is Melissa," Melissa said in a canned, pleasant voice. "Would you be interested in taking a quick survey about the upcoming local elections?" The words rolled off her tongue. She'd given the same survey dozens of times a day for over a month; the words were branded into her memory.

"Um, I'm actually on my way out the door right now..." stammered the woman on the line.

"No problem; is there a better time I could call?"

"Not really."

"No problem, you have a good day now." Melissa hung up before the woman could respond. She leaned back to peek down the row of cubicles to her boss's chair on the end. Hopefully, he hadn't listened in on her calls that day. He'd been pushing the employees to finish the surveys, to say it would only take a moment, to start with the first question before the unfortunate person on the other end was off the line. No matter how hard Melissa tried, she couldn't make herself care. She almost always hung up first.

She turned back to the endless spreadsheet of numbers. The empty survey form had been open for the last nine calls. She hadn't submitted a single thing that day, and she'd been working for almost five hours. The supervisors who checked the surveys cared little for excuses. A low completion percentage was grounds for probation.

Melissa peeked over at her boss again. When he set off to the break room with his empty coffee mug, she decided to take a quick breather.

Her cursor flew as she opened Google and typed in her ex-husband's name.

The usual results popped up in the search. The website for his law firm. A few mentions of his awards and high-profile cases he'd worked on. Some newspaper articles. No social media.

She clicked the link to his firm's site, Styre Law. The familiar web page popped up with Paul's picture in the upper right corner. He looked older, with even less hair than he'd had ten years ago and even more gray. Bags sagged under his colorless eyes. Her stomach clenched.

Ten years ago next month. She hadn't seen him since he'd walked out of the hospital, leaving her alone with Nolin in the mental ward. He'd never contacted her since sending divorce papers, which she'd promptly signed and returned. She doubted he'd contacted Nolin, wherever she was.

He never removed her or Nolin from his insurance. Both of their treatments were covered. Child-support checks had arrived like clockwork each month until Nolin turned eighteen.

Now Melissa's only source of income was this job, taking surveys for outside companies for nine dollars an hour. She made enough to cover the mortgage, utilities, a bus pass, and a hundred dollars per month for food and anything else she needed.

She clicked through the website, skimming his biography though she'd read it a million times. The website said he practiced in Maxwell, a town a few hours north. It listed his company address and phone number, both of which she'd memorized.

Often, she fantasized about meeting him on the bus or out at lunch. In her imagination, she screamed at him, swung her fist into his face. Sometimes she thought about turning up at his office, picturing herself much taller, glaring down at an unsuspecting secretary, demanding to speak to him. He'd appear, unable to conceal his surprise, and she'd say something that would cut deeply. She was never sure what. From then on, his only goal would be to earn her forgiveness, no matter what it took. She'd withhold it, just so he could know how much she'd had to bear on her own. Not just since he'd left, but before that, when he'd leave for work as early as possible in the morning and, in the evening, not come up to bed until she was already asleep, sometimes not at all. He'd let her waste away in fear and depression without trying to pull her out.

He'd left her long before he'd moved out. That was the unforgivable abandonment.

She knew she was being irrational. He did what anyone would have done in his situation. He'd been generous to send money, at least for a while.

But he'd left her with Nolin.

The rational part of her mind wondered what life would have been like if he'd stayed. Maybe she'd be happy, maybe she wouldn't. Maybe she'd still be in and out of the hospital, staying shut in the bedroom to ride out her highs and lows. Nolin might still live at home.

No, she thought, *Nolin still would have left.*

She heard her boss's dry cough. She should get back to work.

As she closed the browser window and clicked back to the empty survey form, the third tab in her browser flashed, announcing an email. She opened the message. Despite the contents, a summons to the floor manager's office, she felt nothing.

***

Melissa rode the bus home three hours early. The piece of her mind that lived in the real world whirled—the sliver of determination that carried her from day to day, reminding her to eat a scoop of peanut butter or a handful of crackers a few times a day, to pay the power bill and do laundry.

Fired.

How will I pay the mortgage now? her rational self cried. *How will I find another job?*

While her rational mind chattered, the rest of her felt still as death.

The bus stopped. She exited to walk the half mile home, not noticing children playing in the yards, dogs barking through fences, or whispers of the neighborhood housewives as they sat on their porches. She didn't hear birds singing, didn't see blossoms opening on the trees, or feel the cool spring wind in her hair. Every inch of her felt numb. She reached her empty house and let herself in.

Five years had passed since Nolin's disappearance, since the day Melissa realized she hadn't seen Nolin in days and that her things were gone. No note or any sign of a good-bye. That was the day she locked the door to Nolin's bedroom from the inside. There'd never been a key to that room. She never intended to enter it again.

Without Nolin, the emptiness of the house seemed massive. Melissa could almost hear it—a distant, low howl like wind in a faraway tunnel. Years later, she realized that it wasn't the house. The emptiness was inside of her.

Paul's abandonment was nothing next to Nolin's. Some small piece of her, an important piece, had disappeared with Nolin. The last shred of hope had fled, leaving her completely alone.

She wasn't worried about Nolin; she could take care of herself, and she wouldn't want to be found. Melissa didn't look. It was better this way.

With shaking hands, Melissa made herself a cup of tea. The hot liquid soothed her rattled nerves, brought life back to her numbed body. Nothing was wrong. She'd find a job. Everything would be all right. Then she noticed the mug she'd chosen: the white mug with pink polka dots. The one she'd used as a child. The one Nolin had always used.

Her eyes filled with burning tears. Before she could stop herself, she hurled the mug against the kitchen cabinets. It shattered, raining tea and ceramic shards over the counter and floor.

They'd both abandoned her, Paul and Nolin. She didn't know whom she blamed more.

Anger. A tiny point of heat glowed within her. Melissa held onto that, clung to the scraps of strength that still burned somewhere inside her. It was all she had left.

***

Miraculously, Melissa managed to sleep that night. Shreds of dreams floated in and out of her mind. A familiar dark eye appeared. She caught a glimpse of dark hair, a smooth cheek, a chin. Never the whole face. The smell of the woods filled her, strangling her from the inside, wrapping her in terrible memories.

Stop it, she thought. *Just let me forget.*

The images swirled together. She felt cold wind in her hair, numbing her face.

A whisper broke her sleep, the words too low for her to hear. The whisper repeated, louder, again and again, until sharp words hissed in her ear.

You never tried to find me.

Melissa's eyes snapped open. The bedclothes were tangled around her. She was cold with sweat. She sat up, her head spinning, taking in her surroundings until she remembered she was in her bedroom, in her own bed, safe.

Surely, she'd dreamed the whisper.

Still, she felt unsettled.

She had to go to the bathroom. Heart thudding, she slid off the bed and padded to the master bathroom. She stopped.

No, not that bathroom. She still rarely entered that bathroom. She'd never showered there again, preferring the bathroom in the hall instead.

She stumbled toward her bedroom door and noticed a strange sound. She smelled wood, fresh air.

Her blood froze. Slowly, she opened the door and peered out into the hall. A bead of cold sweat rolled down her spine.

On the other side of the hall, Nolin's bedroom door stood wide open. Trees thrashed in the wind outside the open window.

No.

That door had been locked for over five years. It couldn't be happening again. It was quiet for so long.

Leave me alone, she pleaded in her mind. *I can't help you. Just go away.*

Melissa thought she heard a tinkling laugh, so soft and strange it might have been the rustling of leaves outside. It could read her mind. Melissa was sure of it. She clamped her hands over her ears, forcing the horrible laughter out.

"Leave me alone!" Melissa shrieked. The girlish laugh assaulted her again though her hands pressed her ears shut.

Chapter 18

THE CHILLY MORNING breeze bit at Nolin's legs. She dangled her bare feet over the edge of the roof, swaying them back and forth and pointing her toes like a dancer. The headstones in the surrounding graveyard cast long fingers of shadows in the dawn, splitting the early sun into pale yellow slices on the frosty grass.

She loved the graveyard in the morning. She breathed the sharp air and soaked in the silence so she could carry it with her the rest of the day. Mist hovered like ghosts. She felt alone, like she and the ghosts were the only ones in the world, hidden behind the wall of trees that separated the mortuary from the network of narrow back roads. She could have pretended she was anywhere, not just a few hundred miles from where she'd grown up, on the other side of the woods she'd watched from her bedroom window as a child.

She'd already been on her morning run through the woods. Her cold skin was slick with sweat and dew, but she felt warm and alive.

A cherry-red Camry rumbled down the long gravel driveway, kicking up pebbles and blaring classic rock. It jerked to a halt under Nolin's window. The music stopped like someone had cut it with scissors. Rebecca, with her mass of red spirals pulled into a ponytail, got out of the car and swung a black duffel bag over her shoulder. Though it was only April, she wore a black tank top with no jacket. Sleeves of colorful tattoos wrapped around her arms. Rebecca looked up at Nolin, honey-colored eyes twinkling behind her glasses.

"Don't do it!" she called. "I don't want to clean up the mess!"

"Don't worry. I wouldn't want to splatter guts all over your new car," Nolin replied, grinning.

"Damn straight you wouldn't." Rebecca cracked a smile and sauntered to the door of the mortuary while she fished a bundle of keys from a pocket of the duffel bag. "I've got plenty to do today. You're welcome to come down to watch if you want."

Nolin nodded. "There's a funeral today," she said. "I mowed and trimmed yesterday, so I'm free."

"Okay, come on down when you feel like it," Rebecca said. She disappeared into the building.

Maintaining a graveyard was well worth a free room in the attic of the old church. Eli, the funeral director and Rebecca's grandfather, told her it was abandoned in the mid-nineteenth century before it was converted to a mortuary. Nolin thought the old church was beautiful with its dark brick walls, peaked roof, stained glass windows, and steeple stretching into the sky. The building had an aura about it; perhaps the lingering force of uttered prayers lived in the walls and held the place together for the past two centuries.

She'd felt more at home there than she ever had in Calder. Every morning and evening she sat atop the pointed roof near the steeple to watch the sun rise and set. Counting on something felt good. For the first time in her life, she could rely on something. She loved getting up every morning, knowing the sun would be there to greet her.

Mourners would arrive soon. Eli would have a heart attack if they saw Nolin perched on the old church like a crow.

Nolin bent down to grip the edge of the eave and stepped off. The muscles in her arms tightened as she swung off the roof and dangled in front of her second-story window. Sometimes, she liked to hang there awhile and watch the ground under her feet. No time this morning. She kicked a leg forward to rest on the sill of the open window, then pulled herself into the tiny room.

Nolin's bedroom in the attic of the church had originally been a small storage room. It wasn't much, just a twin bed and a two-burner range on top of a mini-fridge. The only other objects in the room were two cardboard boxes—one full of clothes, the other with books.

It was all she needed.

She slipped on a tee shirt and worn jeans; thrift store finds Rebecca had bought her when Nolin had shown up five years earlier with only the shirt and sweatpants she was wearing. Her worn-out work clothes felt soft and familiar on her skin. She slipped on her sneakers and opened the creaky door of her room. Her shoulders nearly scraped the sides of the narrow staircase as she descended.

When she reached the ground floor, a floral aroma filled her nose. The church was always filled with fresh flowers on funeral days. Morning light filtered through the stained glass windows, casting dancing colors on the tiled floor. Dust particles glittered in the blocks of colored light.

She always made herself scarce on funeral days. She couldn't stand the tears or the heaviness in the air. All the crying, the whispering. It reminded her of the mental ward. Her stomach rolled as she hurried through the lobby. Before she disappeared down the stairs to the basement, she caught a glimpse of Eli in his office. He sat at his desk, writing, with his white hair standing on end and his jaw clenched.

The basement was bare and industrial compared to the upstairs, just a square cement room with a few tall, narrow, stainless-steel coolers and a door with a window at one end. Nolin peeked through the window of the old-fashioned embalming room. Rebecca stood with her back to the door, bending over the pasty white corpse of a middle-aged woman with cropped brown hair, massaging the arms to relieve the rigor mortis. The bottom of Rebecca's black tank top inched up to reveal swirling tattoos nestled in the small of her back.

Rebecca's body was a treasure map of tattoos. Flowers and swirling planets wrapped around her arms. Winding leaves curled behind her right ear. A giant deer skull stretched across her back, antlers poking out the shoulders of her tank top. Tree branches down the back of her calf. Words she loved across her collarbones. Tiny leaves floated down the crevice between her breasts. Her body was her storybook; each mark was the heading of a new chapter of her life, or a nod to an old one.

Sometimes Nolin wondered if she should get tattoos also, but what did she have to celebrate or remember? And the needles. She would never let needles near her again.

Nolin pushed the door open. Usually, Rebecca played music while she worked. Today, there was only the sound of the pumps. That usually meant she was in an exceptional mood, because she didn't need the music to drown out her thoughts.

"I like working with the dead," Rebecca had once told her. "They don't lie or whine; they don't rush or get worked up about things they can't control. The living could learn a thing or two from this."

Rebecca looked over her shoulder as Nolin entered and then turned back to her work. Nolin walked around the table to the stool Rebecca kept in the corner. Rebecca worked silently. Nolin watched, thinking her usual thoughts as if she were unwinding a massive knot.

She'd watched Rebecca perform hundreds of embalmings over the years. The process wasn't difficult to watch. The cadavers didn't look like people anymore, but more like lifeless movie props. It was no longer a "someone," but something empty, left behind. The same way someone would leave behind a house or a stamp collection.

"You look tired," Rebecca said, glancing up.

"Do I?"

"You have bags under your eyes."

Nolin leaned to catch a glimpse of herself in the glass door of one of the supply cupboards. She'd been tired for so long that she hadn't really noticed how she looked. Two deep grooves were already forming between her eyebrows at twenty years old. Two little wounds. Her eyes, once bright green, had faded to a murky brown framed by purple shadows. Her thin lips, pointy nose, and straight, dark eyebrows cut her face into a permanent frown.

"Have you been sleeping lately?" Rebecca asked as she inserted a needle into the corpse's neck.

"Not really," Nolin said. Right on cue, she yawned.

"Are you still having nightmares?"

Nolin nodded. "Sometimes. I almost sleep. Then I have those dreams that happen in between, when you're not awake but not sleeping either. Then I wake back up."

"What do you dream about?"

"Still that tree, and the girl with dark eyes," Nolin said. "My mom sometimes."

Rebecca shook her head. "You really need to talk to a professional, Nolin. This isn't going to go away on its own. It's been going on for way too long."

Nolin bit her lip. They'd had this conversation so many times. She'd told Rebecca about her mother, the mental ward, and what she could remember about the day she ran into the woods, which wasn't much. Sometimes she wished she'd never said a word. Rebecca cared; Nolin appreciated that, but she didn't always understand. Nolin had more than enough experience with "professionals," and little to show for it.

Rebecca left late that day, just as the sun started to set. Nolin planned on spending the evening alone. She loved the cemetery at sundown when it was mostly shadows. It scared her a little. She loved to walk barefoot on the cold grass and imagine ghosts walking alongside her. Surely they were there, watching her drift through the trees and tombstones. She regarded them as invisible friends, not good or evil, but more honest than most living people. Death had a way of making people honest.

She reached the edge of the woods, looked over her shoulder to make sure no one was looking, and stripped down to her undershirt and boy's boxers. She started running.

Nolin leapt into the trees like a deer, challenging herself to see how fast she could sprint, how high she could jump, like a child in an open meadow. She smiled as she scrambled up and over a boulder. She didn't feel human when she ran like this.

She felt like so much more.

Chapter 19

SHE COULDN'T SLEEP.

Nolin perched on the roof where she watched the sunrise each morning, but the sun wouldn't be up for hours. The outlines of the headstones around the church glowed in the moonlight, casting their long shadows toward her like pointing fingers.

The dream again. Her heart thrashing in her ribs as she ran through narrow spaces between the trees, not sure if she was running to or away from something. Melissa's hollow face, and a pair of dark, searing eyes—all spun together in a maddening slideshow, too quickly for her to think or focus on anything.

Nolin hugged her arms tightly around her thin legs. So tired. Exhaustion sunk into her bones, swam in her mind. Most of the time, she didn't realize how tired she was because it felt normal. She pushed through the days.

At night, though, she couldn't avoid it.

Will it always be like this? Would the little sleep she managed always be poisoned with dreams, her body weighed down with fatigue, her heart heavy with the guilt of leaving her mother?

Maybe I should leave here.

The thought came from nowhere. It seemed so obvious. How could she let go of her past when her hometown was a three-hour drive away? It would always be right behind her, watching over her shoulder.

She loved her life here, her independence, her job, her friendship with Rebecca. But, she realized, very little had changed in five years. What were her plans? What would she do with herself? Part of her would be content to stay here forever, in her familiar routine of work, running, visiting Rebecca to read late into the night with mugs of tea on the small couch in her apartment.

Another part of her twitched like a restless animal, itched for something new, the answer to a mystery she'd been trying to solve all her life.

She could leave her past behind, farther than just a few hundred miles south.

Nolin slid back through the window. Without bothering to turn on the lights, she grabbed her wallet, slipped out of her room, and descended the narrow stairs.

Eli never locked his office. Nolin let herself in, settled into the old office chair behind his desk, and turned on the computer.

She'd never bought a plane ticket, or even flown before. It was the fastest way to get as far away as she wanted. But where? She didn't have a passport. She'd have to stay in the country, at least for a while. She cast her mind around, thinking of places she'd ever thought of visiting. Her mind fell on the box of books in her room, mentally flipping through the worn covers with faded titles. Finally, she remembered the old copy of Jack London stories.

The Yukon. Alaska.

Glaciers, snowcapped mountains, evergreen forests. Sparsely populated. Something clicked in her mind.

She searched for flights from the nearest airport, scanned the list of options and before she could talk herself out of it, clicked "purchase." Her stomach fluttered as she punched in her debit card number and clicked "confirm."

It was done. In two weeks she'd fly into Fairbanks, Alaska, and go from there.

In that frozen paradise so far away from where she'd started, she could forget everything. Whatever she'd been searching for, whatever she was missing, she was on her way to finding it.

***

The cell phone rang at three-twenty in the morning, the generic three-toned trill jerking Nolin out of her doze. She swore, cursing herself for never getting around to picking a less-jarring ringtone, and groggily took the call.

"I'll be there in ten minutes," she croaked before snapping the phone shut.

She'd fallen asleep at Eli's desk. The computer screen lit up as she wiggled the mouse, and she shut it down before shuffling into the lobby.

She slipped down to the basement and out the door to the driveway, where a white van was parked next to her own tiny blue Toyota. She climbed into the mortuary van.

This was the other part of her job, the important part. The van started with a roar, and she guided it out of the mortuary driveway and through the back roads to the freeway toward the city. Her hands guided the steering wheel along the familiar route. She liked driving at night when she had the dark road almost all to herself.

Within minutes, Nolin pulled off the main road and into the back of the Maxfield City Hospital complex. The van sputtered as she turned it off.

Behind the hospital, she gripped the steering wheel tight, head bowed and her eyes squeezed shut. Her job didn't make her nervous, but hospitals did. Always hospitals. Her heart thudded, hard, rapid. She filled her lungs and squeezed them out again. *Calm down*, she told herself over and over until her heartbeat softened to almost normal. Memories flooded her: the glint of needles, the acrid smell of medicines, echoing footsteps, the moldy-green blur of hospital walls and floors.

Calm down.

She'd done this several times a week for two years. She was being stupid.

When her breathing slowed to normal, she let herself out, walked around the van, and opened the door to retrieve the ancient, squeaky gurney. It creaked as she unfolded it and placed it on its wheels. Finally, she took a deep breath and entered the building, nerves tingling. Her senses sharpened to a point, instinctively ready to fight at the first sign of a needle.

The wheels of the gurney squealed like a shopping cart. Her eyes darted sideways into the doorways of storage rooms, then patient rooms as she got deeper into the hospital. Snoozing patients tangled in tubes, tired-looking nurses, echoes of raspy coughs and beeping respirators. Her heart started to pound again. She forced herself to breath slowly. *Not a pleasant environment, but not threatening*, she reminded herself. *Not anymore.* She unclenched her hunching shoulders and concentrated on softening the muscles in her neck and face.

On the third floor, a young male doctor in a rumpled white coat leaned against the wall, writing on a clipboard. Nolin had seen him before. She never remembered his name. He didn't look at her. She cleared her throat.

"I'm here to pick up the body," Nolin said.

The doctor looked up. His eyes moved to her feet, then back to her eyes. She was used to this, doctors and retirement home nurses taking in her short, thin stature and wild hair. Her arms crossed impatiently.

"Can I see some ID?" the doctor asked, as he did every time she came in for a pickup. She wrenched the slipcase out of her pocket and flipped it open, dangling it in the doctor's face. He nodded, satisfied.

"I'll get someone to take him down for you."

"Don't bother, I've got it."

The doctor smirked. "Aren't you a little petite to be hauling bodies around the city?"

Nolin's jaw tightened. "I can handle it."

He shrugged and led her into a room across the hall. The shape of a man lay under a sheet on a gurney. The bulge, though clearly defining a face, chest, flat stomach, and limbs, didn't seem human. Just an oddly shaped sheet.

"Only forty-five. Shot himself in the head," the doctor said, shaking his head.

Nolin shifted her weight uncomfortably. The cause of death wasn't her business. She preferred not to know. Maybe these weary doctors wanted something from her—empathy or reassurance, a sounding board even—but she refused to give it to them. She knew mistrust of doctors was irrational, but she didn't care.

They exchanged signatures on paperwork that neither of them read. With practiced motions, she then wrapped her arms around the stiff torso and the sheet and jerked it onto the gurney, then did the same thing with the legs. The body clunked as it hit the metal frame.

Eager to leave, she wheeled the body out of the room and down the hall to the oversized elevator. She glanced over her shoulder. The doctor watched her bend forward to push the heavy load, but when she turned, his eyes darted back to his clipboard.

Men's gazes still surprised her. At best, Nolin considered herself plain. Her body was a tight wad of sinews and muscles taut as bowstrings; everything about it was thin and straight. Though she preferred undershirts to the fancy bras Rebecca tried buying her, her tiny swells often attracted downward glances.

The corpse already smelled a little ripe—oddly sweet and a bit pungent, like meat that had been sitting out for too long. The first time she'd experienced that scent, she'd smelled it for days, caught it everywhere she went. The odor followed her, the way Rebecca always smelled very faintly of formaldehyde.

Nolin pushed the gurney out the back door. The sky was a flat stretch of black velvet, all the stars drowned out by city lights.

She opened the back of the van and irreverently shoved the gurney inside, its wheels tucking under itself like a bird taking flight, then slammed the doors shut.

Poor stiff; this would be his second car ride on a gurney tonight.

Nolin rarely listened to the radio when she drove. She preferred quiet, but tonight she switched on the college station that only played local indie bands. It was noise to her, blocking out the music of the silence. Tonight, she didn't want that empty solitude. Something about this night unsettled her. She gripped the wheel a little tighter than usual and drove a little faster.

Streetlights passed overhead and illuminated her pale hands on the steering wheel before they faded into a moment of darkness. A web of veins stood out on the backs of her hands. She could almost hear the blood pushing through them.

She exited onto the back road that led to the cemetery. The old church loomed in the darkness as the van made its way up the driveway and backed into the garage. The old engine clunked as Nolin yanked the key out of the ignition.

The back of the van smelled sweet, like something fermented. The wheels of the gurney snapped down and clattered on the cement floor. One of the wheels squeaked its usual tune as she rolled the body through the door and into the basement. The sheet snagged on the rough wooden doorframe, exposing an icy white shoulder. Nolin tugged the sheet back into place, her fingers tingling slightly where she brushed the cold flesh. She took a breath and suppressed a shudder.

The ancient cooler stood by the door of the embalming room, a large, gray refrigerator two feet taller than Nolin and about seven feet deep. She pulled the heavy door open. A blast of cold air laced with the same sweet smell poured out in nauseating waves. Two pale scalps poked out of the bottom shelves—a balding man with a scalp splotched with black bruises, and an old woman with dyed tufts of red hair. Rebecca hadn't finished today; Nolin would have to get the new body onto the higher shelf.

She pulled the metal shelf out and wheeled the creaky gurney beside it. Then, she wrapped her arms around the stiff legs to shift them. They clunked on the cold metal. She shoved the hips, and the rest of the body went with them, firm with rigor mortis.

The sheet snagged the edge of the gurney and unveiled the white face.

She should have screamed, or cried, or something. Instead, Nolin stood still, watching the cold face for several seconds, minutes, maybe an hour. She didn't know.

Finally, she closed her eyes, swallowed hard, and pulled the sheet back over her father's face before pushing the shelf back in the cooler.

Chapter 20

NOLIN SAT IN front of the cooler the rest of the night.

Maybe if she spent the night staring at her father's body, she'd get a twinge of sadness or remorse. The awful emptiness gnawed at her like termites.

Her elbows rested on her bent knees, and she tipped her head into her hands, digging her fingers into her tangled hair. She stared into the blurry green eyes of her reflection in the cooler. They never blinked.

Anger. The void gave way to a dull ache in the hull of her stomach, boiling like the underground chamber of a geyser.

Nolin didn't remember him leaving. Her life was a haze of sedatives back then. She just knew that when she finally came home, briefly, he wasn't there. Melissa hadn't seemed angry; she just retreated deeper inside her shell until she was in a perpetual cocoon. In some ways, she got better. She was able to work again and picked up a stream of temporary jobs to pay the bills. When the shift was over she'd lock herself in her room. Nolin would never hear a word, never make eye contact. Melissa took on a hard, frightening calm.

After he left, Nolin wasn't enough to hold her family together anymore. Was she mad at him for leaving or mad at herself for not being able to take his place?

If he had stayed, would she have run away?

Nolin pressed her temples.

She thought about opening the cooler to see his face. Dead bodies never looked like the people they once were. It was just a shell without answers or apologies. Nolin's eyes stung. She wiped her face and forced the tears back into her head. Deep breaths.

Finally, she leapt up and swung her foot against the side of the cooler as hard as she could. She kicked it over and over, the clanging sound echoing off the decrepit stone walls like a giant brass drum.

"You son of a bitch!" she shrieked, hair whipping her face.

It was his fault she'd been stuck alone with her mother—that she'd had to take care of her all by herself. How could he do that to her?

She hurled curses and kicked until sharp pains shot up her leg. She pounded her fists into the door instead, slammed into it with her shoulder and her elbows, attacking it like she used to fight in school. Her knuckles cracked and ached. She kept kicking until she knocked a dent in the door.

"Nolin, what the hell?"

She hadn't heard Rebecca come in. Nolin slowed her attack and finally stopped, but didn't turn around. Her shoulders slumped with exhaustion. She leaned into the cooler, her sweaty forehead pressing into the cool metal. A hot tear dripped down her nose.

Rebecca placed a cool hand on Nolin's shoulder. Her faint chemical scent, masked by a mist of expensive sandalwood perfume, burned in Nolin's nostrils. Rebecca shook her gently, cooing concerned words. Nolin only heard a soft buzz. Nolin felt herself being coaxed into a sitting position on the floor, leaning against the wall. The cooler was streaked with orange-tinged blood where she had kicked and punched it. She looked down at her own bleeding toes and knuckles.

"Shit, Nolin, what happened?"

Rebecca opened the door to the embalming room and disappeared inside. Nolin heard her rifling through the cupboards and turning on the sink. She returned with a stack of white cloths and gauze.

Rebecca sat down next to Nolin and took her hands to wipe them with the wet cloth and wrap them in strips of gauze. They looked like a fighter's hands, wrapped and ready for a street fight. Nolin breathed deeply, tearing her eyes away from the cooler.

"I'll clean that up," she said, nodding toward the bloody streaks. Rebecca glanced over her shoulder at the cooler and then turned back to Nolin.

"I got worried when I didn't see you on the roof. I thought maybe you really had jumped."

Nolin chuckled and wiped her wet cheeks with the back of her bandaged hands. Rebecca pulled a bottle of Coke out of her bag, twisted it open with a soft *shht*, and took a long swig as if it were something much more powerful than soda. Next to her duffel bag was a paper sack smelling of something warm and greasy. She picked it up and dumped it on Nolin's lap.

"Here. Have a breakfast burrito. Your gut will be so traumatized, you won't be able to think about suicide." Rebecca reached into the bag and pulled out a tube-shaped thing in blotchy white paper. When Nolin didn't respond, Rebecca picked up Nolin's hand and shoved the burrito into it. She pulled another out for herself.

"So, is there anything you want to tell me?" Rebecca said as she took a bite.

Nolin squeezed the burrito slightly. She wasn't hungry. The warmth felt good in her hands.

"I picked up my dad's body last night."

The burrito halted halfway to Rebecca's mouth. Her pale eyebrows lifted, and she shook her head. "Shit. Lousy family reunion." She shoved the burrito into her mouth and bit off half in one bite. Her eyes rolled up to the ceiling in pleasure. "How did he die?"

"He shot himself."

Rebecca froze, a horrified expression on her face. "Oh, god. I'm sorry about that suicide comment. That really wasn't funny."

"It's fine," Nolin said. "I haven't seen him in ten years. He means nothing to me."

Rebecca smiled grimly. Nolin knew she didn't believe her. "Well, on one hand, the jackass left you and your mom in the hospital. I can see how you wouldn't be upset to shove him in the cooler."

"And the other hand?"

"Life probably wasn't easy for him either, then or now. He probably felt like he didn't have a choice."

"But he did have a choice," Nolin said darkly. "He always had a choice."

"He did, and it doesn't make what he did okay. Leaving you or killing himself. But, I don't think he did it to hurt anybody. He's only human."

Nolin said nothing.

Rebecca took a breath and went on. "What he did was selfish, but he didn't do it to hurt you or your mother. He probably didn't know what else to do."

"I'm not going to forgive him."

"You don't have to. Maybe later we can get a big fat cake and have them write 'Congratulations, another one bites the dust' in purple buttercream."

Nolin cracked a weak smile. Rebecca had a strange way of making Nolin feel better and worse at the same time. Nolin finally considered the warm burrito in her hand. She unwrapped it and took a bite; it tasted like deep-fried cat food in a tortilla.

Rebecca sipped her Coke and stared into space. The upstairs was silent; Eli hadn't arrived yet. He got later and later as he got older. Sometimes, he didn't show up at all.

"So," Rebecca said, gulping the last bit of Coke. "Do you think your mom knows?"

Nolin had been wondering that all night. She thought of her mother every day. Sometimes she'd get out of bed at night and go for a walk around the cemetery to distract from her aching guilt. She loved her mother, no doubt about it, but the thought of her was terrifying; that cold, empty corpse taunting her, a soulless marionette acting the part of a mother.

"I don't know."

She hadn't heard from her mother in five years. What if something happened and it was Nolin's fault, for leaving her? As a child, Nolin sometimes felt she was the glue that held her family together. After her father left, she was the glue that held her mother in reality. Anything could have happened after that security was gone.

She was no better than him. She'd abandoned Melissa too.

Heat welled up inside Nolin again, and her eyes grew wet. A choked sob escaped her.

Rebecca took her hand and squeezed gently. She wore contacts today instead of the horn-rimmed glasses. They could have been sisters, alike but different. Rebecca's small, curvy body perched on the floor with her legs curled to the side. Curly hair floated around her beautifully sculpted faced like flames.

Nolin's usually lively curls, on the other hand, hung in a tangled mass, like kelp washed up on a beach. Weak sunlight seeped through the dingy basement window. Nolin didn't want to face the morning; she shut her eyes—a child hiding under the covers from a thunderstorm.

"You're worried about your mom." It wasn't a question. Rebecca pushed a mass of curls off Nolin's face, wiping the dampness of old tears across her cheek. "Look, you did what you had to. You had to take care of yourself. You're human; you can only handle so much. No one should have to go through what you did."

Nolin tried to hold back another sob. It escaped with a strange sound somewhere between a gasp and a hiccup.

Rebecca went on. "She had a job. She was better. She was taking care of herself. You wouldn't have left if she were still sick."

Nolin nodded. "She might be sick now though. Something might be wrong, it's been so long."

Rebecca nodded. Nolin dipped her head into her hands again. Rebecca stood to wad up their breakfast paper into a ball and toss it in the trash.

"Do whatever you need to do," she said. Nolin nodded. "I'd ask if you felt like watching today, but I get the feeling you'd rather not."

Nolin looked up at her, and then to the cooler. She shook her head.

Rebecca opened the door to the ancient embalming room and disappeared inside. Nolin listened to the clanking of Rebecca preparing her equipment. Heavy metal didn't seem to be on the playlist today.

Nolin pulled her knees to her chest and pushed her chin in between them. A loud clunk echoed in the embalming room. Rebecca swore loudly. The door opened, and she stepped out, sucking her index finger. She pulled the finger out with a pop and examined it, her eyes crossing as she held it in front of her nose.

"Ugh, right to the quick." She wiped her hand on her jeans, pulled a pair of surgical gloves from her pocket, and slipped them on, snapping them on her wrists like a television doctor.

"Well, I need to get in there. Unless you want to get run over by a cold gurney, I suggest you scoot."

Nolin pushed herself off the floor and stepped toward the stairs. She heard the cooler open behind her and a shelf sliding out. A soft thud as Rebecca moved a body onto the rickety gurney. Nolin couldn't help it; she looked over her shoulder.

Her father's face poked out from under Rebecca's arm as she shifted him over. The last ten years hadn't been kind to him. His hairline was farther back than it was when Nolin last saw him. He was thinner, with only a few wisps of pale hair. The skin around his eyes wrinkled like a white tee shirt tossed on the floor. Luckily, Nolin couldn't see the exit wound. She sighed with bitter relief.

She knew this was Rebecca's way of giving her closure. Rebecca closed the embalming room door behind the gurney.

Nolin's thoughts rolled around in her aching head as she climbed the stairs out of the cold basement. Was Melissa all right? When she'd last seen her mother, she'd been as pale as those people in the cooler.

She remembered what her father always used to say to her before he'd go to work on the weekend, when he made her repeat their address and phone number back to him while she was a small child.

Keep an eye on your mother, Nolin. Check on your mother.

Hours ago, nothing in the world could convince her to go back. Now here she was, teetering on the edge of the precipice she'd spent years avoiding. Now she realized she'd been walking along the edge all along.

This whole disaster was a chain reaction set off by Nolin's unwelcome arrival into this world. She was the first domino. If it hadn't been for her, her mother wouldn't be sick. Her father wouldn't have left. He'd probably still be alive.

She had no choice. She had to go back.

She marched up to her room, stuffed her clothes into her old school backpack. She remembered the plane ticket she'd bought early that morning. Images of snowcapped mountains, leaping salmon, and aromatic pine trees flashed through her mind.

She wouldn't leave for two weeks. She had time.

She left a note on Eli's desk, explaining that she had to leave, thanking him for everything. She didn't look back at the mortuary, didn't glance sideways at the stone angels who stood silently, seeing her off. Her little car groaned up the long, winding drive with the window down and cold spring air blasting her face. Nolin let the chill sink into her skin to freeze out the slow-burning fear pooling in her heart.

Chapter 21

NOLIN FLIPPED THE car radio on. Then off. Then on again, twirling the dial through crackly radio stations—static voices of DJs, country fiddles, electric guitars, and car dealership ads. Finally, she cursed and slapped the dash. The radio sputtered off. She couldn't stand the noise, but the silence ate at her.

The needle on the speedometer inched up to eighty miles per hour. Her tiny car rattled. She took her foot off the gas. For the fifth time, she rolled the window up. Five minutes later, it had slid back down again.

Just check on Melissa and get the hell out. Quick and painless.

Images of Melissa flashed between thoughts. Ragged, emaciated Melissa. Melissa scalded and bleeding, huddled in the corner of the shower. Melissa unconscious and bandaged in the hospital ward that reeked of chemicals and madness. Melissa, silent and stoic for years afterward, floating through the house like a ghost, fading more and more each day.

What am I doing?

The city had given way to suburbs, which trickled into vast fields laced with trees. Mountains loomed in the distance on either side of the road, forming a wide corridor that ran down the state. Spindly tree branches twisted into the sky, some already fluffy with opening leaf buds. Grass starting to turn green and a few wildflowers dusted the open land with color.

The sun arched across the valley. Her head ached with thoughts bouncing off the inside of her skull. She'd forgotten to bring anything to eat or drink. Her stomach rumbled, the perfect harmony to her dry mouth and scratchy throat.

A sign flew past: *Calder — 8 miles.*

The car slowed. Nolin pumped the accelerator. Her eyes fell on the gas gauge; the needle hovered squarely over the E. She threw the car into neutral to coax more distance from whatever drops remained in her fuel tank. Finally, the car rolled to a stop on the shoulder of the deserted road.

Idiot. Idiot. Idiot.

How many gas stations had she passed? But no, she had been so busy working herself up to deal with Melissa that she never bothered to glance at the gas gauge. Fan-damn-tastic.

Time to start walking.

With a resigned sigh, Nolin reached into the back seat to retrieve her backpack and popped the car door open.

It was colder than it had been in the city. Sharp wind cut right through her denim jacket and tousled her hair like icy fingers on her scalp. She threaded her arms into the straps of the backpack and kicked the car door shut, not even bothering to lock it. The car wasn't worth anything. Nothing inside it was worth stealing. Not even a CD.

Gravel crunched under her sneakers as she walked with her arms folded tightly over her chest and head bowed against the wind. The bitter air found its way into the sleeves of her jacket, under the hems of her tee shirt and pant legs, down the neck of her shirt, and somehow between her toes in her sneakers. After ten minutes of walking, a tiny, cold water droplet landed on her hand.

Well, shit.

She had no umbrella, or even a hood on her jacket. Another drop fell, then another. Dark spots speckled the asphalt.

Soon, a torrent of freezing rain pelted the road. Nolin huddled against the downpour, cursing the rain as her wet feet squished in her shoes. Her soaked jeans and denim jacket weighed down on her. She shivered and peered up into the distance. Nothing yet. No "Welcome to Calder" sign, no houses or gas stations, no sign of anything but grass and rain.

Lighting split the sky like a jagged smile. Nolin stomped through the puddles. The rain didn't feel like it did when she was a child. It wasn't magical anymore; now it was just cold and wet.

This wasn't helping her feel better.

A clattering sound swelled behind her, coming closer. Nolin stepped off the shoulder and walked in the grass. A rusty pickup truck slowed beside her, rattling like a dumpster full of tin cans. She kept walking.

The truck inched forward to keep up with her. The young man in the driver's seat leaned over and rolled down the window. His messy hair and mischievous blue eyes gave him an elfish look. He smiled, revealing a set of shiny white teeth with pointy little canines.

"Do you want a ride?" he called over the rain. He reached to straighten the window, which was rolling down crookedly.

"I'm okay, it's not much farther," Nolin lied. It was still a few miles to Calder. She'd rather trudge through the rain than trust some random guy on the road. She stuffed her hands in her pockets and watched the cracks again. *Don't step on a crack, or you'll break your mother's back.*

"Wait," the young man said. "I think I know you." Nolin stole another glance at his face. Recognition flickered behind his eyes. She realized she knew him as well.

Her stomach fluttered. Images spun through her head. The school cafeteria, walking to the library, reaching up to touch the leaves on the willow tree. She knew him. But she didn't want to be seen. She turned away and kept walking.

"Nolin!" Drew said. "Wow, what are you doing out here? Get in before you drown."

Her teeth chattered. Drew leaned forward and popped open the passenger door. Nolin hesitated, her shivering arms wrapped tightly around herself. Finally, she stepped forward and climbed into the truck, swinging the door shut behind her. It banged like a lid slamming down on a trash can. The truck shook as Drew yanked the stick shift and they jumped forward.

"Was that your car back there? That little blue Corolla?" he asked.

Nolin nodded. "I ran out of gas."

"Well, that's easy to fix. I'll run you to the Shell station."

"Thank you." Nolin curled her hands around the seatbelt that crossed her chest and peeked over at Drew. The corners of his mouth turned up on their own, his resting face still a slight smile that carved faint dimples in his cheeks. He was long and lanky in a gray tee shirt, worn blue jeans, and a tattered blue baseball cap. He seemed to be thinking carefully.

"So..." he started. "It's been a while hasn't it?"

"It has." Her throat suddenly felt dry.

"You never were much of a talker, were you?"

Nolin swallowed hard, trying to untangle her throat.

"I'm surprised you recognized me," Nolin said.

Drew chuckled. "It wasn't hard. I'd know you anywhere. I've only known one girl with hair like that."

Nolin's hand jumped out to touch her wild curls. "It's not a bad thing," Drew said quickly. "It's just, you know...distinct. I always liked your hair."

Nolin was confused. Was she supposed to thank him? She'd never been in this situation, alone with a guy who reminded her of a friendly Labrador puppy. She had no idea what to do.

"I don't mean to be awkward," Drew said again, guiding the truck through the torrential downpour, "but it's really good to see you. I haven't heard from you since, well, since that last day when you ran off. I always wondered what happened to you."

"What happened to me," Nolin repeated. She wasn't sure if he meant where she'd been, or why she'd snapped that day on the playground, broken a child's nose, and fled into the woods.

"You just disappeared. I heard a few different things. I didn't just want to believe anything people said."

Nolin said nothing. She folded her arms tightly. Drew spun a dial on the dash to turn up the heat.

Why should she care what people said? People had always whispered about her and her family. Besides, she'd never see him again after he dropped her off at the car. He'd just fade into the fog of her memory along with the rest of her childhood.

Her silence didn't seem to bother him. Rain pelted the roof and ran down the windows in streams. He drummed his fingers on the steering wheel as he drove slowly through the storm, bobbing his head to some song only he could hear. Nolin was starting to regret getting in the car, or coming back to Calder at all. She opened her mouth to ask him to just let her out, then her stomach growled like a grizzly bear, loud enough to hear over the roar of the engine.

"I think I'd better buy you a burger," he chuckled. He looked over at her. This time she met his gaze. He was different. Not the shy, skinny kid she remembered from school, but he still gave the impression that he'd be up for a game of freeze tag at any moment. A playful child. He smiled at her, and something fluttered in her stomach.

Nothing to worry about, just hunger.

He jerked the truck into the parking lot of a small burger restaurant. Nolin had been there once with her father when she was seven or eight. She shook her head, like an Etch A Sketch erasing an image.

Drew stopped the truck. "Don't move." He hopped out, ran to the other side, and opened her door.

"What are you doing?" she said.

"This is how you treat women. It's in the rules."

"What rules?"

"*The Rules of Not Being a Jerk.*"

Nolin slid off the high seat. Drew shut the door behind her. She'd never seen her father open the door for her mother. She couldn't decide if it made her feel special or strange.

"Do you need another jacket?" Drew asked her, eyeing her soaked clothes.

She shook her head. Her feet squished in her soaked sneakers as she padded into the restaurant. Griddles hissed behind the order counter. Clouds of steam hung in the air. The heavy smell of frying meat filled her nose. Her stomach growled louder than ever.

"Get whatever you want," Drew said. The stocky teenage girl behind the register eyed him. He examined the menu with his hands in his pockets, shifting his weight from one foot to the other.

"I'll have the Big Nasty burger with no onions, a medium fry, and a Coke," Drew told the cashier. He stepped aside and motioned for Nolin to order.

"Um, a double cheeseburger, please. No ketchup," Nolin said.

"Anything to drink?" asked the girl behind the counter.

"Just water. Thanks." The girl handed Nolin a clear plastic cup. Drew offered the cashier a ten and a five. She slowly counted out his change, her lips moving as she plucked quarters, nickels, and dimes from the drawer and clinked the change into his hand. He nodded appreciatively and dropped the coins into the tip jar next to the register.

"Thank you," Nolin said.

"Of course. It's great to see an old friend," Drew said, slapping her lightly on the arm. Nolin blushed, then turned to fill her water cup at the fountain. She pressed the cup into the ice dispenser a little too forcefully, and a spray of crushed ice spilled out onto the floor.

"Shit! Sorry," she said, blushing even more furiously. She shook the spilled ice off her shoes and kicked what she could under the machine before filling her cup with water.

Drew retrieved their tray. Nolin followed him to a booth near the corner of the restaurant.

Nolin's burger was massive, but nothing compared to Drew's. Bacon, cheese, and slices of ham poked out of the bun in all directions. She had no idea how he managed to hold onto it, let alone bite it. He expertly scooped up the whole mess and took a bite without getting ketchup on his face. Clearly, this wasn't his first time.

Nolin bit into her burger, glad for an excuse for her silence. Drew leisurely twirled a fry in the little paper cup of ketchup.

"Why do they call it the Big Nasty?" Nolin finally asked, taking a stab at conversation.

Drew swallowed the french fry he'd just eaten and grinned. "Really, I have no idea. Probably because it's such a ridiculous mess to eat, but there's a trick to it, you see. You have to squash it a bit first." He demonstrated, carefully cupping his hand around the burger and squeezing it slightly. Nolin suspected his technique was much more difficult to master than it looked. "Then you have to hold it just so, so most of the stuff is on the side you're going to bite. That way, it doesn't all squish out the bottom. Then, of course, it just takes practice."

"And you've had lots of practice."

"I probably keep this place in business single-handedly. Well, when I'm home from school, of course."

Nolin bit into her burger again. Drew ate his fries, perfectly content to be here where he was, doing what he was doing. She liked the way the edges of his mouth turned up even when he was resting.

"I'm sorry, I'm not very good at conversation," she said. Drew chuckled and picked up another fry.

"Are you bad at conversation, or are you just bad at small talk? There's a huge difference. And if you're still the girl I knew in school, you're far too interesting to be bad at conversation."

"I guess I just get nervous. And I don't have much to say."

"No need to be nervous. This isn't a job interview." He sipped his soda, his blue eyes probing hers. Not an invasive look or a judging one, just a curious gaze. Nolin didn't know what there was to be so curious about. Usually, eyes slid over her like she was a hole-in-the-wall restaurant. She was the place someone could walk past a thousand times and never notice.

"And anyway, an honest silence is better than a fluffy conversation," he added, tapping his cup back onto the table to punctuate his point.

"That's why I hate small talk," she said. "It's fluff."

"Good. I like that about you already." He smiled again. This boy was always smiling. It wasn't a forced smile, but an infectious one that seemed to bubble up from his depths. He couldn't help it. She even felt a small smile bloom at the corners of her mouth.

"I would like to know, though," he started. "Where have you been? It's been, like, ten years."

She'd known this was coming, and she hadn't prepared an acceptable answer. Excuses, euphemisms, explanations chased each other around her head. Her panic must have shown on her face because he quickly added, "You don't have to tell me if you don't want to. I'm just curious, that's all. People talked after you left, and I just wanted to know the real story. From you. Not just a bunch of people who don't know anything. You're the only one who really has the right to tell that story."

"What did people say?"

"Most said you were in the hospital for a while, that you got hurt in the woods or something. After that, it's everything from military school to juvie to a foster home in Santa Fe. You really don't have to tell me," he repeated.

"The hospital is true."

"Did you get hurt in the woods? I'll never forget when you climbed that fence and jumped. I didn't know what to think; I was worried you'd get eaten by a bear in there."

Nolin actually laughed. "No, I don't think there are any bears in those woods. To be honest, I don't remember much about it. They just found me a few days later and took me to the hospital where my mom was."

"She hurt herself, didn't she? That's why she was there?"

Nolin's smile faded a little. "Yes."

Drew shook his head. "I could never wrap my head around that. Hurting yourself, I mean. How is she doing?"

"I don't know, actually. That's why I'm here."

"Really? When was the last time you saw her?"

Nolin swallowed hard. Her throat was getting dry again, and she sipped her water. "Five years ago," she said. "I left home when I was fifteen."

"When you were fifteen? You were still home then? I never saw you in school."

Nolin shook her head. "I was actually done with school before then. I finished online while I was at a group home."

"A group home?"

"For wayward teenagers."

"Wow. How long were you there?" He leaned forward on his elbows, his head resting on his hands like a child listening to an

162

exciting story. Nolin felt herself relax. Her tense shoulders lowered, her jaw softened, and the maelstrom in her stomach calmed. Now that she was talking, it wasn't so hard.

"It's complicated," she went on. "I was in the local hospital for a while, then I was transferred to the state hospital. Then I was sent to a wilderness program for five months, then a coed group home in Arizona, and then a girl's home in New Mexico. I finished school online there, and they released me to be with my mom."

"I take it you still didn't get along very well."

"No."

"But why you were in the hospital for so long? Did you get hurt in the woods?"

"I wasn't really hurt, physically. I'm sure I had some cuts and bruises, and I might have been a bit dehydrated. I was actually in the children's psychiatric ward for a year." She'd never admitted that to anyone but Rebecca. She glanced up at his face, expecting a look of shock or even disgust, but he didn't look ruffled at all. His eyes still twinkled with that ever-present smile.

"After that," Nolin continued carefully, "the state decided I needed reform. So they sent me to Wilderness and the group homes."

"Wow," Drew said, sitting back in his seat. The vinyl cushion squeaked. "So that's what they do with kids who don't take shit from bullies?"

"I broke his nose."

"You did, and maybe that was a bit much, but he had it coming. He really did, Nolin. That kid needed to learn his lesson before he pissed off someone bigger and meaner than you. If anything, you did him a favor. Trust me, he wasn't so tough after a girl half his size put his nose in a cast."

Nolin chuckled, then mentally slapped herself. What she did had been wrong. That's the kind of thing they'd discuss in therapy back at the group homes until her ears rang. Those group sessions still rattled in her brain whenever she thought about the crunch of that kid's nose under her fist and how, even now, she'd do it again in a second.

"I wasn't a bad kid," she said quietly. "I didn't want to hurt anyone. I felt horrible after I did it. I knew I was in huge trouble and if I did it once, I could do it again. Maybe worse next time. I was just protecting myself and my mom, and I knew the teachers, principal, whoever, wouldn't understand that. They'd only punish me. If I stayed, I'd hurt even more people. So I ran. It wasn't a decision at all, just something I did before I'd even thought about it. I couldn't stay there."

The words spilled out of her, and she stopped to take a breath. She hadn't talked this much at once in...well, she wasn't sure how long. She was used to the quiet of the graveyard, of Rebecca's living room as they read, communicating with minimal words. Rebecca understood her, but words between them were sparse. Not like this, where she felt like she could sit in that booth and talk for hours. She liked it, the comfort of letting the words flow from her like water from a dam.

Drew studied her face and leaned forward on his elbows again, his hands clasped in front of him. "No," he said, "people probably wouldn't have understood. And they wouldn't try to, because you were a kid and they were the grown-ups and that's how it worked. No one really understands why someone else does something or what they really need until they stop and see the other person as a person, not just a deviant or some device there to make your life tougher."

"You should be a counselor," Nolin said.

"I want to be. That's what I'm going to school for, to counsel teenagers."

Nolin smiled. The sensation of her eyes crinkling at the corners was odd, yet pleasant. "You'll be a very good one," she said.

He tipped his hat at her. "Why, thank you."

Drew finished his food, crumpled his napkin and French fry tray, then stuffed them into his empty drink cup before replacing the lid on top.

"What are you doing?" Nolin asked, then realized she sounded rude.

"I like to consolidate my garbage."

"How fastidious of you."

He shrugged. "It seems neater. Makes things easier to throw away."

Nolin picked up her tray.

"Are you finished?" he asked.

"I need to get to back to my car."

They left. Nolin bought a gas can at the station next door and filled it. Drew let her in the truck, and she decided she liked having the door opened for her.

"Want heat?"

Nolin nodded, and he flipped the dial so hot air rushed out of the dusty vents. The pounding rain muffled the clanking of the truck. Every time they hit a bump, Nolin flew off the seat a little bit. She squeezed the handle on the door until her hand hurt.

The truck ambled out of town. Soon, Nolin's little blue car came into view. Drew made a U-turn and pulled up behind it. Once again, he left the truck first, circled around, and unlocked her door. The rain had slowed. She slid off the passenger seat and onto her feet.

"Do you need help filling her up?" he asked.

"I've got it," Nolin said. "Thank you."

"You bet," he said. "Are you sticking around for a while?"

Nolin shook her head. "No. I mean, I hope not. I really don't know. I was just planning to check on my mom and get out." She thought of the plane ticket she'd purchased the night before. The flight was two weeks away; she'd definitely be gone by then.

Drew's head tilted. Was he disappointed? "If you change your mind," he said, "we should get another burger."

Nolin smiled weakly.

He pulled her into a quick, one-armed hug. His strength surprised her, but she was more surprised when she discovered she didn't mind touching her cheek to his shoulder. He climbed into the truck and waved as he backed out. The truck roared down the street.

Nolin didn't want to leave yet, didn't want to drive to her old house and knock on that door, so she watched him disappear down the road.

***

The familiar street looked almost like it always had. A few things had changed; several trees had been cut down. A few yards were re-landscaped. Some of the houses were repainted. A couple of unfamiliar dogs barked at her rattling little car as it splashed down the repaved street.

The windows of her old house were dark, and dead weeds spilled out of the flower beds. Half of the tree in the front yard had been trimmed away. Maybe it was dying. The garage was closed. No car in the driveway.

Nolin slowly turned into the driveway and shut off the engine. Was she really here? She gripped the steering wheel, staring at her hands until her knuckles turned white.

Just go in. Check on her and go home.

Finally, she popped open the door, climbed out, and forced her feet to move. She walked the cement path to the front door, then stepped onto the porch. It would be okay. Melissa would be fine and if, for some reason, she didn't live there anymore, Nolin would just go back to the mortuary and get on that plane in two weeks.

She took a deep breath and pressed the doorbell.

No lights turned on. The house remained silent.

She's not home. Get back in the car and drive out of here, fast as that tin can will go.

She rang again, just to be sure.

I should just go. What was she planning to do anyway? She couldn't make things right, not after what she'd done. Maybe she was better off disappearing.

Nolin jumped when she heard the door unlock. It creaked open. A wiry woman appeared. Stringy hair fell over her shoulders. Sharp elbows poked out of an oversize tee shirt that didn't hide the jutting collarbones. Icy eyes widened with surprise, then instantly hardened, glaring. Nolin didn't know what to say.

As she opened her mouth, her mother reached out and smacked her across the face.

Chapter 22

NOLIN'S FACE STUNG. Melissa twitched. Maybe she itched to follow through with a backhand. Instead, she withdrew her hand and clenched it into a tight-knuckled fist. She'd probably been saving that smack for years.

Nolin wanted to raise her hand to her face to rub away the sting. She didn't. She wouldn't let her mother think she'd won. Instead, she straightened to meet Melissa's cold glare, arms crossed over her chest. She fought to keep her face calm. Melissa's icy stare drilled into her.

Nolin was taller than Melissa now. Though she looked much healthier than she had ten years ago, it finally struck Nolin how tiny and frail Melissa was.

"What the hell are you doing here?" Melissa growled, her voice low and dangerous.

Nolin felt her resolve buckle. She stuck out her chin and imagined her feet growing roots, planting her into the ground, strong and straight as a tree. "I came to see how you were," she finally responded. She tried to match Melissa's tone, low and frightening like faraway thunder. Her voice quavered slightly. She hoped beyond hope that Melissa didn't notice.

"I'm fine, thank you. Now get your ass off my porch before I call the police."

"You can't have me arrested for ringing your doorbell," Nolin snapped. *Just leave. She's fine. You got what you came for. Now leave and never, ever come back.*

"I can if you refuse to leave." Melissa leaned against the doorframe, blocking Nolin's view inside the house. Nolin realized she was bluffing. Melissa hated cops, doctors, and anyone she felt got a kick out of their own perceived authority. Nolin wasn't going anywhere.

"Look," Nolin started, holding up her hands in a gesture of goodwill. "I don't want to be here any more than you want me to. I just had to make sure everything was all right. Then I promise, I'll leave and you'll never see me again."

A vein twitched in Melissa's forehead beneath her papery skin. Her pale lips pressed together until her mouth was nothing but a thin, angry gash.

"Why would I need you to check on me?" she said, looking Nolin up and down. "I got by without you, didn't I? You and Paul. I didn't need either of you."

"That's not true," Nolin said. Melissa was less bony than she used to be, but she clearly wasn't eating enough. Nolin waded through dangerous waters now. Seeing her mother alive and standing upright wasn't enough; Nolin had to be absolutely sure that everything was fine, or the guilt would follow her for the rest of her life like an injury that never quite healed. "I know Dad sent you money, at least until I left. This yard looks like shit, Melissa. Who knows what it's like in there." Nolin nodded toward the interior of the house.

169

"I'm just fine." Melissa said stubbornly. A red tinge bloomed on her pale cheeks.

Nolin took a deep breath. "Dad's dead," she said bluntly.

Melissa's mouth opened slightly, then closed, and her eyes darted downward for a split second before returning to Nolin's. They'd lost the icy burn they'd held before. Suddenly, she looked old, exhausted.

"How do you know?"

"I saw him. Last night."

"You were in contact with him?"

"No. I just happened to be at the hospital... after he died." Nolin leaned back on her heels and looked away. She didn't want to give details about where she'd been or what she did for a living. A moth fluttered around the porch, attracted to the light coming from inside the house. A cool breeze blew. Nolin shivered, though she wasn't really cold. "I just wanted to see how you were, because he won't be helping you anymore."

Nolin forced herself to hold Melissa's burning glare. Fury and fear mixed into a sickening boil inside her. She would not crumble under that stare; she would not back down. Melissa stood in silence for a moment. Nolin could almost see her thoughts whirring behind her eyes like a slideshow. Melissa gripped the doorknob tightly, knuckles bulging under thin, waxy skin. The door shook back and forth slightly.

"What happened to him?" Melissa asked flatly. The muscles in her neck were still tense and her eyes glowered.

Nolin swallowed, crossing her arms. "He shot himself."

Melissa drummed her fingers on the doorframe, looking down at her slippers. They didn't speak for a moment. Nolin couldn't

170

read Melissa's expression; her eyes looked flat and emotionless. Finally, she opened the door another foot and stepped back, allowing Nolin inside.

It was like stepping into a ghost of the house she'd lived in before, a shipwreck at the bottom of the sea. Darker than she remembered, a thick layer of dust coated every surface like dirty snow. Fine dirt crunched under her feet. She could see grime built up in the corners where the walls met the floor and ceiling. The air smelled stale, like old clothes, and she thought she caught a whiff of mold. Cobwebs gathered in the corners of the ceiling. She could barely make out the photos in the picture frames for all the dust.

Surprisingly, the kitchen looked like no one had used it in years. From the filth in the hallway, she expected a sink piled high with dirty dishes, maybe food left out and rotting. Instead, the same fine dust spread over the counters and cupboards. The kitchen table was stacked high with mail, mostly unopened. Piles of envelopes littered the floor where papers had slid off.

"This place is disgusting," Nolin said frankly.

"I allow you in, and the first thing you do is insult my home. I thought I taught you better than that."

Nolin smirked. *You taught me nothing.* "I guess what I mean to say is, why?"

"You're reasonably intelligent, Nolin. Certainly smart enough to know the answer on your own: Obviously, I haven't cleaned recently."

"Again, why?"

"Couldn't be bothered."

A kettle on the stove whistled. Melissa turned off the burner and the whistle tapered off. "I have chamomile or Earl Grey," she said. Melissa opened a cupboard and retrieved two mugs, the same ones Nolin remembered. She'd filled them with tea to take up to her mother so many times, but she'd never seen Melissa make tea.

"Er... chamomile." Nolin sighed. She perched on a barstool and glanced around the downstairs, taking in the details, running through tasks in her head, questions to ask, places to check for dangerous mold.

"Has anyone else been in here since I left?"

"No."

Melissa fished two tea bags out of a box and dropped one into each mug before pouring hot water over them. Steam rose from the mugs. Nolin imagined the steamy bathroom, the angry hiss of the shower, the smell of blood.

Melissa plunked the mug in front of Nolin.

"I don't have any lemon. I know you used to take it with lemon."

Nolin stared into her mug as the tea bag slowly tinted the water dark. She didn't remember telling Melissa she liked lemon in her tea.

"Thank you."

"Drink fast, because I might throw your sorry ass back out before you're done."

Nolin fiddled with the string of the tea bag, turned the paper tab around to read the message printed on it: *You will rekindle an old friendship.* Nolin rolled her eyes.

Finally, she sighed. "Look," she started, her heart thudding. "I'm here to help. This place is a mess, and Dad won't be sending any more checks. I don't know if he has life insurance, but I can help you clean the place up and figure out if insurance will pay out. Then I'll leave."

Melissa leaned against the counter across from Nolin, swirling the tea bag in her mug. "He had insurance," she said quietly, staring into her mug, "but I doubt it will pay out for a suicide. And I'm not the beneficiary anymore."

"What? Then who is?"

"His girlfriend, I imagine."

Nolin glanced up the stairs and recalled the night when she woke up from a dream, crept into the hallway, and overheard her father on the phone. He'd sat on the very stool that Nolin occupied. She wondered if it was the same woman.

Nolin shifted, then stood up and paced as she carefully sipped her tea. She felt Melissa's eyes follow her.

"Well," Nolin said. "We'll figure something out."

"We?" Melissa repeated, venom in her voice. "No, you're a stranger to me. I don't need help from stranger."

"Why? Am I any more a stranger now than I was before?" Nolin slammed her mug down on the counter. A drop of hot water sloshed out onto her hand, but she didn't flinch.

"You were a child, and I was obligated to take care of you. I'd have thrown you out the moment you turned eighteen anyway."

"Take care of me? When did you ever take care of me?" Nolin spat.

"Who do you think fed you, changed your piles of diapers, taught you to speak?"

"I was a baby. I don't remember you ever taking care of me. You never did a damn thing besides hide in your room while I tried to get you to eat." She hoped her words stung like a slap. Melissa calmly sipped her tea. Her body seemed to dangle weightlessly from thin sinews in her neck. She had the look of a new baby bird, mouth too wide for her thin face and elbows jutting out like little wings. Pale fuzz covered her arms like the down of a newly hatched robin. The whites of her eyes looked yellow and poisoned behind the lenses of her glasses.

"I don't need you or your father. Leave me alone and crawl back into whatever hole you've been hiding in."

"Melissa, look at yourself. Look at this house! Everything's falling apart and you look like you've been...vacuum-sealed or something. I've seen corpses that look healthier than you."

Melissa lifted a sparse eyebrow. Nolin kept going before her mother accused her of being a mass murderer. She was sure Melissa thought she was capable.

"Look," Nolin went on carefully. "Let me help you get things sorted out, get you into a better situation or something, and I'll leave. You'll never have to hear from me again."

"I don't need your help."

"What did you have for breakfast, Melissa? When was the last time you ate anything?"

"None of your damn business, that's when."

"That's what I thought. I'm taking you to a doctor tomorrow, and then this house is going up for sale. You're in way over your head here."

"I'm in over my head? You have the nerve to tramp your muddy feet back into my life after years and tell me what to do? You have no idea what the last five years have been like. None. And don't you dare tell me I'm in over my head, young lady." She carefully set her mug on the counter with a clink before turning to Nolin, arms crossed, head cocked to the side. "Nolin, why are you really here?"

"I've told you." Nolin clenched her fists, breathing deeply. Melissa was prodding her, feeling for weak spots, looking for a chink in the armor where she could drive her blade through.

"You came to help me, to check on me. I haven't heard from you in five years and now that you think someone else isn't taking care of me, you show up. Out of the goodness of your heart."

One, two, three...

"I think I can guess. You feel responsible for me. Like I'm your problem," Melissa spat on the last word, a fleck of spit flying into Nolin's eye. Nolin blinked, stared down at her mother, and held her ground. Four, five, six...

"That's why you're here, Nolin. For yourself." Melissa leaned on the edge of the counter, picking up her mug, and stirred with a metal spoon that clinked inside like a tiny bell. "You feel guilty for abandoning me, so you came crawling back for redemption."

Nolin looked down at her feet. Melissa sipped from her mug, a soft smile on her face. Heat swelled in Nolin's body. Her hands shook, but she unclenched her fists and softened her jaw.

Melissa held her mug to her chest and studied Nolin. Suddenly, Nolin felt exhausted, drained as a dried-out leaf. "You can stay, but you pay rent, you buy your food, you help with bills. Clean if you feel inclined, but you are not helping me, and I did not ask for help. You are just a boarder. Do you understand?"

Nolin sighed deeply. She didn't have the energy to protest. "Fine," she snapped.

Melissa nodded slightly, placed her mug in the sink, and brushed past Nolin toward the stairs.

"Your old room is locked, by the way. You can sleep on the couch."

"Yes, *Mother*."

Melissa paused as if someone had shocked her. She didn't turn to look at Nolin. She brushed a strand of hair over her shoulder and disappeared into the hall. Nolin heard her bedroom door click shut.

Nolin stood in silence for a moment, sucked dry, worn out. The surrealism of the moment pressed on her. She felt like she'd been cut out of her new life and pasted into her old one like a clipping from a magazine. The two just didn't fit.

Why the hell was her bedroom door locked? *Probably sheer spite*, Nolin thought. So that just in case Nolin ever did come back, she'd have to sleep on the lumpy couch.

Maybe there was another reason. The thought briefly touched the edges of Nolin's awareness. She was so tired. One problem at a time.

I'll be on a plane in two weeks, Nolin thought. *I'll be out of here and never come back.*

She clung to that thought as she looked around the filthy room, a nauseating soup of anger, disgust, and guilt brewing in her stomach.

Finally, she sat down at the table, piled high with papers and unopened mail and started to sort, dreaming of glaciers and frozen wind and the smell of pine, cleansing her from the inside out.

Two weeks, and I'll get the hell out of here.

It would all be over soon.

Chapter 23

THE SHADOW FELT her coming.

Something electric crackled in the air like an approaching thunderstorm. How fitting that the rain started when Nolin pulled into town.

As the Shadow rested under the Claw Tree and dusk fell around her, she heard it. Felt it. Whispers almost too low and quiet to hear emanated from the tree, echoes of thoughts she hadn't heard in years.

Her bed of dried leaves rustled around her. She reached up and pressed her palm to the underside of the tree with her long fingers spread wide. The whispers grew clearer. Goose bumps spread over her skin. Bits of Nolin's thoughts drifted through the Shadow's mind, hazy, almost impossible to distinguish from her own. The Shadow knew the taste of that guilt, the fear that was unmistakably Nolin. Nolin's veins rippled with it, each heartbeat pushing and pulling the shame through her body. That same shame pulsed in the Shadow's body. She knew the shame she felt wasn't her own, for she had nothing to be ashamed of.

But Nolin. Oh, Nolin.

My fault, my fault, my fault... the guilt pounded like a drum.

The Shadow scrambled out from under the tree and set out for the house, running the route she knew so well, arms pumping joyfully. She laughed as she sprang over bushes and clumps of ferns, rocks, and fallen logs.

For years, the Shadow had watched and waited, patient as the dead, with little to occupy her in the meantime except watching Melissa slowly crumble on the inside. Sometimes, the Shadow watched Melissa pace from room to room in the empty house, open and close cupboards, slip books out of the shelves before immediately replacing them. Whatever she was searching for, the Shadow knew she'd never find it.

The Shadow reached the edge of the woods just as a pair of headlights rolled into the driveway. She clamped a hand over her mouth to keep from laughing out loud. Even the woods felt different. The trees seemed to lean forward with interest in the wiry figure with the mop of curly hair. They watched Nolin drive up, hesitantly walk up the driveway to Melissa's porch. The Shadow watched her ring the bell, saw the door open, saw Melissa strike Nolin. Noticed the steel in Nolin's eyes.

This was good. This would make things much easier.

A happy tear dripped down the Shadow's face, rolled off her sharp chin, and fell onto a leaf with a soft *pat*.

The Shadow's hope ignited. She waited just inside the forest, watched until the lights went out in the house, just to make sure it wasn't a dream.

***

I should have just slept on the floor, Nolin thought. She shifted on the couch, her hands folded over her stomach, staring at the high ceiling of the living room. Her back muscles felt like a mass of knotted yarn. Weak light faded and then brightened as the moon slid in and out of the clouds in the dusky night sky. Her ears pricked at every sound: the soft creaks of the house, the swish of the trees in the woods, the gentle groaning of the old couch cushions when she breathed in and out. She wasn't sure what she was listening for.

If sleeping at home in the mortuary was difficult, here it was impossible. Or was this home? She wasn't sure anymore. What was home, anyway? Where you live? Where your family is? Where you spent your childhood? Or, where you are most comfortable?

Home is elusive. Home shouldn't put you on high alert, listening to every sound for the slightest indication of a problem or danger. She knew every crack in the ceiling and every creaky spot in the floor, and this house seemed to know all of her sore spots, every crack and fissure where it could reach in and jab at the tender places.

Home is where you are welcome.

She shut her eyes and willed herself to sleep, tensing and releasing her muscles one by one, starting with her feet and ending with her facial muscles the way Rebecca had taught her.

Less than forty-eight hours ago, she'd sat on the mortuary roof to watch the sunrise. She hadn't thought about her father in months. Her mother was almost reduced to a figure that lived only in nightmares. Now, here she was at the last place on earth she wanted to be, the last place she thought she'd be in less than two days' time.

Sleep obviously wasn't going to happen. Nolin sat up, her stiff muscles screaming. She tilted her head from side to side to stretch her neck and felt a kink in the right side. Her hip hurt where she'd lay on her blocky cell phone. She slipped it out of her pocket and flipped it open. 2:12 a.m.

She sighed and massaged the right side of her neck. Finally, she stood and slipped on her jacket and shoes. Walking carefully to avoid the squeaky spots on the floor, she tiptoed to the back door and let herself out.

Her first gulp of chilly air scrubbed out any traces of tiredness. The yard was smaller than she remembered it. The fence was a little shabbier. Frost sparkled on long grass—tangled and dead in some places and just starting to green and soften in others after a long winter.

Immediately, her conditioned mind listed tasks for the next few days. Mow the lawn, maybe fix and repaint the fence, weed, then get started on the house. How long would this take? The house was a disaster. The yard was in disrepair. God knows what else was wrong with the place. She hadn't even been upstairs yet. Melissa obviously couldn't handle the place on her own.

At least she'd managed to hold down a job all these years. Nolin had found unopened pay stubs from a telemarketing company when she sorted mail the previous night. That was good. Melissa couldn't be completely helpless then, right? She was thin, but still up and moving around. She hadn't starved herself to death, so didn't that show she was taking better care of herself? She actually went outside now instead of shutting herself in her room all day. Wasn't she better?

Nolin could clean up the place and get out. Maybe get Melissa into a smaller apartment that she could handle on her own. Maybe she should help Melissa get back in touch with a doctor, or at least someone nearby to come in and check on her sometimes.

That could take a lot longer than she'd wanted to hang around here. After all, she only had two weeks until she stepped on a plane to leave for good.

In the morning, she'd hash all this out. One step at a time.

The icy grass crunched under her feet as she walked to the fence. She wiggled it to test its strength, determined it would hold her weight, and climbed up, swinging her legs over and perching carefully on the top board, facing the woods.

The tall meadow grass between her and the tree line swayed in the slight breeze that was no stronger than an exhale. The half-moon slipped out of the clouds and bathed the scene in pale silver light.

Nolin peered into the trees where the moonlight didn't reach. The darkness seemed thick, made of more than just empty space.

She barely remembered the three days she'd spent in the woods all those years ago. She remembered she wasn't afraid. If anything, she remembered feeling calm there in a way she never had at school or home. The woods only seemed menacing when she watched them from the outside.

Her fingers drummed on the peeling fence post. She gazed up at the moon before her eyes snapped back to the deep woods. Had something moved? She squinted into the darkness, scanning the tree line for a deer or fox, any sign of life.

The hair on her arms stood up. Her eyes trained on the darkness between the trees. Her mind wound back to countless evenings in her childhood, watching the forest from her bedroom window, and how, more than once, she'd thought there had been something hovering just inside the trees. She'd always thought it was her imagination, but this time she was sure she'd seen something.

She slid off the fence, then pulled her jacket tighter around herself as she strode across the open field between the yard and the edge of the woods. It occurred to her that she'd never actually been on this side of the fence. Tall weeds brushed against her legs, soaking the ends of her jeans with cold dew.

The forest looked a lot more intimidating from this close. The trees were taller, sharper, stretching into the sky like church steeples. The woods looked deeper. Trees farther back loomed into view—thin aspen with pale bark, tall evergreens bristling against the silence. Nolin's ears pricked for any sound. All she heard was the soft crunch of grass and weeds under her feet.

Ten feet from the edge of the trees, she paused. For the first time, she realized what a bad idea this was. What if she did see something? What if it was something dangerous like an aggressive animal, or a serial killer hiding out in the shelter of the woods?

She should be afraid. Though her mind thought it, she didn't feel it.

Now that she was close she saw nothing. Not even a leaf waving in the breeze.

The full moon illuminated the trees for about twenty yards into the woods. The thick canopy blocked out any light farther in. Nolin slipped her phone out of her pocket, snapped it open, then turned the glowing screen to the forest. She wished she'd sprung for the fancy smartphone with the flashlight app instead of relying on a dim little screen. The light of the screen did absolutely nothing, so she flipped the phone closed and stuffed it back into her jeans.

She could see back a little farther now. The darkness of the woods seemed like a dark mist rather than the simple absence of light. This darkness had form, maybe even a mind of its own.

Nolin shook the thought from her head. Darkness couldn't think. It didn't have mass. The canopy was just very good at blocking out the moonlight.

I really need sleep.

Satisfied that she'd simply imagined something moving, Nolin turned back toward the house.

A light breeze rose. The leaves of the trees hissed.

Then, a soft laugh from somewhere in the trees.

Nolin whirled around.

"Hello?" she called.

Again, a gentle sound like a child's giggle, so soft that it could have been leaves rubbing against bark, or wings soaring between the tree trunks. Did she just imagine it? Nolin didn't feel chilly anymore. Adrenaline rushed through her veins, and her heart thudded in her throat. She took another step forward, then another, until she could reach out and place a hand on one of the thin tree trunks.

Sweat beaded at her hairline. She leaned forward, supported by her hand on the tree. She didn't dare enter the woods, so she strained to peer farther into its depths.

"Hello!" she shouted. Her cry fell flat against her ears. The sound didn't penetrate the murky darkness. She might as well have hollered into a tiny closet. Nolin fought to keep her breath steady while she listened and watched.

In her ear, she heard a soft sigh, like an exhale. Nolin held her breath.

Again, the tiniest hush of a breath against her ear. She jerked her head to the side, but there was only open pasture and moonlight.

She was really losing it now. *I need sleep. I just want to sleep.*

Finally, Nolin stepped back from the edge of the trees and turned to walk back to the house. Her heart started to slow. The cold night air nipped at her nose and fingertips again.

This is all a dream. A vivid, lucid dream.

With one hand, she pinched her other arm. It stung. She blinked. Nothing changed. She was still walking through the field, her pant legs were still soaked, and she'd hardly slept at all though it was early in the morning. Definitely not a dream. A hallucination, maybe. Didn't that happen to people who were severely sleep-deprived?

She reached the fence and scrambled over it, back into the yard. Casting a nervous glance over her shoulder at the woods, she crossed the lawn to the back door. She could have sworn she felt eyes on her, the same feeling she got in a hospital full of security cameras. The same feeling that had followed her as a child.

She jogged the last few steps to the door. As she let herself in, the soft laugh echoed again, not from the trees this time, but inside her head. Violently, she shook her head, stepped into the house, and locked the door behind her.

Chapter 24

NOLIN'S MOUTH TASTED like sawdust when she woke on the lumpy couch later that morning. Her limbs were heavy as lead. For a moment, she didn't remember where she was.

Memories of the previous night rushed back to her. Driving into the town she'd thought she'd left forever, Melissa's rail-thin body in the doorframe, the stinging slap across her face. She remembered the woods, the smooth bark under her hands, the chill of the dew on her feet as she stared into the forest's depths, and the tinkling laugh inside her own mind.

It wasn't a dream, she was sure of that. It was far too vivid. A hallucination, on the other hand...

Nolin shoved herself into a sitting position on the couch. Bright sunlight streamed through the window, stinging her groggy eyes. She rested her elbows on her knees and placed her face in her hands, palms pressing gently into her eye sockets. When was the last time she'd gotten more than two hours of sleep in a row? She couldn't remember.

A thump above her startled her out of her grogginess. Melissa was awake. Nolin lifted her face from her hands to gaze up at the ceiling. The filth of the room dawned on her, and something inside her withered. This awful house, the stacks of junk, and the thick layer of dust that covered it all... she'd take care of it and finally leave this whole train wreck behind her forever.

Nolin pulled her phone out of her pocket and flipped it open to text Rebecca.

This is going to take longer than
I thought. I'm not sure when I'll
be back.

Should she tell her about the hallucination from the night before?

Nolin could guess what she'd say. *I know you don't want to hear this, but you need to see a doctor. Find out what's wrong. Get some sleep meds. Whatever you need to do to sleep, do it.* The thought of seeing a doctor made Nolin feel sick. If she never saw another doctor again as long as she lived, it would be too soon. And she would never, ever take medication again. She'd had enough drugs to last a lifetime. And then some.

Nolin pressed *send* and snapped the phone shut.

Melissa's footsteps pattered above her. Nolin sighed and heaved herself off the couch to make breakfast.

Nolin remembered when she needed to stand on a chair to cook. Now, she still had to stand on tiptoes to reach anything higher than the bottom shelf. The kitchen felt smaller than she'd remembered. She'd grown since she left five year earlier.

In the entire kitchen, she only managed to find a bag of white rice, pancake syrup, and some raisins hard as gravel, all of which had probably been there for years. After determining that all of these were still safe to eat, she concocted a sort of rice pudding with raisins. Though it wasn't something she'd ever crave, it was definitely edible.

Looks like I'm going shopping today.

Her mother was still shuffling around upstairs. Nolin assumed she'd be leaving to work soon. Hopefully, she'd remember that Nolin was there and wouldn't just regard the previous night as a bad dream.

Nolin washed the dust out of two cereal bowls and scooped the porridge into them. A few minutes later, Melissa appeared on the stairs, dressed in a white button-down shirt and a khaki skirt that were both too big. Her thin hair was clean and combed. She kept her eyes down, veiled behind her glasses and bangs, and retrieved a tan jacket off the back of a kitchen chair.

"I made breakfast," Nolin offered, sliding a bowl and spoon across the bar.

"I'm not hungry," Melissa said flatly.

Nolin reached over the bar, picked up the spoon, and stabbed it into the porridge so that it stood up like an exclamation point.

"Yes you are. Eat something. It's good for you."

"What the hell is that?"

"Pantry Surprise. I had to get creative. I'll go shopping today."

Melissa wrinkled her nose, but she approached the bar and spooned a minuscule bite into her mouth.

"Is this really all I have?" she asked quietly.

"That and some stale saltines."

Melissa took another small bite, her expression blank.

"Huh." She slung her purse over her shoulder and walked down the hall and out the door without another word.

What was that supposed to mean? Nolin hadn't expected gratitude, but it wasn't like Melissa to leave without making a biting comment. "What the hell..." Nolin mumbled, and she turned to the front window. She split the blinds with her fingers and peered out. Melissa walked down the front walk, then turned down the sidewalk toward the bus stop at the end of the street.

Nolin's phone buzzed in her pocket. She pulled it out and glanced at the screen.

Don't take too long. Stay in touch.

It definitely won't take longer than two weeks. Buoyed by the thought of icy Alaskan rivers, Nolin finished what she could of her porridge and got to work.

Empty tissue boxes, plastic cracker sleeves, gum wrappers, old newspapers and piles upon piles of junk mail littered the kitchen and living room. Empty toilet paper rolls and hand-soap bottles piled up in the corners of the bathroom, spilled out of the garbage cans.

There were no signs of feminine hygiene products in the bathrooms. No wrappers, no empty boxes. Melissa wasn't menstruating, Nolin realized. She was too malnourished.

I have to get some food in her.

She stuffed trash bags with armloads of garbage until the shiny black plastic bulged, then hauled the bags out to the dumpster in the driveway. When the dumpster was full, she wheeled it to the curb and stacked the remaining bags beside it, praying that trash day would come soon so she wouldn't have to make trip upon trip to the dump in her tiny car.

With another armload of bags, she marched upstairs, bracing herself for what she'd find. An odd, stale smell filled her nose in the familiar hallway. Her mother's room on the right, the studio straight ahead, the bathroom at the end of the hall on the right, and her old room. All the doors were closed. The night-light flickered, the same one she remembered from her childhood. She always hated that light, the way it cast sickly yellow light over the narrow hallway like a scene in a horror movie.

Her room was locked. She felt around the doorframe for a key. Nothing. She made a mental note to keep an eye out for the key or, failing that, a tool kit. Next, she tried the door across the hall, her mother's room.

The downstairs was practically spotless by comparison. Piles of laundry covered the floor and the unmade bed. Dust and debris stood out on the dark carpet where it showed through the clothes strewn about, and it felt gritty even under her shoes. Books, papers, and notebooks were scattered over the floor and half of the bed, the side her father used to sleep on. The nightstand was stacked high with books, prescription bottles, and half-full water glasses, a few of which were also spilled around the room. The same thick layer of dust that coated everything downstairs was present here as well, making the room look like a faded old photograph.

It's like Boo Radley's house.

The books were first. She picked them up carefully, one by one, and stacked them against the wall. Some of the pages were bent, maybe to hold a place. Bitterness rose inside her. She bit her lip and straightened some of the corners. She hated it when she lost her spot in a book she was reading.

189

Then she carried the water glasses down to the counter in two trips. She stacked papers and kicked the laundry into one massive pile in the corner of the room. She avoided the bathroom. Thankfully, the door was shut. A few times, she thought she heard the hiss of the shower or saw a wisp of steam streaming under the door.

It's your imagination, you baby. Calm down.

For the rest of the afternoon she hauled trash out to the curb, bags and bags of it. The trash collector had probably been doubting whether anyone lived in this house by how rarely Melissa seemed to take trash out.

How was this more exhausting than landscaping a massive cemetery all day? In the hall, Nolin slid to the floor with her back against the wall, eyes closed.

Was this really helping? Hauling all this trash out, cleaning up —what was the point? It would probably all accumulate again over the next five years anyway. She was just chasing her tail. Nolin bounced the back of her head against the wall.

Cleaning was just a placeholder until she figured out what else to do. Nolin would make sure Melissa was secure before disappearing for good. She'd never have to worry about her again. She'd never be free as long as Melissa pulled at the corner of her mind.

Though she knew it was pointless, Nolin reached up and tried the knob of her bedroom again. Still locked tight. Finally, Nolin pushed herself up from the floor and dragged herself down the stairs. There was no way she could try to sleep on that couch again, so she might as well look in the garage for some tools to get into the bedroom. Her creaky old bed would be worlds better than a lumpy sofa.

The garage smelled like a moldy shoe. Nolin flipped on the light, which buzzed like an insect. There was still an oil stain on the floor from her father's station wagon. The storage shelves on the walls showed their empty gaps like missing teeth; the toolboxes she remembered were gone, along with the boxes of old Mad magazines and yearbooks labeled "Paul."

Lacy cobwebs draped the shelves and the corners. The typewriter in Nolin's head rattled off more items for the To Do list.

Find out what that smell is.

Put out rat traps.

DUST, for hell's sake.

There had to be a tool set around here somewhere, or at least a decent screwdriver. Starting with the bottom shelves, Nolin opened box after box that produced nothing but stacks of old paperwork, clothes long overdue at Goodwill, dusty old books, and odds and ends that probably belonged on the curb with the other trash, but no tools. Not even a pair of pliers.

On the end of the second shelf sat a faded blue tote-box. She yanked it out and popped off the misshapen lid, hoping for the glint of a screwdriver.

The box was full of spiral-bound notebooks and loose papers, yellowed with age and covered with Melissa's scratchy handwriting.

Nolin froze, suddenly feeling like she'd walked in on something private, but intriguing. She glanced over her shoulder through the open door into the house, then knelt on the dirty cement floor with the box in her lap. Her ears pricked for the slightest sound of footsteps on the front walk or the turning of a doorknob. She reached into the box, aware that she was plunging into a well of secrets.

She slipped out one of the sketchbooks. The spiral binding rubbed on the binding of the book next to it and made a zipping sound. Her heart thudded faster. She peeled the cover open.

The inside of the bent cover read "Melissa Michaels, 1988" in black ink. The first page was covered in swirling doodles in pencil, patterns of looping spiral drawing dotted with tiny leaves.

She touched her index finger to the page. It came away dark and shiny from the loose graphite. Gingerly, she turned the pages; more of the same aimless doodles. The spirals twisted into different shapes, crisscrossing, growing rougher and rougher with each page. The smooth, curved lines turned harsh and scratchy. The tiny leaves started to look less like leaves and more like letters. Nolin held the book closer to her face and squinted at the tiny writing.

stop stop stop stop stop stop stop stop stop

The same word, over and over, the line of text running along the doodled lines like train tracks beside a road. Nolin flipped pages. The shapes repeated, though slightly changed each time. The lines grew to a rounder shape. Eventually, she realized she was looking at a human face, slightly feminine with high cheekbones and a thin, pointed nose. It was impossible to tell if it belonged to a woman or a young girl. Nolin turned back a few pages to watch the distortion of the drawings. The lines had transformed so gradually that she couldn't pick out the point where they'd ceased to be an abstract design and had become a face with hollow eyes and wild hair. The words that formed the lines had also changed, though she couldn't pinpoint where.

sorry sorry sorry sorry sorry sorry sorry

Nolin realized how tightly she gripped the book. Her heart was pounding. Was it fear? Excitement? This intimate look into her mother's mind both thrilled and terrified her.

As she neared the back of the sketchbook, the pages became wrinkled. The back part of the book must have gotten crumpled at some point. The lines became darker and more smudged. The strange face still appeared on every page, looking in different directions, mouth opening and closing as if it were speaking.

Nolin's ears pricked to the sound of light footsteps up the front walkway, floating taps that could have been the footsteps of a cat. Melissa. Was it late afternoon already?

Damn.

Nolin snapped the sketchbook shut and replaced it, quickly and quietly. Trying to look casual, she stepped back into the house, expecting to see Melissa. She bristled, ready for glares, stinging words.

There was no one.

"Mom?" Nolin called softly.

Nothing.

Nolin shut the door behind her and paused to listen. Something smelled strange, fresh like a breeze. Her skin prickled. Someone had been there.

You just imagined you heard something, she told herself. You're being stupid. You're tired.

Nolin shook her head, shaking off the thoughts. Still, she could smell green wood, and she thought she felt the softest breeze through the hair on the back of her neck.

Chapter 25

FROM HER CLOSED bedroom, Melissa smelled something delicious wafting up from downstairs. Her stomach turned, both attracted and repulsed by the thought of roasted chicken. She hadn't eaten since those bites of porridge made from scrounged pantry ingredients. Nolin must have shopped. Melissa imagined her kitchen stocked with cans of soup, jars of peanut butter and jewel-colored jams, her freezer stacked with frozen steaks and chicken breasts.

Usually, she ordered groceries online at work. Every two weeks, a box of dry ingredients showed up on her doorstep. For the past month, there had been no groceries. No job, no internet access to order groceries from, and no money to buy them with. She'd stretched the last box, eating the least she could get away with, and she'd stumbled into an old pattern. The constant, gnawing hunger was oddly comforting. It grounded her, distracted her, and slowed her down in every way, especially her thoughts. Now, she remembered why she'd left all the meals Nolin used to bring to her room untouched; it gave her a handle, an anchor, something to pull her out of her mind and hold her into her body, to remind her she was alive and breathing.

She felt ashamed that Nolin had bought food. When would she tell Nolin she'd lost her job, that she'd fallen behind in the mortgage payments? Her lips bunched together at the thought. No. Nolin wouldn't find out. She could stay, clean up, do whatever she needed to feel like she'd patched her wounds, and she'd leave. Melissa would solve her problems on her own. Besides, she told herself, she'd rather be homeless and starving than accept help from Nolin.

Still, that chicken smelled so good.

She closed the small book of poems she'd been reading and tiptoed to the door. Her mouth watered; her knees buckled in her pajama pants. The hollow of her stomach roiled with hunger. Part of her realized how far her ribs poked out as she rested her hands on her concave stomach.

Finally, she slipped out of the room and padded down the stairs. Nolin stood in the kitchen with her back to Melissa, carving the legs and wings off a rotisserie chicken and portioning them onto two plates, along with rice and some sort of vegetable.

Nolin looked over her shoulder at the stairway. How could she hear so well? Melissa hadn't made a sound.

"Hi," Nolin said.

Melissa cleared her throat, stuck her chin out slightly, and continued down the stairs, trying not to look around the living room. Nolin had cleared all the trash away, the piles and stacks Melissa hadn't found the motivation to get rid of in years.

"I see you've thoroughly taken over my home," Melissa snapped.

"I grew up here. It's my home too," Nolin retorted. "But you can have it. I'm done with it."

Melissa rolled her eyes. Nolin slid the two plates to the edge of the bar in front of two of the stools. She sat and began picking at her chicken.

"Eat," Nolin ordered.

"Screw you."

"You need food."

Melissa snorted. "I didn't ask you to cook." Still, Melissa approached the bar, eyeing the pile of chicken and steamed broccoli on the other plate.

Nolin took another bite of chicken, pressing her lips together in a thin line, just like Melissa did when she was biting her tongue, or annoyed. The light outside faded. The setting sun illuminated the room in a brief bath of orange and yellow. Nolin glanced at Melissa. Her eyes travelled to her rolled-up sleeves and narrowed slightly. Melissa followed her gaze to the downy hair covering her arms and blue veins shining through her papery skin. Melissa cleared her throat and yanked her sleeves down.

"What are you looking at?" she demanded. Nolin shrugged and turned back to her food, but her eyes weren't focused.

"Eat," she said again.

Melissa scooted her plate an inch away.

"Mom..." Nolin said slowly, without correcting herself. "You need to eat. You're sick. If you don't start eating more, you're going to get worse."

Melissa stared at the chicken getting cold on her plate. Her pale, dry lips pressed together. Nolin reached across the bar and scooted Melissa's plate back to her.

Melissa's arm shot out. The plate flew across the bar like a hockey puck and careened off the counter into the wall, breaking into three big pieces. Shreds of chicken and bits of vegetables scattered around it.

"Don't tell me what to do," Melissa hissed. She glared at Nolin. Nolin glared right back, green eyes like steel. "You cannot come to my house and tell me what to do, do you understand me? This is my house. You do not give orders. I didn't ask you to stay, and I certainly didn't ask you to force-feed me. You are more than welcome to leave. In fact, I suggest you do."

Nolin folded her arms over her chest, an action she'd probably learned from Melissa. A smile curled Melissa's lips.

"Of course. You won't leave until you feel you finally have the moral high ground and can walk out of here with your conscience intact. This has nothing to do with me. You just want to be rid of me."

Nolin tightened her jaw.

Melissa went on. "Do whatever you feel you need to do. You abandoned me the moment you had the chance, and you'll do it again as soon as you feel justified."

She slipped off her barstool and marched up the stairs, but before she disappeared into her room, she threw a glance over her shoulder as Nolin bent down to pick up the pieces of the broken plate.

Chapter 26

NOLIN BIT HER lip. She wanted to scream at Melissa to pick up the broken plate, to wipe up the food mess, but Melissa's feet were bare and so pale. Stepping on even the tiniest bit of the broken ceramic would slice her skin like paper. She watched her mother march up the stairs. Biting words perched on the edge of Nolin's lips like a person about to jump from a ledge.

Melissa's words stung. Nolin longed to fire back, to march upstairs, kick open the door, and throw those words back at her. Unfortunately, she couldn't deny her mother's accusations. Not one word. Her guilt burned like a brand.

After she dumped the mess into the trash, Nolin picked at the rest of her dinner. She didn't feel like eating anymore.

Her arms and legs felt heavy, weighed down by an exhaustion that seeped into her bones, into the deepest parts of her mind. Part of her wanted to collapse on the couch and sleep for days, and another part wanted to go outside in the cool evening air and run until her legs gave out.

The exhaustion won. Nolin collapsed on the couch with one arm hanging off the edge, knuckles scraping the scratchy carpet. Her hair spilled over her face, catching in her eyelashes. She opened and closed her eyes, willing herself to sleep.

Please, I just want to sleep. I'm so tired. Just let me sleep.

Floating between waking and sleep, she drifted in and out of strange dreams of climbing up an endless tree that reached into the sky. The bark and branches scratched. Her arms and legs screamed with exertion, pushing and pulling her heavy, tired body up the trunk.

But she kept climbing because of what was below her. She wasn't sure what it was, just that it was dangerous. She had to get away from it. No matter how her body ached, how exhausted she was, she couldn't stop or slow down. The thing below could not get her.

She never found out what, exactly, it was.

***

Nolin sat up and craned her neck to peek out the window. Moisture gathered at the corners of the glass. Brisk spring air nipped at her nose and the tips of her ears, even inside the house.

How could she be so exhausted and restless at once? If anything, a night of fitful sleep had only worsened both.

Finally, she stood, slipped off the jeans and tee shirt she'd fallen asleep in, unhooked her bra and let it drop over her shoulders. Goose bumps erupted over her arms and legs, up and down her stomach. She quickly fished a sports bra, tee shirt, and running shorts from her backpack and wriggled into them before stuffing her hair into an elastic. The little loft in the mortuary was usually much colder in the mornings than this, but something about this heavy chill sank into her skin. She stepped into her sneakers and tiptoed softly to the front door to let herself out.

Biting morning air ran its icy fingers down her arms and legs; a different cold from the empty chill in the house, a more aggressive cold. She glanced down the road both ways before darting across the street and falling into a slow jog down the sidewalk.

Not a soul out except for an old woman in a kerchief walking an equally ancient-looking mini schnauzer. Neither acknowledged Nolin, who cut a wide berth around them. Her eyes darted from side to side, taking in the familiar houses. Nothing had changed. The same houses, the same porch swings and homemade bird-houses hanging from the same trees. The same types of flowers bloomed in the gardens. Nolin might as well have stepped back in time to her childhood, the morning of the day she ran into the woods.

She pumped her legs a little faster, settling into the familiar rhythm of feet landing lightly, the toe a fraction of a second before the heel, arms pumping and cold air rushing in and out of her lungs like waves on a glacier. Street running was never her first choice. She felt too exposed on the sidewalks, too easily watched. At the mortuary she'd run the familiar trails in the woods under the cover of trees, sometimes running off the trails to leap over logs and pick her way through the dense ground cover.

She didn't dare run in these woods. The woods here were darker. If she felt watched and exposed on the roads, it was nothing compared to the invisible eyes of the woods.

She shivered and lengthened her stride.

Soon, she reached the end of the small town. The steady stream of yards and houses slowed to a trickle. The only things down that long road through the hills and trees were more hills and trees. That road that way was narrow and winding, edged with carrion and white crosses and flowers where people had died in accidents. She stopped and leaned on her knees to catch her breath. In the grip of her ribcage, her heart thudded. Veins popped along her forearms and hands, pulsing with the flow of blood, *whoosh, whoosh, whoosh* in her ears. Frozen sweat glued her tee shirt between her shoulder blades. The tips of her ears stung in the chilly air.

Above her, wispy clouds glowed pink, then salmon, then orange. A bright sliver of sun peeked over the tip of the hill, its rays slicing the clouds like shining daggers. The white sun crawled over the edge of the horizon until its round base finally kicked off the tops of the trees and launched itself into the sky. The trees and lawns around her sparkled as the morning dew burned off in the warming sunlight.

Nolin decided to weave through the side roads, get a few more miles in before she ran out of excuses and had to return to the house. With a last glance at the colorful sunrise, she turned and bounced back into a comfortable, mindless pace.

People were starting to trickle out of their houses to retrieve newspapers, have a morning smoke, or let dogs out to squat on the lawns. Some of them looked at Nolin as she passed, their eyes meeting hers for a brief moment before flicking away. It reminded her of the teen group home she'd lived in where they weren't allowed to make eye contact, but stayed isolated in their own little worlds while dozens of other bodies practically pressed into them in the overcrowded dorms and computer labs. If two sets of eyes ever connected, they'd dart away just as quickly.

She recognized a few of the people, though she didn't know them by name. Several were a little more wrinkled than she remembered, hair dusted with a few more grays. One woman huddled on her front porch in a fuzzy pink bathrobe, hair dirty, gray bags under her eyes. She clutched a steaming blue mug, watching her white terrier sniff around the lawn. The dog looked up at Nolin and wagged its stumpy tail a few times before returning to its business. The woman's eyes lingered on Nolin's for a fraction of a second longer than the others. Nolin recognized her as Mrs. Carson, her sixth grade teacher. Recognition flashed behind the woman's eyes, and she immediately switched her gaze to the terrier before taking a deliberate sip from her mug.

Nolin turned another corner instead of going straight back to the house. Her body still crackled with ragged energy that she knew she'd need to smooth out before she got back, or she'd be climbing the walls all day. She needed that delicious blankness, the smoothness of the mind that only came after a long run, a good day of shoveling snow, or digging up the mortuary flower bed.

About a hundred yards ahead of her, a tall, slim figure in a white tee shirt, shorts, and blue knit hat loped across an intersection. That easy, yet energetic, gait felt familiar. Then, Nolin remembered it from elementary PE ten years earlier. The figure casually scanned the road from side to side as he crossed and did a double take in Nolin's direction.

"Nolin!" he called.

Nolin's cheeks tinged red. She slowed to a bumpy jog, then stopped. Her legs twitched, unsure whether to run toward him or in the opposite direction.

Drew waved and jogged toward her. "Hi!"

"Hi," she called back weakly. She took a few awkward steps toward him.

"It's a nice morning, isn't it?" he said.

"Yeah, it is."

He stopped a few paces in front of her. She froze like a statue.

"You're a runner?" he asked.

Nolin shrugged. "I usually run on trails. I don't usually run on the road."

He smiled, not breaking eye contact, unruffled by her awkwardness. "Well, I've got a few miles left. Join me?"

Nolin nodded nervously. She didn't feel like going back to the house yet. He motioned for her to run beside him on the sidewalk while he ran on the shoulder of the road. He was fast for his gentle stride. His long legs covered so much distance, Nolin had to run faster to keep up.

"I'm training for a half marathon in August. I've never run one before, have you?" He wasn't at all winded. His words ran smoothly between his quiet breaths.

Nolin shook her head, then answered "no" when she realized he was looking straight ahead at the road.

"I've done shorter races," he continued. "They're a lot of fun. There's a full marathon next year through the canyon by Maxfield. I'm going to go for that too."

Nolin smiled. She'd never met anyone so enthusiastic. It was refreshing. Her mind raced for something interesting to say. She was so accustomed to her comfortable silences with Rebecca, who said nothing unless she had something important to talk about. Nolin was used to spending her days alone in a silent graveyard with birds and graves for neighbors. Silence usually comforted her. Now the pauses in the conversation glared like blank pages. Nolin always got the feeling that normal people didn't like silence and had to fill it with words or music.

"I've never thought about running races," Nolin finally said. "I just run for me, to clear my head. I've never run with other people before."

Drew nodded and grinned, carving deep dimples in his cheeks. "It's a different experience, for sure. I love it. By the end of the race, you feel like everyone's your friend. And running with someone is a great way to get to know them. If I learned anything from running cross-country in high school, it's that. When you run with other people, you learn who they are. And you can't help but like them."

Nolin felt herself smile. Her cheeks ached. They weren't used to working that way.

"Does it look different? The town?" he asked, looking over at her. Nolin glanced around at the houses, the trees, the cracks in the pavement.

"Not at all."

"I bet it's weird being back."

She nodded. "It's unsettling. It's like it was waiting for me. Everything is just how I left it."

He chuckled. "There's nothing unsettling about this place. It's the same people, same places, same everything. Nothing ever changes. That's one reason I like coming home for the summers. It seems that everything in life changes so quickly. Here, it's always the same."

"Everything changes," Nolin repeated, trying to remember how untethered and carefree she was only two days earlier.

She listened to the rhythm of Drew's gentle breaths, in time with the beats of her shoes on the sidewalk. Again, her mind whirled for something to say. "I'm sorry, I'm not very good at this. Conversation." Her cheeks grew hot.

"Why do you have to be good at it?"

"Well," she went on, "isn't that the main component of socializing? Conversation? The verbal exchange of ideas and feelings?"

Drew chuckled. "Do you always talk like a textbook?"

Nolin felt her cheeks grow warm. "I told you I'm not good at this."

Drew chuckled again and reached out to lightly tap her elbow. "I was teasing. You just have a very formal way of speaking, that's all." His eyes flicked sideways at her, crinkled at the corners.

"Oh," Nolin said. "I don't pick up on teasing, I guess."

"It's okay, you'll learn."

Nolin studied his face. He looked straight ahead, that odd, resting smile still etched into his cheeks. She'd never seen someone look so content. Maybe he, like her, didn't care to waste words either. He simply had more of them to share. His words weren't pushing out the silences, but just coaxing, gently easing her into a place where she'd have something to say.

"I don't talk to people much," she told him. "I live alone. I work alone. There's just no need."

"No pressure, Nolin. We're just two people hanging out, on a run, just talking. It's not hard. Just say what's on your mind. You seem like you have a lot on your mind."

"So I should just tell you absolutely everything I'm thinking?"

"No, just anything you want to say. And ideas or feelings you would like to exchange."

Nolin felt a smile tug at her mouth. "You're teasing me again."

Drew chuckled. "See? You're learning," he said, punching her lightly in the shoulder. His touch felt strange. If conversation was foreign to her, touch felt downright unnatural, but not unpleasant.

Drew went on. "If there's anything you'd like to say, say it. If not, we can watch this pretty blue sky together. It's up to you."

Nolin thought for a moment, rifling through her thoughts, testing their weight in her hands as if they were stones she were about to hurl into a serene pond. How far would the ripples spread?

She took a deep breath. "I probably talk like a textbook because I read a lot of textbooks."

"There we go; this is a step. Textbooks about what?"

"Everything. A lot of biology. Psychology. Mostly my friend's old college textbooks. They're fascinating."

Drew nodded, approving. "Excellent. What do you find fascinating about them?"

Nolin's heart pounded, but not from the running. "I suppose I like the relationship between emotions and chemicals. Abnormalities. How much our personalities depend on a delicate balance of chemical reactions and electrical impulses in the brain. It's really beautiful, actually."

"And complicated."

Exhilarated, she started to speak faster. "Very complicated. So many tiny events add up to a human being, a unique individual with hopes and fears and dreams and talents. Nature is incredible."

"You're right, it's fascinating. Humans are so complicated. Any little tick in their machinery can completely alter the way they work, for better or for worse. See? This isn't so hard." He paused. "Are you thinking about anything else?"

Nolin chewed her bottom lip, waiting for the words to come. Finally, she spoke. "I have no idea what I'm doing."

Drew looked over at her, his brow furrowed. "Er... what you're doing right now?"

Nolin shook her head. "What I'm doing *here*. Back in this place. And in general. Two days ago, everything was fine, and now I'm back here and my mother is falling apart. I don't know what to do."

Drew pressed his lips together and crinkled the corners of his eyes. He stared straight ahead. "Well, I guess you should just do what you *can* do."

"What I can do," Nolin echoed. "I feel like I can't do anything."

Drew shrugged. They turned a corner. Nolin's shoulders grew tense; they were nearing her house.

"Well," Drew started, choosing his words carefully, "if you can do something, do it. Even if it's not very much. That's what I tell myself when I'm working with kids. I can't make them understand. I can't make them want something. Beyond that, I do what I can."

"That's a good thought."

"Don't give me too much credit," he smirked. "It's something my mom always said. 'No one can do everything, but everyone can do something.'"

"Your mom sounds like a smart woman."

"Ah, don't give her too much credit either. She usually said that when us kids were being lazy and not doing our chores. She does believe it, though. It's just something I keep in the back of my mind."

He glanced at his watch and slowed his pace. "That should be seven miles for me. How long have you been out?"

"I'm not sure." Nolin's heart sank when they turned down her road. The house squatted like a toad at the end of the street, duller than the others without the usual spray of daffodils or grass just starting to green. Her legs twitched from exhaustion, or from resistance. Drew slowed in front of the house and turned to Nolin. His cheeks were red and blotchy from the cold air. Nolin tightly folded her arms over her chest, willing herself to go back inside though her legs refused to move.

"I'll run by here around seven tomorrow morning if you want to do this again," Drew said. "I'll see if there are any trails around if you'd rather not run on the road. I could afford to branch out a bit."

Nolin nodded. "Okay. I'll be out here."

"Sounds good," he reached up to adjust his knit hat and stuff a few stray chunks of hair underneath. Then he paused. "Just do what you can do. That's all."

With one last smile, he turned to jog back down the street. Nolin watched him disappear. Something inside her glowed warm, a tiny point deep in her stomach, like a sip of hot tea. For the first time since she'd brought her father's corpse back to the mortuary, since her mother had dug her way back into her mind like a relapse, she felt hope that, one way or the other, everything would be all right.

Chapter 27

THE DOOR CLICKED quietly when Nolin stepped inside the house, blinking while her eyes adjusted to the dim light. The house was quiet. Somehow, she knew her mother was still asleep. Maybe she should go upstairs and check anyway.

She tiptoed into the living room, slipped off her running shoes, and padded up the stairs in her socks. Her soft steps sounded unnaturally loud in the silence.

Maybe today she'd find some tools and get her bedroom door open. The dust in there must be piled up six inches thick.

Melissa's door was shut. A slice of light shined out of Nolin's old room.

The door was cracked open.

She was sure that door had been locked the night before. Had Melissa opened it? Nolin had barely slept. She would have heard Melissa get up during the night, unless Melissa opened the door while Nolin was out on her run.

The still air in the house felt strange, settled, yet alive at the same time, the way a house felt early in the morning as its occupants were just beginning to stir. Nolin climbed the rest of the stairs and pushed the door open, bracing herself for the creak of a stiff door that hadn't been opened in years. To her surprise, it opened easily, like it had been used often.

She peered into the room. Breath caught in her chest. It looked more or less the same as the day she'd left it. A black-and-white picture of her past, the colors muted with a fuzzy film of dust. The bed was unmade, blankets crumpled at the foot of the mattress just how she left them. The plants on her dresser were dried-out stalks. Dead leaves littered the floor.

Despite the dust, the room smelled oddly fresh, though there was a definite musty undertone. A slight edge of something familiar tugged at her memory; perhaps her childhood smell still lingering on the bedclothes. Nolin sneezed as dust filled her nose. Tiny clouds puffed from her footfalls on the stiff carpet. This room was even quieter than the rest of the house somehow. Nolin felt as if she'd dropped into the past, the ghost of her present, a world devoid of sound and color. She could pass through the walls and the furniture like a specter if she'd wanted.

Nolin lowered herself carefully onto the edge of the bed, splitting the silence with a brief creak. She twisted to look out the window at her old view of the woods, unchanged. The jagged outline of the treetops against the sky was so familiar she could have drawn it in her sleep. The top of the tree line jerked up and down like a heartbeat monitor, the pulse of her memory.

Something felt hard underneath her. She reached into the stiff, dusty covers, and pulled out a small book.

It was faded, like an ancient manuscript in a tomb. Feathery dust bunnies peeled off the cover and the golden title showed through.

A Midsummer Night's Dream. Ten years overdue.

She calculated the overdue fee in her head; over two hundred dollars. She was so tired, and the idea of a two-hundred-dollar library fee was so absurd, she chuckled. Icing on the cake, two hundred dollars of her mother's debt was one hundred percent her fault.

She found the dog-eared page, permanently creased and brittle, then read a few lines out loud to settle back into the rhythm. She'd always loved the way Shakespeare felt in her mouth, like small, sweet fruits that rolled around on her tongue. She flipped through the parts she'd already read and restarted the scene she hadn't finished. The fairies in the forest, the fairy king Oberon asking his wife, the queen Titania, for possession of the changeling boy.

Changeling.

The word hit her like a bucket of cold water, stirring a memory of reading this scene the first time, how that word had fascinated her. Her eyes returned to the same footnote. "*A child exchanged for another by fairies or goblins.*" She remembered the illustration that used to be taped above her bed until she tore it down, the gnarled tree surrounded by thin, wild-looking children with pointed ears and devilish grins. A cold prickle of anxiety formed in her stomach.

Why did that idea interest her so much? She'd always loved fantasy, but she'd never believed in monsters in the closet, or Santa Claus, or the Tooth Fairy. She'd never gotten presents from Santa Claus, and she unceremoniously dropped her baby teeth in the trash after pulling them out. So why was this word *changeling* so special?

She'd never heard of changelings anywhere else. They weren't like vampires or witches or other common creatures in movies

211

and books. Maybe that's why the word fascinated her; it was something new and strange. The idea of creatures stealing a human and leaving behind their own spawn was frightening...yet fascinating. A goblin child growing up among humans...what would that be like?

The anxiety in her gut flexed. She understood perfectly. Being treated like a freak, always an outsider, not belonging anywhere. She related more than she wished to admit. This disturbed her even more.

The bright morning sun punched through the window. She'd forgotten how hot her room got sometimes. Nolin twisted around to open the window and noticed clean tracks through the dust on the windowsill. It looked like something large had slid over it, wiping the dust away.

"What the hell?"

The clean mark was about a foot and a half wide, dust piled to the sides like snow flanking a freshly plowed road. Her eyes traveled up to the silver window latch, down instead of up. Unlocked. Gently, she pushed on the window, which swung open easily on well-used hinges.

A fresh spring breeze blew in from the open window, carrying the smell of the woods and playing with her hair. She poked her head out and looked down. Only smooth wall below her. Nothing to climb, no scuffs or marks on the wall or indentations in the grass where someone could have put a ladder.

Nolin pulled the window shut and locked it, pausing to think. The hair on the back of her neck stood up, and that familiar feeling of being watched, the feeling she'd experienced so often, settled upon her. She remembered thinking that the woods had eyes and gazed into her window while she slept, whispered to her at night to invite her into its depths. Suddenly, she didn't want to be in her room anymore.

Stepping into her previous footsteps from the bedroom door, she tiptoed back into the hall, shutting the door behind her.

Dread and fear roiled within her. Something familiar lurked under that anxiety, flitting out of sight before she could identify it. Descending the stairs, she saw the house anew, not as an unwelcome reminder of a past she wished to forget, but as a future she might never have. Her childhood home transformed into something foreign and unfriendly, though she knew every inch. Now, she saw it through the eyes of an intruder.

***

Soggy grass squished under her feet. Worms wriggled on the sidewalk, washed out from the rain. The willow tree looked just like she remembered it, vines hanging motionless in the still air. The library hadn't changed at all. The bushes were a little bigger, the metal letters above the door were a little orange with rust, but it was as good as a warm blanket.

Nolin stepped inside, filling her lungs with the delicious scent of paper and leather. The rush of the climate control blew her hair off her shoulders. The shelves stood in the same places, the same round tables and saggy couches and the same ugly, multicolored carpet. It was like stepping into a dream.

The woman behind the desk with glasses, thick makeup, and tight, brown ponytail looked up from typing. Her dark-blue eyes widened, and her mouth dropped open, her berry-colored lips forming a perfect O.

"Oh my... Nolin! Is that you?"

Nolin grinned. Ms. Savage stood up, ran around the desk, and threw her arms around her, surrounding them in a cloud of lavender perfume.

"Oh my goodness, hon, you're gorgeous! Look at you, all grown up!"

Ms. Savage hadn't changed any more than her library—same ponytail and glasses, similar sweater and slacks. A few wispy lines fanned from her eyes, but it was still Nolin's old friend.

"I can't believe you still work here," Nolin laughed. "I wasn't expecting to see you."

"Well, you too! Where the heck have you been? How many years has it been? I worried they'd locked you up for good!"

Great, has everybody heard what happened? Nolin brushed it off. Her mother and her condition had never exactly been a secret. More of an urban legend, really. Of course a daughter moving in the same direction would excite the gossipers.

"I've been working in Maxfield."

"Well, good for you. What brings you back here?"

"Just visiting my mom."

"Well, a decade is a long time to be gone." Ms. Savage stood back and smiled without showing her teeth. "Welcome back. Your account's expired, of course. We can sign you back up in just a minute..."

"Actually," Nolin started, holding up *A Midsummer Night's Dream*, "I just found this. I checked it out a while ago—okay, ten years ago, sorry about that—and I thought I should return it."

Ms. Savage cocked her head to the side.

"I wondered where that went."

Nolin's face grew hot. "Yeah, I'm really sorry. I found it in my old room; I don't think anyone's been in there since I left. I can pay you back for it."

"Oh, don't worry about it at all," Ms. Savage said, waving her hand dismissively. "Just keep it."

"Oh," Nolin said. She looked down at the book that was now hers, getting reacquainted with it, then hugged it to her chest. "Thank you."

"Not a problem. Listen, I'm going out for an early lunch. Would you like to join me?"

"I... um, yeah. Is there anyone else here to watch the library?" Nolin asked, looking over her shoulder.

"There's an assistant around here somewhere. She can handle it." Ms. Savage bent down to type something into the computer and then stood up to sling her purse over her shoulder.

"I usually just get a salad at the deli up the street."

Nolin shrugged and followed her out of the library.

Ms. Savage walked quickly, neatly clipping along the sidewalk with short little steps while Nolin bumbled along in her flip-flops.

"So...why are you still here?" Nolin blurted. She felt her cheeks grow warm. She hadn't meant to sound so rude.

Ms. Savage smiled and examined her unpainted fingernails, flicking a speck of dirt off her cuticle. "I haven't had a reason to leave," she said. "I'm a creature of habit, and I like comfort. The library is comfortable. I have my books, peace and quiet. I like this town. If the day ever comes that I want something different, I'll do something different. Until then, I'll love my cozy little library."

Nolin chewed her bottom lip and kicked a pebble that skittered across the sidewalk before ricocheting into the grass. Nolin couldn't imagine staying in one place forever, especially Calder. Maybe Ms. Savage's experience was different. Perhaps the old houses and the single stoplight in town charmed her. Nolin found it strange that a woman who loved Chaucer and wore tweed would be happy in a tiny town with a one-room library and no art galleries, theaters, or museums within fifty miles in any direction. She seemed cut and pasted from one world into this one, snipped out of a college professor's life or from a Parisian sidewalk cafe with a thick book and expensive cappuccino. Maybe that's why Nolin was always drawn to her; Ms. Savage didn't belong here anymore than Nolin did, though they seemed cut out for very different lives.

"I know you don't care for it here," Ms. Savage said.

"To put it mildly."

Ms. Savage chuckled. "This town has just the right amount of loneliness for me. It keeps my mind working because it has to. If there's too much going on around me, my mind stops and has to keep up with the flow, go in a certain direction whether it wants to or not."

"So you find the monotony...stimulating?"

"It's like an open meadow for my mind to romp around. Compare that to, say, a crowded freeway, full of noise and action and speed, direction. Though it seems exciting, it's very restricting. Go one way at a certain speed or crash, get a citation, impede other drivers. I prefer my open field where I can run around in circles."

Nolin shook her head incredulously. "I think it's suffocating. You can't buy a pack of gum around here without the whole town knowing about it. Then they'll judge you for buying cinnamon instead of spearmint."

216

Ms. Savage chuckled. "Screw 'em. Screw 'em all," she said.

Nolin fiddled with her book, running her thumb along the aged spine. A thought hit her: Maybe Ms. Savage knew more about changelings. She could probably even recommend some more books about them.

"I have a question about this play," Nolin said, drumming her fingers on the cover. "I left off at the first scene with the fairies. I even remember the exact line, when they ask about the changeling child." Nolin's eyes darted to Ms. Savage's face, which was calm and staring straight ahead. "I remember wondering what a changeling was because I've never heard of them before, and the footnotes said that it's a goblin or fairy child exchanged for a human one. I feel like there's more to it than that. I know people back then believed in fairies, but why did they think they stole children?" Somehow, she felt Ms. Savage would understand. If anyone would understand an odd obsession with something from a book, it was her.

"Well," Ms. Savage said, "it's just a legend people thought up to explain sickly children and oddballs. Western European mythology, that's all."

"Oddballs?"

"Well, the *changelings,*" Ms. Savage indicated quotations with her fingers, "were usually children who just didn't fit in. Sometimes they had a physical or mental condition, and sometimes I think they were just...different. Society's full of them. This was the way to rationalize them. Or mistreat them. They didn't feel so bad neglecting or abusing a child they didn't even consider human."

The wad of anxiety in Nolin's stomach writhed. If she had been born then, would she have been one of those odd children, shunned or feared because she was different? Believed to be the spawn of a goblin, traded for an innocent human baby?

Her mind flipped through her memories of elementary school: the teasing, the fighting, lunches alone at the end of the long cafeteria table. She might as well have been a changeling for the way she was treated. "That's awful," she said.

"Listen, Nolin," Ms. Savage continued. "I think I get it, why you'd find that concept so interesting. I know you've always felt out of place and like you don't belong." Ms. Savage looked over at Nolin, her dark-blue eyes focused and piercing. For the first time with Ms. Savage, Nolin suddenly felt very uncomfortable. She stuffed her hands in her pockets and watched the sidewalk in front of her.

"I can relate to feeling like some inhuman...thing," Nolin said, "stuck in a place I don't belong. Maybe I wish I could just *be* something like that. At least then I could have an excuse to feel so weird with people. I would make much more sense."

"Well, that's exactly how those people felt," Ms. Savage said. "Weird isn't a bad thing, Nolin. Like I always say, there are only two kinds of people in the world: the weird and the boring. Take your pick."

Nolin smiled grimly, though she didn't feel any better. Her fingers twisted inside her pockets.

A crack was forming in her mind, breaking open along the seam of something sealed up long ago. She felt she was on the verge of unraveling some mystery. The crack deepened like a fissure in the earth, and she feared what was hidden underneath.

Chapter 28

*M*ELISSA WALKED THROUGH *the forest, barefoot. She knew where she was going. She always did.*

The massive tree rose in the darkness. She approached its powerful trunk as she had many times before. This time, there was someone else beneath the tree.

A thin, wild figure with long, dark hair and even darker eyes sat cross-legged under the trunk, waiting, peering up at her with a grim smile. Dark circles carved out hollows under the creature's eyes. The lips were pale blue. Large, black eyes glittered dangerously. The ragged girl was pale as a corpse.

Melissa froze, an odd mixture of terror and longing fixing her to the spot. The figure's blue lips moved slowly, carefully forming words with no sound.

"I... I can't hear you," Melissa said, her voice and body trembling.

Grinning with a smile that didn't reach the eyes, the creature pushed herself to her feet and approached Melissa. They were exactly the same height. The creature's lips moved again. Her voice was rough and low, like stones rubbing together, her breath like cold wind.

Come and find me, *she said.*

Melissa's eyes snapped open. She lay paralyzed in her bed, arms and legs splayed. Inside her bony chest, her tired lungs struggled to draw breath.

The fear and cold she'd felt in the dream still engulfed her. These were not ordinary dreams. She learned that long ago. She wanted them to stop.

For years, Melissa had tried to convince herself that the strange things she saw were in her imagination. The dreams, the voices, the dark-eyed face that watched from the shadows, the face that both thrilled and terrified her, that she longed for and dreaded all at once.

She forced herself to breathe slowly and deeply. Her eyes darted around the room, scouring the shadowy corners for the white flash of a face.

She was alone.

***

Nolin thumbed through Melissa's books, half-watching the stairway. She heard the groan of the bed only once, followed by soft creaking and footsteps to the bathroom. Melissa was definitely awake. Did she ever plan on leaving her room? Nolin's restless fingers twitched. There was much she wanted to know. Should she go looking while Melissa was home?

The box of notebooks in the garage. The studio, full of Melissa's sketches and illustrations of strange creatures, and the drawing of the tree that she'd stumbled across when she was ten.

She'd completely forgotten about that drawing until her walk home from the library. The memory came to her in a flash, and she felt the textured drawing paper under her fingers again, saw the scratchy ink lines, felt the weight of the sketchbook in her hands and the sudden pounding of her heart as she'd realized what she was looking at: a drawing of a tree that only existed in her dreams.

Nolin found the old copy of *The Bell Jar*. Nearly every page had been dog-eared at some point, and now those corners held on for dear life, some dangling by the last fibers of the worn seams. How often had she read that book in her childhood? How many times had Melissa read it before her?

Nolin remembered turning those pages, thinking of her mother under the bell jar of madness, strapped to a cold metal table with wires attached to her head, electricity jolting through her body.

"Are they going to shock her?"

"No, they don't do that anymore."

Nolin's heart skipped a beat. She recalled that horrible day in the hospital and her father telling her Melissa was even sicker than they thought.

Are they going to shock her?

Nolin shuddered, snapped the book closed, and shoved it back into the bookshelf.

She slinked up the stairs and tiptoed down the hall, skipping the squeaky spots and listening for movement in Melissa's bedroom. Praying the studio door wouldn't creak, she pushed it open.

The studio was silent, as if the room were holding its breath. It was a much dustier version of the studio she remembered, everything still in its place right down to the configuration of watercolor brushes sprouting upright from the jar on the desk. The drawing taped to the desk was the same one that had been there when she'd run away. The mermaids. Nolin's heart dropped. Melissa probably hadn't been in this room at all.

Nolin glanced over her shoulder one last time to make sure her mother hadn't crept up behind her, like she tended to do.

She squatted down in front of the lowest shelves to run her finger across the aged spines of the sketchbooks. In which book had she found the drawing of the tree? She couldn't remember. So many of the books looked the same.

Nolin chose a book near the middle. It didn't slide out easily. Once it did, the other books exhaled with relief as they expanded to fill the space. The spine creaked when Nolin pried its covers apart. The book had been closed for so long that she had to peel each page from the one behind it in order to turn them.

This wasn't the right book. It was just pages and pages of doodles, spirals, and swirls that turned into tree branches, rough sketches of human figures growing more and more stylized. Nolin did her best to wedge it back into the shelf where she'd found it.

There were dozens of sketchbooks; how was she supposed to find the one she was looking for? She ran her eyes over the rows of sketchbooks again. Nothing leapt out at her. Sighing, she stood up to examine the higher shelves.

Her vision swam when she stood up. The room melted together in a muddy wash. Nolin rubbed her eyes and blinked the dizziness away. The room came back into focus, and her gaze fell on a small, pale-gray object on the top shelf.

Something in her heart twanged like a guitar string, and she plucked the object off the shelf.

It wasn't actually gray, but light pink and covered in dust. The object was made of yarn, stiffened with age. Nolin peeled two knitted flaps apart with her thumb and realized it was a tiny shoe, bunched and curled up. Three tiny roses decorated the toe.

Nolin's forehead wrinkled. She struggled to unearth whatever it was in her mind that was fighting to rise to the surface. She flicked one of the little roses back and forth with her index finger. She'd seen this shoe before, in this studio, but somewhere else too. *Where?*

Her mind strained as if it were untying a massive knot. She turned the shoe over in her hand, poking her fingers inside it and fiddling with the little roses, waiting for the tactility of it to dislodge her memory. Though the windows were shut, for a moment she thought she smelled tree sap and the musty smell of dead leaves.

Nolin gasped. An image flashed in her mind's eye.

She remembered holding an identical shoe when she was a child, and she'd been sitting beneath a gigantic tree that had nearly fallen over, holding to the earth with five massive roots like fingers clinging to the ground.

The tree in her dreams. The tree in her mother's drawing. She'd been to that tree, and she'd found a shoe just like this beneath it.

The tree was real.

She'd been dreaming about it all her life, and it was real.

Suddenly, she felt dizzy. Sick. How had she known about it if she'd never been there until that day in the woods? This shoe, this meant something. How had the shoe's mate gotten so far into the forest?

Her memory rolled over like a hibernating beast, something from when she'd found the mysterious tree, something even older and darker that drew her in, though she wasn't sure she wanted to see it. She closed her trembling hand around the shoe and slipped it into the pocket of her jeans.

Sooner or later, she knew her memory would crack wide open like Pandora's box. The answers to every question she'd ever had would fly out, whether she wanted to know them or not.

Chapter 29

WINTER WAS OVER, but the spring nights were still chilly. The Shadow had to dig into the ground each night to keep warm. Sometimes she wished she could just get hypothermia one night and not have to wake up to this game anymore.

Tiny buds dotted the skeletal branches, opening a little more every day. She tried to be patient like the trees. The trees could stand for centuries, withstanding the storms and terrors around them. They surrendered their leaves in the autumn, coating the forest floor with a lush carpet of red and orange. They waited through the winter, the sap slowing to almost stagnation. Everything about the trees waited.

Now, in the spring, the buds returned and uncurled into leaves that would soak in the sunlight. They'd nourish the tree through summer storms, the heat. In autumn, when the fruit was harvested by scurrying creatures and carried off to winter dens, the leaves would fall again.

How appropriate that her hope should be reignited in the spring.

A soft breeze blew. Instead of the rustling of leaves, budded branches bumped together, filling the woods with a symphony of creaks and knocks. The Claw Tree swayed above her. The wood groaned. She sometimes wondered if the roots of this tree would collapse on her someday. It had stood for her entire life. She had been reborn under this tree; her life had ended and begun here, when she'd been Changed to the creature she was now.

She had been human once.

Sometimes she tried to recall the feeling of being human. It was so long ago, such a brief period in her life. Her old identity had disappeared. Human suffering no longer concerned her, only disgusted her. That's why she chose to live in the forest and not as a human. The forest made sense. It took care of itself.

Of course, some aspects of the human life still haunted her, and that was why she chose to pursue it. She could have the best of both worlds, couldn't she?

A fat robin sang in a tree just outside her den. The Shadow could watch birds for hours. They let her get close to them. Sometimes they even landed on her as if she were just another tree. The robin swooped to the ground and landed, hopped along until it found a nice sprig of dead grass. It collected its prize in its beak and flitted back to its branch, where it poked the grass into a half-formed nest. It would be a mother soon.

Mother.

The Shadow nestled deeper into her pile of leaves, snuggling down into the warmth. Spring, with its new life and tiny young birds, reminded her of the night she became a true outsider—not human, but not goblin, either. The only time she'd held a baby in her arms.

What kind of monster kidnaps a baby? The idea had always sickened her. Even worse, what creature takes the baby and leaves a twisted, demented substitute in its place? She thought of the hu-

226

man mothers of changelings who spent their lives knowing in their hearts that their baby was gone. Mothers always knew.

The goblins, as the Shadow had thought of them, had their reasons, of course.

The race was dying. The few goblins that remained were just the genetic dregs of fairies, wood nymphs, sprites, true goblins, and other magical folk that once ran wild in the forests of Northern Europe, their powers so diluted by centuries of interbreeding that they hardly resembled their ancestors. The switching of children simply delayed extinction and provided a way for the sickly goblin spawn to survive in the care of humans and their superior medicine. The hardier human children were brought to the woods and Changed, like the Shadow had been, until they were no longer truly human, but something much stronger that could survive in the woods with power so ancient and nuanced, she had only begun to explore it.

The Shadow understood why children were taken, but every time she thought of that evil deed, her stomach recoiled. Nothing could justify that atrocity.

She didn't remember the night she was stolen from her cradle. Images of her true mother haunted her memory when she was very young, before she understood what she was. For years, she wasn't sure where those images had come from until the time came for the goblins to steal another child.

A goblin child had just been born—a male, ugly and ill. The goblins watched the town for weeks, searching for a strong male infant to trade. They found one—a healthy baby boy in a loving family with many children. One odd child wouldn't stand out so much in a large family. They formed their plan to steal the child on a hot summer night.

The Shadow watched it happen.

She'd watched the goblin mother spider up the outside wall of the two-story house, slip into the nursery window and return, seconds later, with a squirming bundle in her arms. Wearing a hideous grin, the mother ran to the others hiding in the woods, carrying her prize in one hand, the blanket wrapped around it in a crude sack. The goblin baby wailed inside the house.

They all ran back to the Claw Tree, their sacred place, for the baby to be Changed. The goblin mother placed the boy beneath the Claw Tree, the Tree of Dreams, as they sometimes called it, and placed a tiny drop of the tree's sap on the boy's tongue. The baby giggled and reached for the thin branches that extended down to cradle him, wrapping him in a gentle web of twigs and leaves. The boy would spend the night this way, as the Shadow had when she'd been Changed. The magic of their sacred tree would seep into his veins and connect his mind to the woods, to the goblins. By morning he would be a part of the forest, like them.

The Shadow couldn't sleep that night. She lay in the dirt, her eyes fixed on the sleeping infant beneath the tree. The other goblins slept around her, their hulking shapes rising and falling gently with their breath.

Less than an hour before, this baby had been asleep in his crib, in a house with his family. Now a sickly curse lay in his place. This poor boy was doomed to a life like hers, trapped between two worlds and isolated among these creatures who cared only for their own survival.

She rose to watch the infant sleep in the embrace of the tree. His feathery eyelashes brushed the tops of his smooth cheeks. The tree had wrapped its woody tendrils around his head like a crown. She didn't know exactly how one was Changed, or whether it really took the whole night, and she had no idea how much the boy had been Changed already. He looked the same. His skin was still soft, pink. Something about him still felt right and different from the woods around him.

A strange thought visited her: he could be hers.

For a moment, images of a little boy running through the woods with her flitted across her mind's eye. She thought of teaching him the little she knew about the forest, and life, teaching him to speak the goblin language or even the English she'd learned from observing humans. Perhaps life in the woods wouldn't be so bad if she had another stolen human to share it with. Maybe she'd raise the boy herself. They were the same, two humans snatched from their families and cursed to live in the woods like animals. They'd understand each other. She'd have a companion, a child, someone to care for and fill the empty place in her heart that should have been occupied by her own family.

The boy opened his eyes. He didn't cry. He stared back at her, his blue eyes shining in the darkness. He had no idea what was happening to him, what he was becoming.

A hot tear spilled out onto the Shadow's cheek. She couldn't do it. She couldn't watch this innocent child Change and have the burden of a damaged family on her conscience. Glancing over her shoulder at the sleeping creatures, she untangled the boy from the branches, praying he'd stay silent. He gazed up at her with enormous blue eyes, unafraid and curious. His stubby arms reached for her. His toothless mouth broke into a smile.

When he was free of the tree's grasp, the Shadow snatched up the baby and crept away from the sleeping goblins. She sprinted back toward the house, clutching the warm child to her chest. The jostling didn't alarm him—he squealed with delight at the unexpected ride. He snagged a handful of the Shadow's hair and tugged. She kept running. Even over the sound of the child's glee and the fall of her footsteps, she could hear her own breathing and the pounding of her heart.

The boy's house stood silent and dark. She had no idea what she was doing; she didn't know how to sneak into a house the way the goblins did, didn't know how to climb walls. She'd never tried, especially with a squirming infant in tow. Had her years with the goblins been enough to endow her with these gifts?

There was only one way to find out.

The boy stayed quiet. Perhaps he understood the importance of what she was about to do, could sense her concentration as she approached the back of the house. The white wall glowed in the moonlight. It felt more like an immense tower than a two-story suburban home.

She realized she couldn't hear the goblin child's cries. Maybe it had fallen asleep. Or worse, maybe the human mother had already heard the cries, gotten out of bed to comfort her child, and discovered the creature. What if it was too late?

The Shadow looked down at the baby. Her heart swelled. She wanted him to grow, to be safe and happy. Warmth bloomed in her chest as the baby stroked her arm with his chubby hand. He spit and blew bubbles that popped on his pink little lips. She stifled a laugh. The thought came to her again; this child could change her life. She could run away with him, raise him as her own.

No.

He was human, like she had been once, untainted by the evil lurking in the forest. He'd only been with them for an hour or two. He was still pure.

The Shadow looked up the wall again. Stars glittered in the endless sky above the roof. She took a deep breath, tucked the baby under her arm, and pressed her hand to the smooth wall. It felt warm under her touch—unnaturally warm. Her hand tingled. Finally, she bent her knees and jumped.

Gravity seemed to look the other way as she crawled up the wall, hand and feet somehow adhering to the surface when she pulled herself up. It was easy, even fun, like scaling a tree trunk. She hung on the wall outside the nursery window and peered in. The crib rested against the wall under the window. A soft glow from a light in the hall poured into the room. The room was empty except for the infant goblin that lay still in the crib. She pressed a hand to the warm glass and felt the same electricity tingle in her hand as she slid the window open and slipped into the room, climbing over the crib and dropping silently to the floor. She listened to the even breathing of the parents and other children sleeping in their rooms. They hadn't discovered the goblin yet.

She held the human child against her chest, enjoying his warmth. The walls bore textured wallpaper of tiny teddy bears riding rocking horses. A padded rocking chair stood still in the corner. Next to it stood a small bookshelf filled with colorful, slim volumes. A bundle of stuffed bears and circus animals sat atop the bookshelf, smiling with stitched mouths. Everything about the room was soft and safe. Innocent, unlike the dark, tangled forest. The contrast of the cozy nursery to the cruel woods was staggering. She wished she could stay there forever, hide in the closet like a secret, forbidden pet.

Somewhere down the hall, a mattress creaked. The Shadow's heart leapt, and she instinctively tightened her hold on the child before remembering that he was no longer in danger, but she was.

She planted a soft kiss on the infant's forehead and gently placed him in the crib on his back. For a moment, he lay alongside the still goblin baby. Though they were nearly the same size, the human child's healthy glow overpowered the sickly green of the goblin. A guilty ache clenched her stomach. She thought of all the changeling parents who'd awaken to find an ill, ugly creature in the place of their healthy baby.

Footsteps in the hall. She scooped up the goblin child, climbed out the window, and slid down the wall.

When all traces of civilization had disappeared behind her, she paused to catch her breath. The goblin infant was cold in her arms; dead. The wretched thing had been too frail to survive the night. She'd have to get rid of the body. She could just leave it on the ground or under a bush and be rid of its revolting touch on her skin, but even this loathsome creature deserved better than that. It had no part in the evil of its kind. At least not yet. Gently placing the goblin on the ground, she dropped to her knees and sunk her hands into the soft earth, scooping soil into a pile until she'd dug a large-enough hole. After laying the goblin in the hole, she pushed the soil back, smoothed out the mound, then swept sticks and dead leaves over the spot to camouflage it. When she was finished, not even she could tell it was a grave.

At dawn, the goblins would wake to find her and the human missing. They'd know what she had done. The vengeful hunt would begin. Though she knew these woods as well as they did, she was outnumbered and no match for their brutality. No matter where she hid or how far she ran, they'd find her.

She did have one other option. She steeled herself, cradling her anger and hatred in her heart, and set off for the Claw Tree.

Her skin tingled. She neared the edge of the clearing where the goblins slept.

She bent down and closed her hand around a sharp, heavy rock.

She had no choice. They'd find her and kill her when they woke, and when they had the chance, they'd steal again. And again. The trail of broken families would continue. The woods would be filled with the echoing cries of stolen children. The cycle would never end.

She stepped into the clearing and struck each creature on the head, one by one.

The dull crack of rock on bone raised the hair on her arms. Some of them died in their sleep. Some didn't. A few stirred, the thuds of the rock rousing them from sleep. The Shadow saw their glinting eyes flashing with anger or fear before the light in them went out with a swing of her arm.

Then the last, the goblin mother who only hours earlier had traded her ill baby for the human boy. When the Shadow reached her, the jagged stone in her hand dripping with blood, the goblin shrieked, wrapped her thin hands around the Shadow's wrists. Pregnancy and delivery had left her weak. The Shadow was stronger. The goblin's wide, dark eyes bored into the Shadow's as they struggled.

No more children, the Shadow snarled. Ropey muscles in their arms popped and strained. *I am the last.*

The goblin's dark, fearful eyes left the Shadow's and drifted to the Claw Tree. Was she looking for the human baby? She opened her mouth to say something or call out, then her strength failed.

The sound of the rock echoed in the silent woods.

The Shadow stood and dropped the rock. Every limb shook. Her muscles ached. Her skin was slick with blood.

In only minutes, she'd done what the goblins had tried to prevent since they'd stolen across the ocean in the bellies of ships. The goblins were extinct. Only the last of the changeling children remained in the human world. Eventually, they'd be gone too.

The Shadow remained alone in the woods, beneath the ancient tree that had crossed the sea as a seed in the pocket of a goblin centuries before. Now she had only her vengeance, desire, and unfathomable loneliness.

Nestled in her bed of dead leaves, the Shadow wept. Her humanity could never be reclaimed, but she could still have what she had been denied. And she'd stop at nothing to get it.

Chapter 30

MELISSA HADN'T LEFT her room at all the previous day, at least
not that Nolin had seen. Nolin had fallen asleep on the couch
around five a.m. and woke just as the sun was coming up. She sat
at the kitchen bar sipping hot, black coffee, willing the caffeine
and bitterness to shock her awake. Normally, she didn't like coffee,
but she'd found some old instant granules in the cupboard and she
was desperate. The coffee tasted stale and burnt, like a tea made
with the char at the bottom of a burned frying pan. Subtle buzzing
filled her head, but her eyes still slipped in and out of focus like an
old movie projector. Sighing with frustration, she slid off the
barstool, stumbled to the sink, and dumped the rest of the coffee
down the drain.

She stared blearily out the window down the street, watching
the way the opening leaves on the trees twitched in the morning
breeze. A tall, slim figure in a tee shirt and shorts rounded the
corner and jogged toward the house.

Drew.

She'd forgotten all about their plans to run that morning.
Springing from the couch with energy she didn't realize she had,
she tore off her tee shirt and jeans and yanked on her running
clothes. She jammed socks on her feet and stepped into her sneak-

ers, then skittered down the hall to the front door, winding an elastic around her tangled hair.

A gasp burst from her as she stepped into the cold morning air. The thinnest dusting of frost glittered in the grass. Her breath puffed like steam. Normally, she liked the cold, but today it slipped between her clothes and skin like ice cubes sliding down her body. She drew her arms around herself and shivered, wondering whether she should have put on something warmer.

She glanced back up the street at the figure running toward her. He raised a gloved hand to wave. Her dry lips cracked into a small smile. She waved back, suddenly feeling a little less cold.

Drew was smiling as he slowed in front of the house. "Hey," he said, "it's freaking freezing out here. Do you need a jacket or something?"

"Don't worry, I'll warm right up," Nolin said. She gave a violent shiver. "Let's get going, though. I need to move."

Drew's eyebrows knit together in concern. He pulled the blue knit hat off his head, releasing a wild mop of dark hair that stood up in all directions. "Here, at least wear this until you do."

Nolin took the hat and pulled it onto her own head. It was a little big, but that gave her plenty of room to stuff her hair into the end. She patted the odd lump, knowing she probably looked ridiculous, like an alien with a bulbous head. "Thanks." She really did feel warmer.

"It looks good on you," he said with a teasing smile.

Nolin rolled her eyes, grinning back.

Drew shrugged and broke into a jog. Nolin fell into step beside him. Exhausted as she was, running in the fresh air felt good. More than anything, she was glad for the company.

"I found a trail we can try today," he started. "I thought we could run to the top of one of those hills at the edge of town. There's a nice lookout up there."

Nolin nodded. She'd never been up there, but she'd run just about anywhere right then. The farther and faster, the better.

"I forgot to mention something yesterday," Drew said. "I ran into that Max kid from school the other day, the one whose nose you broke? I haven't talked to him since then, and I haven't even seen him in years. You really did a number on him. His nose never did heal right; he looks like one of those squashy-faced cats now..." he laughed a little. Nolin even chuckled, then stopped when guilt twanged in her chest.

"I feel really bad about that," she said.

"I know you do," Drew said, "but it was a long time ago and there's not much you can do about it now. We might as well laugh about it."

"I'm sure he's not laughing," Nolin said bitterly.

"Ah, he's fine. I'm sure it taught him not to bully people. Anyway, he turned out to be an okay guy. He works down at the grocery store in produce, helped me pick out the best bunch of asparagus in the place; he even brought out some fresher stuff from the back. I guess they taste better when they're small..."

Nolin smiled and listened. She'd never met anyone who talked so much. It refreshed her as much as the cool spring air. People in her life were somber, intense, weighed down by lifetimes of trouble and pain. Drew was an untarnished penny, light where she felt dark.

"...and I never ate rutabaga again. I learned my lesson." He laughed again. "That was the worst; I thought my face was going to turn inside out." She'd also never met anyone who laughed so much, or so easily. His laugh felt like bubbles in her stomach, like tingling in her cheeks.

"Drew, what's your favorite book?" she asked suddenly. She wasn't aware of thinking the question. It popped out of her like soda from a bottle that had been shaken. Afraid she'd been rude by changing the subject, she nervously glanced at him. The corners of his eyes were still crinkled in a smile.

"Good question," he said, and he pressed his lips together in thought. "I've never been a big reader, to tell you the truth. I mostly just read when I had to, for class and stuff. I really liked *To Kill a Mockingbird* when I read it for school. I don't really remember what happened, just that I liked it."

"I love that one too," Nolin said. "Do you read Shakespeare?" Suddenly, she wanted to know everything about him—this person who laughed and smiled and talked like he had an unlimited supply of joy to give away.

Again, he laughed. Nolin felt herself smile widely, the edges of her eyes crinkling. What an odd sensation. "Hell no," he said. "We had to read a few plays for school. I'm pretty sure I just watched the movies and called it good. I still have no idea what anyone was saying. Just a bunch of guys in pumpkin pants and tights, speaking gibberish... not my thing at all. I'll stick to textbooks and my old Hardy Boys, thanks."

"Shakespeare is wonderful once you figure out how to read it," Nolin blurted. "Once you start to understand it, you can't get enough. It speaks to a deeper part of you that normal language just can't reach. It's like you understand it deep down. You could never quite explain in regular words..."

Drew was looking at her, she realized. Her cheeks grew hot. She couldn't quite explain how she felt at that moment—like she'd been cracked wide open. She just wanted to talk, to hear him talk, especially about things that didn't matter. No talk about her mother, her nightmares, or the growing dread that lurked in her stomach. She wanted to talk about books, his schooling, his first pet, her favorite tea, how the sky looked that day, and adventures they each wanted to take. It felt frantic, this strange desire to talk and listen, to understand and be understood.

"You'll have to teach me sometime," he said. "Show me how to like Shakespeare. I kind of get what you mean though; it's like music. How music reaches you in a way that words don't. You know?"

Nolin nearly tripped over a weed growing through a crack in the sidewalk. She didn't know. "I don't actually listen to music," she said sheepishly.

Drew's eyes grew wide. "You don't...*what*? Who doesn't listen to music?"

"A person who is very used to silence."

Hills rose ahead of them. Drew veered to where the trees opened to a tiny dirt trail she'd never noticed before, then held out his hand, indicating for her to go first. Nolin hesitated, then plunged forward into the trees.

Sunlight glowed through the sparse canopy in patches. The woods smelled like earth and damp frozen over; a sharp, yet fresh smell. She ran faster.

"Well, you can show me some Shakespeare, and I can show you music," Drew said behind her. Nolin kept running, faster. His words started to falter as he breathed harder, struggling to keep up.

Nolin's limbs tingled with heat, either from running so fast as the trail sloped upward, or from the idea of sharing Shakespeare and music with Drew. Her legs propelled her forward and upward. The wild feeling she often felt when she ran through the woods near the graveyard crept through her veins like electricity. A wild grin spread across her face. Faster, she flew up the hill.

"Hey, slow down!" Drew called behind her. Nolin glanced over her shoulder and realized he was a lot farther behind her than she'd thought, maybe thirty feet. His cheeks were red and his chest expanded and fell as he struggled to keep up. "Damn, you're fast," he wheezed.

Nolin stopped to allow him to catch up. "Sorry," she said, "I just felt like running fast for a minute there. It felt good."

"Are you sure you're not running away from me?" he said, bent over with his hands on his knees, catching his breath. "I need to do more trail running, my lungs are killing me..."

"Let's walk then," Nolin said. Drew nodded. Nolin let him go first. The trail grew steeper. Soon they were carefully picking their way up the hillside, stepping over rocks that jutted, maneuvering around fallen logs and overgrowth.

"Somebody needs to come through here with a bulldozer," Drew muttered. He swung his arms and leaned forward. His legs pushed him up the hill, the runner's muscles in his calves tightening.

Before long, the slope evened out and the trees thinned, opening up into a meadow dotted with wildflowers: red prairie-fire, sunny yellow dandelions, and tiny bluebells.

"Here we are," Drew said, turning in the direction from which they'd come. "I haven't been up here in years." He sat in the grass and patted the ground next to him. Nolin sank into crossed legs beside him, propping her chin on her elbows.

"I didn't even know this was here," she said. "I would have loved this when I was a kid."

Drew smiled. "I sure did. I used to come up here sometimes when my family was driving me nuts. I'd ride my bike over and hike up to just sit and watch the town. It was the only place I could get some peace and quiet. Not that I wanted peace and quiet often, but sometimes."

Nolin smiled grimly. "I had all the quiet I could stand. Not peace, though, just quiet."

"Only child, right?"

"Yes. I was even an accident."

Drew smiled sympathetically, though it was clear to Nolin that his experience was entirely different. "How many siblings do you have?" she asked.

"Five sisters, one brother. Also twelve nieces and nephews, ten aunts and uncles, twenty-one cousins, and pretty much all of them will be at my parents' house at least once within any given week. It was a lot of fun growing up, but sometimes it was just a madhouse. And then Christmas and Thanksgiving, when they were all there at the same time... I'm *still* recovering from some of those."

Nolin's eyes widened. "Wow," she said. She tried to imagine the stony silence of her house pierced by a gaggle of laughing family members. She couldn't do it. "I'd like to meet them sometime."

Drew smirked. "Really? A whole herd of Carringtons? I mean, they're awesome, but they're pretty overwhelming."

"Really," she said. "I want to see what a big family's like."

Drew turned to look at her, eyes narrowed slightly, maybe trying to tell if she was kidding. Then, his face softened. "Okay."

For a few moments, they sat in comfortable silence. Drew shifted his weight and his elbow brushed her arm. Nolin flinched as if he'd shocked her. Drew hadn't noticed.

Nolin brushed the spot on her arm where he'd bumped her, half expecting it to feel different. She wanted to reach out and touch his arm again, or his knee. Why did this fascinate her? It dawned on her that she'd hardly ever touched another person on purpose unless she was punching them in the face. Her parents always kept their distance. Her teenage years spent in group therapy homes were strictly no contact with others. Other than her evenings with Rebecca sitting feet to feet on the couch while they read, she couldn't recall touching or being touched.

Growing bold, she reached out and brushed Drew's arm.

He turned to look at her curiously. She felt her face redden again.

A sly smile slowly spread across his face. "Was there a bug on me?"

"I...um, yes. A big one," she said lamely. *A bug? A BUG?*

"Thanks," said Drew. "I'd hate to get bitten or something."

Nolin wanted to disappear. Drew didn't seem bothered at all.

"Well," Drew said, slapping his knees, "My butt's totally numb, and I've got to get to work. Shall we?" He scrambled to his feet and held his hand out to help her up. She took it, the same strange electricity tingling in her hand.

Nolin tugged at the hem of her shirt and looked up to see that Drew was looking at her. Something like curiosity twinkled in his eyes. There was a strange softness there too, something that made Nolin feel warm and oddly uncomfortable all at once.

They froze for a moment, then Drew blinked and cleared his throat. "How about I lead so you don't outrun me, huh?"

With Drew in the lead, they made their way down the hill and fell back into a brisk run on the road. It wasn't until they reached the house and said good-bye that Nolin remembered how exhausted she was.

Chapter 31

MELISSA DESCENDED THE stairs draped in a too-large beige dress. She hated her work clothes. The fabric felt scratchy and stiff on her skin, crinkling against her legs as she stepped down each stair, rustling against her concave stomach every time she slid her arm farther down the banister.

This was the time she normally left for work, though now there was no work to go to. Still, she would pretend nothing had happened. Nolin couldn't know.

Nolin bustled around the kitchen, scooping oatmeal dotted with black raisins into bowls, pouring creamy white milk into glasses. Melissa's famished stomach roiled. As a child, she'd hated oatmeal for its bland glueyness. Now the thought of it in her mouth, moving down her throat, and weighing in her empty stomach sounded like heaven.

Nolin turned with two steaming bowls in her hands and started when she saw Melissa, her eyes wide for a split second. She recovered quickly and put the bowls on the table with two loud *clacks*.

"Good morning," Nolin offered tonelessly, not looking at Melissa.

Spittle pooled in the corner of Melissa's mouth. Her eyes fixed on the steaming bowls. She wiped it away and approached the table slowly.

"I'm late," Melissa croaked. Unable to resist, she bent over and spooned two small bites into her mouth. It was hot. Her tongue stung. Her stomach roared.

Nolin paused at the sound, a spoonful halfway to her mouth, and stared at Melissa's middle.

"I can put it in a container so you can take it with you."

Melissa shook her head, though an unwilling spark of gratitude flared in her chest.

"No thanks, I'll be all right." Her spine cracked as she straightened. Melissa grabbed her purse from the back of a kitchen chair and slung it over her shoulder. The movement knocked her off-balance. Her vision swam. She felt Nolin's eyes on her, but she stared straight ahead and walked down the hall, carefully placing one foot in front of the other before stepping into the cool morning, playing her part, pretending she had somewhere to go.

***

The moment Melissa disappeared down the street, Nolin darted into the garage. Finally, she had a chance to root through the boxes on the shelves, where her curiosity had been tugging her all weekend. Something she wanted was there, information she craved. She didn't know what exactly, but she'd know when she found it.

The ancient cardboard bulged as Nolin hefted the heavy box down from the shelf. A thin layer of tawny dust plumed in wood-scented clouds that made her sneeze when she folded back the limp flaps.

Inside were faded papers jumbled on top of slim, hardbound books. Nolin slipped one out; it was patterned in ugly green-and-yellow stripes with sketch of a badger baring its teeth and crouching atop bubble letters that spelled "Cromwell High."

Cromwell was the next town over. Melissa must have attended high school there before Calder had built its own tiny high school.

The style of the drawn badger on the yearbook cover was familiar. It looked like something from a storybook, though it was ferocious-looking, not only by its expression, but an underlying boldness and aggression in the pen strokes. Nolin knew that hand well. The spine creaked as she flipped the book open to scan the title page until she found the words she was looking for.

Cover-drawing contest winner: Melissa Michaels

Her mother had never struck Nolin as one to enter contests or bother with school clubs. Nolin thumbed through pages until she got to the M's in the sophomore section. She opened to the page where her mother would have been, then immediately noticed one of the black-and-white pictures was scribbled out with angry black pen, pressed so hard that it ridged the shiny paper. Nolin scanned the list of names that flanked the row of pictures.

Alexa Mitchell

Just above that, the name *Melissa Michaels* was printed. To the left of the scribbled-out picture, a much younger version of Melissa smiled without showing her teeth. Even in the fuzzy picture, her eyes sparkled with mischief. Her long hair was brushed smooth. She didn't have her fringy bangs or glasses. Her face was much fuller, her cheeks a flush of dark-gray dots. Without the name and unmistakable pointed nose, Nolin wouldn't have recognized her.

Nolin squinted and held the page close to her face to examine the scratched-out picture. She could see only the outline of dark, curly hair. The entire face that had been inked into oblivion.

She browsed the extracurricular pages and was surprised to see the same apparition of her mother with that coy smile gazing at her from the creative writing club and the studio art club, painting backdrops for the school production of *The Sound of Music*, and voted "Most Creative." Nolin was even more surprised to see full hips, a curved waist, a figure teenage boys would have ogled in the hallway between classes, and absolutely no hint of self-consciousness in Melissa's stance. On the contrary, the teenaged Melissa angled her hips and shoulders to accentuate the curves, something Nolin could never imagine her doing as an adult.

Every so often, there were more scrawled black patches where a face was scribbled out, leaving only a mane of curly dark hair that almost faded into the pen scribbles. Always Alexa Mitchell—in the group photo of the track team, on the spread reserved for the science club, holding out a beaker in one photo and, in another, leaning over a glass tank with a coiled-up snake inside, dropping food into its den. Without the face, she could have been a teenaged Nolin, in tee shirts and jeans, wild hair, and a slim, boyish body.

Nolin hadn't attended high school. Sometimes she thought about how it would have been. Would she have been involved in science or art? Would she have run cross-country or received awards for athletics or academics? Part of her had no interest whatsoever in clubs or awards; at the same time, she fantasized about collecting medals and certificates to hang on her bedroom wall, about running her heart out on a track with her proud parents cheering in the stands.

This Alexa person made her believe it could have been possible. This is exactly how it would have looked.

Nolin reached the end of the book and picked the yearbook from the following year. She flipped to the M's in the junior pictures.

Melissa Michaels, now with bangs, the same coy smile and a glittering chain around her neck. Next to her, a scribbled-out photo of Alexa Mitchell.

Again, Nolin swiped the pages aside, pausing on the inky patches. Alexa, voted "Future Einstein;" Alexa, cross-country champion; Alexa, holding a trophy and standing next to a science fair exhibit about genetically modified seeds. Then there was Melissa—not in quite as many photos, Nolin noticed—painting sets for *Fiddler on the Roof*, bending over an illustration board with a pen poised in her hand in the art club.

Something stirred in Nolin's memory, a sensation she was getting used to. She pinched her eyes shut and took a deep breath, rummaging through her mind to bring that memory to the surface. Alexa. She'd heard about her before. She could hear the name spoken aloud in her head, in her father's voice. The taste of chamomile tea...and the dark feeling of guilt deep in her gut.

Her father had told her about Alexa, Melissa's best friend that died when they were teenagers. She remembered now. Nolin's stomach backflipped as she looked down at the page to the scribbled-out face. Alexa died not long after those photos were taken—two years at most.

But if they'd been best friends, why had Melissa scribbled out her face? Had she done this before or after Alexa's death? Did they have a falling-out? Something told Nolin that asking Melissa would be a bad idea.

Nolin picked out the third book and flipped it to the M's in the senior section. There was Melissa again, her face thinner, her hair not quite as shiny, and the sparkle gone from her eyes. There was no Alexa.

Nolin thumbed through the rest of the seniors, then the juniors and sophomores in case Alexa's photo ended up somewhere else by mistake. Nothing. Nothing in the M's. No scribbles. Nothing in the extracurricular pages, of Alexa or Melissa. Alexa was nowhere in the yearbook at all. Nolin supposed there was a chance she'd moved away or transferred schools, but Melissa's drawn appearance in her senior photos and the absence of any other images of her told Nolin that her life had taken a downturn.

Alexa had already died.

She turned pages until she came to the last one, or at least where the last page should have been. The page was missing, with only one jagged fragment of the top corner remaining and the top of a printed letter showing an I or a J. Nolin ran her finger along the edge of the rip, no doubt in her mind that it had something to do with Alexa.

Chapter 32

NOLIN SHOVED THE heavy box back into the shelf. Her phone vibrated in her pocket. She opened it to see she had a text from Rebecca.

I'm in town. Where are you? I'll take you to lunch.

Nolin's heart leapt with joy. Suddenly, she realized how much she missed Rebecca. She thumbed her reply:

I can meet you at that burger place on the edge of town. Do you want to meet now?

Nolin didn't want Rebecca to see the house. For some reason, those two things needed to stay separate.

Rebecca's reply came almost immediately.

Yes. I'll see you there.

Until she turned the key of her old blue Corolla, Nolin hadn't realized how desperate she'd been for an excuse to leave the house and her mother's strange mysteries. When the house disappeared behind her and she felt the warm spring air rustling her hair through the open window, she almost forgot the secrets she was unraveling and the lurking presence that followed her in those silent moments in the house.

Rebecca's red Camry was waiting in the parking lot of the burger joint. It was uncharacteristically dirty, probably from the long, dusty drive from the city. Nolin pulled up beside it. Her car sputtered as she turned off the engine.

Rebecca was sitting alone at one of the booths with her back to the door, her head tilted downward. At first, Nolin thought she was looking down at a book or her phone. When she rounded the booth to sit down, she saw that Rebecca was only looking at the blank tabletop, her hands clasped together, one thumb absentmindedly picking at the peeling black polish on her other thumbnail. She glanced up at Nolin, then returned her gaze to her hands.

"What's wrong?" Nolin asked. She slid into the booth across from Rebecca.

"Eli had a stroke," she said, her voice gravelly.

Nolin's mouth suddenly went dry.

"He's okay," Rebecca went on. "He's decided to sell the mortuary, though. The graveyard, the whole thing."

Nolin's jaw tightened. On some level, she'd known this was coming. Eli was old. He was always worrying. Hadn't Rebecca told him for years that his stress would get to him? It was only natural that he'd want to sell the mortuary and retire once his health caught up to him. What about her little room in the attic?

Then she remembered the plane ticket she'd bought only a week earlier. She'd be leaving for Alaska in just a week. Until that moment, she'd forgotten all about it. She still had no idea what she planned to do there, just that it had felt right in the moment. She wouldn't be going back to the mortuary anyway, but to have that door close behind her made her feel rootless, transparent, like she didn't belong anywhere.

"So..." Nolin said hoarsely, "what's going to happen?"

"The mortuary's been in the family for a long time," Rebecca said, "but I always told Eli I didn't want it. There's no one else now, at least no one else that we talk to, that Eli would ever consider trusting. He's decided to just sell. It won't take long. He's had some guys from the city pushing him to sell for years. I'm not planning to stick around, though...I think I'm done."

"Done?"

"It doesn't feel like my place anymore." Rebecca shrugged and flicked a shred of black nail polish off the table. "I'm actually thinking of going back to med school, or maybe graduate work in biology. I've been thinking about it for a while."

Nolin imagined Rebecca in a slick hospital with her tattoos poking out of the sleeves of a white lab coat, being with people all the time. She knew it had been her dream once. Nolin couldn't picture it now.

"That's great," Nolin said.

"I'd be moving away," Rebecca said. "I don't want to go to school in Maxfield; they don't have the programs I'm looking for. You're welcome to come with me, of course, but it's up to you. You can do whatever you want."

Nolin nodded. The hope and excitement she'd felt when she booked the flight had mostly crumbled into anxiety, but she was going to get on that plane. She'd made the decision. When she got there, she'd figure it out.

"I might travel a bit," Nolin said. "I've barely been outside the state. I need to see what's out there. I can't make decisions if I don't know what my options are." She stared at the table as she talked, but she felt Rebecca watching her with her gentle eyes. Nolin knew she understood. "I actually bought a plane ticket last week. I forgot to tell you. I'm going to Alaska."

She finally looked up at Rebecca, who looked back with a soft smile, eyes twinkling behind her glasses. "Good," she said. "You need to go somewhere."

A middle-aged woman in a red polo and visor approached their table with a tray piled with two wrapped hamburgers, two steaming cartons of fries, and two tall fountain drinks. She set it down on the table and walked away without a word.

"I ordered you a mushroom burger," Rebecca said. "Sorry I didn't wait. I figured you'd be hungry when you got here."

Nolin unwrapped her burger eagerly. Rebecca's intuition was spot-on, as usual. Nolin was very hungry, even though she'd eaten breakfast.

They ate in the same comfortable silence that they enjoyed during their long nights on the couch with stack of books and a pot of tea split between them.

Everything will be okay, Nolin thought as she chewed her burger. Her stomach filled with its warmth and weight. It was almost as good as sleep. Once she'd eaten the whole burger, she almost felt that she could sleep dreamlessly.

"So," Nolin said, "you really didn't have to drive all the way out here."

Rebecca shook her head and nibbled on a fry. A few loose curls swayed. "I needed a drive. And I wanted to make sure you were okay."

Nolin was hoping the conversation wouldn't turn that way. "I'm fine," she piped automatically.

"Hey, have you slept at all? You look exhausted."

Nolin didn't answer.

"You can come home, you know," Rebecca said, her voice softening. "You don't owe her anything."

Nolin wanted so badly to agree. Rebecca was right, but if Nolin left now, she would never feel right again. "She's my mother," Nolin croaked, her insides wrenching.

Rebecca sighed. "Nolin, I think you need to finish up whatever you're doing here and get out. Come back home. We'll get you to a doctor. You can't go on like this. You're not functioning."

"I'm fine!" Nolin snapped. Dry pain tingled in her throat, as if her words had clawed their way out. "Just... I'm fine, okay?"

"No, you're *not*," Rebecca said. "You're exhausted. At least get yourself a sleep aid or something. Listen to me. You are not thinking clearly. Do you understand that?" A hardened tone crept into her voice, a sternness she usually employed with Eli when she told him to take time off or learn to manage his stress. "Sometimes, these kinds of relationships are better from a distance. A significant distance, in this case."

Nolin sat with her hands on the table. She stared at her crumpled burger wrapper, spotted with grease. Suddenly, the burger didn't sit so well in her stomach. Far from feeling pleasantly satisfied and grounded, she felt she might be sick.

Rebecca's voice dropped lower. "This won't end well," she said. Was that pleading in her voice? Nolin didn't look at her.

"I can't leave until it's over," Nolin said tonelessly.

"Until what's over?"

"I don't know." Nolin shrugged. "I'll know when it is. When it feels right, I guess. But if I leave her like she is, I'll never forgive myself. I'll always think about it. That's how it was when I left the first time, and I won't leave now until I'm sure it won't follow me."

Rebecca shook her head. "I get that, but this is just going to hurt you, Nolin."

Nolin shifted in her seat. "I don't want to talk about this anymore," she said flatly.

Rebecca sighed and sat back. The vinyl seat squeaked. "Fine. But I don't think this is about her; I think it's about you. Your mother's an adult. She might not act like one, but she can take care of herself, or someone else can. It doesn't have to be you, Nolin. Letting her suck you dry won't make you feel better." She sipped her drink until the last drops scraped through the straw, then plunked her cup on the table.

Nolin squirmed in her seat. Rebecca was right. Leaving or staying. No matter what she chose, it would rip her apart.

Rebecca finished her food in silence, and they left. The outside air felt hot and smothering compared to the air conditioning in the building. Outside the restaurant, between their cars, Rebecca wrapped her arms around Nolin and pulled her in tight. Nolin stood still for a moment, then returned the embrace. Rebecca rarely hugged Nolin, but now her arms were tight around Nolin's shoulders. Her loose curls tickled Nolin's face.

"Call me. I want to hear how you're doing," Rebecca said when they broke apart. Nolin nodded.

They both climbed into their cars, and Rebecca drove back up the road toward Maxwell.

Nolin didn't feel like going back to the house yet. Her mind was a carousel of worry, exhaustion, and confusion. The car lurched out of the pockmarked lot and onto the road. Her mind wandered as she rambled aimlessly down the street and around the town.

She wasn't getting out of this unscathed.

Either she'd stay and let the poison of her mother's presence work its way through her, or she'd leave and let the guilt eat her from the inside out like maggots. One way or the other, this would be over soon.

Soon, she found herself at the edge of town by the hills where she and Drew had run. Warmth filled her stomach as she passed the sign for the trailhead, tucked into the trees. If she hadn't known it was there, she never would have noticed the small wooden plaque on the worn fence post. She smiled. The car ambled into the hills.

She was sure she'd been this way before, but the wooded hills and the winding road looked unfamiliar. The woods here were thinner than they were closer to town. She could see far into their depths, lush and green in the late spring. Sprigs of colorful wildflowers bloomed along the edge of the pavement. Trees cast shadows over the road, and she drove through stripes of light and darkness.

The road sloped upward. A yellow sign warned of a sharp turn. The car lurched and made a scraping sound as she downshifted. The car swung around the corner, and Nolin's hands tightened on the wheel as the force of the turn threw her shoulder into the door. She eased onto the brakes. That sign wasn't kidding.

For just a second, her eyes flicked downward at the RPM meter on the dashboard. When she glanced up her, heart leapt into her throat.

Melissa was standing in the road.

Nolin slammed on the brakes and jerked the wheel. The car skidded off the road. Gravel crunched beneath the tires, spraying pebbles over the doors. It groaned to a stop only inches from the tree line.

The world was still for a moment. Nolin froze, her mouth open in shock and her heart slamming in her chest. Her limbs burned with adrenaline.

In the rearview mirror, Nolin saw her mother standing in the middle of the road, looking up at the trees with her lips parted slightly and eyes wide. She looked like a child in grown-up's clothes. Her work shoes dangled from one hand. Nolin's eyes traveled down her mother's spindly legs to her bleeding feet.

Melissa glanced over her shoulder at the car and started as if she'd just noticed it. Then, she turned down the road and started walking away.

Nolin snapped out of her daze and threw the car door open.

"Melissa!" she shouted as she climbed out of the car. Her blood boiled.

Melissa didn't turn. She walked faster, her feet dotting the pavement with spots of blood. "Hey!" Nolin screamed. "What the hell are you *doing*?"

She jogged to catch up with Melissa, who broke into a run at the last second. Nolin grabbed her shoulder and whirled her around.

"Look at me!" Nolin shouted. "I almost killed you!" Melissa shrank back, then stiffened her jaw. Her icy claw grabbed Nolin's hand and threw it off her shoulder.

"I'm walking," she said simply.

"Yeah, I can see that," Nolin hissed through her teeth. Her limbs shook with anger and ragged adrenaline. She could still hear her heart ripping blood through her veins. "Why, exactly, are you walking? You're supposed to be at work."

Melissa looked away again. Her stiff jaw slackened. Nolin thought she saw her chin quiver.

"What?" Nolin spat.

Melissa straightened again and crossed her arms. "I'm on a lunch break."

"The hell you are!" Nolin snarled. "We're miles out of town."

It was surreal. Nolin had never lost her temper at her mother before. She couldn't remember the last time she'd lost her temper at all. Normally, she would have expected Melissa to fight back, to punish her. Nolin would have been terrified to yell at her. To see her now though, as thin as she was in those plain work clothes, barefoot in the road and at a loss for words, Nolin felt like a monster. She'd never seen Melissa look so vulnerable, not even when she'd been unconscious in a hospital bed.

Nolin sucked in a deep breath and forced herself to calm down. Slowly, the pounding drumbeat of her heart slowed. Her fists unclenched.

Melissa still had her arms folded. She was looking off into the trees, deliberately avoiding Nolin's gaze.

"I don't have to tell you anything," Melissa said curtly. "I'm allowed to take a walk. I wonder, though, why are *you* out here, Nolin? Just a casual drive?"

Nolin pressed a palm to her forehead, summoning all the strength she had to keep from grabbing her mother and shaking the truth from her like a candy bar stuck in a vending machine.

"Don't give me this shit," Nolin said, her voice quivering. "Tell me what on earth you're doing out here, right now."

Melissa chuckled and adjusted her glasses. Nolin wondered if she'd really lost it this time, casually adjusting her glasses behind her ear as if she weren't barefoot in the middle of the road with her feet bleeding. "Or what?" she said. "You'll yell at me? Oh dear, I don't know how I'll endure it."

Nolin bunched her hands into fists again, the muscles in her shoulders tight. "Fine," she said simply. "I'll leave your ass out here then. Have fun walking home." She nodded to Melissa's bleeding feet.

She turned back to the car, cursing quietly, then something clicked in her mind. She slowly turned back to your mother. Her throat felt dry.

"Did...did you lose your job?"

Melissa glanced at her briefly, her eyes stony, then looked back to the woods.

"You did. You don't have a job."

Melissa pretended to examine her cuticles. Nolin sighed wearily and brought her hands to her face. *Shit. SHIT.*

Melissa still didn't look at her.

Nolin frantically looked around her feet for something to kick. Her foot swung at a scrap of bark and sent it skittering into the trees. Melissa's eyes followed it as it spun off the road, only mildly interested.

"Did you get fired?" Nolin demanded.

Melissa nodded.

"Today?"

Melissa's shoulders dropped slightly. She picked up one bloody foot to kick at a pebble in the road. "A month ago," she said quietly.

"But...do you have savings? Severance? Anything?" Nolin questioned desperately, though she guessed the answer.

"Nothing."

Nolin thought of the house, of the unopened envelopes she'd cleared off the table. Unpaid bills, she now realized.

Shit, shit, shit.

Nolin ran her hands into her hair, pulling it back from her face, and looked to the sky. It was smooth, perfect blue, completely cloudless. The trees that lined the road cut a jagged line in the sky on either side of her vision. She breathed in deeply and smelled the woods, letting the aroma fill her. Squeezing her eyes shut, she looked back to her mother.

"Get in the car."

Melissa kept her jaw tight, but didn't protest. Arms still crossed tightly over her thin torso, she stepped deliberately to the passenger side of the crooked car, popped the door open, and plopped down into the seat.

Nolin sucked in another breath of forest air, then turned back to the car and climbed in.

Neither of them spoke on the way home. Nolin's temples throbbed. She drove back to the house in a daze, her mind whirling through possibilities and problems, wondering how much time had been added to her sentence in that house. Somewhere, there was a vague thought of Alaska, cold water, and glaciers she would never see.

Chapter 33

IN A WAY, Melissa felt relieved.

No more leaving the house each day, pretending she had somewhere to go. No more wandering aimlessly while blisters bloomed on her feet. Nolin knew she was a failure. Of course, she'd probably known all along.

Melissa perched on the kitchen chair. Nolin knelt at her feet, tending to her bleeding blisters, cleaning them and wrapping them in gauze. Melissa watched her daughter's face, focused and serene. Nolin's green eyes narrowed as she carefully wrapped the gauze around Melissa's toes and tilted her head from side to side to see what she was doing.

Something in Melissa's heart flickered. A burning tear slipped from her right eye, trickled down her face, off her chin, and landed with a tiny plop on Nolin's arm. Nolin paused, glanced at the wet spot on her arm, and then continued wrapping without bothering to wipe it off.

"We need to figure out what you're going to do," Nolin said hoarsely. "You need a new job, and, honestly, I think you should sell the house and find an apartment or something more affordable." Her eyes darted upward at Melissa's face, gauging her reaction. The flickering part of Melissa's heart jumped when she briefly met her daughter's gaze.

"I know it's probably hard to sell the house," Nolin said quickly. "I know you've been here for a long time, but it will be a lot easier for you to support..."

"No, it's fine," Melissa sighed. "I want to sell."

Nolin sat back on her heels and looked up with wide eyes. "Really?"

Melissa nodded. "I hate this place. I want to leave."

Nolin's mouth set in a grim line and her emerald eyes blazed. "Well, all right then." Then she went back to tending Melissa's feet.

She was right, Melissa thought. *I do need her help.* For the first time since Nolin had arrived, Melissa was glad she was there.

***

Nolin walked to the library to clear her head. She took long strides, gravel crunching under her sneakers. Sweat dampened the back of her tee shirt.

Find a realtor. Set an appointment. Go from there. She'd never sold a house before. She was in over her head. They both were.

She couldn't believe Melissa hadn't told her she'd lost her job.

Then again, maybe she could. Maybe she just couldn't believe she hadn't noticed.

The willow tree stood in front of the library to greet her, its vines swaying as though it were underwater, like a giant jellyfish. She reached up to run her fingers through the ends of a vine and feel the smooth leaves against her thumb and forefingers. It felt like greeting an old friend with an almost-forgotten secret hand-shake.

She expected to see Ms. Savage at her usual perch behind the information desk, but a pale young girl around Nolin's age sat there instead, her thin lips parted slightly as she typed. As Nolin stepped in, the girl jerked her head in surprise, as if the last thing she expected was for someone to walk into her library.

"Can I help you?" she said nervously.

"Um," said Nolin, still taken aback that it wasn't Ms. Savage. "May I use the computer?"

"Oh, sure." The girl leapt up from the desk. She skittered to the line of computers along the back window, wiggled the mouse of one to bring the screen to life, then typed something.

"There you go," she said, not looking at Nolin as she retreated to the desk.

Nolin sat in the hard chair and set to work.

Calder realtors, she typed, and then scrolled through pages of names, smiling headshots, reviews, and appointment information until her brain felt numb.

Maybe she should take a quick break.

Her fingers poised over the keyboard. *Changeling*, they typed the moment the word popped into her mind.

Her mind still couldn't shake the strange word, couldn't explain the odd curiosity it awakened in her. Ms. Savage had told her about it, but she wanted to know more. At least to find out why this silly concept intrigued her so much.

She scrolled through the titles that popped on the search page, filtering out the fluff related to movies and TV shows until she found articles related to actual lore. Her eyes whipped back and forth as she scanned; for what, she wasn't sure.

...ill, disordered, or unusual children were often thought to be the offspring of fairies, trolls or goblins left in the place of the original human child...

Just like Ms. Savage had said.

She clicked on "Means of Identifying a Changeling." Something in her mind told her to get back to finding realtors, but her unrelenting curiosity drove her further.

Voracious appetites...malicious tempers...dislike of shoes...a greenish tint to the skin...vastly intelligent...

The page was illustrated with sketches of children with twisted, evil-looking faces, pictures of screaming mothers holding monstrous-looking babies. The drawings reminded her of her mother's illustrations.

Bitterness rose in her throat. The fluttering in her stomach stopped and gave way to a lead weight.

She flipped through article after article, dismissing each as folklore and paranoia. She felt sorry for any child who lived among that superstition and was forced to bear the label of changeling. Goblin.

Stop. You need to find a realtor.

Nolin closed the article and started searching realtors again, her mind slipping into a bland numbness. She propped her elbow on the desk and rested her head in her hand. Her eyes slid closed.

Her bedroom was dark, different. Instead of an empty room coated with dust, there were decorations on the walls. Instead of her bed, Nolin lay in a crib with a mobile hanging above it. Shiny stars and moons turned slowly in a breeze from the open window.

The room smelled of the woods, that unmistakable scent of earth, leaves, and panic, hot and metallic. She kicked her tiny legs and gig-

gled, beating her fists in the air and on the mattress. The crib shook as she wiggled. The stars and moons on the mobile twitched. Something crunched in her hand, and she held up a chubby fist to examine it; a dried leaf, crushed to papery shreds. How strange.

She kicked again and realized one of her feet was bare while the other was stuffed into a little pink shoe with tiny roses on the toe. She squealed with delight and she looked up to the open window.

Something pale and slender was slipping through the window above her crib, and Nolin realized it was a hand and an arm, white as aspen bark. A face followed, wild and shadowed in the darkness, surrounded by dark hair. Nolin squealed again and reached for the face. Her hand closed on a handful of matted hair.

The soft, white hand closed around Nolin's chubby wrist. The creature brought Nolin's hand to its lips and kissed it softly.

"Good-bye," it whispered. A woman's voice, soft and quiet as the breeze. Then, the creature released Nolin's arm and slipped out of the window.

Nolin reached farther, her forehead wrinkling as she struggled to understand. Why had she gone?

"Ma," Nolin babbled. She didn't know she could make that sound, or what the sound meant, but it seemed like the only thing to say. "Ma," she said again.

Nolin jerked awake, scanning the room madly. She scrambled out of her chair. The chair fell over with a clatter.

"Are...are you all right, miss?" the girl behind the desk stammered.

Nolin meant to nod, but she just stumbled across the room to the front door, fumbled with the handle, and staggered out into the yard of the library.

She struggled to gather her thoughts. She'd fallen asleep and had a dream...hadn't she? But it felt so real.

Nolin rubbed her wrist. She could almost feel the creature's cool touch on her skin, feel the breeze on her face and in her short baby hair, the breeze on her bare feet...

What if it wasn't a dream, she thought. *What if it was a memory?*

Head swimming, Nolin broke into a jog down the street toward her house. Her legs pumped faster and faster until she was sprinting. She reached the house in no time and burst through the front door, vaguely acknowledging that Melissa wasn't downstairs.

Nolin found her backpack resting beside the couch, unzipped it, ripped out the jeans she'd worn a few days ago, and fumbled with the pocket until she found it.

The faded pink shoe uncoiled in her hand from its bunched-up ball, exactly like the one in her memory. This shoe had a mate in the woods, under the tree she'd visited in her dreams, and once in her waking hours.

Or maybe, she thought, she'd been there even before that.

Nolin remembered two dark eyes, a wild face. She gasped like she'd been punched in the stomach. She'd seen someone in the woods that day, under that tree. She tried to recall the face. The harder she tried to focus on it, the further it drifted from her mind.

The tiny shoe fell from her hand and landed on the floor without a sound.

Changeling.

The word rose in her mind like something dead floating in water. It all made sense. Her mother never let Nolin call her "Mom."

She never showed any attachment or affection at all. As if she knew.

Of course she knew.

No wonder Melissa hated her; her baby was replaced by an awful creature—a changeling.

Changeling.

Nolin mouthed the ugly word.

She looked down at her hands, her arms, and noticed the greenish tone of her skin. She'd noticed before, and it never struck her as odd before now. No human had skin like this. Her sinewy muscles, the green veins in her hands, her constantly tangled hair. Air caught in her lungs, and she choked. Her stomach roiled. She ran to the bathroom down the hall and threw herself across the toilet to retch.

Clambering to her feet in front of the sink, she turned on the faucet and cupped her hands under the flow to wipe her mouth. Her skin burned with fever. She splashed cold water over her scorched face, then stuck her head under the tap, soaking her hair, letting the cold streams run down her neck and into her ears. Without wringing her hair, she tossed her head back. Water ran down her chest and back. Dark spots appeared on her shirt where the water seeped through. She could breathe again, but now she breathed too hard. She was still fiery hot. She crossed her arms over her chest and peeled off her tee shirt. Her muscles rippled with her rattling breaths, her shiny stomach pinching in and out, shoulders tensed up by her ears. The more she watched her reflection, the less human she looked. She looked less like a woman and more like the willow tree in front of the library—her body a hard, toughened thing, rooted down, while her wild hair hung down like vines.

She locked eyes with herself. Her emerald eyes burned brighter. She searched her own wild face for some shred of humanity. Someone she recognized.

Now she understood why the woods fascinated her, why they called to her. That was why she'd fled to them that day on the playground. The shadow that had followed her all her life, the face in her dreams, the face that stared into hers when she woke up under the tree all those years ago wasn't her imagination.

Without meaning to, without knowing it, she'd stolen someone's life. Someone's child.

Melissa wasn't crazy—she'd lost her baby. Nolin, the real Nolin, now lurked on the edges of their lives.

Chapter 34

THE SHADOW FUMBLED with the thin branches that hung under the Claw Tree. Thoughts rolled through her head, none of them actually hers. There were fewer and fewer thoughts to sort through these past few years. The tree was getting quiet. The humans and goblins who were connected were dying out.

Though it was night, it didn't take her long to realize Nolin wasn't asleep. No dreams to shape.

Nolin didn't sleep often. The Shadow wondered if she avoided her dreams on purpose. Most nights, Nolin would drift into slumber for a few minutes at a time. Her dreams would flow through the tree into the Shadow's mind and back again, but tonight there was nothing. Nolin was stark awake, not even trying to sleep.

Something was keeping her awake.

Something had happened; the Shadow was sure of it.

***

The faucet dripped. For the entire night, Nolin didn't move from where she lay in the fetal position on the bathroom floor. The steady drip marched along with her slow heartbeat, her even breathing. Her eyes focused on a single crack on the wall until her vision blurred. Her eyes felt dry. She'd forgotten to blink.

So what now?

She could stick around and try to get Melissa out of this mess.

Or, she could return to the forest.

Maybe she could find her real family, the goblins or fairies or whatever she was.

Nolin smirked bitterly, shaking her head. No way was she a fairy. She thought of herself as a child, a wild little thing with dirty feet and a hot temper, digging holes in the schoolyard just to feel the soil between her fingers. How could she be anything else *but* a goblin?

Nolin pulled herself into a sitting position. The knobs of her spine dug into the drywall. She tilted her head back and let her hair cover her face like a shroud.

Melissa wasn't her mother, so was Nolin obligated to help her? Nolin could pretend this never happened, go back to the forest, and forget everything about her human life, the way she did before when she fled into the woods.

Nolin hugged her arms around her knees, trying to make herself small enough to disappear. Tears spilled from her eyes and burned trails down her swollen cheeks.

No, she couldn't leave.

As much as she wanted to be free, she couldn't abandon Melissa now. She had burdened her. She'd driven Paul away, then left Melissa alone to manage herself. Human or goblin, she couldn't leave now. She didn't know how to be a goblin, anyway. She only knew how to be Nolin, whoever that was.

Her joints cracked as she clambered to her feet and to the living room. Slowly, she laced her sneakers and tied her hair back, all sound and feeling muffled as if she were underwater. She needed a walk.

Quietly, Nolin slipped out the front door.

How strange that the trees, the houses, the sky, everything about the quiet street in the small town was exactly the same as the day before. And yet the trees felt different. The sky felt different. She felt like she was seeing everything for the first time, through different eyes that didn't view trees and the sky as something outside of her, but something inside of her, part of her. She was part of the earth and the forest, just like the trees.

In a daze, she rounded corners, marching in a solid rhythm though she gave her body no orders. She realized she was still avoiding the cracks in the sidewalk. *Don't step on a crack or you'll break your mother's back.* Biting her lip, Nolin planted her foot over a crack in the sidewalk. *She's not my mother. I don't know my mother.*

Once she finally looked up to see where she'd wandered, she realized she was at the end of town, on the road that wound into the hills where she'd found Melissa the day before, where the trail she'd run with Drew snaked through the trees and up the hillside.

She broke into a run. The muscles in her legs screamed as she propelled herself up the steep hill, pumping her arms to the sound of her breath, the rhythm of her pulse thrumming in her ears. She'd never run so fast in her life.

Within minutes, she reached the top of the hill. Thick trees gave way to the open clearing bathed in morning sunlight. Startled, she paused at the edge of the trees, because she wasn't alone.

Drew sat on the same rock where they'd sat together only days before, or was it a lifetime ago? He leaned forward on his elbows and watched the sunrise.

He turned when he heard her coming and beamed at her.

272

"Hey!" he called. "Sorry, I ran by your house this morning, but you weren't outside, and I didn't want to knock in case you were asleep." His smile faded and his words trailed away. "Are you okay?"

Nolin's limbs shook from the run, so she hobbled forward and clumsily dropped down next to him. She opened her mouth to speak. Nothing came out. For a moment, Nolin forgot how to speak, as if losing her human identity had also cost her human speech. She dropped her head into her hands. Her hair curtained her face, wrapping her in a dark cocoon that blocked out the sunrise completely. She didn't want to talk. She didn't want to see. She just wanted to sit there and know he was beside her, not requiring her to do or be anything, except be there.

"I don't think I can do this anymore," she said. "Any of it."

She felt his large hand on her back between her shoulder blades. He inhaled to say something, then thought better of it. Nolin was grateful. She didn't have the energy for words—for speaking them or for listening.

His arm wrapped around her. She leaned into him. The thoughts that had been blowing around her head like a tornado slowed.

"Whatever it is, it'll be okay," he said softly. "You're tough enough to get through anything." Nolin felt herself smile, though she wasn't sure she believed him. She appreciated it all the same.

Did it matter if she was not human? What if she chose humanity—was that the same thing? Melissa, Rebecca, Drew, people she'd cared about as much as a human could. Nothing had changed, in reality. Just her perspective. Perhaps she could choose to belong, choose to be what nature had decided she was not.

Nolin's hands slipped away from her face. She opened her eyes, gazing into the blazing sunrise. Her muscles stopped twitching, and a heavy sleepiness overtook her. Maybe she'd sleep later.

For now, she would sit and watch the sunrise in Drew's arms and welcome a new day, this new discovery, and watch the world go on.

Chapter 35

THEY WALKED HOME together. Nolin watched the ground while Drew looked straight ahead. Occasionally she'd glance up at him and find him looking at her. She'd smile. He'd smile back.

Just do it, she thought.

She took his hand. It was so much larger than hers, warm against her cool fingers. Rough in some places. He squeezed her hand gently, ran his thumb over her knuckles. Nolin's heart thudded. Could he feel her pulse in her hand? She looked up at Drew, at the gentle smile that could mean anything.

He had no idea. No clue what she was. Would he care? Did it matter?

No, she thought defiantly, *I don't care what I am.* Something at the back of her mind flickered in protest. She snuffed it out, like kicking dirt over a stray spark from a campfire.

It doesn't matter. It doesn't matter. The thought ran through her head until it carved grooves in her mind.

"You don't have to go home, you know," Drew said. "Whatever happened, you don't have to go back."

"No," Nolin responded, her voice calm. "It's all right."

She understood now; she wasn't afraid of Melissa, or the house. She was afraid of herself.

***

When Nolin walked into the house, Melissa was standing in the kitchen clutching a steaming mug. Nolin startled; she hadn't expected Melissa to be up, much less in the kitchen, making tea as if this were a lazy Sunday morning. Another mug sat on the counter with the tag hanging over the side, the vapor rising in curls.

"I made you some tea." Melissa stared out the living room window at the woods. There was no wind outside. The tops of the trees were still for once, fluffy and green with new spring leaves.

"Thanks," Nolin said. She watched Melissa take a tiny sip of tea. A strange cocktail of emotions stirred deep in Nolin's stomach. Anger, pity, sadness, fear, and relief twisted into a heavy wad in her gut. This was the woman she'd grown up believing was her mother, who'd raised her, but never treated her as a daughter. This broken shell of a woman, whose love she'd always desperately wanted.

Melissa took a slow sip from her mug. "I'm going to look for a job today," she said quietly.

Nolin took in Melissa's clothes for the first time, her neat sweater and skirt. Too big, but clean and unwrinkled at least.

"Oh, good." Nolin said. Really, she was happy for her, also glad she'd be leaving for a while. "Good luck. I'll stay here and clean some more." Nolin smiled tightly, reaching for the extra mug of tea on the counter and raising it to her mouth, inhaling deeply before taking the first sip.

Nolin slipped into Melissa's room once she'd gone.

She'd never seen any baby pictures of herself. She dug through the bookshelf in Melissa's room, but she couldn't find any photo albums. There had to be pictures somewhere.

Nolin found boxes under the bed, stacked to the brim with papers and folders. Financial records; college and high school transcripts; a high school diploma; a few award certificates from art shows. Things that any normal person would keep in a filing cabinet. Melissa must have shoved her entire life under that bed. It was interesting how she and Melissa dealt with things they didn't want to face: Nolin ran, Melissa hid. Run and hide. Both cowards.

She looked under the bed. Nothing left.

She swore as she grabbed handfuls of papers and dumped them back into random boxes, not caring if she crumpled or tore anything. She slid a box under the bed, stretching her arm to shove it to the far side. The underside of the box spring sagged. In the far corner, she noticed the gauzy material that was was ripped and held together with safety pins. Something poked through the fabric. It felt like a book. There were other shapes poking through the fabric, more corners and edges.

Nolin wriggled under the bed and unhooked the safety pins, then reached through the tear.

One by one, she pulled out book after book, nearly a dozen. Then, she realized they were journals, ranging from cheap ones with pastel art printed on cardboard covers to soft, leather-bound notebooks. Nolin spread them out on the floor and picked what looked like the oldest of the lot, patterned with kitschy pink flowers. She flipped the pages; it was filled.

The inside cover even had a *This book belongs to...* stamp, under which was *Melissa Michaels* printed in blue pen. She recognized Melissa's unfeminine scrawl. Nolin started at the first page.

April 17, 1979

I've never kept a journal before. Mom says if I don't, no one will know about my life after I die. I don't care if no one knows. She bought journals for everyone from the dollar bin at the grocery store, and now every night after dinner is "journal time." Most families watch TV together in the evening, or just do their own thing. Mine spreads out over the living room and writes in cheap notebooks for an hour.

My life isn't very interesting anyway. I'm eleven years old, I have long blond hair, and I'm supposed to wear glasses, which I hate. I always take them off before I get on the school bus. I have a grumpy dad, a mean mom, and a stupid little brother named Donald. We call him Donny. Sometimes I call him Donald Duck, mostly when he's being annoying. Then he cries and Mom yells at me to be nice to my little brother. Ugh.

My best friend's name is Alexa. She comes over a lot because she doesn't like her foster mom, but she likes my family for some reason. Mom just loves her. She makes treats every time she comes over and offers to let her spend the night. I've never been to Alexa's house. She says they're not allowed to have friends over. Alexa doesn't think she'll ever get adopted; she just wants to wait till she's eighteen so she can move out. Oh good, journal time's over.

The margins were filled with scribbles and doodle of curling vines, echoes of the Melissa's adult illustrations.

Nolin turned another page and skimmed the entry. Every day, Melissa wrote and mentioned how stupid she thought it was. Stupid Donny this, Mom yelled at me for that. Alexa's name appeared on nearly every page. Nolin stopped turning halfway through the book, when Alexa's name caught her eye.

August 8, 1979

Alexa came over for dinner tonight because Mom told her she's getting too skinny. She worries she doesn't get enough to eat at home. Of course, if she eats with us, she gets to stay for journal time. Mom even bought her a nice journal, a nice black one instead of one like mine that looks like a Kleenex box. Alexa likes writing. Mom tells her what pretty handwriting she has, and how pretty she is. Mom never tells me I'm pretty. I look so boring. Alexa has long, dark curly hair and brown eyes. I'm just boring dishwater blond with blue eyes.

Alexa is spending the night. It's been really warm at night, so we like to sleep outside. Sometimes, after my parents are asleep, we sneak into the woods a little ways. Alexa loves the woods. She says she feels like an animal when she runs through the trees. She doesn't even use a flashlight. It's like she can see in the dark while I'm always tripping over something. It scares me sometimes.

Last week, she took me into the woods because she said she wanted to show me something. I was scared and I didn't want to go. She went anyway. I didn't want her to go alone, so I followed. She's so fast; I fell down a few times and scratched up my legs. She finally stopped in a little clearing. The moon was out, and it lit everything up.

"Right here!" she told me. She was standing by a hole in the ground, and she stepped in when I came over. She told me to go down with her. The opening of the hole was as big around as a hula hoop and led to a little underground cave big enough for both of us to lie down in. It smelled amazing, like rain and fresh-cut grass. Like earth.

"Did you dig this?"

"With my own hands. Do you like it?"

We were lying on our backs, looking up at the sky though the hole. It was like putting the sky in a frame, so it felt right on top of us instead of millions of miles away.

"It's incredible," I told her. I don't know how long we lay there, just watching the sky. I even reached up to touch it. It looked so close, and I thought maybe I could. If I held my finger just right over the edge of the moon, it looked like I was touching it. I imagined I could feel it. What would the moon feel like?

"I sleep in here sometimes. When I don't want to be home." Alexa said.

"You sneak out? You'd get in so much trouble!"

"I've never been caught. No one cares anyway; I come back long before anyone knows I'm gone."

I told her I wanted to go home. I was starting to get scared, and I wanted to go home. I didn't even want to sleep outside anymore, so we slept in the living room. Alexa was grumpy the rest of the night.

That was the end of the first journal. Nolin sat back on her heels, her feet almost numb from sitting for so long. How strange that Melissa was best friends with someone so similar to her daughter, who loved to dig and be in the woods, who lived in a home where she wasn't wanted.

She shivered and ran her hand down Melissa's words. A strange thought entered her mind.

Was Alexa a changeling?

Chapter 36

A STACK OF finished journals grew at Nolin's side. A picture formed in her mind—a movie reel of Melissa's childhood, full of constant family rifts and a strange girl who was so much like Nolin, and with whom Nolin was becoming more and more fascinated.

This girl was wild as the woods, brilliant, and reckless. Though Melissa called Alexa her best friend, Nolin couldn't ignore the bitterness in Melissa's descriptions, or how her handwriting became less neat and more jagged when she wrote about Alexa.

Nolin noticed the time when she finished the fifth journal, right when Melissa and Alexa were entering high school. The sun was now making its way to the west horizon. She replaced the journals in the box spring.

Nolin was cooking dinner when she heard the door open and Melissa's light footsteps in the hall.

"How'd it go?" Nolin asked casually. She pushed the stir-fry around the pan. Melissa sat at the bar.

"Fine." Melissa's eyes were glazed like those of a dead fish. Clearly, she didn't want to talk. Nolin didn't push it.

Nolin dumped the stir-fry over the rice waiting in two bowls on the counter and slid one across the bar to Melissa, who didn't acknowledge it at all.

Nolin leaned against the counter and stabbed her food with her fork. "Have you drawn anything lately?" she asked lightly. Melissa didn't seem to hear her at first, then blinked.

"What? Oh, no. It's been years."

"Why don't you get back into it?" Nolin suggested. "This seems like a good time. Maybe you could do some freelancing."

"Huh," Melissa responded. She still didn't touch the food. Her eyes slid back into focus, though she still looked deep in thought.

How strange to talk to Melissa like there was no animosity between them. Nolin settled into this odd feeling. Perhaps now that she realized Melissa wasn't actually her mother, the tension had dissolved.

But Nolin couldn't ignore the sinking feeling deep in her stomach. Part of her still wished things had changed and that they could be this way, mother and daughter, comfortable, talking in a kitchen like civilized humans. This was, of course, impossible, because Nolin was not human. She suspected that Melissa was aware of this. Why else would she have hated her so much, put her through hell as a child, and loathed her as an adult?

This wasn't a truce. It was just a quiet day in monsoon season, calm before yet another storm.

***

Melissa didn't leave to look for jobs the next morning. Or the next. Or several afterward. Nolin scrubbed, met with realtors, and put the house on the market like an actor in a play, reciting lines, smiling the way she should have, pretending this was her game and not some strange role in a performance she never signed up for. The date on her plane ticket came and went, and with it her painful visions of pristine snow, sparkling glaciers, and silent ever-green forests. Finding her place seemed less important now that she knew she belonged nowhere.

Her morning runs grounded her. She ran until her legs shook and her chest ached, until her mind was still. The smell of the town in the morning was starting to feel familiar. She looked for-ward to those mornings, even more so when she spotted the lanky figure jogging up the street toward her.

Drew was a strange fixture in her life, like an actor from a com-edy who had wandered into a soap opera on the next station. They never planned on meeting each morning, but she started to expect him.

The same route each day: the same turns around the town, down the long road into the hills, then up the hillside to the clear-ing, where they'd watch the sunrise and stay as long as they dared before Drew had to go to work at his first job and Nolin couldn't justify the stolen moments any longer.

The mornings were getting warmer. They had to run faster to catch the earlier sunrises. On a particularly warm morning, Nolin sat with her legs long in front of her, feet bare, leaning back on her hands. Drew stretched out on his stomach beside her, propped up on his elbows. The sky changed from pink to light blue. She watched the way the sunlight brought out the yellow in the leaves and flecks of gold in Drew's messy hair.

She was starting to tan; the tops of her thighs were now lighter than her lower legs. Her arms were darkening to their summer bronze. Nolin noticed that Drew's calves were slightly darker than just above his knees where his shorts had slid up. Summer was on its way.

This summer felt different, though. She was a new Nolin, back in her hometown, her life twisted inside out. Summer was cracking her wide open. A strange recklessness stirred in her. Perhaps she was antsy with Melissa's drama, or simply embracing her true nature.

"We should meet for lunch today," Drew said. "Before I go to the school." He worked two jobs in the summer, both at his father's landscaping company and as a summer activities counselor at the local junior high.

"I'd like that," Nolin said. Any excuse to get out of the house was okay with her.

They'd stay for a few more minutes. Nolin rolled up the sleeves of her shirt. A few minutes later, Drew peeled off his shirt and tucked it underneath him for padding.

Unlike Nolin, his torso wasn't crisscrossed with tan lines. He was slim, his lean muscles long and smooth. The slight ridges of his ribs and shoulder blades moved under his skin when he breathed; the curve of his spine flexed when he shifted his weight on his elbows.

The recklessness that had been brewing in Nolin's gut for weeks twitched, itching in her arms and legs. Her fingers tingled. Curious. She wanted to touch him. What would happen if she did? Before she could think it through, her hand reached out and placed itself on the small of Drew's back.

She worried he'd flinch or push her away. He didn't. She thought she saw the corner of his mouth twitch into a grin.

Her hand slid upward, her middle finger gliding up his spine like a boat cutting water.

Drew sighed happily and dropped his head down so Nolin could touch the back of his neck.

"Keep doing that," he said.

Nolin smiled. She felt surreal, touching someone like this. Normally, she lived in a bubble that she preferred no one ever enter. No physical contact. His skin, smooth as clay, rooted her to some deep and immovable part of her that felt unchanging despite the turbulence of the last month. Surprisingly soothing. This act of touch made her feel more and less human; more connected to another person, yet more animal as well.

Nolin wished the sun wouldn't rise any higher in the sky, and they could stay in this special spot on the hill. She could forget anyone else existed. She wanted to hang onto this peace for as long as she could.

Drew's smile faded; maybe he didn't want to leave either. Finally, he reached for her hand on his shoulder and pressed it to his lips. Nolin's entire arm tingled, and her stomach fluttered.

"We'd better go," he said quietly. He pushed himself up to his feet and reached down to help Nolin up.

They ran down the hill in silence, Drew first. The run back passed far too quickly. They paused in front of Nolin's house to catch their breath.

He'd be late soon. Drew pulled Nolin into a hug, his arms wrapped tightly around her shoulders and hers around his slender waist. Then, he kissed her forehead, pulled away, and threw her a quick smile before turning to run down the street.

Her forehead burned a little where his lips had been. The rest of her felt unusually warm, though that might have just been from the hurried run home. When he was out of sight, she turned and walked up the front walk to the door, ready to step back into her life and face whatever new, ugly discoveries the day had in store for her.

Chapter 37

NOLIN FOUND A note from Melissa on the bar.

I have a job interview this morning and another in the afternoon. I'll be back later today. For the love of God, don't panic and come looking for me.

—*Melissa*

Nolin didn't know whether to roll her eyes or be suspicious. Better to not dwell on it, she decided. With Melissa gone for the day, she was free to dig through the journals.

Those journals drew her like a moth to a porch light. The strangeness of Melissa's mind before it cracked open, the odd girl she spent her time with, the turbulent relationship with her own family that echoed her treatment of her future daughter, it all meant something. In those journals, she'd find out who her mother was, who this Alexa really was, and most importantly, who she, Nolin, was.

Alexa. Nolin had a feeling they'd have gotten along if they'd known each other. The more she thought about it, the more she was sure Alexa was another changeling. They were too much alike.

Nolin stacked the journals in order from oldest to newest, ten journals in all, then started where she'd left off. She barely noticed the passing of time as she followed Melissa and Alexa through junior high and into high school. During their junior year, things grew stranger.

Alexa is doing this weird scholarship project, Melissa wrote. *She's studying local flora and fauna, and she's completely obsessed. She spends all her time in the woods, making drawings and writing in her notebooks. Mom says I should take that kind of initiative and keep a notebook on my own instead of only writing during journal time, when I have to. I could seriously puke.*

Alexa might be onto something, though. She keeps finding these "nesting" sites, like how deer and elk sleep in the grass and leave it all matted down, but these are much smaller. During the winter she found some huge holes in the ground, or burrows like the ones she dug back in elementary. They're full of grasses, small animal bones, and berry pits. I told her it's probably hobos and she should stay away from them, but she thinks she's found some nomadic, omnivorous mammals who bed down in the grass in the summer and burrow in the winter. I think she knows more about it than she's telling me.

Nolin's insides froze as she understood.

Alexa had found signs of the goblins in the woods, where she'd come from. Where *Nolin* had come from. *No wonder she was obsessed*, Nolin thought. *I would be too.* She read on.

Now Alexa wants to go camping out there to see if we can find any of these things. I don't know what she's thinking. She's totally obsessed! The weirdest thing is, I talked to our biology teacher and she said Alexa hasn't told her anything about a project. Alexa's lying to me, and I want to know why.

Her heart pounding, Nolin flipped the page.

Blank. The rest of the journal was empty.

But tucked into the back of the book was a folded, wrinkled piece of paper. Nolin carefully unfolded it.

It was the missing page from the back of Melissa's yearbook. A picture of Alexa, larger than any of the others in the yearbooks, the face marked out with black sharpie. There were words along the top:

In Memory of Alexa Mitchell

June 1, 1969 - May 18, 1985

Rest in Peace

Nolin ran her fingers over the scribbled-out photo. Alexa died on that camping trip. Why hadn't Melissa written anything after that?

Her back ached from hunching over on Melissa's bedroom floor. She got to her feet and pressed her shoulders back, then slowly straightened her sore legs. Her hamstrings and the backs of her knees screamed. She'd probably never sat in one position for so long.

"What...the...HELL...are you doing?"

Nolin felt like she'd been doused in a bucket of ice water, and she jerked around.

Melissa stood in the doorway, face red with fury, blue veins shining through the papery skin of her neck.

"I..." Nolin stammered, her blood turning to ice.

"You little bitch!" Melissa's gnarled hands balled into fists and she lunged.

Nolin shot to her feet and instinctively grabbed for Melissa's forearm. Melissa lurched forward and slammed into Nolin with every measly ounce of her weight, shoving her into the wall. How could she be so strong?

Her face turned purple with rage. She hissed, flecks of spit flying into Nolin's eyes. "How dare you. How dare you!"

Nolin didn't want to hurt her mother. She shoved Melissa off her and Melissa stumbled backward. Nolin ran for the stairs. Melissa pursued.

Before Nolin reached the top step, she felt her mother's claws on her shoulders, then Melissa's weight hurling into her. Melissa's enraged howl turned to a scream of fear as she slipped. Nolin stumbled and they both fell forward, tumbling down the stairs.

Nolin caught herself on the banister, but Melissa rolled over her and landed with the sickening crack of bone as her head hit the tile floor at the bottom.

Melissa gasped, eyes bulging and then blinking slowly, laying nearly upside down on the stairs. Her leg jutted out at a very wrong angle. The arm she'd tried to hit Nolin with splayed oddly at her side.

"Oh my god...Mom...*Mom*." Nolin scrambled to her mother's side. She brushed Melissa's cheek with trembling fingers. Melissa's head twitched. She tried to move and a small, red smear appeared on the floor from a head wound. Nolin fumbled for the phone in her pocket and dialed 911.

A voice crackled on the other line. "911, what is your emergency?"

"Hello? My mother's fallen and she has a head injury..."

"Do you require an ambulance?"

She gave the operator the address. Melissa's eyes rolled up to meet Nolin's, the whites visible all the way around the gray irises.

"Oh god, I'm so sorry Mom. I'm so sorry."

Nolin was afraid to move her in case her spine was damaged. She threaded her fingers through her mother's. Melissa didn't resist.

"Help's coming, Mom. Tell me about your drawings. Can you tell me about your drawings? Anything?"

"My...drawings..." Melissa wheezed.

"Yes, what do you like to draw?"

She had to keep her talking. Melissa's eyes opened and shut slowly. Nolin had to keep her awake before she was swallowed by sleep.

***

Nolin didn't tell them what happened, except that she slipped. No one questioned it, or at least, they didn't show they did. Maybe they just didn't have the time to show suspicion, or perhaps they simply didn't believe a daughter could harm her mother.

Nolin rode in the ambulance, tears searing hot trails down her cheeks so that she could barely see the figures hunched over her mother's skeletal form on the stretcher. Melissa looked so fragile, like a child.

Once they reached the hospital, an hour seemed to stretch into days. Nolin waited for a doctor to tell her what she'd done, what was broken, how Melissa was. Eventually, a middle-aged man with silver-rimmed glasses and a white lab coat approached her.

"She has a nasty concussion and some stitches in her head," he told her. "She also broke her hip. She's extremely undernourished, so her bones are quite fragile. A tumble down the stairs could injure anyone, but was much more serious for her. She has the bones of someone much older. She dislocated a shoulder as well, but that's back in now and shouldn't leave any lasting complications."

Nolin sighed with relief, but her stomach still churned with anxiety. "She'll be okay?" she croaked, her voice edged with pleading.

"We'll need to operate on the hip, and healing will be slow. She might not heal completely. She should heal, though." He inhaled, breaking eye contact.

What had she done?

It happened so fast. Melissa burst in and within seconds, was on the floor bleeding with her limbs splayed out every which way. Just one touch; that's all it took.

"I have some other concerns though, that I'd like to discuss with you..." The doctor cleared his throat and looked down at the clipboard again, his face growing pale. "She's very malnourished, you see, and her liver and kidneys are failing. She actually had a minor heart attack in the ambulance on the way over. We've got her on a feeding tube, but her organs might be damaged permanently."

Nolin swallowed hard. "What does that mean? Is she going to be okay?" Nolin glared at him. He met her gaze only briefly before his small eyes darted back to his clipboard. He cleared his throat again.

"It's too soon to tell. Her injuries are serious, but we're far more concerned about organ failure. To be honest, I'm surprised she's still alive."

His words hit like a kick in Nolin's gut. *Surprised she's still alive?* Had it gotten that bad?

"We're doing everything we can," the doctor added quickly. "She might be just fine, but again, it's too soon to say. She'll need to be here for a while. If she's still kicking after so many years of malnourishment, she's tough."

Nolin stuffed her hands in her pockets to keep them from lashing out and throttling the man, just to have a way to release her fury at herself.

She should never have run away. She should have stayed home, forced Melissa to eat, even if that meant sitting on her and prying her jaws apart. She should have checked Melissa into rehab. Now, it might be too late.

The doctor reached out a hand in what might have been a comforting gesture. Nolin jerked away.

The doctor left, scribbling something on his clipboard and shaking his head. Nolin sat on a chair in the hall and buried her head in her hands, her fingers digging into her scalp. She rocked back and forth just like she'd seen Melissa do during anxiety attacks.

I really am a monster, Nolin thought miserably.

She'd better leave, she decided. The farther away she was from Melissa, the better. She was too dangerous to stay. She stood to leave, but realized she'd ridden to the hospital in the ambulance and had no way to get home. Could she walk? No, the house was miles away.

Finally, she pulled her phone from her pocket and dialed Drew's number.

"Hey," he answered. "Weren't we meeting for lunch? I was about to call you..."

"Drew," Nolin wheezed, another wave of tears rising in her eyes.

Drew paused, the line silent for a moment. "What's wrong?"

"Melissa's in the hospital," Nolin whimpered. "She fell down the stairs..."

There was a rustling sound, like he was suddenly moving. "Are you at the hospital?"

"Yes."

"Okay, I'll be right there."

Nolin nodded and remembered he couldn't see her. When he hung up, she sat and stared at the wall, feeling utterly alone. Guilt ripped at her insides.

Nolin checked the time. Drew wouldn't arrive for at least another ten minutes.

Her legs shook as she pushed herself out of the chair and craned her neck to see into the room where her mother was. There didn't seem to be anyone else in there, so she slipped inside. She felt like a criminal even standing next to Melissa, knowing what she had done. It was an accident, she told herself. But maybe some sick part of her had wanted it to happen. Some evil part of her made it happen.

I'm a monster.

Melissa was asleep, or maybe she was drugged. A bandage wrapped around her head. A thin, clear feeding tube was taped to her cheek and threaded up her nose. Just looking at it made Nolin feel sick.

Melissa's mouth slacked open. She looked much, much older than forty-one. Thin, bony arms poked from the sheet-like hospital gown. She looked tiny and alone in the sterile hospital bed.

She stepped forward and carefully placed her hand over Melissa's, half-expecting her to jump, to snap awake and yell at her. She was still. Melissa's hand was cold and dry. It felt more like a wadded-up piece of paper than a human hand.

Drew texted her.

I'm in the lobby. I'm not family, so they won't let me up. Come on down when you're ready.

"I'm so sorry," Nolin said quietly to Melissa. "For everything. I'm sorry for what I did. I'm sorry for what I am." She could say more, but the words dried up in her throat.

She met Drew in the lobby. He wrapped his arms around her, hugging her tighter than he ever had before.

"What happened?" he asked.

The tears spilled over. Nolin told him what happened, that Melissa had slipped and was a broken pile of bones in a hospital bed, that she'd found her reading her journal, and that it was an accident. She hadn't meant to hurt her. Nolin told him about the blood on the tile and the stitches in Melissa's head. Words spilled from her like her tears; she couldn't have stopped if she wanted to.

"It's my fault." Nolin finished. A wet spot bloomed on his tee shirt from her tears.

"This was an accident," Drew said, his voice low and steady. She pressed her ear to his chest, and his voice rumbled inside. "It's not your fault. That's a dangerous track you're on; get off it now."

"If I hadn't been looking through her stuff, she wouldn't have come at me and this wouldn't have happened," Nolin said. "And now she's got this on top of everything, and it's because of me. She might not even heal properly because her body can barely function. She might have a cane for the rest of her life if she ever gets out of here."

Drew brought a hand to her face and twined his finger through her hair. She felt him kiss the top of her head. "Come on," he said. "I think you need to get out of here."

Chapter 38

Nolin didn't think it was possible for that house to be more uncomfortable, more hollow than it already was. Without the ever-present shadow of Melissa, the beating heart of that house, it stood silent and empty, like a vacated battlefield after the carnage is over and all that remains are the dead bodies and crows, the echoes of gunfire and cannon blasts.

Nolin paced, just like she'd watched Melissa do when she was very young. Some of her earliest memories were of watching Melissa cross the room again and again. Melissa would drift from room to room, sometimes talking to herself very softly, looking out the window, making nervous gestures. Nolin had never understood; Melissa was looking for a place for her mind to crash. She was a mess of dangerous, runaway thoughts that wouldn't stop for anything except a head-on collision.

Drew waited patiently on the couch, watching Nolin without saying a word, his hands in his lap. Nolin wasn't sure how long she paced. She didn't know what else to do.

For once, she didn't want to be alone.

She was sick of the house, full of secrets and memories and layers upon layers of bitterness like dust sticking to the shelves.

Everywhere she looked, a memory. A scolding, a worry, a tear. She couldn't be alone here.

Finally, she sat next to Drew and pulled her knees to her chest, tucking her arms in front of her to be as small as possible.

"I don't know what to do," she whispered.

"Why do you have to do anything?"

"It's *my fault*. I came back here to help her, and I hurt her."

"Nolin, you don't have to take care of everyone. It's not your job."

"It's my fault," Nolin protested, her voice a low hiss. "I'm the reason she's like this in the first place. It's always been my fault." She gulped and yet another tear dripped off her chin. "She'd probably be fine if it weren't for me."

"You can't know that," Drew said quietly. "And you can't know why she's sick. It has nothing to do with you or anything you did."

A hot tear rolled down Nolin's cheek. She immediately swiped it away.

"Nolin..." Drew started, his head cocked to one side while he searched for words. "Look at me."

She turned to face him. She'd never seen him look so serious, without a trace of a smile, no twinkle in his eyes. He didn't blink.

"You don't owe anyone anything," he said. "You have a right to be happy, no matter what she's going through. None of this is about you."

Nolin let out a breath she didn't realize she was holding and rested her forehead on her knees. She wanted to believe it, that her happiness was somehow separate from Melissa's. Protests flew through her brain so quickly she couldn't have articulated any of them. At her core she knew: this was her fault.

"You don't believe me, do you?" Drew said.

"I want to." Nolin clamped a hand over her mouth to suppress a sob. "I'm sorry," she said. "I'm being an idiot."

"Nolin, I have five sisters. I've seen girls cry over lost earrings and shit like that. You have nothing to be sorry for."

An odd sound burst from Nolin, a sharp laugh mingled with a sob. She wiped her eyes. Drew watched her patiently, leaning forward on his elbows.

She wanted to ask something. She was afraid, but she asked anyway.

"Will you stay with me tonight?"

Her toes curled. Though something inside her recoiled with embarrassment, she couldn't be alone in this house. If he said no, she'd drive her car somewhere and sleep in the front seat. She stole a glance at his face. He looked calm, with the ghost of a smile on his lips.

"Okay."

They could have slept on the living room couches, but they'd wake up with their backs full of knots. Most of all, Nolin wanted to be close to someone, close as she could possibly get. Maybe then, she wouldn't feel alone.

So they moved upstairs to Nolin's room.

Nolin scooted to the wall to make room for Drew on her narrow twin bed, lifting the blanket for him to slip under. The mattress creaked as he climbed onto the bed beside her. He stretched his legs out. His feet hung off the end.

"This is just like my bed at my parents' house," he chuckled. "I feel right at home."

They settled, facing each other. "You probably think I'm ridiculous," Nolin said.

"Not at all."

The corners of his mouth lifted into a small, encouraging smile that Nolin tried to return. She didn't feel it. At least she didn't feel alone. She knew he didn't fully understand—how could he—but at least he cared. That was more than enough.

And he was warm. Nolin wiggled her feet out from under the blanket until she felt cool air. She brushed her toes against his legs.

"Sorry if I talk in my sleep," he said. "My brothers tell me I mumble a lot, or that I dream about meeting Eddie Van Halen and stuff. I giggle. So...I pre-apologize if I wake you up."

"I'll be fine," Nolin said. "I don't sleep much anyway."

"How come?"

"I have dreams," she said simply.

"About what?"

"The woods."

"Oh. I do too, sometimes."

Nolin didn't expect that. Suddenly, she was wide awake. "Really? You do? These woods?"

"Sure," Drew said, shrugging. It was a strange motion for someone who was lying down. Only one shoulder seemed to jump towards his ear. "They don't bother me, though. I just figure my subconscious wants to go for a walk or something." He smiled. His arm draped over her waist. "Do those dreams scare you?"

"Sometimes," Nolin admitted. "Mostly they just make me...uncomfortable, I guess. I feel like I might find out something I don't want to know."

"Something you don't want to know," Drew repeated. "So you aren't being chased by bears or something in your dreams? Because other than that, I'm pretty sure there's nothing in those woods that can hurt you."

Nolin's thoughts strayed to a dim memory of a dark-haired figure crouching above her under the Claw Tree.

"I'm not sure what's in there," she said.

"Then why do you need to be afraid of it? Is it scary just because you don't know what it is?"

Nolin paused, her fingers fiddling with the edge of the blanket.

"That's a good point," she said.

Drew reached up to brush her hair off her face, smoothing it back from her forehead. "Everything is fine. Just try to get some sleep, okay?"

Nolin nodded. Drew slipped his arm back around her waist and closed his eyes. Soon, his breathing grew slow and even. Nolin settled closer to him, with her cheek pressed into his chest. Even in his sleep his arm tightened around her. The trees rustled and moved outside, swishing their leaves in the wind. Bright moonlight streamed into the room, bathing everything in a silver glow.

She finally closed her eyes and listened to Drew's heart beating through his tee shirt, in time with her own. It was warm with him under the blankets. Comfortable. Drew giggled softly in his sleep. Nolin smiled. The rhythm of their pulse was steady in her veins.

***

The Shadow had fallen asleep with the tips of the thin branches still entwined in her fingers. She'd been dreaming she was in the arms of a man, in a tiny bed, in a room she recognized. Then she jerked awake.

The dream wasn't her own. It was Nolin's.

The Shadow sat up under the tree, and the piled-up leaves around her rustled. The light of the full moon poured into her den beneath the trunk of the Claw Tree and illuminated the woods around her. The fog cleared from her mind and a thought emerged: *I want to see them.*

She scrambled out of her den and shot off into the trees.

***

When she awoke, Nolin's fingers were entwined in Drew's tee shirt. Her forehead pressed into his chest. Her tank top had ridden up to her ribs somehow, and Drew's arm was draped across her bare stomach. His skin was warm; Nolin was slightly sticky with sweat, and her head felt heavy. She was sure she'd only been asleep for a few hours, but she couldn't remember the last time she'd slept so deeply.

Drew was dead to the world. His chest rose and fell against her cheek, steady as the tide until he giggled again and shifted.

"Thank you, Mr. Van Halen, it's an honor..."

Nolin smiled. Pushing her feet against the mattress, she lifted her hips to ease herself onto her back. Her eyes fluttered open and focused on the window.

Someone was staring back at her, pale, with wild hair and dark eyes that widened before the face disappeared.

Nolin bolted upright. She'd seen it. The one in the woods was real. It was only there for a moment, but it was real.

She leapt off the bed.

"Nolin, what's going on?" Drew mumbled sleepily. Not pausing to answer, Nolin ripped into the hallway, down the stairs, and out the back door.

The damp grass was cold on her bare feet. She ran faster than she'd ever run in her life. Ahead of her, a figure vanished into the trees, dark hair whipping behind it.

"Nolin!" Drew shouted somewhere behind her.

Nolin didn't stop. Her eyes fixed on the spot where the figure had disappeared, and she pumped her legs even faster, her feet pounding the ground so hard that they felt numb.

"Nolin, wait!" He sounded like he was getting farther away. Nolin didn't pause to check.

Finally, she reached the edge of the woods and plunged into them, leaping through the undergrowth and darting between the trees like she'd been running through them all her life. She thought she saw a pale flash of a body ahead of her.

Nolin leapt over a fallen log, but her foot caught the edge of the rotting bark and she fell forward, catching herself on her hands and knees in the dense cover of the forest floor. Her legs and lungs screamed. She lifted her head and squinted into the trees.

She'd lost her. Whatever she'd seen was gone.

Nolin stayed on her hands and knees, breathing deeply to slow her pounding heart until she heard Drew behind her.

"Nolin!" he panted. His shoes appeared in Nolin's peripheral vision. He crouched by her side, and she felt his hand on her shoulder. "What's wrong? What happened?"

Nolin breathed heavily, debating whether to tell him everything, something, or nothing at all.

"I..." she wheezed. "I thought I saw something. In the window. And then it ran into the trees."

"So you ran after it? What were you thinking?"

"I don't..." she coughed. Her lungs felt like dried-out sponges. "I don't know."

"I don't know how you saw anything," he said, still catching his breath. "I can't see a damn thing out here."

"Really?" Nolin looked around. She could see perfectly. It was night, of course, but everything around her was clear. She looked up at the moon that seemed to illuminate everything around her, expecting it to be full and wide, but it was a waning sliver. A slim crescent in the dark sky.

"You really can't see?" Nolin asked warily.

"I can barely see you," Drew said.

Can I see in the dark?

Finally, she sat back on her heels and looked into the trees. They waved their leaves gently. Stars twinkled innocently above the canopy.

"I think you are really, really stressed about your mom," Drew finally said. "Come back to bed; come on."

He helped her to her feet.

"You don't have shoes..." he said.

"I'm fine," she croaked. Her feet were numb. Drew wrapped his arm around her shoulders, then looked at her and paused.

"What?" Nolin said.

"I just...it looked like your eyes were glowing for a second there. Like a cat's."

"My eyes glow?" Nolin asked.

"Well...I think I'm just tired. Come on."

Drew walked her back through the woods to the house. Just before they stepped out of the trees, the canopy hissed in a breeze that grew stronger, pressing against their backs, pushing them out of the forest. Nolin turned to look back into the woods and thought she heard a light, lilting laugh carried on the wind.

Chapter 39

NOLIN WAS ALREADY awake when Drew started to stir. They laid twined together as the sun rose, past the time when they'd usually be out for a run. Nolin didn't want to leave the bed. More than anything she wished to stay where she was, fall into the blissful blankness of sleep, and forget everything about her life that shouldn't have been her life at all.

Drew pressed his lips to the back of Nolin's shoulder. She felt his warm breath on her neck.

"I have to go to work soon," he said quietly, pulling her closer. "I'm worried about you."

Nolin didn't say anything.

"What happened last night?"

"I just... I thought I saw something outside."

Drew sighed. "Nolin, if you see something creeping around outside, you call the police. Or animal control, or the ghostbusters, whoever. You don't chase it down."

Nolin snuggled farther down into the covers, pulling the blanket up to her chin. "I wasn't thinking."

"You're under a lot of stress."

"You don't know the half of it," Nolin said groggily. "She started getting sick when I was born. She didn't want me. She still doesn't.

I'm not even sure she's my real mother anymore." Nolin sucked in a breath through her teeth. She couldn't believe what she'd just said. She braced herself for his reaction.

Drew paused. "You...you think you're adopted?"

"Something like that. Worse, actually. I think...I think I might have been switched for her real baby."

Drew's arm stiffened around her waist. "Like, in the hospital? Some nurse screwed up or something?" His voice grew louder in her ear, the sleepiness gone. Nolin decided that was enough. No more.

"More or less. It's a long story, but I have...reason to believe that."

Nolin felt him shake his head. "Damn," he sighed. "But you know, even if that's true it's not your fault. You were a baby, for god's sake. It's not like you could crawl around and trade yourself for some other kid."

A smile flickered across Nolin's face. In her heart, she knew he was right, but it didn't change the fact that a wrong needed to be made right, and it was her responsibility to do it.

"Should I call in sick?" he asked. "I feel bad about leaving you alone with all this."

Nolin shook her head. "No. I'll be okay."

They lay in silence for several minutes before Drew finally pushed himself up and slid off the end of the bed. He pulled on his jeans and stepped into his shoes while Nolin watched, still wrapped in the blankets.

He didn't know what she was. He had no idea.

Would she ever be able to tell him?

Drew knelt to tie his shoes and looked up at her. His usually sparkling blue eyes looked tired, with light shadows beneath them. Nolin could only imagine how tired she looked.

"Are you sure you'll be okay?" he asked.

Nolin nodded, the scratchy sheet rustling against her ear.

Drew didn't look convinced, but he pulled his baseball cap over his head and stood up.

"Call me or text me if you need anything," he said. "Meet me for lunch? For reals this time?"

Nolin nodded again, looking at his chest instead of his eyes. Drew made a funny jerking movement, as if he wasn't sure whether to walk out of the room or move toward her, but then he took a step forward and crouched beside the bed. He brushed her hair off her face and kissed her forehead. Nolin shut her eyes, resisting the urge to grab his arm and pull him back into the bed so she could curl around him and pretend that nothing existed outside that room.

"I'm okay," she insisted.

Drew nodded, but his eyes were still clouded. For once, the corners of his mouth weren't curved upward in their perpetual smile.

"I'll text you in an hour," he said, then kissed her forehead again and walked out of the room.

Nolin listened to his footsteps down the stairs, through the kitchen, and then heard the front door open and close. The stark silence rang in her ears.

Her stiff muscles and joints screamed as she pushed herself off the bed. As she dressed, her bones cracked in protest. Her eyes felt dry and chapped. Though she'd slept a few hours that night, never before had she experienced such exhaustion. The heavy fatigue cut through to her bones.

What should she do now?

She knew she'd seen a face in the window, seen someone running into the woods, and heard the softest laughter drifting out from the trees. She'd seen her.

Nolin couldn't decide if she felt angry, violated, or afraid. Did she have a right to feel any of those things? Did she have a right to anything in her life? After all, she, Nolin, was the interloper. The imposter. The girl in the woods, the shadow who'd always lurked at the edges of her life, was the real Nolin.

Her mind coiled around the only thread she had, the only other possible changeling she knew about.

Alexa.

Her feet carried her out of her bedroom. She found herself opening the door to Melissa's room. The journals were still sprawled over the floor, exactly where she'd left them.

She knelt and began to gather them up, stacking them so she could shove them back into the box spring where she'd found them. It was too little too late, but it gave her something to do, just for a minute.

She reached for a journal near the side of the bed, and her eyes caught on something beneath the nightstand. She slipped her hand underneath and her fingers closed on what was unmistakably a book.

Another journal?

Her heart leapt in her chest. It was bound in fake brown leather and looked newer than the others. The spine creaked as it opened. It was blank.

Nolin flipped through the pages. All blank.

"Come on!" Nolin yelled. She threw the book, and it smacked the wall. A few pieces of paper slipped out as it flopped to the floor.

Her heart beat faster. She crawled to where the book had landed and carefully picked up the papers.

Two photos, slightly faded. One of a shiny wooden casket, crowned with a spray of flowers and surrounded by people dressed in black. Blue sky and green grass. She didn't recognize anyone in the photo.

The other was a man and a woman standing on the other side of the same coffin, not looking at the camera. They were flanked by a young boy and a teenaged girl Nolin recognized as Melissa. The woman was crying; the man was solemn. The boy looked sad, but Melissa's young face was a mask. Her lips pressed together, and her eyes were blank. Arms folded tightly over her chest.

There were also newspaper clippings, stiff and yellow with age.

The first headline set her heart racing.

Teenage Girl Missing in Camping Accident, Found Dead

Alexa Mitchell, 16, was found dead last Saturday near Swallow Ridge. She had gone on a hiking trip with her friend, Melissa Michaels, 16. The two girls were hiking alone when Alexa reportedly slipped and fell down the ravine and into the river, where she was washed downstream. Michaels claims to have climbed down the ravine after Alexa, but was unable to find her friend. After searching for some time, Michaels returned to town to report the incident. Searchers discovered the body nearly a mile downstream from where Michaels claimed the fall occurred.

Nolin felt like an ice cube had slipped down her throat and dropped into her stomach, coating her insides with chilling dread.

The next clipping was a short obituary accompanied by a grainy photo of Alexa that looked like a school photo. Alexa's face was reduced to a grid of black-and-gray dots, though Nolin made out a sharp nose, high cheekbones, and piercing dark eyes on an unsmiling face.

Alexa Mitchell, 1969-1985

On Saturday, May 18th, Alexa Mitchell was killed in a hiking accident in the hills near Calder, Colorado.

Alexa attended Calder High and was an honor student, well-liked by her teachers and peers, and showed great promise in the fields of biology and chemistry. She planned to apply for college during her senior year. She was considered for many scholarships to universities throughout the western region and was the recipient of several local and national academic awards.

An orphan, Alexa was a resident of Colorado foster care, though she was well-loved by the family of her best friend, Melissa Michaels. The family was planning to adopt Alexa before her untimely death and made all arrangements for Alexa's funeral. Alexa will be buried in the Maxfield City Cemetery.

A great loss to the community, Alexa will be missed.

Nolin sat back on her heels and stared. *Maxfield City Cemetery.*

Her cemetery, where she'd lived and worked for five years, probably seeing that grave every day without even knowing it.

Nolin moved on to the last clipping. Her hand shook as she read.

High School Student Suspected in Teen's Disappearance

Melissa Michaels, 16, was questioned by local police about the death of her friend, Alexa Mitchell, in a hiking accident along Swallow Ridge. Suspicion was aroused by a doctor who treated Michaels' cuts and bruises from what Michaels claimed was a desperate search along the ravine for her friend. Scratches on Michaels' face and arms appeared to be made by human fingernails rather than branches, and the pattern of bruises on her arms were consistent with finger marks.

Searchers also noticed that the slope of the ravine that Mitchell had supposedly fallen down was dense with trees and foliage, and that it was unlikely a person could have fallen all the way into the river from the trail above.

Students and teachers at Calder High confirmed suspicions that the relationship between the girls was a tense one, that Michaels was often jealous of Mitchell's achievements and that the two often quarreled.

Authorities are reviewing the case. The site of the accident will continue to be searched for further evidence.

Nolin stared at the paper in her hand, shocked, scanning through memories of teachers and neighbors whispering about the "incident," something that had to do with Melissa that Nolin had never understood.

This was it. The whole town thought her mother was a murderer.

Could Melissa actually kill someone?

A girl who outshined her at school, who her family loved more than they actually loved their own daughter, while Melissa felt shunted to the background.

Could Melissa have been jealous enough to push her down the ravine?

Nolin's mind whirled. She snatched up the photo of the funeral again. Melissa's blank face. Her crossed arms. She sure didn't look sad that she'd lost her best friend.

Maybe this was why Melissa was sick. She couldn't live with what she'd done.

This was why Melissa had always treated Nolin like a monster: because Nolin reminded her of someone she hated.

Another thought ran through Nolin's mind: *If Alexa was a changeling, had Melissa known? Did she suspect that Nolin was as well?*

Nolin ran her thumb over of the faded photo, smudging it slightly. Then she noticed something. Nolin held the picture up to her nose and squinted. Melissa had something tucked under her arms in the photo. It looked like a book, the size of the journals she'd read. Black. It blended with Melissa's dress, which is why Nolin hadn't noticed it before. Then it hit her.

Melissa's first journal said that Alexa kept a journal as well. The book in the photo. It didn't look like any of Melissa's, so maybe the book Melissa held was Alexa's.

But why would she bring it to the funeral?

Nolin struggled to string her thoughts together. She was so exhausted. Her temples throbbed.

A connection formed. Nolin tried to brush it off as ridiculous, but something about it fit. It was exactly something Melissa would do. Morbid. Desperate.

What if that journal contained something Melissa never wanted anyone to read?

What if she slipped it into the casket so its secrets would be buried along with Alexa?

It was crazy, insane.

At this point, Nolin was willing to bet on crazy.

Nolin pulled out her phone, flipped it open, and texted Drew, a twinge of guilt burning her stomach.

I'm sorry, I'm going to have to skip lunch again today. I'll make it up to you, I promise.

Before closing the phone, she vaguely noted that her battery was low, but she had other things to think about.

Nolin crossed the room and scrambled down the stairs, down the hall, and into the driveway with purpose. She started her little blue car and sped down the road, her mind spinning with obsession.

She had a grave to rob.

Chapter 40

THE FREEWAY PASSED in a blur; the ghosts of hundreds of trips to hospitals and nursing homes to pick up cadavers in the middle of the night. Everything looked different during the day. The day belonged to the living, but the dead ruled the night. Nolin always felt it while driving back to the mortuary in the white van with a body behind her, or walking through the graveyard at night. The graveyard and the mortuary pulsed with the presence of passed souls who never slept. Daytime felt different.

Nolin shook her head to rattle her crazy thoughts and tightened her grip on the steering wheel. Images of rotting hands pressing up through the soil of the graveyard haunted her. She thought of yellowed eyes meeting hers on the embalming table, invisible gazes following her journey since she left the mortuary.

Nolin had watched Rebecca handle hundreds of dead bodies. Rebecca never showed a hint of anxiety; she was like any other industry worker hauling bolts of cloth or car parts. When the body died, it was no longer a person. It was just a body.

Finally, she exited the freeway onto the busy city streets of Maxfield. Honking horns and roars of car motors faded to a buzz in her ears. She dimly realized that perhaps she shouldn't be driving, tired as she was. Somehow, she managed to navigate the chaotic streets until the buildings and lights gave way to trees and faded stop signs. She reached the outskirts of town, and finally, the arched sign over the entrance to the cemetery rose in her view.

The grass was a little long. Whoever was mowing the lawn lately hadn't done a very good job. The gravestones and old church looked more foreboding under the clouded sky than she remembered. Gravel crunched under her tires as she pulled into her old spot. It felt strange not to see Rebecca's Camry right next to her. The graveyard was silent as she climbed out of the car. No birds, no rustling of leaves in the breeze, nothing at all.

The mortuary seemed to be empty, but it was unlocked.

Eli's office was neater than usual. His framed photographs and candy dish were missing. Whoever had bought the place might not have moved in yet.

Eli had never computerized the records. Her best bet for finding the grave would be to check the ancient filing cabinet in the corner of the room. Nolin yanked open the file drawers. The tabs of the ancient manila folders were labeled, but Eli's scrawl was so untidy that she could barely read it. She squinted at the handwriting on the tabs; last names in alphabetical order, some folders obviously older than others. In the middle of the row, a few folders with the name "Mitchell" caught her eye. "Mitchell" wasn't an uncommon name, so one by one, she slipped out the folders, opened them, and then stuffed them back in when they weren't what she needed. She slipped out the last one and let it fall open.

Mitchell, Alexa

Nolin examined the wrinkled, yellowed form. The graveyard was set up on a grid system, and it didn't take her long to picture the exact area in her mind where Alexa was buried.

It occurred to her that digging up a grave in the daylight might be a bad idea; dusk wasn't far off. She climbed the stairs to her room to wait.

Her old room felt foreign. She'd only been gone for a few months, but it felt like several lifetimes. The smell was different, musty. The orange light of the sunset felt hotter, more slanted than she remembered. She threw open the window, took a seat on the floor, and waited.

The sun sank lower and lower, setting the sky on fire. The red clouds faded to purple, then blue. The first stars of the evening appeared, opening their eyes one by one.

It was time.

She climbed down the stairs and out of the mortuary to where the paperwork said Alexa was buried. The fireflies that usually flitted about the headstones at night were absent.

She was completely alone.

Finally, she found it.

The small, unimpressive headstone lay flat on the ground. The name etched into its surface was still crisp even though the grave was over twenty years old. She'd never been interested in the newer graves and rarely noticed their names. She was drawn to the older graves, with old-fashioned headstones that stood up and whose names were barely legible. No wonder she'd never noticed this one before.

Good. She knew where she was going now. She turned and ran back toward the mortuary where the gravedigger's backhoe was parked. He always left the keys inside.

She'd only driven the backhoe once, but she managed to maneuver the large machine back to the gravesite. The friendly

317

gravedigger had let her help dig a grave years ago. Digging up an occupied grave couldn't be much different.

Through the windshield, she looked down at the tiny head-stone, her heart drumming. *I can do this.* Finally, she tilted the lever and dipped the bucket toward the ground.

She dug carefully, making slow progress. The bucket scooped up lumps of dirt that she carefully dumped into a pile, swiveling the machine on its base.

Finally, the teeth scraped the top of a concrete box. Her heart leap and she withdrew the bucket from the hole. Grabbing the shovel she'd found, she climbed out of the backhoe and into the grave to finish.

She worked silently in a slow rhythm, scooping and swinging. The shape of the concrete box appeared as she dug out the cor-ners. The exertion calmed her; the images of rotting corpses and zombie movies dulled. It was almost over.

Finally, she pulled herself out of the grave and climbed back into the backhoe to retrieve the chains she'd brought in the shed. She hoped this worked.

Carefully, she wrapped the chains around the bucket, then jumped into the grave to dig the hooked ends of the chains under the lip of the concrete lid. Then, she scrambled back into the backhoe. Her hair was soaked with sweat.

Please, please, please, she prayed as she restarted the machine and started to lift the bucket.

The arm struggled, but the lid moved. Slowly, it lifted out of the grave.

For a moment, she paused, staring down into the hole. The smooth surface of the closed casket gleamed in the moonlight, still glossy after all these years. Since she'd arrived, her heart had been pounding in her chest. Now, it seemed to stop completely.

Carefully, she lowered the lid to the ground, then climbed down and approached the edge of the grave.

Maybe she'd made a mistake. Why had she thought Melissa would put the journal in the casket? She hadn't been thinking clearly. She was so *stupid*. This was a terrible idea.

But the hole was dug. The lid was off. All there was left to do was open the casket and look.

She clambered down into the grave, carefully placing her feet on either side of the casket where she'd dug a little extra space to stand on. Her fingers fumbled for the lip of the lid. Taking a few deep inhales and then holding her breath, she mentally counted to three.

The old casket opened with a creak.

The coffin was lined with rotted silk. Nestled into the lining was Alexa. Masses of dark hair surrounded her dry, sunken face. Brittle lips drew back from a set of yellowed teeth. The mouth cracked open in a silent cry. The top of her ribcage poked through the remains of a dark green frock and her limbs were nothing but dried-out sticks, shrouded with papery shreds of skin.

Nolin fished the latex gloves from her pockets and slipped them on, struggling to get her fingers in the right places. Her hands didn't want to work right. She'd been holding her breath, but her lungs screamed for oxygen. She briefly tilted her head to the sky and gulped in a mouthful of air.

Even in that brief inhale, she could taste it—the edges of decay on the dust that floated up from the casket.

Nolin crouched over the body and gingerly felt along the corners of the casket, under Alexa's stiff arms and legs. Finally, she found something under the left hip. It slid out easily.

A book, the black book Melissa had been holding in the photograph, sealed in a plastic zipper bag.

It struck Nolin as odd that Melissa would bother to put it in a bag. Maybe she'd planned to come back for it someday. Her mother's strangeness never ceased to amaze her. Yet here she was, Nolin, digging up a body for something that might or might not have been buried with it.

Before climbing out of the grave, Nolin looked at Alexa's face, imagining eyes beneath the sunken, crepey eyelids. In some ways, she felt like she knew her. They shared their strangeness, their origins, perhaps. Nolin hoped that whatever she found in the journal would be the truth, would either confirm or deny her theory that she wasn't the only changeling to darken Calder.

Nolin closed the casket and climbed out. Back into the backhoe to replace the cement lid, scoop the dirt carefully into the hole, and cover the dirt patch with patches of sod. She took her time, because the prospect of getting caught wasn't nearly as terrifying as what she might find in that book.

***

Melissa opened her eyes, but all she could see was pain. She didn't know pain had a color. It was a bright red film over her eyes that hid the real world. Tubes and needles hung out of her famished body—her stomach, her wrists, her nose—pumping nourishment into her. She felt so light, like she could float right off the bed. Was she lying on a bed? She must be. Softness cushioned her sharp joints.

She felt something brush past her, then a gentle hand on her face, adjusting the feeding tube.

"You're going to be okay," crooned a soft voice. A woman's. Familiar.

She'd heard that voice many times.

Her.

Melissa tried to look. Her eyes were open, at least she thought they were. All she could see was pain—jagged, dark shapes against a crimson scrim. Fabric brushed her fingers, the thick material of nurse's scrubs. A soft, icy hand closed around her arm.

Terror shot through Melissa's body.

"There, there," said the voice, cold and amused. Melissa felt the frigid hand on her hot forehead. It brushed her tenderly, though fingernails raked Melissa's skin as the hand slowly pulled away. Melissa tried to scream, but only a managed a choked squeak through the tubes and the pain.

"I'll see you soon," said the one from the woods.

The cold hand touched Melissa's arm again. After a sharp prick, the red pain dissolved into thick, black nothing.

***

Melissa was asleep now.

The Shadow slipped into the hallway, which was conveniently empty.

Melissa had recognized her. She hadn't seen the Shadow's face, but she'd known.

The Shadow smirked and ducked into a restroom to shed her nurse's scrubs and change into street clothes. On the way out, she checked the mirror; she didn't resemble herself at all, with her hair back and her lips and cheeks coated with rouge.

Not that it mattered. No one here would know her anyway.

Amazing how easily one could masquerade as a nurse on the night shift.

She stuffed the scrubs into her bag, stepped out of the restroom, and glided confidently down the hall, even smiling at the doctor who'd directed her to Melissa's room earlier. He nodded politely, with no flicker of recognition. She smiled. Coming here was stupid, unnecessary, but she had to see Melissa for herself. Invading her dreams wasn't enough anymore.

Those feeding tubes would hold Melissa for a few more days, maybe weeks, but it was too late. Nolin would come running sooner or later, and they would all finally meet and see each other as they were.

Mother, daughter, and imposter.

Chapter 41

HERE WE GO.

She'd stalled long enough. Sitting cross-legged in the middle of her bedroom floor, Nolin picked up Alexa's journal, drew in a breath, and opened the stiff cover.

No words on the first unlined page—just a drawing of a fern in soft pencil, slightly smudged. The next page: powdery, brown smudges of dirt. A pressed cottonwood leaf, perfectly preserved. Nolin flipped the pages through beautiful sketches of leaves, flowers, and a few pressed plants until she found the first words scrawled in a childlike hand:

Last night I dreamed I was running through the forest, and I fell in a hole. I wasn't hurt, but I didn't want to leave. I decided to stay there forever, and I did. I woke up disappointed to find myself in a sleeping bag on Melissa's floor. When I finally got back to sleep, I dreamed about that tree again, the giant one that's starting to fall over.

Nolin felt a jolt somewhere in her stomach. She knew exactly which tree Alexa dreamed about.

Alexa must have lost interest in writing that day, because a leafy pattern covered the rest of the page.

Nolin turned the page. She followed Alexa as she explored other holes like the ones she'd dug, and found strange tracks and objects in the woods. She recognized herself in the writing, a friend tucked between the pages like pressed leaves.

The only place I feel at home is Melissa's or in the forest. I love being in the woods, but I always feel like I'm being watched. I can't explain it.

Nolin noticed the pages were lightly smudged with dirt. The ink was smudged in a few places. Had Alexa carried this journal around with her, outside, even into the woods? A few of them were wrinkled with water damage. She hoped to hell that it was actually just water and not another fluid from the coffin. She shuddered and read on.

Alexa discovered areas where a patch of edible roots was neatly dug up in a manner unlike any other animal. She found symbols freshly scratched into trees and rocks, carefully carved animal carcasses, and strange scraps of fabric, light and translucent gray, like no cloth she'd ever seen. There were holes filled with soft grasses and small animal bones with odd teeth marks—almost human, yet deeper than human teeth could make in hard bone. Sometimes, she stumbled across simple traps, like snares fashioned from sticks and woven grasses.

She also found footprints. *The tracks look almost human, only they're smaller and longer. I've mostly found them near the big holes. I don't think these things are human. They don't seem like animals, either. Could they be something in between?*

Nolin folded a sketch between the pages, a rough drawing of the town and the forest that wrapped around it. In the woods on the map was a circle of dots with a larger X in the middle. A shiver rattled through her, and she read the page.

I've plotted the sites on a map, Alexa wrote. *They form a perfect circle, which makes me wonder what's at the center. I have a feeling that their "base," if they have one, is in the center of that circle. I'd find them there.*

The Claw Tree, Nolin realized. That was their home.

Nolin turned the page.

We're all set up to go, Alexa wrote. *Melissa's never been camping before, and technically, I haven't either, but I can handle the woods. We'll be fine.*

Melissa can't figure out why I'm doing this. I'll explain everything on the way. She'll be upset, but she'll never be able to find her way back if she walks out. She won't like it. I know she'll believe me. It will make sense to her.

That was the last entry. Alexa never made it back from that trip.

Nolin closed the book. Her brain scrambled to fit pieces into the puzzle she'd been working on the entire week.

Alexa had planned to find the goblins and tell Melissa everything. Had she gotten that far? Had Melissa learned the truth?

Nolin remembered, years ago when she asked her father about Melissa. He said she'd always had troubles, but she really went off the deep end when Alexa died. Seeing her best friend die would've been traumatizing, but did learning of Alexa's true identity have anything to do with it?

Nolin wished this would all go away. She knew it never would. Like Alexa, she'd never belong anywhere, never feel settled. All her life, she'd feel caught in between.

Maybe Alexa had the right idea, she thought. *Maybe I should find them.*

With Alexa's map, she could get there.

Nolin struggled to string her thoughts together. From the haze of her half-formed thoughts, clouded by exhaustion, she had an idea.

Her daughter.

I'll go find Melissa's daughter.

If Nolin could find Melissa's true daughter anywhere, the real Nolin, it would be at the Claw Tree. That was where she'd come from, where they'd *both* come from, Nolin and Alexa.

Nolin thought of the face she'd seen in the window the previous night. That face had always been there, watching, wanting to be found.

Nolin folded the map and slid it into her pocket. *I'm coming to find you,* she thought. *You win. I'm coming.*

Chapter 42

THICK BLOOD PUSHED through her veins. Nolin clambered to her feet, leaving the journal on the floor. Before she left the room, she glanced at the bed under the window, where her crib once stood, years ago.

That was where it all started, where she was exchanged for an innocent human baby and left to torment a poor mother for years while the true child was carried away into the woods. Who knows what happened to Melissa's daughter after that? How had she turned into the wild, haunting apparition of Nolin's dreams?

Nolin descended the stairs feeling heavy and slow, like she'd been asleep for days. The carpet felt rough under her feet. Her backpack was still propped against the couch where it had been for weeks. She bent to unzip it. Fumbling around inside it, her hand closed around the soft crocheted baby shoe. Without looking at it, she stuffed it into the pocket of her shorts along with the map.

There was something she had to do first, before she was swallowed by the woods. She had to see Melissa. She didn't know why. To apologize? To say good-bye?

Her car keys glinted on the bar in the kitchen. As she reached for them, there was a knock at the door; three sharp raps, then a pause followed by three harder ones.

Nolin froze. No one ever knocked on their door. Melissa didn't take visitors, and Nolin sure didn't want any.

She stayed quiet, hoping the visitor would leave.

Three more pounds on the door.

"Nolin, I see your car out front!" came a familiar voice. He sounded scared, frantic almost. "I know you're home."

Nolin's heart sank. *Drew.*

He pounded again. "Nolin, seriously, I'm worried about you."

Nolin's blood turned to ice, and she felt sick. He'd probably been trying to reach her, but her phone had been dead for hours. Slowly, she slunk down the hall, unlocked the door, and opened it. Drew rushed in and wrapped his arms around her, holding her tight to his chest.

"Why didn't you answer my calls?" he asked. "You were really weird the other night and I haven't been able to get a hold of you. I was really worried."

"I'm all right," Nolin said quietly. His bare arm touched her cheek; his skin was cold. She could hear his heart thudding through his tee shirt. Nolin wrapped her arms around his waist and pressed her face into his chest. She heard air rushing in and out of his lungs and felt his ribcage ripple along his back as he breathed.

"Yeah, well, I didn't know that. I was scared something happened to you. Don't scare me like that."

"I'm sorry." She didn't know what else to say. She was sorry she'd worried him, and even more sorry for what she was about to do.

He kept hold of her shoulders when he pulled away. Nolin didn't want to look at him. She felt his eyes boring into her. His thumbs pressed into the front of her shoulders.

"Look at me," he said quietly. Stubbornly, she trained her eyes on the well between his collarbones. "Nolin."

His hand slid up her neck and lifted her chin so that her eyes met his. His face was cast in shadow, but his eyes were bright, flaring like blue flames. The lines around his eyes were laced with concern.

"Nolin, what's going on?"

"You wouldn't believe me," Nolin said in what she meant to be a flat and determined tone. Her voice cracked on the word me. Her throat felt dry and constricted.

"Is this about your mom?"

Nolin nodded without breaking her gaze. What could she say?

Drew sighed deeply, his jaw tightening. He brought his other hand to her cheek to cup her face, holding her focus to him. "Nolin," he started, his voice quivering with frustration, "I don't know what the hell is up with you. Something's going on. I don't know what it is or if I can help, but I'm not an idiot. I don't like being left in the dark. I'm worried about you."

Nolin bit her lip. Part of her wanted to tell him every last thing, no matter how ridiculous it sounded. Maybe then it would dissolve into nothing like a bad dream. Maybe she could forget all about it.

No. She'd hidden from it all her life, and she could never outrun it. She'd have to go.

"I don't belong here," she whispered. For the first time, fear welled up inside of her, about what she was about to do, what she'd find out there.

"Of course you don't; you belong somewhere way better than here," Drew said.

"That's not what I mean. I don't belong..." she nearly said *with people*, but that wasn't quite right, either. Instead, she pressed her lips together.

"Where?" Drew said. "Here? Like, *Earth*?" His eyes grew wide and his eyebrows disappeared under his messy dark hair. "Nolin, please tell me you're not thinking what I think you're thinking."

Nolin shook her head. He didn't understand. Then again, maybe he did. Maybe that was *exactly* what she meant.

She had no plans for what would happen after she entered the woods. She wasn't sure if she'd ever come back out. All she knew was that Melissa's real daughter deserved her life back, and Melissa needed to see her true daughter again. Maybe she couldn't fix things. Even so, she had to do what she could.

Maybe he understood perfectly.

"You are..." he said breathlessly, releasing her and running a hand through his hair, looking down at his feet, chewing his lip.

"Drew," Nolin said, forcing her voice to stay steady. "Everything's all right."

"No," he said hoarsely, "no it's not. I may not have known you for long, but I know you. You're not telling me something, and you're thinking of doing something stupid. I know you are."

Nolin crossed her arms, standing up straight. "Look, I'm sorry I came barging into your life. I just came back to check on my mom. Just...just forget I ever came back, okay?"

Drew looked at the floor and shook his head slowly. "Nolin," he said, "I could never forget you because I never *forgot* you. You were gone for ten years, and I always wondered what happened to you." He glanced up at her, his cheeks tinged red. "Sorry if that's weird, I mean...I didn't think about you all the time...you were my friend, though. Then you came back, and it was like you'd never left. And now all this, everything we've done and talked about... you think I could just forget all that?"

Something inside Nolin was tearing in two. "*Why?*" she asked.

Drew shrugged. "You're the most genuine person I knew. You see things differently. You're strong. You don't take shit from anyone, even if it bites you in the ass. And I've never known someone who *cares* so much, about anything."

Nolin's steel faltered. She drew in a sharp, painful breath. "I'm sorry, I really have to go..." She stepped toward the door. His hand slipped around her arm, gently holding her back.

"Nolin..." he started. He took her face in his hands, his thumbs brushing over her cheekbones. Then, he lifted her chin and kissed her.

The ice in Nolin's veins melted. Through the pain and terror inside her, something else rose to the surface.

Drew pulled away and held his forehead to hers. "I should have done that weeks ago."

Something in Nolin screamed for her to stop, but her hands rose to his waist, and she found herself tipping her mouth upward to meet his.

He took the invitation and backed her against the wall, pressing his body into hers. She ran her hands beneath his shirt, up the sides of his ribs, his back. His mouth moved on hers as he slid his hands into her hair, then down her neck and over her back. Goose bumps prickled on her arms and legs. Nolin inhaled as Drew kissed her neck, her collarbones. His breath was warm on her skin. She felt his hands inside her tank top and the warm skin of his stomach on hers. She groped for the hem of his shirt and reached up to pull it over his head.

For a few moments, Nolin forgot what she had to do, lost in a blur of skin and heat. She hadn't realized how much she wanted this. For weeks she'd stuffed her feelings down until they broke through. It felt like the most natural thing in the world. Nothing existed outside the two of them. Nothing else mattered.

She wrapped her arms around his neck to pull him closer, breathing in his scent of soil and freshly cut grass, pressing her lips to his shoulder.

Then her eyes fluttered open and fell on the window in the living room. The trees swayed, and she remembered. She had to leave, though she didn't want to. But how? He'd never let her out of his sight after this.

"Drew..." she whispered.

"Mmm," he responded. He kissed under her ear and slid his fingers beneath the waistband of her shorts.

With every ounce of willpower she possessed, she put her hands on his chest and gently pushed him away. He didn't protest. His hands stayed on her waist.

"I'm sorry," he said. "I didn't mean to make you uncomfortable."

"You didn't," Nolin said. It was true. Her mind wandered briefly, playing out the scenario to its inevitable conclusion. She could still feel the ghost of his touch on her bare hips beneath her shorts. "This just isn't the right time," she finished.

He closed his eyes and nodded. "I know."

Nolin trickled her fingers down his chest. The sooner they got this over with, the better.

"I'm sorry for everything," she said. "A lot of strange things have been happening, and I'm just not thinking clearly. I think I need to go see my mom."

He nodded again. "I'll take you." Nolin was afraid of that. He kissed her forehead and bent to retrieve his shirt from the floor. Nolin watched sadly as he turned it right-side-out and pulled it over his head. Her entire body still tingled.

"No, it's fine," she said quickly. "I'm not going to make you spend your evening in a hospital."

"I don't mind," he insisted. He was suspicious. Nolin could tell because he wasn't looking at her.

He kissed her briefly before taking her hand, and they left the house. Nolin resisted the urge to take one last look inside before she closed the door behind them. She allowed Drew to lead her to the truck and open her door, and she stole a final glance at the house. Was she happy to see it for the last time? She couldn't tell. Maybe she'd be happy if she were going somewhere better. She wasn't sure if where she was going was better or worse.

Drew's hand slipped into hers and squeeze gently as they drove away. Her eyes drifted to the woods.

Maybe she could forget it. She could stay with him, follow him when he left for school and never think about this town again. Whatever lived in those woods could stay there.

But Melissa might be dying. Her real daughter was out there somewhere. Nolin had to make things right, one way or the other.

She squeezed back a little harder, drawing strength from him, because she would need more strength than ever to risk seeing him for the last time.

Chapter 43

DREW DIDN'T LET go of her hand until they reached the waiting room.

"Family only," said the nurse at the desk, a thin, middle-aged woman in blue scrubs.

Drew squeezed Nolin's hand before letting go. Her hand felt cold without his. Suddenly, she felt alone.

Drew chose a chair that faced the hallway where Melissa's room was. Nolin wanted to tell him good-bye, or at least turn to look at him, but he'd know she was up to something. She felt his eyes on her as she walked down the stark hall to Melissa's shared room. She was careful to walk steadily, unflinching under his gaze, to give no sign of her intentions.

Good-bye, she thought as she stepped into the room. She hoped beyond hope that she'd see him again, but she knew better than to get optimistic.

Melissa was asleep, still wrapped in a web of tubes. Nolin raised a hand to her neck, remembering the sting of tranquilizers, painkillers, and who knows what else being shot into her own veins years before. The fine hairs on her arms stood straight up. Her breathing grew shallow and her legs twitched to run away. She forced herself to stand fast. She wouldn't be here long.

Melissa looked so weak in the hospital bed, barely a bump under the thin blankets. Nolin tried to imagine her as that young, wild girl in the yearbook photos, her face streaked with paint as she swept the brush over a theater backdrop. She imagined Melissa laughing, eyes sparkling and hair long and full rather than brittle. That girl was a ghost. Now, Nolin only saw sharp cheekbones, deep purple circles under Melissa's sunken eyes, and hair dull as straw.

Now that she was there, she wasn't sure what to say or do. Melissa wasn't even awake. She took Melissa's limp hand. It was cold; the skin was dry and rough. Nolin gathered words that floated around her mind, tried to wrestle them into coherent sentences.

"I'm sorry," Nolin finally said. "I'm so sorry. For everything."

She paused, half-expecting Melissa to wake, for her features to take on the constant glare she wore around Nolin. Nothing. Her chest rose and fell softly, her nest of tubes rising with her.

Nolin went on. "I just want you to know that I never meant to hurt you, or anyone else. This isn't what you bargained for. You had a daughter, and she was stolen, and you got me. I was never your daughter. You knew that. Maybe not consciously, but on some level, you knew what I was. What I am. And now I know it, too. I know I don't belong here, so I'm going to make things right." She swallowed hard. "I'm going to find your daughter."

Nolin carefully placed Melissa's hand at her side on the bed.

It was time.

Nolin chewed her lip, thinking how she could leave the room without Drew noticing. The room had one door. Hospital windows didn't open—she'd learned that in the mental ward. Could she tell him she had to use the restroom? No, he'd wait by the door like a watchdog. He'd know she was going to do something stupid.

How could she leave without being seen?

A tingling sensation prickled in her fingers, up her arms, and down her legs. A thought popped into her head, one that didn't seem to come from her own mind: *I won't be seen if I don't want to be seen.*

It made no sense. Her legs moved on their own. She approached the door and peered down the hall as far as she could without poking her head out of the doorway.

There was a stairwell across and down the hall about twelve feet. If Drew wasn't looking for just a second, she could dart out of the room and down the stairs. How would she know if he looked away? If she peeked to see whether he was watching, he'd see her.

Nolin stood on the side of the doorway where she could see the stairwell. Her fingers tingled, and a thought that she suspected wasn't hers drifted across her mind.

He's not looking. Go.

Voices moved down the hallway from the direction of the waiting room. Without thinking, she stepped out in front of a group of doctors making their way down the hall. She peeked over her shoulder. Five male doctors walked behind her, all taller than she was, hiding her from view of the waiting room.

When she got to the stairwell, she stepped inside it. She paused, listening for frantic footsteps down the hall, Drew calling her name, or the protests of the nurse at the desk. Nothing. He hadn't seen her.

Nolin ran down the stairs, adrenaline pumping, and dread pooling deep in her gut like ice water.

Four floors down, Nolin reached the lobby and nearly ran out the front door, throwing one more look over her shoulder to make sure she wasn't being followed. It wouldn't be long before Drew realized she'd left. He'd come looking her. By then, she'd be somewhere he wouldn't know to look.

Nolin crossed the parking lot and the street to the woods. She groped at her pockets for Alexa's map. She felt nothing. It was gone. The shoe was missing, too. Frantically, she checked all of her pockets and scanned the ground around her. *Damn.*

Time was tight; she couldn't backtrack.

She'd find the way on her own. She knew she would. At the edge of the woods, she stared into the trees and took a deep breath. The dreams of walking to the Claw Tree played in her mind. They always started somewhere in the woods, never at her house or anywhere she knew.

Maybe it was always supposed to be this way.

She knew where to go. Without looking back, Nolin stepped into the trees and veered slightly to the left, walking purposefully, letting her insides go numb, willing herself to forget what she was leaving behind.

In her pocket, her phone vibrated. She didn't need to look to see who it was.

Grief sliced through her as she reached into her pocket, slipped out the phone, and dropped it on the ground.

She walked deeper into the trees.

***

The Shadow sat before the Claw Tree, gazing into its canopy. The thick, serpentine branches cut the blue sky above into puzzle pieces. Her eyes traced their familiar lines, and she waited.

Nolin was coming.

Chapter 44

NOLIN HAD NO way of knowing how far or even how long she'd walked through the silent woods. She crept like a thief, constantly glancing up to the treetops, half-expecting a goblin ambush at any second. No sounds of birds or insects. The whole forest watched.

Though she didn't know where she was going, something told her she was headed in the right direction. After all, she'd found the Claw Tree once before—that day she'd fled the playground and run into the woods. The tree was like a beacon. She'd always known the way.

What would happen once she got there? She hadn't given it much thought.

Did Alexa have a plan when she entered the forest with Melissa? Did she intend to find her human counterpart, to return to the woods for good, or did she have something else in mind? Nolin suspected Alexa hadn't thought it through either, that she was driven into the woods by the same force that propelled Nolin: desperation, guilt, and the exhaustion of living in a world where she didn't belong.

Nolin shivered. She wrapped her arms around herself and trudged forward, stepping over fallen logs, clumps of bushes, rocks, around holes. Without thinking, she steered herself to the right.

It was like walking through her dreams. She felt surreal, her mind full of fog and the edges of her vision not quite clear. The woods took on an odd glow, like the trees were giving off their own light instead of being lit by the columns of sunlight that managed to shine through the thick canopy. In a way, it was magical.

Still, she couldn't shake the feeling she was walking to her execution. She felt like a condemned woman climbing the steps to the gallows for a crime she hadn't meant to commit. Whether she'd meant to commit that crime or not, she had to try to make things right.

But how? When she found Nolin, the real Nolin, how would she get her back? How would she get her out of the woods and to her mother?

Her temples started to throb. She'd have to figure that out when it came up, she decided. She didn't know what she was getting herself into; there was no way to prepare for the unknown.

The real Nolin.

Nolin.

That name was stolen, like everything else in her life.

Melissa wasn't her mother.

The house she'd grown up in wasn't her house.

Would Drew have wanted to be with the real Nolin?

The thought of him felt like a punch in the gut. She pushed him out of her mind, along with the name that was never hers.

Do I have a real name?

It didn't matter, she decided. Nothing mattered except getting to the Tree and finding Nolin. Only then would the relentless guilt leave, and when everyone was back where they belonged.

The light faded. Night would fall in a few hours. She clambered on, feeling more and more like she was entering a different part of the forest, something mysterious and ancient. The ringing silence took on a deeper, lower tone like a gong. The trees stood straighter. The rocks and boulders became larger and more jagged, coated with soft, green moss. The smell stirred something inside Nolin: excitement, memories she couldn't quite place.

She noticed rocks, a few misshapen trees, and a berry patch that looked familiar. The farther she walked, the surer she was she'd been there before.

Not much farther.

***

Melissa's head throbbed. The painkillers in her system were wearing off. Her limbs were full of needles. Her face was a tangle of tubes poking into her nose and down her throat. Horror pulsed through her veins.

Nolin was going into the woods. What had she learned?

Melissa made her decision in an instant: She was going after her.

One by one, she pulled out the tubes. Needles slid out of her skin, and she dropped them on the mattress. Flecks of crimson blood speckled the starched white sheets. Finally, she peeled up the tape on her cheek that held the feeding tube in place and grasped the thin hose that threaded into her nose and down her throat.

Her hands shook as she slowly pulled on the tube. A sharp pain in her nostrils made her eyes water, and she forced herself not to cry out. Something in her throat tickled, then scratched. The end of the tube climbed up her esophagus. She started to gag.

She paused, a short rest. Pinching her eyes shut and taking a deep breath, Melissa counted to three in her mind, then gave the tube one last tug.

The end of the tube shot up past the back of her throat and through her nose until it dropped out in her hand. She retched on the bed, her eyes watering and throat burning. Her torso heaved. Drops of blood splattered on her arms from her nose, and she wiped them on the bedsheet.

Now she had to get out. She knew she could do it. Slipping out of the hospital unseen wouldn't be the problem.

The woods...the thought of what she'd find there wrapped her with terror. Something deep and primal stirred within her, a long-dormant instinct: protective, intuitive, benevolent. She'd felt glimmers of this feeling over the years, but nothing like this. The pain dimmed, and a manic strength returned to her body.

She had to save her daughter.

***

She was close.

Nolin didn't think it was possible for the woods to grow quieter. Instead of ringing in her ears, the silence whooshed, like the wings of a bird taking flight. It was almost nightfall. The ground felt different beneath her feet. It seemed to move, rising and falling softly. Grasses and ferns around her twitched in unison with the whooshing noise and the rising and falling of the soil.

Nolin looked down. Trickles of soil fell away from her feet, and she thought she rose an inch. She heard an unmistakable inhale that seemed to come from her own mind. The ground was moving.

Were the woods...*breathing*?

As she inhaled, the ground swelled. When she exhaled, it fell. *The forest is alive*, she realized. She wasn't sure if this scared her or comforted her. No wonder she'd always felt like the trees had eyes.

Nolin's instincts told her to run, but she kept walking. Even if the ground was breathing, breathing couldn't hurt her. Within minutes, the trees thinned. Ahead, Nolin saw a clearing. Her heart slammed against her chest. This had to be it.

She stood before the massive, tilted tree, its ancient black bark twisted and lumpy, its branches speckled with small leaves. Her dreams had come to life. Her foggy childhood memories of the place suddenly felt razor sharp. The smells, the sounds, the strange feeling of this part of the woods—she remembered everything.

At the foot of the Claw Tree sat a pale figure, her back to Nolin. A mass of tangled dark hair fell down her back. She wore a long, gray garment that reflected the dying light like soft metal. The girl sat still, legs crossed, watching the sparse canopy of the tree. Her white skin was almost transparent, ghostly in the fading light.

Nolin froze, her breath caught in her throat.

Was that the real Nolin? Another goblin? She had no idea. Why didn't she think of what to say or do when she found her? Now that she was here, her mind was blank.

Nolin cleared her throat to kick-start her voice. "Nolin?" she said. The name felt strange in her mouth. The girl didn't stir.

A soft voice whispered in Nolin's ear. It didn't seem to come from the figure before her, but from the forest itself.

You're here, it said.

The voice was gentle and delicate, with an edge of suppressed emotion. It was like a cold touch to the back of Nolin's neck. Goose bumps erupted over her body.

This *was* her, the real Nolin.

There was no turning back. She had to finish this.

"I know who you are," Nolin said. Her voice quavered like a leaf in an icy breeze. "I'm here to bring you home."

No. I am home. You've *come home.*

Nolin hadn't expected that. It never occurred to her that perhaps the girl wouldn't want to leave the woods. Nolin didn't understand.

Sit with me.

The ground beneath Nolin's feet heaved slightly. The rushing sound filled her ears again, like a sigh. She took a tentative step forward. The leaves of the Claw Tree twitched as the ground beneath it exhaled.

Nolin approached the figure slowly. The girl was small, about Nolin's size. She was very thin. Though her wavy hair was matted and dirty, it shone in the evening sun.

Nolin's calves twitched. Something inside her wanted to run. Ignoring her impulses, she rounded to the girl's side and lowered herself to a sitting position a few feet beside her. Nolin's stomach twisted itself in knots. Sweat beaded in her hairline, palms, and the groove of her back.

The girl gazed up into the canopy serenely. Nolin knew that face. She'd seen it in her dreams, staring back at her when she'd woken beneath the Claw Tree when she was ten, and in the window only nights ago, but somewhere else, too. There was something oddly familiar about her. Nolin couldn't quite place it.

The girl's eyes were so dark they were nearly black. Nolin couldn't see a difference from the irises to the pupils. Her narrow face was smooth and ageless; she could have been in her twenties or her forties. It was impossible to tell. Her frosty-white lips parted slightly. The cheekbones, nose, and chin were sharp. Her eyelashes were long, strangely pale like feathers.

I've been waiting for you for a long time.

Her lips moved slightly. The voice was curiously disembodied, emanating from the girl but at the same time, from Nolin's mind. It was so soft and sharp at once, like a cold puff of air.

I've been calling you for years, in your dreams, in your mind. I was starting to worry. No matter, you're here now.

This wasn't what Nolin was expecting at all. She'd expected anger or fear, for this girl to be completely feral, anything but this.

Still, something about it made sense. All her life, she'd felt the woods calling her, both in her dreams and when she was awake.

"It was all you," Nolin said. "You...you spoke to me in dreams? Those dreams about this tree, those were from you?"

The girl turned and looked Nolin in the eye. The face was expressionless, the eyes cold and flat. Her gaze fell on Nolin like a bucket of ice water.

I had to show you the way. The girl said. *I had to remind you. That's how you got here all those years ago, when you hid here. You already knew the way because I showed you.*

"You've been following me all my life," said Nolin. "Following Melissa. You've watched us both."

Yes. I have.

"You wanted me to come here."

The girl nodded, her eyes never leaving Nolin's.

"You always knew who I was, who Melissa is. That she was your mother, and that I was"—she fumbled for words—"who you were supposed to be."

The girl's eyebrows knit together.

No.

"No?" Nolin repeated. Something wasn't adding up.

Melissa isn't my mother.

"But..." Nolin was confused. "Are you, weren't you Nolin Styre?"

The girl's expression softened. She looked away, her eyes focused straight ahead on the trunk of the tree.

No. I'm not. I wasn't.

Nolin couldn't believe it. She sat up straight and her mouth dropped open slightly. Her mind spun. What was going on?

"Then who are you?"

The corners of the girl's lips turned up. The effect didn't warm her cold face. *You read my journal. Your mother knows me well. Much better than you know.*

Realization dawned on Nolin like a punch in the stomach. The threads she'd woven together into a flimsy understanding of her life unraveled before her eyes.

"Alexa?"

Chapter 45

ALEXA SMILED, HER features softening for the first time. Now Nolin saw her age. It wasn't marked in lines on her face because there were none. It was her demeanor. Nolin sensed a weariness about her that echoed the weariness Melissa wore like a shawl. This was Melissa's childhood friend, the one whose supposed death triggered decades of mental illness and led the whole town to believe that Melissa was a murderer. All these years of being followed and watched. It was always Alexa.

"Does Melissa know?" Nolin asked.

Alexa nodded.

"She knows you're alive. She knows you're still here."

Alexa nodded again, then chuckled. The curve of her throat twitched. The sound might have been branches clicking together in the treetops.

No wonder Melissa is half-insane. At least that much made sense. Nolin had so many questions, she didn't know where to start.

"You've been spying on me. On us," Nolin said. "*Why?*"

Alexa's smile faded, and she looked at her hands in her lap, fiddling with her fingers.

"I was lonely."

Her voice startled Nolin. She spoke out loud this time, truly out loud, not in Nolin's mind or through the woods. Nolin wondered if Alexa could tell the difference, if she could control it.

"You were lonely," Nolin repeated.

Alexa nodded. "Of all people, you understand what it's like to be alone, stuck in a world where you don't belong. I wanted someone who understood. That's why I called you here." She twined her fingers around each other in her lap. "I wanted a daughter."

"A daughter?" Nolin's mind grasped at what she heard. Her head wasn't working properly. She felt like she could only stupidly repeat Alexa's words.

Alexa nodded again, more eagerly. She turned around to face Nolin. Nolin could see the outline of her slim torso through the sheer material of her garment. Alexa took Nolin's hands in hers. Nolin wanted to pull her hands away, but she didn't. She wanted answers.

"Whose body did they bury?" Nolin asked. "In your grave. Who is it?"

Alexa looked down again. "It was a goblin."

"A goblin." Nolin didn't like this at all.

"I came back to the forest to make sure I belonged here," Alexa went on. "With your mother all those years ago. It didn't go as I'd hoped, but here we are. It didn't take the goblins long to find me." She shuddered. "They took me because I knew their secrets. They were vicious. I'm probably lucky they didn't eat me."

Nolin couldn't believe what she was hearing. Alexa continued.

"One night, years later, they stole another child. It's their way, to ensure their survival and widen the gene pool for breeding. It still felt wrong to me. So I returned the baby boy they'd stolen. I thought about raising him, but I couldn't. It wasn't right." Alexa swallowed. Her dark eyes pleaded with Nolin. "Something happened to me that night," she went on. "It changed me. I was so lonely. That night I realized I wanted a child, but not just any child."

"You wanted...me?" Nolin said, her throat dry. Alexa nodded.

"My old friend Melissa had a special daughter. She didn't deserve you. I watched how she mistreated you, Nolin, and I knew I could do better. I would never have hurt you the way she did." Alexa's eyes filled with tears. Her white lips buckled. "I couldn't just steal you, though; that would be wrong. I'd be no better than the goblins. I knew you'd have to come to me by choice. I wanted you to *choose* me." Alexa's frigid hands shook.

"So I showed you the way. I took you from your crib one night and brought you here." She looked up at the tree, smiling. "This tree is special, Nolin. It was sacred to the goblins. It connects all our minds together. It connects us to the woods and to what little magic we still have. No one can find this place if they don't already know where it is. You have to be shown."

It was too much. Everything Nolin ever wanted to know poured on her at once. The dreams, the confusion—it was always Alexa, with the Claw Tree as her instrument.

Nolin sat, dumbfounded. "How?"

Alexa scrambled to her feet excitedly, dragging Nolin with her toward the tree. Panic rose in Nolin's throat. She forced herself to calm down. Alexa led her under the tree into the pile of leaves, then reached for a thin vine that dangled from the trunk.

"Take this," she ordered.

Nolin took the branch in her fingers, uneasily wondering what to do while Alexa watched expectantly.

"Listen," said Alexa.

Nolin didn't know what she was supposed to be listening to. She trained her ears hard, searching for any subtle sound, anything Alexa wanted her to hear.

A bolt of panic shot through Nolin's body and she gasped, nearly dropping the branch. It felt strange, like the panic wasn't hers. Alexa grabbed Nolin's hand and held the vine in place. "You feel it, don't you? Close your eyes."

Nolin obeyed. A blurry vision of the town swam in her mind's eye. She was driving a truck, frantically wheeling around corners, panic-stricken. She realized her hands weren't hers. They were larger, rougher. Her body felt too big.

Alexa released her hand so the vine would slip out of Nolin's fingers.

"What the hell was that?" Nolin demanded.

Alexa smiled. "That's how I know you so well. How I speak to you. Through this tree, I can see what you see and feel what you feel."

"So I was seeing through someone else?" Nolin asked, breathless. "Wait...was that Drew?"

Alexa beamed and nodded eagerly. "That's how the tree works. Once the tree knows you, it's always with you. It can see you. And we can communicate."

"You've been spying on me through this tree?" Nolin asked, flabbergasted. "When you're not peeking through my window or sneaking into my house?"

"Sometimes," Alexa admitted. "I can only *show* you things when you're asleep, in dreams."

Nolin wasn't sure how she felt about this. The word *violated* came to mind.

"So, the tree has to know you. So why Drew?" Nolin asked. "Why does the tree know..." Then it dawned on her. "Drew? It was *Drew*? The boy the goblins took?"

Alexa smiled, her eyes glazed like she was recalling a treasured memory. "He wasn't here for a full night. He won't remember, but the tree remembers him. It doesn't matter. He wouldn't understand. It's *you* I wanted."

Nolin shook her head incredulously.

Alexa leaned over, plucked something from a lump of leaves, and offered it to Nolin—a pink crocheted baby shoe.

Nolin took the shoe and rolled it over in her hand. It was exactly like the one she'd found in Melissa's studio.

"I'm not a changeling," Nolin said tonelessly.

Alexa shook her head.

"Melissa's my real mother."

"Yes."

Nolin let that sink in. Was she relieved? Disappointed? She couldn't tell. Mostly, she was just confused.

"She shouldn't be, though," Alexa said darkly. "She doesn't know you. She's never seen how amazing you are. She treated you terribly." Nolin flinched as Alexa put a cold hand on her arm.

"I knew you when you were a child," she went on. "You were so smart, so special. I spoke to you through the woods every day, gave you dreams every night. I knew I could give you better. I tried to take your mother's place so I could take care of you and we could be together. Paul would have none of it..."

"Wait, my dad?" Nolin said suddenly. "When did you meet my dad? You disappeared long before he met..." The parts slid into place, and she understood. "It was you?" Nolin said. "The woman on the phone that night?"

Alexa smiled. "Do you really think he wouldn't be looking for someone else?" she said. "Melissa was a disaster. We talked about him leaving her and bringing you with him. I didn't know if you'd ever come here on your own, so I tried to come to you."

Nolin's mind reeled. "Did he know what you are?"

Alexa's smile wavered. "No. I was just a girl in town to him. He didn't need to know. I just needed to look like a better choice than the mess he was married to."

Nolin shook her head. "I don't believe this. What makes you think I would have bought that?"

Alexa smiled gently, like a rusty nail dipped in sugar. "Because," she said, "we were great friends. Paul would always drop you off with me when you had to come home from school early. We thought it would warm you up to the idea so it would be easier when we finally told you."

Nolin saw stars. The world seem to spin, and she was glad she was sitting down. "No, no. Ms. Savage? You? The whole time?" Nolin stared hard at Alexa's face. She could see it now. Contacts, makeup, clothes, hair tied back. A completely different persona.

"That's why your face was scribbled out in all the photos," Nolin said. "Melissa didn't do that. You broke into my house and did it yourself. So I wouldn't recognize you." Nolin doubted she would have anyway. The strange woman in front of her was nothing like the librarian that befriended her.

Alexa nodded, seemingly glad that Nolin was understanding. "I didn't want you to know before you were ready. I thought it would upset you."

"Well you're right. I'm upset," Nolin said, her voice shaking. "You manipulated me. For years."

Alexa's smile disappeared. "I wanted to help you," she said, hurt, a dangerous edge to her voice. "Melissa was a terrible mother. I had to save you, one way or the other."

"So why didn't you just take me when I ran out here?" Nolin demanded. "I ran away from school and came straight to you. Isn't that what you wanted?"

"Your mind was gone," Alexa snapped, sitting up straight. "You didn't choose it. You didn't come to me; you had a nervous breakdown and ran away. I couldn't take you like that." She shook her head. "Letting those men take you away was one of the hardest things I've ever done, but you needed to heal and learn for yourself. You needed to be whole, not just wander here by accident."

Nolin shook her head, then pushed herself up and climbed out from under the tree. Alexa scrambled after her.

"Wait! I know this is hard for you to hear. It's all true. I just want the best for you, I swear."

Nolin tramped toward the tree line. The ground breathed under her feet, and she felt disoriented, unbalanced.

"Melissa was your friend," Nolin said. "Why would you do that? You drove her insane!"

Alexa's hand closed around Nolin's arm, pulling her back. "You don't know anything about her," Alexa said, her voice low and dangerous. "You don't know who she is or what she did. She left me for *dead*, Nolin. Would a friend do that?"

Nolin turned to face Alexa. They were exactly the same height, the same build, had the same wild hair. *She really could be my mother*, Nolin thought.

But she wasn't.

"Melissa looked for you," Nolin said. "You fell down that ravine and she looked, and when she couldn't find you she went back to town to get help."

A vein throbbed in Alexa's temple. Color bloomed in her pale cheeks. "She *threw* me down that ravine when she found out what I was!" she hissed. "When she found out I was alive, she didn't try to find me. She was no friend. She resented me. Always. I'm sure you read all about it." She spat the last sentences. A fleck of spittle landed on Nolin's cheek.

The muscles in Nolin's face stiffened. Was it true? Melissa had been a murder suspect, but she was never tried. There was no evidence; only speculation.

"There were bruises on her arms," Nolin remembered from the newspaper clipping. "Finger marks."

Alexa's nodded, a relieved smile touching her face.

"Yes," she said. "We fought. I told her why we were really there. At first she thought I'd dragged us on a wild goose chase. Then she believed me. She was furious." Her voice cracked, and tears sparkled in her black eyes. "She was stronger than me. I tried to hold on or throw her off me, but I couldn't. She threw me over the edge. I was hurt. And *they* found me." She stood up straighter. "Please believe me."

Nolin didn't know what to think. Alexa's white lips pressed together, eyes glimmering with tears. She took a tentative step forward, then reached her arms out and embraced Nolin.

Her arms and body were like cold stone. Nolin carefully hugged her back. Nolin could feel every bone in her torso. In that moment, Alexa reminded Nolin so much of Melissa.

A wave of sympathy passed through Nolin. Alexa had been alone for years, abandoned, forgotten. Her life couldn't have been easy in the woods or in the human world. Was this the right thing? Was this how it was supposed to be?

Alexa stiffened in Nolin's arms. Over Alexa's shoulder, Nolin noticed a strange rock on the ground about ten feet away, half grey and half brown, about the size of a grapefruit. She wasn't sure why it caught her eye. Before she could think about it, Alexa jerked away.

"Do you hear that?" Alexa said, staring into the trees.

"Hear what?" Nolin listened.

Something moved in the trees. Nolin heard a soft rustling of undergrowth.

Without warning, Alexa sprinted into the trees faster than Nolin had seen any person run. She leapt between the white tree trunks until she was only a pale blur. A yelp, a scream, then a thud, followed by furious thrashing of the ground cover as Alexa marched back, dragging something with her. Someone was screaming.

Alexa stepped into the clearing, her face a mask of fury, pulling Melissa by the hair. The hospital gown had ridden up around Melissa's waist. One of her hips was still encased in gauze and plaster, but that seemed to be the least of her concerns. Melissa kicked and shrieked, clawing helplessly at any part of Alexa she could reach.

"Sticking your nose where it doesn't belong, as usual," Alexa spat. She yanked Melissa to her feet by her hair.

"While you're here," Alexa said to Melissa, "I think you have something to tell your daughter." Melissa put most of her weight on her good leg. The remaining color drained from her face.

Nolin felt sick. Her lungs seized in her chest. Alexa marched the hobbling Melissa closer, only to throw her at Nolin's feet. Melissa shrieked in pain as she hit the ground. Automatically, Nolin stooped to help her, but Alexa tugged Melissa away by the arm.

"No, no. She's fine. Let her stand up on her own." Alexa left Melissa and crossed to stand by Nolin's side. "Tell her who you are," Alexa demanded. "Tell her who I am. She needs to know."

Nolin gaped at Melissa, torn between wanting to help and needing to hear whatever Alexa was ordering her to say. "Tell me what?" she asked quietly.

Melissa panted as she heaved herself to her feet, leaning on her good leg and yanking the gown down to cover herself. Her legs were scratched, and her nose was bleeding. With a sick jolt, Nolin wondered whether Melissa had removed the feeding tube herself. How had she gotten out of the hospital? How had she dragged herself all this way with a broken hip, to a place that couldn't be found except by those who knew the way?

She knows the way, Nolin realized.

Something was missing.

"Tell me what?" Nolin said again, louder, her voice ringing with anger.

Melissa stood, her face screwed up with pain and grief.

357

"I'm not Melissa Michaels," she said finally, her voice raspy and coarse. She nodded at Alexa. "She is."

Chapter 46

"WHAT?" NOLIN ASKED, her voice thin and faint. "What the hell does that mean?"

"She means," Alexa said gently, taking Nolin's hand in what was probably meant to be a comforting manner, "that she is a goblin. She was switched at birth for a human child—me. I was Melissa Michaels."

Nolin's insides felt numb. Only an hour ago, she'd thought she knew the truth, and that disappearing into the woods would make everything right. Now she didn't know what was real.

She wasn't sure she wanted the truth anymore.

Alexa squeezed her hand. It might have been meant as a gentle squeeze, but she was strong. Her frigid skin made Nolin shiver.

"She was never meant to be your mother, Nolin," Alexa said softly. "Her life wasn't supposed to be hers. Everything she's ever had was stolen from me, including you."

A lump formed in Nolin's throat. She thought she might be sick. She pressed her free hand to her mouth and squeezed her eyes shut. Melissa whimpered in pain, but she stayed on her feet.

This wasn't real. It couldn't be.

"You were always afraid to go outside," Nolin said quietly to Melissa. "You were afraid of the woods."

Alexa smiled coldly. "She's afraid of what she is," Alexa said, her voice edged with malice. "She was scared of what the forest would do to her. It would turn her into a monster, so she stayed inside and tried to forget, starved herself into nothing so she could never be what she truly is." Melissa swayed with her hospital gown billowing around her, staring at her scratched and bare feet. Tears rolled off her grimy cheeks and splattered in the dirt.

Alexa went on. "She never embraced her true nature, so she lost it. Goblins are born, but they also have to be made. I was born human, then the forest changed me. We've all chosen what we are."

Melissa said nothing, looking miserably at Nolin. Her empty gray eyes seared like a brand.

Nolin released Alexa's hand and crossed her arms over her chest. "How long have you known?" she asked Melissa.

Melissa tried to clear her throat and coughed before speaking. "Since she brought me here, when we were seventeen. She told me then."

"And you believed her?"

Melissa's eyes turned to her feet. "I didn't at first. Then we came here, and I remembered. I realized that the dreams I'd had all my life weren't dreams. I was different, and that's when I found out why."

"My parents never liked her," Alexa piped up. "They knew, deep down, that she wasn't theirs. I fit in so perfectly. They told me they wanted to adopt me, but they already had two children to support." She glared at Melissa, who returned her steely gaze with her own.

"You lived with humans," said Nolin. "If you were stolen, why didn't you live in the woods?"

Alexa smiled grimly. "I was found in these woods by hikers when I was very young. I must have escaped, and I was very sick. They took me to the hospital and I was placed in a foster home. I grew up like a normal child, more or less. No one knew who I was. I didn't even know who I was."

Nolin didn't think her brain could absorb anything else, but she still wanted to know. So many holes in this story that intertwined with her own. If she didn't know now, she never would. And she would always wonder.

"And you went to school and met Melissa," Nolin said flatly, not looking at either of them. She stared blankly at the forest floor a few feet in front of her. "Did you know what you were, and what she was?"

Alexa shook her head. She looked like she was getting impatient. "I didn't at first," she said, exasperation in her voice. "I thought my memories were only bad dreams or stories I'd imagined. I was so young when the goblins left me. I realized the dreams weren't dreams when I started exploring the woods and finding places I dreamed about. I started to remember. Then I started to dream about my parents. *Her* parents. They were memories too. The more I remembered, the more obsessed I became with the woods, and the more I wanted to go there to be sure. So we went into the woods together, and I told Melissa. Then she threw me down that slope and left me for dead."

"I didn't mean for you to fall," Melissa said, her voice thin and raspy. "You attacked me."

Alexa ignored her.

361

"What?" Nolin said, turning to Alexa. "Attacked?"

"She's lying," Alexa said simply, arms crossed.

Nolin looked from Alexa to Melissa, and suddenly realized how similar they looked. Similar builds, the same pointy nose and chin, same narrow face that Nolin herself also possessed. The middles of their eyebrows creased in exactly the same way when they glared.

"How am I supposed to trust either of you?" Nolin demanded. "I can't believe a damn thing either of you say!"

"She's lying," Alexa said again. "She's been lying to you your whole life."

"You posed as a librarian for twenty years," Nolin shot back.

Alexa shrugged.

"You attacked me, and you slipped," Melissa said to Alexa. Her knees buckled, but she held herself steady. Her hairline was dark with sweat, and her forehead began to shine. She coughed again, holding the side of her fist against her mouth. When she dropped her hand back to her side, Nolin saw drops of blood flecked over her skin.

Alexa shook her head. "None of this matters," she said. "The only important thing is what Nolin thinks."

"I think this is insane," said Nolin.

"I know, I know," Alexa cooed. She turned to Nolin and reached to touch her face. Nolin jerked away. "I know this is confusing," Alexa continued, slightly hurt. She held her hands out in front of her as if she was unsure what to do with them. She was like an actress trying to play a mother, but who had never actually experienced a real mother's warmth before. "You don't belong with her, Nolin. You never did. She never wanted you." She looked at Melissa. "Deny it," she said to her. "I dare you."

Melissa stayed silent. Another tear fell into the dirt.

"She even tried to leave you here," Alexa said. "Did she tell you that? You were just a baby."

Nolin shook her head, not looking at either of them.

"She bundled you up and brought you to the edge of the woods," Alexa said almost gleefully. "I watched the whole thing. She came in just far enough so that no one could hear you cry, and she left you. I think she left you for me, or she left you to die. I can't be sure." She grinned wickedly, triumphantly, at Melissa. "I would have cared for you. It wasn't ideal because it wasn't your choice, but I never would have left you there. I'm not like her."

Nolin felt dead inside. The aching in her stomach ceased, and it was like she had no stomach at all. She felt weightless. Hours ago, her limbs had been heavy with exhaustion. Now she felt nothing, not the breeze on her face, not the ground beneath her feet. She heard nothing, saw nothing. Her glazed eyes saw only a blur of color, darkening in the fading light.

In the middle of that dark blur was a shock of white. Melissa in her hospital gown, standing still. Watching her.

"I'm sorry," Melissa whispered, her voice barely carrying over the breeze. Nolin allowed her vision to focus. Melissa's eyes glimmered with tears. Her mouth bunched up into a tiny slash of crimson on her flushed face.

Nolin opened her mouth to speak, then thought better of it. She didn't want to hear any more.

Alexa moved closer to Nolin. "I know you'll do the right thing," Alexa whispered in her ear. Even her breath was like a cold wind. "You never forgot who you are."

There was a strangled cry, and Nolin looked over at Melissa. She'd fallen to the ground and lain on her side in the fetal position. Nolin wasn't sure if she'd fallen with emotion or if weakness had finally taken over. Nolin hated everything about her in that moment, from her stringy blond hair to the knobby spine showing through the crack of the gown like a string of beads. Dark fury rose in Nolin's heart, and she felt a strange, twisted satisfaction. Melissa, the woman whose love she'd sought all her life and failed to receive, was lying in the dirt, a perfect picture of how Nolin had felt every time Melissa insisted that she not call her "mom," how she felt each time she'd gotten suspended from school, knowing she'd added to the torments of her poor, sick mother.

It had always been about Melissa.

Stop crying, Nolin said sharply. The voice didn't sound like hers. It was lower, terrible, and seemed to issue through the trees themselves. Melissa flinched. She looked at Nolin with wild, terrified eyes.

"Nolin..." Melissa said weakly.

"Shut up!" Nolin barked. She stepped toward Melissa, who scrambled into a sitting position and tried to stand. She fell back down, her pathetic legs unable to hold her, and scrambled backward like a crab. "I'm finished with you," Nolin growled. "All my life, I tried to be the best daughter I could because I thought it was my fault you were so miserable. I blamed myself, always."

"It wasn't your fault," Melissa squeaked.

"Yeah? That's not the message I got. Everything I did was wrong. You couldn't stand the sight of me, don't deny it," she hissed when Melissa started to protest. "You were a terrible mother. You never wanted a child, especially not one like me. You made sure I knew what a burden I was, you sniveling, awful excuse for a human being." Spittle flew from Nolin's mouth. Her temples ached. Her face twisted with rage. Melissa scurried backward, dragging her leg. Nolin drew closer, wanting more than anything to step on Melissa like a bug.

"I wasted my life running after your approval. I almost became as crazy as you. And all this time, you were the imposter, not me. You were the dangerous one that couldn't be trusted. You tried to abandon me!" Nolin shrieked these last words. Melissa flinched.

"I'm sorry," Melissa sobbed. "I'm so, so sorry. It was never you. It was always me that I hated, not you."

Nolin's jaw stiffened so hard it ached. "I want you to go," she said, her voice low and dangerous. "I never, ever want to see you again."

"I'm sorry," Melissa said again. "I love you."

Nolin felt like she'd been stabbed. Never, ever in her memory had her mother said those words.

"You love me?" Nolin hissed. "*You love me?*"

Terror ripped across Melissa face. She struggled to scramble to her feet, shuffling away. Alexa laughed.

"You had years to tell me you *loved* me!" Nolin screamed. "Do you really think I'm going to believe that now? *Do you?* Well I *hate* you. You made my life hell, and I hate you for it." Melissa cowered at the venom in her voice, eyes wide with terror.

Nolin had never wanted to hit someone so badly, just to give Melissa a tiny dose of the pain she'd put Nolin through. She flexed her twitching fist. Electricity rippled down her arm. She felt Alexa's eyes on her; she was probably thinking the same thing—*do it.*

Nolin looked her mother in the eye. Melissa's limp hair was ratted across her face. Between the dirty strands, her eyes were wide, ringed with deep shadows; terror was written on her skin.

Melissa reached the edge of the trees. She backed into a tree, her hands grasping at its narrow trunk behind her.

"Nolin, I'm sorry..." she stammered. "I'm so sorry."

Nolin's fingernails dug into her palm. Melissa looked pitiful and tiny, curled up like a terrified animal.

She hadn't been loved either, Nolin realized. Her childhood had been just as cold and lonely as Nolin's.

No, it wasn't right.

Nolin loosened her fist.

"How did I get back?" she demanded. Melissa looked confused. "After you left me there," Nolin spat. "How did I get back?"

"I...I brought you back," Melissa said weakly. "I didn't even make it back to the house. You weren't there for five minutes before I went back for you."

Nolin glowered.

"I know that doesn't make it all right," Melissa said quickly. "Believe me, I've never regretted anything more. And you were different after that day. You clung to me. You never wanted to leave my side. I never hated myself more than I did after that."

"You still left her there in the first place," came Alexa's voice. "The damage was done."

366

Nolin looked at Melissa and said nothing. She saw her for what she was—a confused, scared woman who couldn't handle the responsibility of a daughter who reminded her of everything she hated about herself. She was sick. Weak. She just couldn't be the mother Nolin had needed. It wasn't in her.

She'd never actually hated Nolin. Nolin was just a mirror, a reminder of what Melissa truly was, a constant echo of the shadow who'd haunted her since disappearing into the woods.

Nolin's jaw softened. Her entire body ached. She was so tired. No longer numb, she now felt ready to collapse.

"Go," she croaked to Melissa. "Just...just go." She pointed into the trees.

Melissa gulped. "I...you can't stay here." She seemed to steel herself, leaning against the tree as she clambered to her feet. "She's dangerous."

"I don't care," Nolin muttered. "I can't try to be human anymore. This is where I need to stay. With the goblins."

"No, Nolin, you don't understand!" Melissa said, louder. Panic rang in her voice. "There are no other goblins. They're gone."

Nolin sighed, exasperated. "And where are they?" she asked.

Melissa opened her mouth to respond, but Alexa spoke first.

"Dead," she said flatly. "I killed them."

"I...what?" Nolin said. "You killed them?"

She faced Alexa, who stood with her feet planted, challenging. "I had to," she said pointedly. Her mouth was a thin line, her eyes hard. "They were monsters. They were just going to steal more children, ruin more lives, just like they ruined ours. I couldn't let that happen."

"I felt it in a dream," Melissa said. "It happened right here! She took a rock and bashed their heads in, all of them!"

Nolin's stomach somersaulted. Alexa's face was hard, not a ripple of regret or emotion at all. "I had no choice," she said plainly.

"She tried to kill me too, Nolin," Melissa pleaded. "She tried to throw me down that ravine first. I fought her off, and she slipped. She grabbed me around the neck from behind."

"Liar!" Alexa shrieked.

Nolin looked at Alexa. "The goblins are gone?"

Alexa nodded. "They're gone. It will just be you and me, Nolin. That's how it should have always been. Just us, in these woods together, mother and daughter."

A gust of wind whipped through the treetops. Nolin stumbled as the ground lurched under her feet. The inhaling, whooshing noise filled her ears again, and the forest seemed to sigh.

"What's going on?" she said, struggling to keep her balance.

"The woods want you back," Alexa said. "These aren't just trees and rocks and plants. These woods are alive. They know you. They're a part of both of us, Nolin." She rushed forward and took Nolin's face in her white hands.

"Listen to me," she said. "You belong here, and you've always known it. You'll never fit in with the humans. There's nothing for you there. Stay with me, and you will never be an outcast again. You will never, ever feel unloved. I promise, I'll make it all up to you. You'll forget your suffering and become part of the woods. You'll be exactly where you belong."

It sounded like going to bed after a long, long day. What would that kind of love feel like? How would it be to belong, to be exactly where she was supposed to be for once instead of feeling like an imposter, hated and feared though she wanted so badly to be loved?

What about Drew?

His face rose in her mind. Nolin thought about watching the sun rise over the hills in the mornings, how he stayed with her when she didn't want to be alone. Could she belong with him?

Alexa looked into her eyes. Nolin could see her own reflection in the shiny black irises.

"I need to try something," Nolin said. Alexa watched Nolin purposely stride to the Claw Tree and crawled into the hollow beneath. The leaves rustled as she found the thin branch, pinched her eyes shut, and closed her hand around it.

A rainbow of Drew's thoughts and emotions shot through her, images flying through her mind like rapidly flipping channels. Her heart started to pound. She didn't know what she was doing, but she watched.

A few moments later, she felt him. Something in her heart twanged. She focused on it, letting the flashing images slow until she could focus on just one.

He was in her backyard. Through Drew's eyes, she looked out at the trees. He gripped something in his hand, a piece of paper. She couldn't see what it was. His anxiety tore through her. Panic rippled down his limbs. She felt helpless. It hurt to sit in those feelings, even though they belonged to someone else. She settled into them, felt into their depths. Beneath them, she found something more.

A quiet warmth stole over her and tinged the edges of her vision with gold. This feeling pulsed down in her chest, and she realized his fear, panic, and anger that pulsed in her sprang from that warmth.

Nolin's face broke into a smile.

She released the vine. The vision faded, but the warmth stayed.

She could belong with humans. She *did* belong.

Drew, Rebecca, even Melissa in her own screwed-up way—they all loved her. The human world was full of books, art, stories, caring and generosity. She'd never known how to access it before, but it was there, and she could have it.

She had to leave. Now.

She scrambled out from under the tree and ran across the clearing to her mother.

"We're leaving," she said to Melissa.

Melissa started to smile, then her face contorted with fear.

Something slammed into Nolin from the side, knocking her to the ground. Alexa fell on top of Nolin and held her down. Then, Nolin felt an icy hand close around her throat.

Chapter 47

NOLIN GASPED FOR air, groping at Alexa's hand. Her grip was like a steel vice.

"Stay," Alexa said, her lips bunched, choking back a sob. "I love you. Please." Her face was stark white. Her bloodshot eyes swam with tears that splattered onto Nolin's forehead.

Nolin writhed, struggling for air. Yellow flashes danced across her vision, and the edges of Alexa's face went black and fuzzy.

Something flew out of the darkness and pulled Alexa off, wrestling her to the ground. Nolin sucked in a deep, gasping breath that burned her lungs. Her throat was on fire.

Her vision slowly came into focus. Melissa and Alexa locked together on the ground with their hands around each other's throats. Veins and muscle in their arms pulled tight as bowstrings. The back of Melissa's gown had almost come undone. Every bone and muscle in her wasted back stretched and heaved.

Nolin's head swam. She scrambled to her feet. Alexa immediately sprang back up to sprint toward Nolin, her eyes burning like coals. Then Melissa launched herself around Alexa's legs. Alexa flew forward and landed hard. She rolled beneath Melissa's grip and seized a handful of hair. Melissa howled and with a swift jerk, Alexa slammed Melissa's head on the hard earth. Melissa rolled over, dazed. Alexa's hand fumbled over the dirt until it closed on the odd rock Nolin had noticed before.

Now, she realized the rock wasn't discolored; it was stained with old blood.

Nolin's vision sharpened. Though her head throbbed, she threw herself at Alexa. Melissa groaned and lifted her head.

"Go!" Nolin gasped as she tried to wrench the rock out of Alexa's hand.

Alexa's other fist swung at Nolin's face. Without thinking, Nolin blocked with her arm and drove a knee into Alexa's stomach. Alexa doubled over, gasping for breath. Her grip on the rock loosened and Nolin pried it from her fingers before throwing it as hard as she could. She heard a "plunk" where it landed. Coughing and bent over, Alexa charged into Nolin's middle, knocking them both to the ground.

Nolin's body moved on its own, some long-forgotten impulse surging through her muscles. She couldn't let Alexa pin her. Her elbow flew into Alexa's face. She snatched a handful of tangled hair and yanked, kicking at whatever she could reach, her free hand clawing at Alexa's face. Alexa shrieked and rolled off her, her face crisscrossed with deep scratches and covered in blood.

Nolin rushed to her feet, panting. Alexa lay dazed, with glassy eyes to the sky,

Then she chuckled.

"There's my little goblin," she spat, locking eyes with Nolin. A crazed smile spread over her face, strings of blood dripping from her teeth. "I knew you still had it in you."

Nolin's insides curled with disgust. Before she could respond, Alexa lunged forward with unreal speed and knocked Nolin's legs out from under her.

Nolin slammed into the ground, and Alexa was on top of her again, hand at her throat. Nolin kicked furiously, scratched at Alexa's hand. She felt hot liquid running down her neck, either her blood or Alexa's.

"You don't know what's best for you, sweetheart," Alexa gurgled. Blood and saliva rained on Nolin's face, and she pinched her eyes shut. "I do, though. Mommy knows what's best."

Nolin heard a thump and a white-hot ribbon of pain trailed from her temple. She felt like her skull was opening along the seam. Her vision went white. She coughed and spat as her mouth filled with her own blood.

"I should have done this years ago," Alexa growled. Nolin braced herself. Then Alexa's weight lifted. Melissa screamed, and leaves rustled as something dragged across the ground.

Nolin shot to her feet, her vision swimming into clarity. She staggered forward and tripped over something hard. Another rock. Alexa must have hidden them everywhere, always at arm's reach.

When Nolin's vision came into focus, she saw that Alexa had her arm wrapped around Melissa's neck and was dragging her toward the tree. Melissa's feet pawed uselessly at the ground. They reached the tree, and Alexa started to climb, pulling herself up with her free arm and hauling Melissa with her.

Nolin sprinted. Wind blew and the ground swelled again as the woods breathed. Her legs wobbled. The Claw Tree shifted slightly, or was it just Nolin's eyes?

Alexa progressed farther up the tilting trunk. Nolin reached the edge of the tree and leapt onto it, groping the deep grooves in its bark for handholds. She dug her toes in and pulled herself up, climbing as fast as she could. Alexa scaled at almost superhuman speed. Melissa's legs flailed; she kicked, screamed, bit, scratched, but Alexa didn't slow her ascent.

Nolin didn't realize how high she was until she looked down. She was nearly thirty feet in the air. She tightened her grip on the bark until her hands ached.

Melissa screamed above her. They'd nearly reached the canopy. The tree sloped enough that Nolin could now crawl up the trunk. Ahead of her, Alexa stood and wrenched Melissa to her feet.

"Let's see how *you* like being thrown off something!" Alexa snarled, and she shoved.

Melissa screamed and fell backward onto the trunk before slipping over the edge. Her hands just caught a trench in the bark and she dangled by her thin fingers fifty feet above the ground.

Alexa sighed, obviously irritated, and stepped toward her.

Nolin got there first.

She slammed into Alexa. The wind blew and the whooshing sound filled Nolin's ears. The ground heaved again, rattling the leaves of the canopy. They both lost their balance.

Nolin grabbed at the edge of the tree, its rough bark scraping and shaving off skin as she fell, but Alexa's weight pulled them over the side. Time froze. Nolin locked eyes with Melissa, who let go with one hand to reach for her.

Nolin fell.

Alexa let go. They hit the ground with a thud and a chorus of cracking bones.

374

Nolin screamed as pain tore up her side, shot down her leg, and wrapped around her neck. It hurt to move, hurt to scream. Each breath burned as something in her side raked along her lungs.

Her vision was painted red when she opened her eyes. A few feet away, Alexa struggled to her feet, arm hanging limply at her side, shoulder strangely deflated. Her left leg bloomed blotchy and purple. She stared at Nolin, her face placid as a porcelain mask, then she looked up at Melissa dangling above them. Alexa smirked and hobbled forward.

"Nolin," she said hoarsely. Nolin tried to push herself up, but a riot of pain wracked her body. "I'm so sorry about this." Alexa winced as she leaned down to pick a rock out of the dirt. She raised it over her head while Nolin frantically tried to crawl with her good arm and leg.

Suddenly, the ground gave an almighty lurch. The trees groaned. Above them, the Claw Tree swayed. Melissa screamed, holding on for dear life. There was an earsplitting groan, and the gigantic tree began to sink into the ground from the base.

Alexa froze, her wide eyes fixed on the sinking tree. Then she looked at her own feet. The ground beneath her swelled, the dirt shifting around her toes. She looked back up at Nolin with sad eyes, opening her mouth to speak. Then the ground cracked.

A dark, yawning hole opened in the earth, and Alexa fell. Her pleading eyes never left Nolin's as she was swallowed.

Nolin lay still, stunned.

Then she realized that the edges of the hole were spreading.

Panicked, she scrambled away.

"Nolin!" Melissa cried. Nolin looked up. Melissa still clung to the tree that was sinking like a ship. Nolin frantically tried to stand. The ground was collapsing everywhere; the entire clearing would be swallowed in moments. Nolin dragged herself as quickly as she could, her broken limbs flailing uselessly and sending fireworks of pain through her body. She kicked her good leg against the ground and pulled herself forward with her arm. In the briefest moment, she noticed her foot had nothing to kick off as the ground collapsed beneath her. Instinctively, she dug her fingers into the soil.

At the edge of her fading vision, Nolin saw the top of the Claw Tree sink into the ground. The clearing was now nothing but a massive hole.

Somehow, Nolin didn't fall. Her fingers held to the ground like roots and, within seconds, she felt cold hands close around her wrists.

Nolin looked up and saw Melissa's blurry face. Melissa tugged. Nolin tried to pull herself up, but she was too weak.

"Don't let go, I'm going to get you out!" Melissa cried. Even as she fought to stay conscious, Nolin could hear the panic in her voice. Melissa's wasted body couldn't lift her. The bones in Nolin's broken arm pulled apart as she held on. She felt sick, dizzy. She was going to pass out and fall, probably taking Melissa with her.

Then another set of bigger hands wrapped around her forearms. She was moving upward, out of the hole, then laid gently on the ground.

Two hazy faces above her: Melissa, pale and exhausted, and Drew, wide-eyed and horrified.

"Mom," Nolin said faintly.

"I'm okay," Melissa breathed. "We're safe."

Drew's warm hand cupped her face. Nolin felt herself smile. A drop of pleasant warmth slipped into the mass of her pain, spreading gentle ripples to the edges.

Drew and Melissa were talking to each other. Nolin couldn't understand them. They were saying something about her, she thought.

Pain twisted and roared through her body. Time escaped her as she floated in and out of a lake of flames, each breath burning her throat and lungs as her ribs stretched and shifted.

At one point, she was aware that they were moving, and she even caught a glimpse of clear, dark sky ringed with pointed trees and studded with twinkling stars. Someone was crying, talking to her. The words swam in her mind as though she were underwater.

"I'm sorry," they said. "Stay with me." Someone kissed her forehead, and then she was being carried. There was screaming, moaning, crying, and she realized those inhuman sounds were coming from her.

Sometimes there were hands on her face, the small ones or the large, warm ones. They were so gentle.

A fleeting thought crossed her pain-wracked mind: *I'm home.*

Chapter 48

EVERYTHING WAS WHITE through the shroud of her closed eyelids. She felt heavy as cement, but at the same time, she was flying. Tiny bubbles filled her limbs, making her giddy. The pain was still there, but she didn't care as much. She hadn't felt so good in years.

Something warm was wrapped around her right hand. Her fingers twitched. Whatever it was moved, squeezing gently. It was another hand, she realized, warm against her cold fingers. She squeezed back.

"Nolin?"

Her eyes cracked opened. Light blinded her. Her eyes immediately pinched shut before slowly blinking open again.

The room swam. Blocks of white and gray bled into each other, moving around her. Her head felt so heavy, yet at the same time light, unattached to her body.

"Nolin," the voice said again.

Nolin turned her head, or rather, let it fall to her right side.

Drew's face, out of focus, yet unmistakably Drew. Soft golden warmth swelled inside her.

"How is she?" Nolin asked. Her voice sounded funny, high and breathy.

"She's here," Drew said, nodding at something on the other side of the bed. "Asleep. She had a heart attack out there, and she really did a number on her hip. It might not ever heal fully, but she'll be okay for the most part. They've got her feeding tube back in and her heart seems to be working."

Relief washed over Nolin. She tried to roll her head to the other side to see her mother. It felt like a giant rock.

Drew lifted her hand and gently pressed his lips to her fingers. Nolin giggled. She felt stupid, slow, giddy. There was something in her body that wasn't her, something pumping in her veins that was making her dizzy.

"I don't think I've ever heard you giggle," Drew said.

"I feel weird," said Nolin.

"The painkillers. You're probably super high," Drew said. "They gave you all kinds of good stuff."

Nolin's head rolled to the side, and she struggled to lift it. Drew's chin was covered in day-old stubble. His usually sparkling eyes were flat, tired, circled with shadows.

"I know you aren't up to it at the moment," he started, "but I want to know what happened out there. You'll tell me sometime, won't you?"

Nolin remembered Melissa suddenly, and then she remembered the woods, Alexa, the Claw Tree sinking into the ground, everything. Another fit of dizziness seized her, and she pinched her eyes shut.

"That was insane, what I saw," he continued. "I don't understand it. I don't know why you went out there. You and your mom almost died." He chewed his lip. "When you disappeared and I couldn't find you, I was asking myself why I got mixed up with this in the first place. It doesn't matter, though. When the girl you love is in trouble, you go after her. That's all there is to it."

The soft warmth flickered in Nolin's stomach, and a smile played on the edge of her lips. "You *love* me?" she said, almost teasingly.

His face swam in her giddy haze. He looked straight at her, not blinking. "Yeah," he said. "I do."

"Aw," Nolin giggled. "So are you my boyfriend then?"

Drew smiled. "You are high as *balls* right now."

"I've never had a boyfriend before."

"What a coincidence, me neither," Drew said, grinning. "But if we're going to be a thing...I need you to be honest with me. No more weird secrets."

He was right. Nolin's head throbbed. "Okay," she croaked.

Drew nodded, then closed his eyes. He looked exhausted. Nolin's fingers flailed, and his hand gripped hers tighter.

"Promise me you're not going to do something stupid like this again," he said. "Okay?"

Nolin closed her eyes and breathed evenly, letting the dizziness and nausea wash through her and retract in waves. "I promise."

She needed to sleep, but memories leaked back into her stupor. The tree, Alexa, everything.

And Drew. He was closer to all this than he realized.

"How did you find us?" she asked. He rummaged through one of the pockets of his jeans and pulled out a piece of paper.

"This," he said as he unfolded Alexa's map. "I don't know what it is. I went back to your house to see if you'd gone there and I found it in the entryway."

"It was in my pocket," Nolin said. Drew turned the map around and looked at it.

"Oh," he said. "I thought I felt something come out of your pocket when we were...anyway, I had a feeling it would take me to you. I don't know, once I got in there, I seemed to know where I was going."

He leaned forward and kissed Nolin's forehead. Nolin realized her head was wrapped in gauze. He kissed her between the eyes, just below her bandages. Then, he softly kissed her on the mouth.

"You drive me nuts, you know that?" he whispered.

Nolin giggled again as a bubble of dizziness burst in her head. "Drive them where?"

Drew rolled his eyes, but he smiled. "I'm going to get some coffee. I'll be right back, okay?"

"'Kay."

He stood to leave, then turned, "Oh, your friend Rebecca is on her way," he said. He pulled Nolin's cell phone from his pocket. "I found this across the street. She tried to call you."

Nolin smiled. She missed Rebecca.

"Drew?" Nolin said, holding out a shaky arm. He took her hand, and leaned in to kiss her again, longer this time. Nolin's mind couldn't form the words she wanted to say, couldn't phrase how grateful she was or tell him how she'd seen his thoughts and felt his feelings through the tree, and how that pulled her back, anchored her to this world where she'd belonged all along. Instead, she kissed him and hoped he understood what he meant to her.

"You'll come right back?" Nolin whispered when they broke away.

Drew nodded, touching his forehead to hers. "Just to the coffee machine and back." He smiled, his eyes twinkling for the first time since Nolin had woken up. "Don't worry. I'm not going to sneak away." He raised his eyebrows pointedly. Nolin stuck out her tongue. Drew smiled, rolled his eyes, and left.

"He's cute," said a voice on her other side.

Nolin rolled her head to see her mother in the next bed. A feeding tube threaded through her nose. She smiled weakly.

"I like him," Nolin wheezed, struggling to return the smile.

They looked at each other for a moment, each too exhausted to speak. Faint spots of color blossomed in Melissa's cheeks. Though she was cut, bruised, and full of hoses, she was more radiant than Nolin had seen her in years.

"I'm sorry," Melissa said. She opened her mouth, maybe to say something else, but then closed it. Her gray eyes were soft.

Nolin's chest tightened, and her head felt heavier than ever. For years, this was all she had wanted in the world: an apology. Now that it was here, she felt oddly empty, tight. There were wounds that were too deep, scars that would never heal.

But Melissa had saved her. She could have run. Despite a healing hip, she'd ripped out her tubes, snuck out of the hospital, and come to the Claw Tree. She'd faced her worst fear to save her daughter.

Tears burned Nolin's eyes. Her mother loved her.

Melissa reached out. Nolin stretched her good arm to take her mother's hand, which Melissa squeezed gently.

A wave of heaviness washed over Nolin again. She dropped into the abyss of sleep that ate the exhaustion from her bones, slowly mended her mind.

382

***

She didn't hear Drew return, sit beside her, and quietly sip his coffee. She didn't hear Rebecca outside the room snapping at the nurse who insisted that there could only be one visitor at a time, or hear her walk into the room anyway, promptly introduce herself to Drew, and then sit on Nolin's other side.

Nolin slept deeply and the golden warmth inside her grew, spreading from her chest to her limbs, healing years of aches, scars, memories. She was home, surrounded by home, dreaming of swaying treetops, and the whispering of soft breeze through leaves.

Epilogue

Eight years later

NOLIN DREW THE BLANKET tighter around her swollen belly
while she settled into her desk chair. It was already dark outside,
though the clock above the fireplace read 3:26 p.m. The temperature hadn't risen above zero in weeks.

The fire and laptop screen were the only sources of light in the
tiny cabin, illuminating shelves stuffed with books, squashy sec-
ondhand chairs, and their little kitchenette. Everything they
owned. Nolin fiddled with the Ethernet cable, hoping for a solid
connection, just for a few minutes.

The familiar sound of a truck rumbled outside. Nolin listened
for the crunch of his boots in the snow, the sound of his key in the
lock. Warmth fluttered inside her as Drew opened the front door
and rushed in, a gush of freezing air accompanying him. That
thrilling cold. He stomped the snow off his boots, pulled off his
coat and knit hat, unwound his thick scarf, and finally stepped out
of his boots and snow pants.

He startled slightly when he saw her in the desk chair.

"Hey," he said, flipping on the light. "Why you are sitting in the dark?"

"I didn't bother to turn on a light when it got dark," she said simply.

Drew crossed the room and leaned down to kiss her, his hand finding its way to her round belly before playfully squeezing her breast. "The girls are getting sassy," he whispered in her ear. He planted a kiss on the side of her neck. "I love you."

Nolin smiled and turned to kiss him again. His hair had gotten long, covering his ears with soft brown waves. He'd let his beard grow. She'd worried he wouldn't like Alaska, but her lanky runner had transformed into a rugged mountain man in no time.

"I'm going to shower," he said.

"Okay." She watched him strip off his sweatshirt, jeans, then his thermals. His clothes fell into a pile at his feet and he kicked them into the bedroom before walking naked into the bathroom, mischievously grinning at her over his shoulder and clicking the door shut behind him.

Nolin smiled and looked at the clock again. Three-thirty.

She opened Skype and clicked the number in her contact list. The call icon flashed on the screen.

Melissa appeared on the screen. She looked different. Her hair was cut smartly to her chin and she wore glasses with purple frames. Her face looked fuller, healthier.

"Hi," Nolin said.

"Hey there," Melissa responded, her voice slightly garbled. "How are you? Is it cold up there?"

Nolin smiled. "A balmy ten below."

Melissa shuddered, shaking her head.

Nolin smiled awkwardly. They spoke infrequently, saw each other even less. Nolin found she liked her mother more and more each time they met. Nolin realized Melissa was slowly morphing into the woman she was always meant to be, the fiery creative she was all along.

"How's the drawing?" Nolin finally asked.

"Oh, very good," said Melissa. "I just signed on to do a new children's series, five books total. They want covers, chapter headings, and a full-page illustration for each chapter! I can't wait to get started." Her eyes twinkled behind her glasses, and Nolin noticed she was also wearing earrings, dangling chains of silver rings. Nolin wondered when her mother had gotten her ears pierced.

"So, how's the little one?" Melissa asked eagerly.

Nolin pushed the blanket aside and sat up straight so Melissa could get a better look. "Healthy. The doctor says everything's perfect." A small bump rolled under Nolin's skin. If she focused hard enough, she thought she could feel the flutter of a tiny heartbeat. "Anyway, I wanted to talk to you because we found out the sex today."

Melissa's smile faded, but her eyes twinkled just as brightly. "Oh?" she said. She leaned closer to the screen, the glow illuminating her rosy face. Her cheeks had filled out. Nolin smiled again, for a moment just staring at her mother's face and wondering at how she'd changed from the woman she'd been when Nolin was a child. Nolin rubbed her belly and swallowed.

"It's a girl," she said, her voice quavering.

"A girl," Melissa breathed.

For a moment, they were quiet. All Nolin could hear was splashing in the shower and Drew's absentminded humming.

"You're going to have a daughter," Melissa said dreamily. "My goodness."

"I know," said Nolin. They stared at each other for moment, then they both smiled, and Melissa broke into an excited giggle.

"Oh my goodness!" she laughed, taking off her glasses to wipe her eyes. "Wow."

"Just a few more months," Nolin said, grinning. "Drew's so excited. He's going to spoil her rotten. I think we knew from the beginning that it would be a girl."

Melissa smiled and nodded. "That's how I felt too, with you," she said. "Your father insisted you were boy, but I knew from the moment I found out I was pregnant that I would have a daughter."

Nolin drew in a breath. "You did?"

Melissa nodded. "I won't lie; that was a rough pregnancy. I was sick, sick, sick. I could barely pull my head out of the toilet. I was glad I was having a girl, though. I used to wonder what you'd be like, what you'd look like."

"Was I what you expected?" Nolin asked, not sure if she wanted to hear the answer.

Melissa looked her in the eye through the screen, a grim smile on her face. "Yes," she said. "You were exactly what I expected. You were everything I thought you'd be and more."

Nolin looked down at her belly, smiling to herself. "I'm sure she'll be exactly the same," she said.

"I'm sure she will be. A rambunctious, wild little spitfire just like you were."

"I hope she gets Drew's patience," said Nolin.

"And your grit," Melissa countered.

Nolin stroked her belly, running her finger over the tiny nub of her navel.

"So, were you excited? To have a daughter?" she asked.

Melissa's looked somewhere above the screen, her eyes wandering, and nodded. "Sometimes, I really was," she said thoughtfully. "Mostly, I was terrified. Motherhood isn't for sissies, and I was afraid I couldn't handle it. And we both know that was true; turns out, I couldn't."

There was a pause. Nolin looked into her lap awkwardly.

"I wouldn't take it back," Melissa went on. "Sometimes, you were the only light in my life. My marriage was failing, I was getting sicker by the day, and there was always *her*..." she trailed off. "But I had you. I got to watch you grow, watch you learn. You were so smart, Nolin. So smart." She shook her head. "And I wanted to teach you everything. Art, literature, about everything I knew. I loved that you loved to read. And I loved you. I just didn't know how to show you. That love was buried so far under all the other mess that I forgot it was there sometimes." She wiped another tear from under her glasses. "But there you are."

They sat in silence for a few moments. The shower was still running. Nolin hoped he still had a few minutes; she might join him.

"Well," said Melissa, an air of finality in her voice, "I'd better let you go. I have a deadline to hit, unicorns to draw. The usual."

Nolin smiled and nodded. "Okay."

They said good-bye and Melissa disconnected. Nolin closed the screen.

Drew started singing "Bohemian Rhapsody." He'd be there for a while. He had to finish the song.

Nolin went into the bedroom and stripped down to her socks, underwear, and undershirt. Though the fire was warm, she shivered in the cold little bedroom.

She crossed to her side of the bed, lifted the mattress, and thrust her hand underneath.

Her hand closed around it—the pink baby shoe.

She held it for just a moment. The faded knit was still tight and secure. Sometimes she pulled the shoe from its hiding place and marveled at how small it was, that her foot once fit inside it. That the baby in her womb would be that small. Would anyone crochet shoes for her daughter?

Nolin slipped the shoe back in its place before padding over to the bathroom, pausing in from of the full-length mirror on the back of the bedroom door.

Her six-month belly swelled, balancing awkwardly on her thin legs. She'd never get used to it. It was cumbersome, hard to sleep with. Drew adored it, but sometimes it got in the way during sex. Nolin didn't recognize her own body. It was still her face, her legs and arms, her wild hair, but everything in between was new to her.

She hugged her arms around her stomach. The little creature inside rolled, and the skin of Nolin's belly rippled.

I'm your mother, Nolin thought.

What a complicated thing, a mother. Something constantly changing, something beautiful and terrifying sometimes, something benevolent and yet always afraid.

Nolin met her own eyes in the mirror. She looked terrified. Had Melissa had ever done this when she was pregnant? Looked at herself and wondered if she could do it?

I'm your mother, Nolin thought again.

The drop of golden warmth glowed in her chest, brighter than ever.

ABOUT THE AUTHOR

M. K. Sawyer has been writing stories since elementary school, often staying in from recess to write in the school library. She started writing *The Goblin's Daughter* while she was enrolled in the creative writing program at Weber State University.

When she isn't writing, M. is usually reading, painting, or exploring the mountains near her home. M. lives in Salt Lake City, Utah, with her husband and cat.

A NOTE FROM THE AUTHOR

I hope you enjoyed *The Goblin's Daughter!*

Online reviews are extremely important for helping indie authors spread the word about their books.

If you enjoyed this book, I'd love it if you could take a few moments to rate and review *The Goblin's Daughter* on Amazon or Goodreads. Thank you in advance!

If you'd like to receive additional exclusive content and updates on my future projects, make sure to sign up for my mailing list at MKSawyerBooks.com

Thank you so much for your support.

-M. K. Sawyer

Acknowledgments

It took nine years for *The Goblin's Daughter* to be born, from the first tiny seed of an idea to this book you hold in your hands.

There are so many people who helped me along the way and who inspired me long before this story was even a thought.

Thank you to my Sam for endless love and patience, for your honesty, for always being there to rescue me from the clutches of technology or from my own emotional meltdowns. Thank you for your help and faith in me during the very long production of this book. I love you so much.

Thank you Mom and Dad for always encouraging me, believing in me, and joking about me supporting you in your old age when I'm a famous writer. Thank you for joking that you'll tell the world all kinds of embarrassing stories about me when my name is a household term. You never doubted me for a second, and I couldn't have written this book without your support.

Chandler, Adam, and Erianne, you guys never doubted me either. You've always made me feel like I can accomplish anything. I love you dorks.

Jernae, Wyatt, and Liesel, I can't thank you enough for your invaluable feedback and encouragement. Without you, this book would still be an unfinished draft rotting away on my hard drive.

And a special thanks to Jernae for being there from the very beginning of this book's journey, and for extending an invitation when I felt like giving up on it.

Thank you so much to Destinee, my best fran (misspelled on purpose, calm down), for your help, your feedback, and for being the president of my fan club. Thanks for listening to endless complaints and frustrations as I wrote and produced this book. I love you to bits and you're the very best friend a girl could ask for.

Thank you to Chandice, Josh, and Missy for being my beta reader guinea pigs. Your feedback and support mean the world to me!

Special thanks to Suzanne Johnson, my incredible editor for your wonderful work on this book, and to my designer David Provolo for making my book beautiful. This book wouldn't be what it is without you!

Finally, thank you to the long parade of teachers and mentors who helped me grow as a writer; to Mrs. Bambrough, my elementary school librarian who took a weird little kid under her wing; and to Dr. Prothero and Dr. Schwiebert for always pushing me, teaching me, and making sure I always carried a notebook.

There are hordes of other friends, family members, teachers, and colleagues who have supported me, inspired me, and encouraged me, so many that I probably couldn't list them all, but thank you all for everything you've done for me.

This book is only the beginning.

M.K. SAWYER

CPSIA information can be obtained
at www.ICGtesting.com
Printed in the USA
BVHW030347040122
625385BV00025B/353